Another Kind of Country

KEVIN BROPHY

headline review

First published in Great Britain in 2013
by HEADLINE REVIEW
An imprint of HEADLINE PUBLISHING GROUP

1

Cataloguing in Publication Data is available from the British Library

ISBN (HB) 978 0 7553 8088 6
ISBN (TPB) 978 0 7553 8089 3

Typeset in Giovanni by Avon DataSet Ltd, Bidford-on-Avon, Warwickshire

Printed and bound in Great Britain by Clays Ltd, St Ives plc

Headline's policy is to use papers that are natural, renewable and recyclable products and made from wood grown in sustainable forests. The logging and manufacturing processes are expected to conform to the environmental regulations of the country of origin.

HEADLINE PUBLISHING GROUP
An Hachette UK Company
338 Euston Road
London NW1 3BH

www.headline.co.uk
www.hachette.co.uk

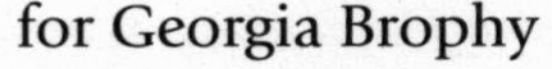

for Georgia Brophy

Acknowledgements

I am deeply grateful to Claire Baldwin, my publisher at Headline, for her help in focusing the thrust of this book. And likewise to my agent, Caroline Montgomery, for her patient nursing of me and my words.

Mairéad Joyce, with skill and good humour, transformed my handwritten pages into a twenty-first-century printout, for which I thank her.

Although I am too superstitious ever to discuss the workings of a novel-in-progress, I am always grateful to friends who inquire about progress, supply the balm of non-prying encouragement and then wisely and kindly move on to the business of sport, politics, films, travel and other important codology. In this regard I am grateful especially to my friend and mentor, Christopher Murray, and to my coffee-drinking mates, Paddy Lydon, Mossy Moran, Maurice Ward, Pat Kennedy, Ralph O'Gorman, Eileen Graham, Andrew Tomlinson, Aidan King and Terry Small.

And, as always, a special thank you for everything to Elizabeth Wölk.

It is too late to start
For destinations not of the heart,
I must stay here with my hurt.

R. S. Thomas

PART 1

CHILE

One

Tuesday, 11 September 1973, 6.30 a.m.
Santiago
Chile

He put the phone down gently but it didn't matter. Elena was standing in the doorway, wearing only his pale blue pyjama jacket.

'Salvador?' An edge of fear in her voice.

A jet screamed overhead in the early morning sky and he saw her body tremble in the thin fabric. He moved quickly towards her, put his arm around her shoulders.

He cleared his throat, tried to force into his voice a smiling confidence he did not feel.

'Yes,' Franco said, 'it was Salvador. He's at the palace.'

'At this hour . . .'

She left the rest unsaid. It was 6.30 on Tuesday morning: this was an early start to the working day even for the workaholic President Salvador Allende of Chile.

'Caro,' he said, 'you know what he's like.'

She leaned into him, glad of the familiar wiriness of his chest hair. Yes, she knew – like all of Chile – how their President burned both ends of the candle in his pursuit of a socialist Chile. Who knew better? It was often after midnight when Franco dragged himself through the door after another crusading day at his Ministry for Industrial Development.

'I know,' she said, 'but this . . .'

Another plane jetted overhead. The house itself seemed to tremble.

'This is different.' Her voice was muffled into his chest. 'Isn't it?'

'Listen to me, Elena.' He held her at arm's length, surprised, even after all these years, by the way her casual beauty could astound him. 'I need to go now, I have to be with him at the palace. I'll send a car for you, with Felipe, he'll take you and Rosa out of the city, to your parents.'

'Rosa is going to school.'

'Elena, there won't *be* school today.'

'Don't be ridiculous,' she tried to swing out of his grip, 'it's Tuesday, of course there's school today.'

A deeper sound outside now, an almost subterranean rumbling. And Salvador's words on the phone: *I had to get through a cordon of armed carabineros to get into the palace, there are tanks in the streets*. And now the tanks were growling mechanically through the leafy streets of the Barrio Alto. Allende's own house was just a few streets away.

'There are tanks in the streets, Mama! What's going on, Papa?'

At the sound of their daughter's voice they started, almost guiltily. Rosa was fourteen, long-legged, dark-haired.

She laughed, looking at her parents. 'Sister Mercedes would be shocked!' The rich, dark hair flounced as she shook her head in mock disapproval. 'And are we so poor that you guys have to share one pair of pyjamas?'

Franco tried to draw his pyjama bottoms higher around his waist. Elena drew the pyjama jacket tighter across her breasts. Their lovemaking last night had been noisy; Elena's hand on his mouth had tried, vainly, to stop his groaning. And yet they'd never before been self-conscious about their sexuality in front of Rosa. Maybe, Franco thought, it's that other growling outside that does it. The tanks at the palace. And now at our door.

'I have to go,' Franco said. 'Felipe will be here as soon as I can arrange it.'

Rosa looked at them both, questioningly.

'We're going to my parents',' Elena said. 'For a few days.'

'But I can't! We have rehearsals this evening, the show is on Saturday night—'

'Rosa, please.' Franco looked at Elena. How did you explain to your teenage daughter that your government was under attack by its own generals?

'But what about the play? And anyway I don't want to go to the fucking country to my grandparents'—'

'Rosa!' Elena's voice was sharp but what could you do to a strong-willed fourteen-year-old? 'We don't use language like that here!'

'No, we just walk around half-fucking naked—'

Elena slapped her hard on the face.

The silence seemed deeper inside, the rumbling of the tanks louder outside.

With a cry Rosa spun away. They listened in silence to the angry footsteps on the stairs, the angrier slamming of the bedroom door.

Franco slumped into a chair.

'I don't know . . .' He wasn't sure of what he didn't know. How could a jokey comment from a beloved daughter become a moment of anger, a flash of violence?

'It's just the way we are these days,' Elena said. She was on her knees beside his chair. 'All of us, waiting, for what we don't know, a match to dynamite as if our whole country is a ticking bomb.' Elena taught German literature at the university; Franco envied the way she could spin pictures in words.

She took his hand. 'You have things to do. You have a government ministry to run. Our President needs you. Get dressed and go to the palace. And don't worry about Rosa. I'll sort it out.' There was a sadness at the edge of her smile.

He raised her hands, kissed them. 'I'd be lost without you, Elena.'

'You manage without me at the weekends.'

'Elena, you know—'

She hushed him. 'It's a joke,' she said. At weekends he went to the country to a wife who refused to divorce him. For fifteen years, from Mondays to Fridays, they had shared a home in the Barrio Alto.

'Now go,' she said. 'My government minister.'

Twenty minutes later he was ready to leave, briefcase in hand. He wondered if she guessed that the briefcase held a loaded pistol.

'She hasn't come down.'

'You know what teenage girls are like.' She made a minute and unnecessary adjustment to his tie. 'She'll cool down.'

'I'll call you when Felipe is leaving, make sure you're ready.'

'And you make sure you take care of yourself.' She wanted to ask when he could join them in the country; she knew also that she mustn't ask, that there was no way of knowing when. The air force in the sky and the army on the streets made that clear.

Their kiss was gentle, a long slow goodbye.

'*Vaya con Dios*,' she whispered.

He touched her face, whispered that he loved her.

She heard the car starting up in the yard, the faint hum of the electric gates swinging open.

The air was rent by the screaming of jets. She thought she

heard the sound of explosions in the distance. She fingered her lips, as though she could trace his kiss on them.

And she whispered again her parting words: *'Vaya con Dios.'*

Two

Tuesday, 11 September 1973, 11 a.m.
Santiago
Chile

The attack planes were flying so low that she could make out their markings. Planes of the Chile Air Force. Hawker Hunters. When you were the daughter of a government minister you picked up things almost without knowing you were doing so. Not that it did you much good, crouched at your bedroom window, hands on your ears as the planes tore across the blue sky, unloading their bombs on La Moneda.

La Moneda. The President's palace. She'd been there a couple of times with her father; the President himself had spoken to her, asked her how she was doing at school. Sometimes she'd hear her classmates at school whispering behind her back, mocking her as a bastard, the illegitimate spawn of a politician's mistress. President Allende didn't give a toss about that. After all, everybody knew that the President spent most of the week with his own mistress.

Anyway, she didn't think of Franco as a politician. He was her father, the guy who loved her and her mother. Although right now Rosa couldn't forget that her father was not just a politician but a minister in a government under attack. From her window high up on the Barrio Alto she could see where the bombs were falling; she could see, too, the puffs of smoke from the tank barrels trained on La Moneda.

She hoped Franco wasn't inside. Nobody was going to walk out of there except with his hands in the air – and she couldn't see her father doing that. The only people she could imagine Franco surrendering to were her mother and herself.

The phone rang.

She broke away from the window, rushed downstairs to stand beside her mother.

'Franco?'

'Caro, Felipe will be with you in a few minutes.'

Rosa's head was close to her mother's, the phone between them.

'But you, Franco, where are you? You have to come with Felipe.'

'I'll come when I can, just get out of the city now.'

'But, darling—'

'Tell Rosa I'm sorry about this morning, tell her I love her.'

'Papa!' She pushed her lips close to the phone. 'I'm so sorry, Papa, I'm so sorry for what I said.'

'I love you, princess.' The line was crackly. 'Look after your mama. Get her out of there the moment Felipe arrives.'

'I love you!' Her mother's voice blended with her own in a single cry into the phone.

'My gorgeous ladies—'

The phone went dead.

'Franco! Franco!' Elena was shouting into the phone, shaking it as if she might spill his voice from it.

'Mama, please.'

Rosa took the phone from her mother, put it for a moment to her ear. Only seashell static came back to her. She put the phone down, looked at her mother's face, made older now with tears, and she put her arms around her, as though she were the mother, comforting her weeping child.

'We have to be ready, Mama.'

'I know.' Her mother's voice choked with snuffles.

'You've packed a few things?'

Her mother nodded, swallowing back tears.

'You can only take twenty-five bags and a dozen cases.'

Elena looked blankly at her daughter, then she laughed. And then started crying again.

'C'mon, Mama.' She took her mother's hand. 'Felipe will be here any minute.'

'If he can get through.' Elena swallowed. 'The radio said the tanks are everywhere in the city.'

'Felipe loves Papa as much as we do,' Rosa said. 'If anybody can get through, Felipe can.'

From behind the gold-tipped, black iron gates Rosa watched the jeep swing into the street. Felipe's bald pate shone like a dark-brown egg in the morning sun. His white shirt clung sweatily to his thin frame. He saw Rosa at the window, shouted as he gunned the jeep through the gateway, into the yard.

'Now, Rosa! Now! We haven't much time!' He swung down from the jeep, the engine still running. 'Señora Rossman!' His voice echoed in the courtyard. 'The soldiers are coming, please hurry!'

He looked with dismay at the line of bags and cases standing at the door of the house.

'Where is Franco?' Elena's voice was steady; she looked immaculate in pale blue slacks and lemon blouse, framed in the open doorway.

'We have to get out of here, Señora.' Felipe was bundling

bags into the back of the jeep. 'And we can't take all of these. Please, Señora, get in the jeep.'

'Is Franco safe, Felipe?' She was like a statue, immovable in the doorway.

'Who knows, Señora? Nobody is safe. There are soldiers and carabineros everywhere, and tanks around the palace. Please, Señora, I promised the minister I'd get you and Rosa out of the city.'

Elena moved then. *We knew this was coming, Rosa and I should have gone yesterday, as Franco wished.*

She looked at the luggage in the jeep, seized two cases, exchanged them for two others from the array at the door.

'Rosa, you have your stuff?'

'Here.' Rosa swung a rucksack. 'I have my script and some books.'

'And underwear and a nightdress?'

'Mama.'

Elena laughed. Felipe tried to hide his smile.

'Please, Señora, we haven't much time.' He waved his sunglasses for emphasis. He had no wish to join the dead bodies he'd passed on the streets, scuttling along back alleys to the Barrio Alto.

'All aboard?' Felipe looked at his passengers, Elena beside him, Rosa wedged between cases on the back seat. Both of them sat stiffly, faces pale under wide-brimmed hats. The sun was high: it was going to be a long, sticky journey in the open jeep.

He eased the jeep round the red-tiled well that was the centrepiece of the courtyard. Overhead a Harrier Hunter roared across the sky. Shells were still falling on the city below.

'There's a car coming,' Elena said. 'Maybe it's Franco.'

The noise drew closer, the unseen car clattering across the cobblestones.

It didn't sound like any car Felipe had ever driven. He pushed the jeep into gear, gunned it towards the open gateway.

A black American automobile, all chrome and fins, slammed across the gateway, blocking the jeep's exit. The driver who leapt from the car was ponytailed in blue jeans and white T-shirt.

'Everybody out!' He stood in front of the jeep, slightly crouched. The black pistol pointing at them seemed like a metal extension of his big hands. 'Now! Everybody out!' He was shouting in English.

'You're American.' Rosa wondered at the calmness of her mother's voice.

'Get out of the vehicle, lady. Now!'

'There's no need to point a gun at us.'

'You.' The American pointed the gun at Felipe. 'Raise your hands higher above your head. Higher – I want to see you stretch for the sky, man – now!'

'We're not deaf.'

'Lady, for the last time, shut your Communist mouth and get out of the fucking car.'

'That kind of language—'

The gun bucked in his hands.

Felipe screamed. For a second his right arm was still upright but his hand was nothing more than a bleeding mass of shattered bone and tissue. He whimpered, cradling his mangled hand in his lap.

'I might not be so accurate with the next one.' A flash of white American teeth. 'And my orders didn't say I had to keep the driver alive, just the minister's mistress and her daughter.' The lank ponytail swung jauntily above the T-shirt. 'Now come to me, ladies, nice and gently and we'll wait until your liberating army arrives and decides what to do with you.'

Rosa started to scream.

'My ears, lady.' The American gestured with the pistol.

Elena turned in her seat and swung her arm. The sound of her open palm on Rosa's face was like another gunshot.

'Stop it,' she hissed. 'I want you to live.'

The screaming died in Rosa's throat.

She looked from her mother to their tormentor. The American's hair needed washing, she thought; maybe he wore it long to cover the spreading birthmark she could make out below his left ear when he turned his head.

Felipe was moaning, blood leaking from the crushed mass of his hand.

'Let me help him,' Elena said.

'Get out of the car, lady.'

He kept the gun trained on them as they climbed out of the jeep. Elena drew her daughter close to her, murmured into her ear.

'Felipe is losing so much blood.' She spoke over her daughter's shoulder. 'Please let me help him.'

'He won't need any help soon,' the American said.

He stood beside them and trained the gun on Felipe. Horror dawned in Felipe's eyes as he realized what was about to happen. The American shot him in the face.

For a couple of seconds Felipe's body remained upright in the jeep. A gurgled moaning issued from the mashed red mass that had been his face and then he tumbled, still moaning, from the jeep. He hit the ground with a thump; his body twitched, blood pooling on the tiles, and was finally still.

The American poked at the body with his feet. 'A bit messy.' He might have been talking about the bloody tissue that stuck to his canvas boot. 'Still, the carabineros would've made him suffer a lot more.' He looked at Elena, white-faced, her arm around her trembling daughter. 'All things considered, lady, you could say that I'm an angel of mercy.' When he grinned, his high forehead furrowed into ridges that ran into the receding hairline of his skull.

Rosa chose that moment to be sick. Her body heaved as she bent beside the jeep. The morning air was foul with the stench of blood and vomit.

'My, my, I'm surprised by such behaviour. I'd have expected more delicacy from the females of a Communist minister.' The American tut-tutted. He shook his head and the birthmark on his neck flashed a dull red in the sunshine. 'I guess you never can tell—'

He was suddenly silent. Elena and Rosa looked up.

A slight man in a grey suit and sunglasses was standing behind the American. His right arm was outstretched, pointing a gun at the American's head.

The American was motionless. The pistol in his hand seemed limp, useless.

'Take it easy, Dieter,' he said. 'No need for anyone to get hurt.'

'Tell that to the driver.' Dieter spoke English with a thick, guttural accent. Anyway, Rosa thought, wiping her mouth with her hands, with a name like Dieter, he *had* to be German.

'Drop it,' Dieter said. 'Slowly.'

The gun clattered on the ground.

'Now push it with your foot towards Señora Rossman.'

The American put his canvas-booted foot on the gun, shoved it away from him. It scraped along the tiles; dark pearls of blood clung to the darker gunmetal.

'Please pick it up, Señora Rossman.'

Elena stooped to retrieve the weapon. Its cold stickiness repelled her. She began to wipe the gun with a white, lace-edged handkerchief.

'Who are you?'

'I'm your friend,' Dieter said. 'Just in case you doubt me, Señora Rossman, I have a letter in my pocket from,' he almost smiled, 'from Rosa's father. My job is to get both of you out of the country to safety.'

The American made a kind of whinnying sound; his ponytail swung like a mane.

'Out of the country, Dieter! You'll be fucking lucky – even the port of Valparaiso is closed. What're you going to do – get out in a spaceship?'

Dieter stepped back a pace. His short, slight body seemed lost in the grey suit. The raised gun seemed monstrous in his small hand.

'Time for you to be leaving us, Mr Dover.'

'No!' Elena took a step forward. 'Please, there's been enough killing.'

'He murdered your driver, Señora Rossman, he was going to hand you over to the soldiers—'

'But you stopped him,' Rosa butted in.

'You'd better stop me permanently, Dieter.' The ponytail swung again. 'You know I always like to settle old scores.'

'Where are you taking us?' Elena let the bloodied handkerchief fall from her fingers. 'And how did you get here? You have no car.'

'I'm guessing old Dieter wants to take you all the way behind the Iron Curtain to the Democratic Republic of Germany. Right, Dieter? And you haven't a prayer – the roads are blocked, the ports are closed, and the skies,' he glanced upwards at the jet trails in the blue sky, 'the skies are ours, right, Dieter?'

Dieter pulled the trigger.

Dover collapsed, howling, clutching at his blasted knee.

Rosa looked in fascination at the blood seeping through the American's blue jeans.

'Please,' she said as Dieter stood above the American, 'he can't harm us now.'

'You'd better finish it, Dieter.' The American spat the words out through clenched teeth. Sweat bled from his furrowed forehead.

'If you kill him,' Rosa said, 'you're no better than him.'

Dieter fired again. Dover bucked on the ground. A pool of redness flowed from his other knee.

'I hope,' Dieter said in his guttural English, 'that I don't regret letting this bastard live.' He looked at Rosa and her mother. 'We have to move. My car is on the next street but this,' he pointed at the jeep, 'this is what we need for our journey. It's what Franco intended. He asked me to tail Felipe in case something happened. I'm just sorry I couldn't get here in time. A couple of carabineros stopped me and it took some time and some *dinero* to get past them.'

It took only moments for Dieter to move the American car out of the way.

'You won't be needing these,' he said over his shoulder as he tossed the car keys into the courtyard well. Herbert Dover heard neither Dieter's words nor the splashing sound of the keys hitting the water; the American had passed out, blood leaking from his shattered knees on the ground beside the jeep.

'*Vamos*,' Dieter said.

The street was quiet, deserted, as he nosed the jeep out of the courtyard but sporadic gunfire rattled through the air from the distant streets around La Moneda.

Three

Tuesday, 11 September 1973, noon
Santiago
Chile

Rosa felt she was seeing her city with different eyes. Dieter swung the jeep left and right along alleys she had never seen. Sometimes she was sure he backtracked but always, when he straightened out, the mountains rose closer in front of them to the east.

From all around came the noises of a city at war, yet it was a war that remained unseen. Strange, she thought, that this saviour, who spoke English and Spanish with a German accent, seemed to know the streets of Santiago better than herself.

She'd given up asking if they were really going to fucking Germany and why the fuck weren't they waiting for her father. Dieter ignored her. Her mother didn't even remind her that such language was forbidden. Elena reached back from the front seat beside Dieter and took Rosa's hands in her own. Elena's hands felt cool, comforting, and she let her mother go on holding her.

'We might make it now.'

They had to strain to catch Dieter's almost whispered words. They were in a short street on the outskirts of the city. Ahead, beyond the tiled roofs and the church towers, the Andes reared, distant, yet seemingly close enough to touch.

'If we can make it to the mountain road . . .' Dieter left the rest unsaid.

He eased the jeep out of the alley on to a long curving boulevard that Rosa recognized. Beyond, she knew, lay the countryside, climbing to the mountains.

'Shit.'

As they rounded the curve, they could see, further ahead, a police van on the shoulder and a couple of carabineros stopping traffic.

'Here.' From his inside pocket Dieter took a pair of plastic-covered ID cards which he handed to Elena. 'You are Señora Medeiros and her daughter, Susi, and I'm your driver-cum-gardener. We're headed for your weekend place in Santa Marta, you're worried by the trouble in the city.'

A photograph of herself stared back at Rosa from the ID card. It wasn't today or yesterday, she realized, that her father had begun to organize their escape.

'And Papa? Where—'

'Hush, Rosa, say nothing.'

Dieter eased the car to a halt beside the carabineros.

'Papers.' The shorter one had his hand out; the taller, thin one stood back, cradling his sub-machine gun.

Dieter gestured towards Elena. She smiled, opened her handbag, handed over the ID card. The policeman waited, staring at Rosa. He wiped at a large blob of sweat on his mouth as he took Rosa's card.

To Rosa it seemed that all of them had stopped breathing as the carabinero examined the IDs.

'Where are you going, Señora?'

He's from the south, Rosa thought, *where the chilling wind narrows your eyes and your words almost to a whistle.*

'We have a summer cottage in Santa Marta. We were worried about—'

He wasn't interested in her worries. 'And Señor Medeiros?'

'He's at work.'

'Where?'

She hesitated. 'At the university.'

The narrow eyes narrowed almost to a slit. 'Señora, the university is closed.'

She tried to smile. 'Yes, my husband had some paperwork to pick up.'

'Which department?'

'Physics,' Elena said. She tried to meet his eyes, tried to look unconcerned, a middle-class lady on the way to the country with her teenage daughter.

'Corporal.' The word spat from deep in his windpipe. 'Get on the radio to headquarters and clear these IDs.' He turned away from the jeep, arm extended to give the ID cards to his colleague.

'Get down!' Dieter's pistol was in his hand. He fired through the doorway of the van, splintering the radio set. The thin one was levelling the sub-machine gun as Dieter pushed down on the accelerator. The engine roared. He swung the wheel, clipping the smaller carabinero. The plastic ID cards flew from his hand.

'Get down! Down!' Dieter yelled again.

He floored the accelerator. The jeep roared away along the road. Gunfire followed them.

Even with her head buried in the seat, Rosa couldn't shut out the deathly pinging of bullets on the steel rear of the jeep. Her insides jellied with fear.

And then Dieter swung the jeep hard across the central island of the boulevard. For a moment, as the jeep clattered against the kerb, it seemed to hang in the air and Rosa held tight, her new fear now that she'd be flung from the vehicle.

Dieter chanced a look over his shoulder.

'I'm OK,' Rosa gasped.

He nodded, went on pushing the jeep to its limit.

'Their radio is kaput,' Dieter shouted. 'If we can get on to the mountain tracks, we have a chance.'

And then Elena, with a tiny sigh, slumped against Dieter in the front seat.

'Señora Rossman?' With his right hand Dieter tried to push Elena upright.

Another tiny sigh came from her lips.

'Mama!' Rosa was staring wide-eyed at the hole in the back of the seat in front of her. 'Mama!' she screamed again. She touched the edge of the bullet-drilled hole with tentative fingers and drew back her hand as though scorched by the ragged edges.

'Get up here in front.' Dieter was handling the heavy steering of the jeep while holding Elena upright with his other hand. 'It's too risky to stop.'

Rosa clambered into the front seat, somehow got herself between her mother and Dieter.

The jeep leapt ahead as Dieter got both hands on the steering wheel and pushed down on the accelerator.

Rosa held her mother close against her. Elena's body was limp, heavy. Another sigh, a bubble of blood leaking at the corner of her mouth.

'We have to get Mama to hospital.' Her words seemed flung backwards in the slipstream of the jeep. 'She needs help or she'll die.'

Dieter seemed deaf.

Rosa kicked out at his leg. 'Take us to a hospital – now.'

Dieter's right hand flew from the steering wheel, backhanding her in the face.

'Every hospital in the city is under guard. We go there and

you will die too. D'you think your mother would want that?' She wondered at the calmness in the blue eyes when he threw her a sideways glance. 'Your father trusted me, that's why he gave me the job of protecting you.'

'And this is how you protect us?' She took one hand from around her mother's body, pushed the blood-soaked palm close to his face.

'Forgive me, Fräulein Rosa.' Only her grandfather, her mother's father, had ever called her *Fräulein*, an echo of the country he had long ago left and never again visited. But her grandfather's voice had never been laden with such dull sorrow as she heard now in Dieter's words.

'I know I've failed.' His words spoken to the fly-splattered windscreen of the jeep. 'But there's going to be no more failing.'

She reached out then, touched him on the shoulder.

The city was behind them now. She tried to hold her mother close against her to soften the bouncing jolts as they hurtled along a narrow potholed blacktop.

Elena gave a long, slow sigh. Her body rattled, seemed to crumple against Rosa like an empty paper bag. A bag that went on emptying blood against Rosa, drenching her shirt with a warm stickiness.

Dieter, too, had heard that long, rattling sigh.

'I'm truly sorry, Fräulein Rosa.' A hard hand on her arm, the briefest of pressure. 'Truly sorry.'

Rosa swallowed. In the rushing blur of sloping fields she could glimpse her mother's face that morning, the intimate look she flashed at Franco. She could hear above the growling of the engine the smack of Elena's hand on her face.

'She slapped me this morning,' she said. 'On the face.'

Dieter glanced at her. 'Maybe you deserved it.'

'Yes,' Rosa said, 'I deserved it.'

Dieter smiled at her and she returned his smile.

For about an hour they rattled along winding roads that climbed higher, narrowing as they climbed. They drove through villages with closed doors and shuttered windows and they knew that eyes followed them and ears listened to the planes that screamed across the sky.

Dieter slowed, pointing at a farmhouse ahead. 'We'll be safe here,' he said, 'for a little while.'

He swung the jeep on to the dirt track that led to the farmhouse. Chickens scurried across the yard. A thin plume of smoke hung in the air above the chimney. Rosa shivered, as though her mother's body had suddenly cooled against her own.

Dieter cut the engine.

In the open doorway of the farmhouse a close-shaven young man in faded dungarees stood watching them. A pair of dark-haired twin boys, maybe four years old, stood beside him.

'You made it this far,' the man said.

'Not without trouble,' Dieter said.

The children's mother came to the door. Her solemn gaze moved from the men to the jeep in the yard. She gave a little cry when she saw the girl and the blood-soaked woman slumped in her arms. She ran across the stony yard to Elena; her husband held the children back.

'Señora Rossman?'

Dieter nodded. 'We almost made it.' He shook his head. 'You know how it is.'

'Eat something,' the man said, 'and get moving.' He looked across at the jeep. 'I'll take care of it.'

'The soldiers will come, maybe soon.'

'They'll find nothing.'

Rosa was ushered into the big kitchen. The twins watched

her, silent, as she sat at the table, shoulders slumped. The woman offered her tea, coffee, water. Rosa didn't even shake her head. Outside in the yard the men moved softly, murmuring to each other, but she knew they were about the business of putting her mother's remains in the stony ground.

Dieter came in.

'Nando?' the woman said.

'He's doing what has to be done.'

From outside came the clanging sound of metal on stone.

They're digging my mother's grave. 'I want to see,' Rosa said, 'I want to say *adios*.'

'There isn't time,' Dieter said. 'We've got to move.'

Something snapped in her.

'I want to say goodbye to my mother!' she shouted.

The twins began to cry.

'Please, please!' their mother said.

Rosa looked at the bawling children, the way they clung to their mother's skirt. She saw the fear in the woman's eyes, heard the clang of danger in every stroke of the spade slicing into the stony earth.

'I'm sorry,' she said. She looked around the kitchen, saw the large old-fashioned radio on the window sill. 'But please, is there news of my father?'

The woman shook her head. *How do you tell a young girl that the army-controlled radio had announced that President Allende had taken his own life in the palace rather than face trial for his crimes against Chile? And that one of his fellow criminals in government, Franco Mendoza, had been shot dead for resisting arrest by the soldiers of liberation.*

'There is no news, little one,' the woman said. 'The radio is silent.'

She turned away, bent over the cooking pot to spoon rice

and beans into a dish for Dieter. He ate in small, neat spoonfuls yet in a few minutes the dish was empty.

'*Gracias*,' he told the woman.

'You should go now,' she said. 'If the soldiers find you here . . .' She drew the twins to her, one on either side.

Rosa stood up. 'Thank you for taking care of my mother, Señora – I don't know your name.'

'It's better not to, little one.'

'The soldiers,' Dieter said. 'If they stop us.'

What you don't know, Rosa thought, can't kill you. *Or anyone else either*.

'*Gracias*, Señora,' she said. 'From my heart.'

The woman embraced her.

'I will come back,' Rosa said.

'Of course you will.' There was a sadness in the woman's voice.

'*I will!*' A kind of fury in Rosa's words.

'Rosa.' She heard something different in Dieter's voice. When she turned to him she saw a different face, harder, but sadder too. 'Socialism in Chile is finished for now, the army generals and the Americans have made sure of that today. What they have done is illegal, anti-democratic, but the Americans will get away with it – for now anyway. Maybe socialism can survive here, even the Americans can't kill us all. We don't know,' his voice softened, 'we don't know if President Allende is alive, if your father is alive, or any other ministers.' The woman caught his eye and he read understanding there: sometimes you had to lie. 'You're fourteen years old, Rosa, maybe your father never talked to you about socialism or democracy . . .'

'The other girls at school called my father a Communist, that he and the President would steal their lands and their businesses.' She half smiled. 'I always told them to fuck off.'

The woman flinched, drew her children closer.

Dieter shrugged. 'Sometimes you have to lose a battle before you can win the war. But if you go to Germany now, as your father wished, it may be a long time before you can come back.'

'Germany? Who wants to go to fucking Germany?' She looked at Dieter, stunned. *Germany, where her grandfather never wished to return?* Outside, the spade went on clanging, digging her mother's grave.

A jumbled blur of images flashed through her mind like a cock-eyed movie. Her father's laugh, his stubbly cheek as he kissed her goodnight. Grandfather Rossman singing '*Stille Nacht, Heilige Nacht*' when they all gathered together on Christmas Eve. The girls at school sneering with raised eyebrows. Her mother's stinging hand. The planes tearing the fabric of the September sky and her mother's life leaking away in the front seat of the rattling jeep driven by a German stranger in a cheap, shiny suit.

She looked at him, this man who had just wandered purposefully into her life. Who had probably saved her life.

'It's what your father wanted,' Dieter said. 'When it's safe, he'll join you.'

She wanted to believe him. There had to be a different place, a different ending – another beginning – from this mountainside where her mother's body would lie unmarked. Just hours ago her mind had been focused on a school play, her lines learned, her moves rehearsed; now there was *this* – the wind on the mountain, the clang of steel on stones, the confusing kindness of strangers. Here the drama was unrehearsed, the plot unscripted.

Dieter was waiting, watching. She saw his stillness, like a rock that belonged on the mountain.

What did it matter now, Germany or anywhere else?

'All right,' Rosa said. 'If my father wished it.'

The twins stood waving in the doorway as Dieter turned the jeep in the farmyard. The back of the jeep was laden with jerrycans of petrol that the children's father had secured with ropes, and Rosa thought again how long they must have been preparing for this day of disaster.

The sky was darkening. Here in the mountains night would fall suddenly, like a curtain on her school play.

When they swung on to the road, she looked back at the farmhouse, retreating into the gloom. In the field beyond the house the dark-haired farmer raised one arm in farewell, then bent again over her mother's grave.

Four

11–14 September 1973
The Andes
South America

Afterwards, in her new life, wrestling with the unaccustomed language, Rosa could not recall clearly how long they had meandered among the lower reaches of the mountains. She remembered the cold of the nights, wrapped in the hairy blankets from the farmhouse, but was it three nights or four, under the icy stars? She remembered Dieter's paleness, face drawn, as though the dentist had forgotten to inject him before pulling resistant teeth. And the peaks themselves, like giant canines, towering above them, mocking their puny attempt at escape.

Even in the mountains there was no escaping the screaming planes.

Dieter pulled the jeep under a hanging rock, killed the engine and stared skywards.

'So much for national airspace.' She had to strain to make out his words.

'We're out of Chile?'

'I hope so.' But he didn't say where they were.

Limbo, she told herself. A place between there and now, between here and yesterday. A place where the unforgiving mountain terrain was ever-changing but always the same.

'Argentina?' The sky was silent.

'Argentina has generals too, Rosa.' Dieter pulled the jeep out from under the rock. 'We can't stay here.'

Generals. In her ears like another word for bogeymen, the kind of monsters who ambushed your dreams and you woke to find your mother dead and your father . . .

She wanted to ask but Dieter looked too tired for questions.

Each day he drove until darkness stopped them. Too dangerous, he said, to chance the lights. Yet whenever she stirred in the night, he was awake, upright in the driver's seat, or standing by the jeep, cowled in the rough blanket. Once she felt him rearranging her blanket, folding it more closely around her. *He loved my father*, she thought. *Or maybe they both loved the same thing*.

She wanted to ask about her father. She didn't want to hear the answer. Something about the woman's attitude, her tenderness, in the farmhouse made her doubt that the radio had been silent all day.

Her mother had died that day. Even though Elena had begged Dieter not to kill that American at their house. You spare one of them but another of the bastards will kill you anyway. She had to believe that her father was alive, that he would come for her in Germany. She looked at Dieter, at that impassive face, and was both frightened and reassured.

Dieter was tapping on a dial on the metal dashboard. He looked at his watch, drew the jeep to a halt. From his pocket he took a piece of paper and unfolded it. Rosa leaned closer, watched him finger a black line on the hand-drawn map.

'Are we almost there – wherever we're going?'

'A few hours.' He smiled at her. 'If the petrol holds out.'

'We still have one can left.'

'But it's no longer full, Fräulein Rossman.'

She watched him uncap the jerrycan and empty it into the tank with small, neat movements. He'd be a good dancer, she thought, and she laughed.

'Are you laughing at me, Fräulein Rossman?'

She was ashamed then, as though the teacher had caught her giggling over some silliness at the back of the class.

'You can laugh at me anytime.' His voice was soft.

'There's not much else to laugh about right now.'

Dieter smiled.

There was something renewed about the way he turned the key now. He banged on the horn, a hoarse, squawky sound like geese over the mountains, as they moved off along the mountain track.

'We have to make time.' He had to shout above the noise of the engine. 'And the petrol has to last. But I think we're going to make it.'

They did.

A long climb along a boulder-edged path, a muffled sound, like a Sunday lawnmower, above and beyond them, and then they emerged on to a narrow, unexpected plateau. In the middle of the plateau, incongruous, a small twin-engined plane, its engine idling with a throaty *put-putting* noise.

Dieter drove the jeep along the levelled causeway. Close to, the surface was rough; jagged splinters flew from under the wheels of the jeep.

A blue van, a white Beetle and a motorbike with a sidecar stood to one side of the plane. A small group of men, jacket collars turned up against the mountain chill, stood watching as Dieter drew the jeep to a halt. Only the rim of the sun edged above the mountain peaks; in the gloom it was impossible to make out faces.

A single figure detached himself from the group. He was tall, painfully thin.

'You made it, Dieter.' He spoke in German but Rosa had spent enough time in her grandfather's garrulous company to understand.

'Just in time, it seems.' Dieter gestured at the plane.

'You know we'd have waited for you.'

Dieter laughed drily. 'Yes, but for how long?'

'You must have more faith, Dieter, in our sense of socialist fraternity.' Now the thin fellow was laughing too. 'What you need is a long spell in the homeland.'

'I forgot to bring bananas.'

The rest of the group – five men and a close-cropped woman, Rosa could see now – were silent, listening to this exchange. And she felt small, childish even, in the presence of these strangers in the deepening shadow of the mountains. She felt their eyes upon her, on the flimsy T-shirt and denim jeans, and she raised her hand to her long dark hair and longed for a shower and a shampoo.

And her mother.

The dark mountains seemed to stoop over them. Rosa looked into the darkness, felt her own smallness before these strangers in this alien place.

'My father,' she said to no one in particular. 'Where is my father?'

The thin man, seemingly the leader of the group, looked from Rosa to Dieter.

'This is Minister Mendoza's daughter?'

'Rosa.' She was glad of Dieter's hand on her shoulder: the long journey through the mountains had created its own bond. 'Rosa Rossman, daughter of Franco Mendoza and Elena Rossman.'

The thin man held out his hand to her. 'You are welcome among us, Fräulein Rossman.' He spoke to her in German, using the formal, adult *Sie*.

She asked again. 'My father?'

'He died defending his President.' She was sure he clicked his heels together, gave her a slight bow. 'My deepest sympathies.'

Her hands reached out but the darkness offered no support. She felt her mind scrambling for something – anything – to hang on to. The school play, she thought, but now even the title eluded her. Hers was the role of the teenage girl at odds with disapproving parents over an unsuitable boyfriend: not even a name came to her.

She felt the men come closer but they were shadows, as unreal as the parents in the play. Only her mother's nameless grave was real. And her father. His smell, his smile. His hard jaw against her face when he hugged her.

And now he, too, was an absence.

My deepest sympathies.

She wanted to know how and where and when and, most of all, *why*, but these considerations seemed less important under the majesty of the darkening mountains. The thought struck her that she was an orphan now – but she was an adult too. She drew herself taller and inclined her head gravely to the thin German and she said thank you.

And then she was falling, crumpling, and she felt Dieter gather her into his arms.

'She's just a child,' Dieter said.

Rosa didn't hear him. She had passed out and they were carrying her up and into the small plane.

Five

14 September 1973
The Andes
South America

They were airborne when she came to. She didn't move, kept her head on the small pillow pushed against the window. Eyes closed. The engines droning like a lullaby off-key.

She could hear Dieter's voice, raised above the noise of the engine.

'You think I'd leave her to those animals?'

'It was her father we wanted to get out.' A female voice, smoky with cigarettes. 'He stood for something, it would have been a triumph if we could have shown him to the cameras in Berlin.'

'He stood for decency and democracy and socialism.' There was an edge to Dieter's voice. 'And Franco Mendoza entrusted me with the safety of his woman and his daughter.'

'He should have got out when we told him to.' The woman snorted. 'Romantic bullshit – was he going to hold off the rebels with a handgun? Talk about tilting at fucking windmills.'

Rosa heard a match struck, smelled cigarette smoke.

When Dieter spoke again, his tone was sharper. 'A man like Franco Mendoza reminds us of the meaning of socialism, of the ideals we strive to achieve in our own country.'

'Dieter, you talk like a fucking textbook. You're full of—'

Rosa never did hear what the woman thought Dieter was full of.

The plane bucked, plummeted through a hole in the mountain air. A shared gasp of fright filled the cabin. Rosa's head was knocked against the seat in front and she grabbed for Dieter's hand. His fingers went round hers.

'It's OK.' He put his arm around her.

The plane righted itself, levelled off, climbed again. Across the aisle the woman's face, framed in its cropped cut, was as white as the cigarette that she held in her thin fingers. Rosa felt skewered by the grey eyes in the pale face. The woman went on staring at her as she stubbed out her butt in an empty cigarette pack.

'We shall see.' The woman turned her head to Dieter but he made no reply.

Rosa felt his fingers tighten on her shoulder.

'Just a little bump,' he said again. 'Feeling better?'

She wanted to thank him for what he had said about her father but she wasn't sure she had fully understood his words.

'I'm tired, Dieter.'

'We'll be home soon.' He let the words rest there, sitting on her shoulder, as the small plane droned on through the Andean night. She knew that the short-haired woman was seated across the aisle; she knew that she and Dieter were not alone but in the dimly lit cabin you couldn't see the other passengers belted into their seats.

Even with a friendly hand on hers she felt alone, ploughing through the dark skies towards a strange place that Dieter called 'home'.

But first there was Asunción, Paraguay. She knew it was Asunción because the woman said so as they were coming to land.

'Paraguay?' Puzzlement in Dieter's voice. 'Why Paraguay?'

'No time to organize anything else – and there was a fraternal visit by a cadre of factory workers to our fellow workers in the great socialist state of Paraguay.'

'Socialist Paraguay!' Dieter's laugh was dry. 'The Americans own the place – so how?'

'American dollars, how else?' The woman's voice bitter. 'Dollars can buy you anything – even a handful of army colonels to get you in and out of Asunción.'

The wheels hit the runway, bounced once, twice, settled and roared to a halt. The silence seemed deafening when the engines were switched off.

The woman was on her feet. 'We must be silent.' The hubbub of landing was quelled.

The thin man who had shaken her hand was standing in the aisle, looking back at Rosa. *He has the words but it's the sharp-faced woman who leads.*

In silence they trailed the woman down the steps on to the black tarmac. The plane had come to rest far from the airport buildings: in the distance a lighted window in a tower hung above the single-storey terminal. The military lorry standing near the plane was dark. A lighted cigarette glowed in the cabin. Instinctively the small group moved together towards the lorry. Only then did Rosa see the soldiers: three of them, rifles held across their chests, standing beside the lorry. The door of the vehicle opened, the cigarette end glowed again. The officer who climbed down was short, pot-bellied, cigarette in one hand, a silver-tipped swagger stick in the other.

'Welcome to my country.' In Spanish, the words spat out below the pencil-thin moustache. 'Alas, your stay here must be brief.' He let the cigarette fall from his hand, trod on it without taking his eyes from the huddled group. 'And your stay must be silent.' The swagger stick swung lazily towards the lorry. 'All aboard – in silence.'

There were no steps to climb into the back of the lorry. Two of the men swung aboard, reached down to help the pale-faced woman. Rosa shrugged Dieter's helping hand aside and hauled herself up. The soldiers stood immobile, arms ready, watching them. Dieter boarded last. Only then did the soldiers move, climbing into the back of the lorry. They stood at the tailgate, gripping the metal frame. One of them faced the night. The other two stared inwards at the group.

Someone coughed as the lorry moved off, tried to quell the noise in cupped hands.

The lorry driver changed gear noisily and metal mangled metal. In the back they could hear the officer's barked expletive, the driver's mumbled apology and they smiled at one another.

The soldiers at the back of the lorry didn't smile.

The soldiers sprang to the ground when the lorry halted, stood back to let the group alight.

They were standing in the shadow of the Tupolev. The Russian-made plane reared above them, a fortress in the night. No lights showed inside. The tail rose in the dark, brooding above the engine tucked below it and the pair of side engines.

She felt Dieter's hand on her shoulder, felt herself drawn closer to him. She wondered about her lost father. Saw the stubble-jawed farmer bend over her mother's grave in an unnamed wilderness. She let herself be led up the gangway steps. At the top she hesitated, looked back down. The moustached officer had another cigarette going, a red glow in the darkness. The silver tip of his stick shone in the glow as he touched it to the peak of his cap in a silent gesture of *adios*. *He's glad to be rid of us*. What was it the woman had said? *Dollars will buy anything.*

The blue-shirted stewardess drew her into the plane's still-dark interior. She could make out seemingly endless rows of seats; her eyes focused and she saw white faces, rows and rows of them staring up at her.

'Take your seats quickly.' The stewardess was pointing at the empty rows in front. In German, unsmiling. 'You're the last. We've been waiting for almost two hours.'

'Comrade.' The pale-faced woman, her lips so thin, so compressed, you wondered how the word escaped. 'You have a problem with our late arrival?'

The stewardess blanched, her own face suddenly whiter than her interrogator's.

'Of course not, Frau Comrade, I merely wish to expedite—'

'Enough.' A single word spoken, a single finger raised in the face of the stewardess, and yet it seemed to Rosa that the entire plane was holding its breath. *Who is she, this woman who thinks Dieter just wasted time on me?*

Behind the frozen stewardess the door to the flight deck swung open. The captain stood there, white-shirted in the lighted doorway.

'Frau Colonel.' The slightest heel click, the slightest bow. He extended his hand to shake the woman's. 'You are welcome aboard. We are ready to leave when you are.'

The woman thanked him. All eyes watched as the captain helped her into her seat, helped fasten the belt across the skinny lap before returning to the cockpit.

Within minutes the Tupolev was climbing from the runway into the night sky. The metal frame shuddered in the dark, strained against the clawing grip of gravity.

Her childhood seemed to fall away into the land lost beneath them. *The house in the Barrio Alto, the little well in the courtyard and your mother wearing your father's pyjama bottoms in the brightness of your morning kitchen. Your mother's impatience with your foul language and your father trying to keep the smile off his face.*

In the metallic clamminess of the plane she dozed and woke, dozed and woke.

She feared she would dream, that she would see her mother rise from her stony grave. Perhaps her exhaustion was more powerful than her fear of dreaming. Maybe her spirit was saving the dreams for later. Maybe it was Dieter's nearness that kept the dreams at bay. Whenever she stirred on the long flight through the night, she checked to make sure he was there, strapped into the narrow seat beside her.

Once she thought he whispered something to her but the loud droning of the engines distorted sound.

'I'm here.' She thought that's what he said. But maybe she dreamed it.

They landed in the white light of day. More soldiers, more jeeps; she watched them on the dark tarmac, looking down at them through the porthole.

'Lisbon,' Dieter whispered.

Nobody was allowed off the plane while they refuelled but the doors were opened and the sunshine spilled into the crowded fuselage. An officer stepped in, in sunglasses and braided cap; he spent a few minutes closeted on the flight deck with the captain and then left without so much as acknowledging the silent passengers staring up at him.

The doors of the plane closed and voices chattered like school kids' when the teacher has left. The thin woman stood up in the aisle and looked back along the plane. The chattering ceased.

Later, on her way back from the cramped toilet, Rosa noticed how all the passengers avoided eye contact with her. They feigned sleep, buried themselves in magazines, looked over her shoulder. What had that woman called them? *A cadre of factory workers*. Factory workers who asked no questions and shunned the eyes of a bunch of latecomers who boarded like refugees in the night. Refugees for whom the plane waited for hours in a remote corner of Asunción Airport.

What kind of country was it that these silent, cowed workers came from?

The Tupolev powered north-east through the skies of Europe. The sky was blue, flecked with clouds as innocent as puffs of cotton wool.

The clouds over Santiago had signalled horror below. She could see her father in La Moneda, knew instinctively that he would have stood close to the President, would have remained beside him to the end. She tried not to think of that end but the blood from her mother's broken body leaked on to her hands like red slime.

The tears came then, great silent tears like rain on her face. She felt Dieter's hand on hers.

His voice was low and soft, the words German.

'We'll be home soon, Rosa.' He squeezed her hand. 'In Germany.'

PART 2

64A WILHELMSTRASSE

Six

September 1989
East Berlin
German Democratic Republic

They knocked on your door but they never waited for your answer.

This time it was Bendtner who pushed in the door and stood there, blue-jawed, close-cropped, fully suited.

'The Herr Direktor wishes to see you in his office.' Hand still on the door handle, ready to depart. 'Immediately.'

Miller nodded. He wondered if it was his office alone that Bendtner walked into with such little ceremony.

He didn't get the chance to ask. He wouldn't have asked anyway, even if the door had not closed as abruptly as it had opened. Even if Bendtner were not already halfway down the marble staircase to rejoin his colleague at the porter's desk in the lobby of 64A Wilhelmstrasse. You learned quickly not to ask too many questions in East Berlin. Not even such innocent ones as why Bendtner was ordered to climb to the fourth floor with a message that Direktor Hartheim (or his secretary) could more easily have delivered by picking up the phone.

Miller stood up from his grey, metal desk and put on his jacket. This September afternoon's sticky heat wasn't much affected by the small fan in the corner of the office but the Director was a stickler for formality.

Miller hurried to the tiled, echoing toilet to check his hair and tie in the small mirror above the equally small washbasin.

The doors along the corridor were closed. Inside the Secretariat for Socialist Correctness in Publishing you learned to value whatever little privacy you could find. *And after a while you learned that the idea of privacy was an illusion.*

Enough, Miller told himself, hurrying along the corridor; it's almost ten minutes since Bendtner delivered his message.

He tapped gently on the glass door at the end of the corridor.

Frau Siedel left him standing there for the statutory minute and a half before she opened the door. And in statutory silence she ushered him into her own box of space, the ante-chamber to the Director's office.

Miller took care to touch nothing on Frau Siedel's desk while the secretary phoned to announce his arrival.

'*Ja.*' The blond head bobbed at the phone. Frau Siedel was young, good-looking, Hartheim's latest secretary selection. '*Alle ist klar.*' Hartheim's appetite for young blondes did not go unnoticed in 64A; like much else, it was not spoken of. There was a certain stiffness about this one, Miller felt, that told you she wouldn't be staying too long.

'You may enter now,' Frau Siedel told Miller.

Miller thanked her, went into the Director's office.

Helmut Hartheim's chair was, as usual, pushed well back from his desk to accommodate his huge stomach. Like his secretary, he left Miller waiting for some internally measured interval before lifting his head from the paper in his hands. Maybe he counts, Miller thought, or maybe he's one of those people you read about, men with metronomes pulsing away inside their heads.

'Ah, Herr Miller!' As though surprised to see somebody standing in front of his desk. 'It's good of you to come.'

The big, round head nodded Miller towards the chair on the other side of the clutter-free desk. Hartheim laid the sheet of paper down carefully – upside-down – on the desk, moving the box of pens a fraction to the left, in line with something that Miller could neither see nor imagine.

Tune in. Hartheim was asking about the English language edition of the nineteenth-century farm labourer's diary.

'Everything is in order, Herr Direktor. I've cleared the final page proofs and you yourself have approved the cover design.' *You could at least read photographs.*

'Good.' A ponderous lifting of the basketball head. 'And you are satisfied that the language adequately conveys the socialist spirit of the original?'

Miller nodded. 'Most faithfully.' Although why a minor university in Western Australia should choose to publish a translation of a nineteenth-century farmhand's memoir of life under upper-crust Prussian landlords was beyond Miller. The print run was agreed at 500 copies; Miller reckoned that at least 400 of them would finish up in remainder bins. 'It's an excellent translation, sir,' he added with extra conviction.

Hartheim's was a corner office; two windowed walls looked out over the rooftops on to the tree-lined stretch of Unter den Linden. Over the Director's shoulder Miller could see, through the glass, the slow-moving traffic on the wide thoroughfare. Most of the traffic was heading east, or swinging on to Friedrichstrasse; westward lay only the barricaded columns of the Brandenburg Gate, at the heart of the Berlin Wall.

'We are fortunate,' Hartheim was saying, 'to have a distinguished writer – a native speaker – to help us with these English translations.'

'It's my good fortune to be here, sir.' In the beginning Miller had been inclined to swallow such compliments. 'And the cause is greater than any of us.' Although after seven years of life in East Berlin, Miller wasn't sure if he was still a believer.

'Still, it was an unusual event, your arriving here like that, Herr Miller.'

Miller nodded. *And more unusual than you ever found out, not even after all the interrogations.*

He spread his hands, smiled. 'The struggle is ongoing, Herr Direktor, but it is worthwhile.' *And you sound like a page from a textbook. Even after seven years you still have an itch to tell the truth, no matter what the bastards in Pall Mall might say.*

'It's a pity those fuckers in Budapest don't feel the same.' With unexpected grace Hartheim got to his feet and moved towards the small television on a corner table.

The hum of the TV set filled the office. The black-and-white pictures fashioned themselves into focus; the sound of a helicopter rotored from the small set.

'The fuckers are still at it.'

It was impossible to tell where Hartheim's venom was directed: at the camera operators in the unseen helicopter or at the shirt-sleeved crowd waving up at the helicopter from the grounds of the West German embassy in Budapest.

'Cunts.' Hartheim had resumed his seat. 'We should drop a bomb on them.' His whole body turned as he looked west through the window. 'And another one on the cunts over there.'

All summer long, since the Hungarians had opened their border with Austria, the roads and trains had been crowded with fleeing East Germans making their roundabout way to West Germany through Hungary and Austria.

The camera swooped low over the waving crowds in the embassy garden; the growling noise of the chopper grew louder in Hartheim's office.

Miller held his breath. Like most people in East Berlin, he

had his television aerial tuned to the West. Like Hartheim and other accredited East German staff, Miller was authorized to do so. Now it seemed almost that such authorization no longer mattered. All of the German Democratic Republic was staring at these pictures of a people in flight and even the Stasi seemed not to know what to do about it.

'Cunts,' Hartheim said again. He waved a hand. 'Please – turn it off.'

Miller wondered why the TV had been turned on in the first place. Some lesson for himself? Or simply further evidence of Hartheim's capricious nature? With Hartheim you never knew – and you never asked.

Miller waited. He knew he hadn't been summoned to Hartheim's office simply to report progress on an Australian edition of an almost-forgotten nineteenth-century memoir. His work consisted in the main of examining new books for any wayward comments on socialism as practised in the German Democratic Republic. Once upon an innocent time, in his life before East Berlin, his own articles in the British press had been a continuous hymn to the glories of German socialism.

Hartheim was taking a bulky manila folder from a drawer in his desk.

And this is where your hymn-singing has landed you.

'I have an important task for you, Herr Miller.' Hartheim laid the thick file on his desk. His left hand rested on top of the file, the one with the chewed-off index finger. In the last days of the war, as the Red Army powered its way through the rubble of Berlin, Hartheim had been one of the Communist provocateurs rounded up by a fanatic Nazi commander. Interrogation was cursory and brutal: the Gestapo officer had slashed Hartheim's hand with his knife and offered the bloodied finger to the half-starved Dobermann pinscher at his side. The crazed dog had devoured Hartheim's index finger with a single bite. Then the Russians arrived and both dog and master died in a sudden burst of gunfire.

Hartheim had a habit of stroking with his right hand the knuckle stub of the missing finger. Watching it always made Miller queasy, as though the wolfish dog were chewing away in front of him. Hartheim was doing it now – fat, sausage fingers poking away at the lumpy knuckle.

Tune in!

Of late, Miller felt he was too easily distracted. Maybe it was all that embassy-refugee shit on the television. The entire country seemed distracted.

Hartheim was droning on in his thick Berlin accent.

'It's a routine reading, a matter of form, the autobiography of a distinguished soldier. The general understood better than anyone that the Party is truly "the sword and shield" of our country. Just set down your reactions in your usual objective way.'

The general? Miller looked longingly at the file but Hartheim's pudding hand was covering the name stickered to the top of the brown cardboard.

Aloud he said, 'Would it be possible for me to see our reports from earlier readers?' *You didn't want to fuck around with the memoirs of a fucking general, no matter which general it was.*

Hartheim croaked a kind of laugh. 'They're not relevant, Herr Miller. What we expect of you is your usual assessment of how the general's book might be received in the Western media. We both know how our enemies distort and murder the truth in the West. We simply don't want to present them with opportunities to do so in our own publications.' An attempt at a smile on the round face. 'Nobody knows better than you, Herr Miller, how a word or a phrase can be seized upon and twisted into an untruth. It is that expertise of yours which has been so helpful to us over the last few years. Just do your usual job of applying your expertise to General Reder's work.'

'General Reder?'

'Yes.'

'General *Hans* Reder?'

'Which other General Reder is there?'

'I mean . . .' Miller swallowed. 'I didn't realize that the general was still – still with us.'

'Perhaps not for much longer, which may be why he wishes to see his story in print.' Hartheim pushed the file across the desk to Miller. 'General Reder has cancer but is presently in remission. His daughter cares for him. The daughter is also looking after the general's manuscript and has asked if she might be told personally of any changes we think necessary. Of course, we wouldn't normally agree to any such thing but, in view of the general's standing in our country, I have agreed to this. I have therefore arranged for his daughter to call at your office on Thursday.'

'But that's the day after tomorrow.'

'Which means, Herr Miller, that you and I will have time to discuss your written comments on General Reder's manuscript tomorrow.' There was no attempted smile now on Hartheim's face.

'Of course, Herr Direktor.' Hartheim pushed his chair back another inch. The interview was over.

The file under Miller's arm felt like a ticking bomb as he made his way back to his own office. Commenting on the memoir of a retired general, a hero of the German Democratic Republic, was a task to be avoided. Miller knew that he would have to be at his most bland: this required fence-sitting of the highest degree. It was a truth he had learned quickly after arriving in East Berlin: the truth was a movable feast. General Reder might be today's hero but he could also be tomorrow morning's scoundrel.

The phone on his desk rang.

It was Frau Siedel.

'The Director wishes you to know that General Reder's daughter's appointment is for three o'clock on Thursday afternoon.'

'I'm sure I'll have everything in order for Frau Reder.'

'Actually it's his stepdaughter, Frau *Rossman* – Frau Rosa Rossman.'

Miller didn't realize the secretary had hung up. He didn't hear the buzz of the dead line in his ear. He was hearing, seven years ago, Redgrave's hee-haw tones telling him that his arrival in East Berlin would be 'a match made in Communist heaven'. For good measure Redgrave had thrown in a handful of plummy 'old chaps'.

Miller put the phone down, crossed to the window. If he stood on tiptoe and craned his neck, he could see a tiny stretch of Unter den Linden.

East Berlin was going home in the September evening. His father would be in the Wolverhampton surgery, rheumy eyes still ogling his private patients. And soon Miller himself would be lodged in his functional flat, turning the pages of General Hans Reder's typescript.

It was going to be a long night in Berlin. But he had to get something suitably non-committal ready for Hartheim.

He didn't give a second thought to Frau Rosa Rossman.

Seven

Thursday, 14 September 1989
East Berlin
German Democratic Republic

On Thursday afternoon Miller was asking himself how he would ever get Rosa Rossman *out* of his thoughts.

The woman waiting for him under the watchful eyes of the porters in the entrance hall of 64A Wilhelmstrasse was of medium height, slim, with straight, jet-black hair that hung below her shoulders. Her rucksack sat on the small bench that was the institute's grudging concession to waiting visitors; Rosa Rossman herself stood beside the bench, arms crossed, looking almost puzzled, as though she had been placed there by mistake. Vulnerable, Miller thought, a porcelain figurine, eminently droppable, breakable.

And then she moved, unfolded her arms, extended her hand to him, and what Miller was aware of was the overwhelming physicality of her, the electricity of her smile, the very *presence* of the body stirring beneath the simple white T-shirt and the navy pencil skirt.

Open your ears as well as your eyes: the woman is talking to you.

Frau Rosa Rossman was introducing herself, saying how good it was of Miller to see her.

Miller tried not to stare at the wide face, the deep, sloe-black eyes, the full lips that seemed to grow fuller in speech.

Miller said it was an honour to be allowed to read the work of her distinguished stepfather.

Frau Rosa Rossman said that she and General Reder would be most grateful for any advice, any assistance, that would expedite the publication of the general's book.

Miller said that naturally he and his colleagues would be pleased to assist in any way they could.

'But don't offer any dates.' Hartheim had been uncharacteristically direct the day before. *'Remind her that the publication date is decided by the publishers.'*

The publishers, housed next door in No. 64, would not go for a piss if the Secretariat for Socialist Correctness did not approve of it.

Miller said none of this to Rosa Rossman as they stood swapping platitudes in the marble-floored entrance hall. Most likely she already knew this. She volleyed his formulaic pleasantries back to him like a pro.

The general, she was saying now, was most anxious to know if any publication date had been set.

The two porters, Miller could see, were hardly bothering to conceal their interest in Rosa Rossman's physical charms.

'Forgive me,' Miller said. 'We shouldn't be standing here like this, we should be in my office.'

No. 64A had no lift. Miller knew that the eyes of the porters followed Rosa Rossman all the way up to the first landing, where they climbed out of view. He couldn't blame the porters. In their place he'd be craning his neck too.

Upstairs, seated in his office, Miller wasn't sure how he felt about the grey metal desk which separated him from General Reder's stepdaughter. It blocked his line of vision to the long legs which were crossed, primly enough, at the ankles; on the other hand, the desk served as a kind of defence barrier against the tangible *womanliness* which emanated from his visitor. Her T-shirt and skirt were the usual nylon material, almost plastic in its hardness, worn by all of East Germany's proletariat but, on Rosa Rossman, the utilitarian clothing seemed almost haute couture.

Miller was about to offer Rosa a cup of office coffee when Frau Siedel entered his office, carrying a gold-coloured tray laid with china cups, a small metal pot of coffee and cream and sugar.

'Director Hartheim thought you might like some coffee.' Frau Siedel's words and frozen smile were directed at Rosa. 'He regrets he is not free to welcome you himself but sends his good wishes to you and to General Reder.'

The door fell shut behind her. Miller would have thought he imagined it but for the unaccustomed tray on his desk.

'Real coffee, I think.' Rosa Rossman was almost laughing at him. 'And sugar cubes with a silver tongs.'

I usually make my own mug of black, bitter powdered stuff.

'I think,' he said at last, 'that our Director knows very well that today we have a very distinguished visitor.'

'Herr Miller, I am a teacher and not a particularly distinguished one at that.'

'I didn't know you were a teacher.'

'Of English at the university. I wanted to study Spanish but my father said that English is the language of the future,' the merest hint of a downturn of those full lips, 'and my father is a hard man to resist. So here I am, teaching English to unsuspecting students at the university.' She smiled. 'Where we are not served coffee on a fancy tray.'

'Oh, I'm sorry—'

'Shall I be mother?' She said the words in English. He stared at her across the desk. *Shall I be mother?* A lifetime had passed since he had heard that expression: usually in jest, often with irony, over teacups and coffee cups in grotty student cafes and bedsits half heated with coin-operated gas fires.

'I told you, I teach English.' She shrugged, smiled. 'The general did a little research on you, Herr Miller.' She poured his coffee, handed him the delicate, gold-rimmed cup and saucer. 'He said you sounded like an interesting man – English by birth, East German by choice. He said that you were probably the right kind of person to evaluate his book.'

Miller could hear the question in her words but his years in this office had taught him a little side-stepping adroitness.

'The general is an interesting man.' He sipped the coffee, black, the better to savour its richness. 'You are, I understand, the general's stepdaughter.'

'No.' The eyes looking at him over the rim of the gold-rimmed cup were deeper and blacker than the coffee. 'I am General Reder's adopted daughter.' He felt himself – the plain office, the metal desk, the inevitable hidden recorders – he felt it all being measured by dark eyes that seemed to him to have known a world wider than where they sat. She laid the cup and saucer on the desk and Miller noticed the silent way she did so.

'I lived with General Reder and his wife almost from the time I arrived here. Just before Frau Reder died, they adopted me.' Her eyes locked on Miller's. 'The general is my father now.'

'I'm sorry if I intruded.'

'You didn't.' She might have been addressing a group of students. 'Now, what can I tell the general about progress with his book?'

Miller spread his hands, tried to hold her gaze. 'Not much, I'm afraid. Here we just read the book and give whatever advice we can to improve the work. The date of publication – and all the rest of it – is the business of the publishing house.'

'But the Berlin Press must wait for the go-ahead from you. So,' the faintest of smiles, 'I think what my father wants to know is whether that go-ahead will now be given.'

'That decision is, of course, made by the Director.' Miller gave up trying to meet the steady gaze of those black eyes. 'It's the decision of Herr Hartheim.'

'Who suggested meeting you, Herr Miller, to discuss the matter.'

'And I'm delighted to do so.' *This is a fuck-up, I've only ever dealt with these affairs through the post or – very occasionally – on the phone.* 'But the ultimate decision is the responsibility of the Director.'

'Ah, I see.' The tiniest clink of porcelain, the gold-rimmed cup raised to the cherry mouth, the black eyes widening at him. 'And how would you describe your responsibility here, Herr Miller?'

Mostly I lie: to my colleagues, to the Director, to the writers whose work lands on my desk. Maybe even the stuff I send to Redgrave and his assorted 'chums' is no more than lies. Mostly I lie: even to myself.

To Rosa he said, 'I read stuff, I evaluate it, I make considered judgements.'

She leaned forward slightly to return the cup and saucer to the desk. Her nearness seemed a threat, a potent mixture of talcum powder and fresh soap and fresh undergarments that would scorch your skin and trouble your sleep.

'I'm sorry I can't be more helpful, Frau Rossman.' He tried to smile. 'But I'm sure everything will be OK – after all, the general is recognized as a hero of the state.'

Shut it: even the most bland of political statements can be replayed on the listening tapes as a form of treason.

'That's what everyone says, Herr Miller, that my father is a hero of the German Democratic Republic.'

Miller could hear a 'but' coming. It didn't come, seemed swallowed behind those inviting lips. For the umpteenth time he asked himself why such a fuss was being made by Hartheim over an innocuous book by a retired general. Maybe Frau Rosa Rossman herself knew the answer.

Miller wasn't sure he wanted to know. Ignorance was almost always the safer option.

Rosa Rossman was getting to her feet, thanking him for his time.

'You are happy here, Herr Miller? You do not miss England?'

He forced a smile, said something platitudinous. There were topics you did not touch, not even in the most apparently harmless of conversations. Especially not with a general's daughter.

The general's daughter, he realized, had something on her mind: he was familiar with that narrowing of the eyes, the glance away, the hesitancy.

Miller waited.

'I wonder,' Frau Rossman said, 'if maybe you wouldn't mind walking me to my tramstop. The streets these days, you know . . .'

You could talk your way out of any street demonstration, Frau Rossman. Even fight your way out.

He said, 'I'd be delighted, the unrest on the streets these days . . .' He shook his head knowingly.

Rosa smiled.

They were playing games with each other. He wondered if Rosa Rossman was also playing to the unseen gallery. He'd know for sure when they were on the street, if she said yes when he asked her if she'd like to go for a drink or another coffee.

Miller phoned through to Frau Siedel to advise the Director that he was escorting Frau Rossman from the office. He heard the slight intake of breath as Frau Siedel prepared to speak but he hung up before she could say anything.

Eight

Thursday, 14 September 1989
East Berlin
German Democratic Republic

Maybe, Miller thought, Rosa Rossman had been right about the atmosphere on the streets. The tension in the city was palpable. The sky was blue, the air clear, but the September afternoon seemed to crackle with electricity, as though a storm threatened.

Pedestrians on their way home seemed intent on their feet. Even Rosa seemed determined to meet nobody's gaze as she strode out alongside Miller, her heels beating a steady rhythm on the cracked pavement. He didn't ask where they were headed, content with her nearness. She said little, just turned her head slightly to indicate that they should cross the wide thoroughfare of Unter den Linden.

On the island in the middle of the road a military policeman was checking the papers of a frightened-looking, middle-aged man with a tan briefcase in his hands. Under the steel helmet the policeman's face was as sweaty as his quarry's, his face unsmiling as he handed back the ID card and waved the man on.

Nerves, Miller thought: the crowds in the embassies and the candlelit protests in the Leipzig church have the bosses spooked, police on the corners, lines of soldiers tramping in and out of their barracks with assault rifles in readiness.

The green man lit up, Rosa touched his elbow to cross the street. Yet another helmeted policeman held up the lines of traffic, hand raised, whistle at the ready.

Miller followed Rosa off the main street, behind a red-brick church. These were his streets but he wondered where she was taking him. In these winding alleys you wouldn't find the kind of fancy cafes suitable for the daughters of generals. And you wouldn't find a bus stop or a tram halt here in these back streets. *Maybe she's after my body. You wish.*

She led him between two tall buildings with cemented-up windows. The sun did not reach in here; the unpaved passageway was rich with flowering weeds, clogged with rubbish.

In front of them was a single-storey breeze-block building with blackened windows. The tar-black door was shut. ZERO, the hand-painted sign over the door said, in black letters on a plain white board. Faint music came humming from behind the closed door and blackened windows.

She seemed to sense Miller's hesitancy.

'It's OK.' She was smiling. 'It's just a cafe the students showed me.'

'Frau Rossman,' he tried to smile, 'my department is part of the Ministry of State Security—'

'And you're afraid you might be compromised?' Eyebrows arched above the black pools. 'Do you think I would make trouble for my father, Herr Miller? The general found out I was in the habit of coming here with some of my students – there's no need to ask *how* he found out – and he assured me that, after a thorough investigation, ZERO was definitely *not* a hive of counter-revolutionary reactionism.' She laughed, a bell pealing in a grim and sunless alley. 'I like to think it's a different kind of place, Herr Miller, but we both know that eyes are watching wherever you go.'

Go home, Miller told himself. If you get yourself arrested and expelled you'll be no use to anybody. Not to Redgrave and his pinstriped acolytes. Not to your mother. Not even to your groper father. *Go home. Now.*

But she was smiling again, opening up those dark pools of infinity to him, and Miller feared that he might swim into any darkness they might lead him to.

The interior of ZERO seemed harmless. Strings of ceiling-hung bulbs compensated for the locked-out daylight; candle stubs in wax-ringed wine bottles made an amateurish attempt at student-type bohemianism. To Patrick Miller it seemed like a poor man's attempt at recreating the student haunts of his own undergraduate days in London.

The students were different. A mixture of shaven heads and pre-Raphaelite shoulder-length hair – and that was the men. The females favoured kohl-ringed eyes and cropped haircuts. The air was smogged with rising clouds of cigarette smoke. And the sweet scent of grass – Miller was sure he could smell it.

He knew that Frau Rosa Rossman was watching him.

He sniffed, smiled. 'The general didn't raise any objections to that?'

'My father has more important battles to fight.'

He wondered what she was driving at. He let it go: better to wait. It wasn't for his pale body that she had brought him here.

He made to move towards the small counter but she caught his sleeve, gestured with her other hand to a small table. 'You sit – they know me.'

Heads were raised to watch her thread her way between the tables to the small serving counter. She nodded, smiled, in response to a couple of hellos.

She came back with two beakers of black coffee. 'I should have asked – they only do tea or coffee.'

He waved away her concern, thanked her. He thought of saying something – anything – to put her at her ease, facilitate the telling or asking of whatever it was she had brought him to this place for. But he said nothing. It was, after all, her choice, her place. Rosa Rossman didn't look like somebody who'd have a problem making her point.

Or making her request. In this battened-down world behind the Wall there was always somebody who wanted something from a fellow like himself – a state employee who had clearance to cross into West Berlin at will.

Her opening gambit was simple. 'You're wondering why I've brought you here, Herr Miller.'

'It's not every day I am brought anywhere by a beautiful woman.' The cigarette smoke from the table behind ringed her like a halo. 'And my name is Patrick.'

'And I'm Rosa.'

'Rosa *Rossman*.'

'Yes.'

'In my office you said you were adopted by General Reder.'

The staccato music from the record player behind the counter was something punk, English words bellowed above the pogo-stick beat.

'I was eighteen when the general and his wife legally adopted me. I asked if I might keep my name and they said it was what they wanted too.'

Miller nodded. 'I suppose our name wraps up our identity.' *Even if you're living a lie, like me.*

'Rossman was my mother's name.'

'Naturally – a fine German name.'

She looked at him then, directly, her back seeming to

straighten on the paint-peeling kitchen chair. 'My father was from Chile.' A pause, pink tongue licking the rose-red lips. 'Like me.'

'Not everyone in England is as nosy as me, Rosa.' *She's a fucking general's daughter.*

An elegant shrug, a rippling of the T-shirt. 'I don't mind telling you – it's not as if it's a secret – but I'd prefer to know about Patrick Miller.'

Miller laughed. The pogo-stick shouting was climbing to a crescendo. 'I imagine that General Reder knows more about me than myself.' *Or he thinks he does.*

'Let me summarize what the general has told me, Patrick.'

Miller was almost amused by the schoolmistressy way she ticked off the main events of his life on her elegant fingers; part of him wondered what it would be like to be touched by those hands.

'One, you are the only son of a doctor, a gynaecologist, whose practice is private, someone whose loathing for your National Health Service is public knowledge. Two, you attended a private school and went from there to the University of London. You started out studying English but switched to modern history. You graduated top of your class in nineteen seventy-two. Three—'

'Three,' Miller said, 'I taught history at a college of further education but was fired after one term for preaching Communist politics in class.' He grinned. 'Blah-blah-blah. It's ancient history.'

'Hardly *ancient*, Patrick – you're thirty-nine years old.'

'So?'

'So my father says you're a man of principle. After you lost your job you survived in London doing odd jobs and writing left-leaning articles for small publications.'

'*Communist Radical*.' He leaned closer to her. Maybe it was the pounding music of ZERO that had led to Rosa's choice of coffee-and-talk venue. '*Marxist News, Fighting Fist* and god knows what else. I made more money washing dishes in the cafeteria at Euston station.'

'But eventually you made it into bigger publications – you became a book reviewer for a magazine called *New Statesman* and then got a job as a feature writer at the *Guardian* newspaper.'

'Where I preached my brand of socialism to middle-class lefties who were senior civil servants and comprehensive school headmasters.'

Rosa looked puzzled. 'Why do you belittle what you were doing? For some time you were one of England's most respected left-wing commentators – you spoke often on radio, you appeared on television chat shows. In your own world you had become famous. And then—'

'And then I resigned in a blaze of publicity and announced that I was going to live in a socialist democracy, a land where ideals were respected, where factory workers and farmhands were the social equals of intellectuals and political leaders and,' he turned in his chair, gestured airily, 'and students.'

'The general says you were a nine-day wonder.'

'Yes.' For a minute he was silent, savouring days that he had tried to banish from memory. 'A nine-day wonder just about says it all.'

'You announced that you were moving to East Germany—'

'And the East Germans said it was the first they'd heard of it.'

'Was it?'

'Rosa!' Miller laughed. 'You know it was – or at least the general knows it was. It's all in the files.' Files showing records of hours of interviews after he'd crossed into the Eastern half of the divided city – files that would be accessible to a general of the National Volksarmee.

'My father wonders if you think now it was worth it. You gave up your country to be here and, well, not to be offensive, but you've been given a job that my father says is,' she hesitated, '"glorified pen-pushing".'

'In that case why is the general so interested in me?' Despite himself, Miller was nettled. 'In a glorified pen-pusher? My work is vital to the state – I evaluate proposed publications and I pay particular attention to how our publications might be used against us by the capitalist media in the West.'

'Patrick.' She laid a hand on his. He became aware that there was a lull in the pounding music, that his raised voice had caused heads to turn. He saw the way the students looked at him, at his suit and collar and tie; he saw the hostility in their faces and then, as their gaze met his, he saw the resentment change to fear as they turned again to their own huddled conversations.

'I think I've outstayed my welcome here,' he said.

'D'you mean in ZERO,' Rosa asked, 'or in East Germany?'

Miller thought it was a good question. But he wasn't about to say that to the adopted daughter of General Reder. His passage into East Germany had been conducted in the headlights of publicity – and under the most twisted of threats. And not threats alone: there had been the seductiveness of living under a banner that he had long championed. Now, having lived under the reality of that banner, and in these days of candlelit demonstrations and soldiers on the streets, he was no longer sure what drum he would march to.

None of which was tellable to Rosa Rossman. You could say less and still finish up in the holding cells of the Stasi at Normannenstrasse. And it didn't pay to think about what might lie beyond that: nobody came out of the Stasi prison at Hohenschönhausen in the same condition – either physical or mental – as they had entered it.

Miller decided it was time to turn the talk in a safer direction.

'General Reder's life is an example to us all,' he said.

'He has been more than an example to me,' Rosa said. 'He gave me back my life, he and his wife both.'

Miller was silent. Maybe now he would learn exactly why he had been brought here, away from the listening tapes of his office.

'Maybe sometime I'll tell you how I came to be here, Patrick.'

And once more Miller knew he was being measured, examined, considered for something – but what? – by those ebony eyes.

'What about your father, Patrick? Were you close?'

You're not slow to use your clout as a general's daughter to ask sensitive questions.

'We got along – up to a point.'

'The point of politics?'

'My father is a dyed-in-the-wool conservative who thinks the sun shines out of Margaret Thatcher's you-know-what.' *And an old lech who can't keep it zipped up.*

'And he is *Sir* Roger Miller.'

Miller shrugged. 'A piece of medieval flummery.'

He knew the examination was continuing, that the dark eyes – and the sharp intelligence behind them – were still probing, still assessing. The metal music was pounding again, loud, threatening. The smoke-thick air seemed edged with menace. *Get up from your seat and go – now.*

He stirred in the chair.

Rosa Rossman said something he didn't catch above the hard rock.

He leaned closer, straining for her whispered words.

'The general would like to meet you.'

'To discuss his book?'

'Among other things.'

Among other things. Get up and leave now, while you still can.

'My boss, Director Hartheim, might like to do that particular interview himself.'

'My father doesn't wish to meet Herr Hartheim.'

They were both whispering now.

'But that's not my call, Rosa.'

She hesitated, shook her head. 'He doesn't have to know you're meeting.'

This had 'out of bounds' written all over it. On the other hand, he might learn something to keep Redgrave off his back for a while.

'But how? You said yourself that we're always watched.'

'General Reder will organize it.'

And if Hartheim finds out later, what then? And Hartheim was not the sole problem: technically, Miller's department was part of the Ministerium für Staatssicherheit – what the people called (disparagingly and fearfully) the Stasi. Even a native-born Englishman who had wilfully chosen to live in East Germany could expect no kid-glove treatment in the bowels of Normannenstrasse or Hohenschönhausen.

All this Miller considered in the moments he looked across the formica-topped table in ZERO at the sculpted face of Rosa Rossman. The invitation to meet secretly with General Reder stank to high heaven; only a fool would think otherwise. And yet . . .

And yet Miller, in his seven years in East Germany, had grown tired of watching, listening, looking over his shoulder. He was tired of the cross-border trips to West Berlin, the delivery of information that must seem worthless even to Redgrave, cufflinked and proper in his whispering club off the Haymarket.

After all of it, he just felt worn and disenchanted. Not to mention how enchanted he was by the voice and face and nearness of Rosa Rossman.

'OK,' he said to her, 'let's do it.'

Her look was unsmiling but the dark eyes were warm.

'It will also give me the chance to hear more about you, Patrick, about your life and how you came here.'

Miller nodded. In his heart he knew he couldn't tell her *all* of it.

Nine

December 1979
Putney
London

He knew she'd be at school, that he would get only her answering machine.

Patrick Miller had known that for the past week but that hadn't stopped him phoning every day, twice, three times, sometimes he lost count, just wanting to hear her voice: *This is Sophie, I'm not here but do please leave a message for me. Byeeee.*

In his mind he could see the phone, white, on the small desk where she marked school essays in the corner of her sitting room. He could see himself sitting on the sofa she'd bought in an Oxfam shop, newspapers littering the space around him, waiting for her to finish, to share a glass of wine with him, talk to him, go to bed with him . . .

It wouldn't change anything, listening to her voice, the trilled goodbye, the hint of laughter in her voice. He could almost taste her voice, the way he'd tasted her lips, her breasts.

He dialled anyway. She'd said it was over, his *obsessions* were too much for her, too intense for a schoolteacher who just wanted an *ordinary* life. She'd had enough of his rants about Thatcher, about the destruction of society, about the virtues of a socialist system.

He'd pleaded, told her he'd change.

Sophie had said she didn't want him to change. He was what he was. She admired his commitment, his idealism. She just couldn't live with it. She'd asked for her key back.

He'd always kept his bedsit in Putney, never moved in completely to her flat in West Ken. Putney was where he wrote, kept his papers, filed his cuttings.

Until Sophie dumped him, he'd never realized how small the bedsit was, how cell-like. From the high window you could see the buses on the Broadway, red galleons of life cruising past while you loitered, marooned amid your sea of papers and books and jottings, the phone in your hand, pressed to your ear, waiting for her voice.

'Hello.' Not Sophie's message, a strange voice. A man's voice.

Miller almost threw the phone to the floor, as though his ear had been stung. He stared at the phone.

A wrong number. Dial again. Carefully this time, reciting the numbers to himself as he dialled.

It rang only once.

'Hello.' The same male voice. 'Who is this?'

This time Miller cradled the phone in the rest with care. Someone else has the key now. His heart seemed to be pounding its way out through his chest. He felt he couldn't get his breath.

And his own phone was ringing.

Miller stared at it, let it ring, picked it up gingerly.

A woman was sobbing on the line.

'Sophie?' Hoping against all hope that she was weeping for him.

'Patrick! Oh, Patrick . . .' More sobbing, hysteria in the voice, in his ear.

Not now, Mum. Not now, I'm trying to stay alive myself.

Miller said, 'What's up, Mum? You OK?'

'Patrick, Patrick, it's the lies they're telling me, the hateful letters – and somebody phoned me yesterday—'

His mother broke off. In a way, he was used to her crying jags. He waited for her to finish, wondering about the new holder of the key to Sophie's flat. Anything to keep his mind off the big house on leafy Compton Avenue in Wolverhampton: the big house where his mother alternated between bouts of depression and frenetic attacks of housekeeping.

'What's wrong, Mum?'

Sniffles. Snuffling. Gulped breath.

Miller hoped this wasn't going to be one of his mother's marathon phone sessions. *Who is this?* But Sophie must at least have mentioned his existence to the new key-holder. Or maybe not.

His mother's snuffling sounded as if it were running out of steam.

'C'mon, Mum, tell me nice and slowly. Whatever it is, it can't be that bad.' Sometimes they changed her tablets or the dosage, you never could tell with this pharmaceutical shit. One of these days he was really going to dig into that stinking industry and expose it for the cesspool it was.

'It's horrible, Patrick. Another letter came this morning, that's the second one, and somebody phoned yesterday – in the morning, I was having a cuppa while I was reading the *Telegraph*—'

'Mum, what letters are you talking about?'

Silence on the line. His mother would be sitting on the piano stool they kept beside the polished occasional table in the hallway, phone clenched in bony fingers, cigarette burning in the cut-glass ashtray on the table beside the phone.

'They're saying things about your father, Patrick, horrible things.'

'What things?'

'I can't . . .' Miller was afraid she'd start crying again. 'They're too horrible for me to say, Patrick, just too horrible and disgusting.'

Poison-pen letters about Dr Sir Roger Miller, distinguished gynaecologist, knight of the realm and avowed enemy of the National Health Service. *How fucking inevitable.*

'Two letters, Patrick, saying these dreadful things and then – can you believe it? – signing himself "a well-wisher". Whoever he is, he's not a well-wisher, is he, Patrick?'

'No, Mum, I don't think so. It's just some nasty person trying to stir up trouble.' *Who is this?* 'Have you told Dad about the letters, Mum?'

'Of course not. You know how busy your father is, night, noon and morning at his surgery and at the hospital and then somebody writes these awful things about him – I can't distress him with these letters, can I, Patrick?'

After all these years, Miller thought, you still love my father. Despite everything, you still keep your eyes closed because you're afraid to open them. And you love being Lady Miller, wife of Dr Sir Roger, ennobled by the Queen herself at Buckingham Palace. No wonder you're on medication. No wonder you escape into your private worlds of polishing and scrubbing and chemical-fuelled fantasy, washed down with sherry or wine or whatever is to hand.

'Why do people do these things, Patrick?'

'I don't know, Mum.' Why did the people of Britain elect a maniac like Thatcher? Why do we aid and abet in the destruction of our own society?

He heard the dragging on the cigarette, saw the jewelled fingers clawing at the untipped Senior Service, knew that she was pulling herself together. Until the next time.

'Are you in that paper today, Patrick?

'It's Thursday, Mum, I'm in the paper on Wednesdays.'

'So you were in it yesterday.'

'Yes, Mum, my piece was in it yesterday.'

'Sometimes I remember to buy it, just to look at your little photograph at the top, but it upsets your father, that paper does, you know what he thinks of it.'

A red rag. A comic. No better than an undergraduate offering – and with even less sense. Any upright British subject – especially one elevated at Buckingham Palace by the sovereign – could only recoil from it in distaste.

'Yes, Mum, I know Dad doesn't read the *Guardian*. But maybe you should tell him about that phone call and let him read those letters.'

'I couldn't do that, Patrick. Maybe I should just burn them. But – you'll come to visit soon, Patrick, won't you?'

'Yes.' Back to a polished mausoleum of the living dead, where the only words ever spoken were words that avoided and/or concealed the truth. Where nobody ever asked, *Who is this?*

'You promise, Patrick? We haven't seen you for so long.'

'Yes, Mum, I promise.'

'Just don't talk politics, Patrick, you know how your father is about all that stuff.'

'Yes, Mum, I know.'

'Sometimes,' she drew on the cigarette again, he could see her powdered cheeks hollowing, 'sometimes I think you don't know your father at all.'

They said goodbye. Miller waited for his mother to put the phone down first.

He remembered her on one of his rare visits home from university. He'd let himself in, found her drunk on the sofa, the wine bottle still upright amid the fallen-over plastic pill containers. His mother had looked at him as if trying to remember who he was. He remembered the red gash of her mouth, the crimson lipstick smeared below her dribbling nose. The multicoloured pills were splashed like smarties across the polished surface of the coffee table. He'd taken her to the downstairs loo, waited while she vomited. 'I didn't take any, Patrick, honest.' He'd lifted her from her knees beside the lavatory, washed her face, settled her against the mound of pillows on the double bed. 'You mustn't tell your father, Patrick, please, promise me, he has enough on his mind.' *Like his round of golf this Saturday afternoon.*

And you never did say anything, did you, Patrick Miller? You couldn't bear to see her hurt but you didn't want to stick around and face the music, did you? You wanted to escape, to flee the Compton mausoleum.

And now Sophie has fled.

Who is this?

The voice on the phone was that of a stranger but Miller knew only too well – and for too long – who and what his father was.

Ten

January 1964
Wolverhampton
England

'Sod it!'

The Compton bus was just pulling away as Patrick Miller came running around the corner. After seven o'clock the buses came only hourly. Sodding dentist, keeping him waiting in the unheated waiting room warmed only by ancient *Titbits* and *Reveilles* and *Woman's Weekly*. Hadn't even apologized, just another schoolboy customer with an overweight bag of books and his school cap folded in his pocket.

'Least you had plenty of time to get your homework done!' Dentist's idea of an apology, concluded with a guffaw and, 'How's your dad, haven't seen him in ages. Tell him I was asking for him.' Fat twit. At least the nurse had smiled her toothy smile at him from behind the dentist's back.

He shook his shoulders, felt the schoolbag settle more comfortably on his back.

'Miss your bus, young fella?' The owner of the newsagent beside the bus stop was fixing the folding metal gate across the doorway of his shop.

Patrick nodded. Mr Mapother was OK, he kept the *Hotspur* for you even if you were a day late.

'You'd better get a move on.' The newsagent pushed the neck of the lock home, tugged at it once, then straightened. 'It looks like rain and it's a good walk to Compton.' He nodded, said goodnight.

Patrick watched him until he turned the corner. He'd never said more than 'Please' and 'Thank you' to the newsagent and yet the man knew he lived in Compton. Wolverhampton was that kind of place. It seemed large, stretching out in all directions, but really it was no more than a big village where everybody knew if you burped or broke wind. And when your father was a doctor who drove a Jag, well, there was no hiding at all. Not even if you did your burping or wind-breaking in the dark.

Queen Square was dark now, shops and banks and offices closed or closing, the last shopkeepers exchanging goodnights at the end of another day. It wasn't such a bad place, Miller thought, but he'd be leaving it as soon as his time at the Royal Grammar School for Boys was done.

He caught a glimpse of his reflection in the darkened window of the newsagent's. He thought he looked ghostly under the dim street lamp. He peered at himself in the window. The half-light hid the spots at the corners of his mouth. He'd hated that, the blonde nurse bent over him, handing the silver instruments to the dentist, no place for the pimples to hide. Pity you couldn't fill the bloody things with something, the way the dentist filled his cavity.

He started to walk, had only reached the corner of the square when the rain started to fall. The clock above the red-brick bank said five past seven: it was just possible that his father was still at the surgery. He turned up the collar of the navy school gaberdine coat and dashed across the street. A car horn blared angrily; through the falling rain he had a glimpse of the driver's face, pale, bespectacled, the snarled obscenity silent behind the thumping windscreen wipers.

He sprinted downhill towards the football ground. His schoolbag bounced against his sodden back. The lights on the ring road were against him but he made a dash for it. Another horn hooted in anger. Rainwater sluiced from the black tarmac over his shoes.

Even in the rain the brass plate on the tall gate pier seemed to shine: *Roger Miller, Obstetrician/Gynaecologist.* Patrick drew the gate shut behind him and stood under the big tree beside the garden path. He shook the rain from his dark hair, loosened his collar, swung the schoolbag from his shoulders.

The bay windows of the big double-fronted house were in darkness. The fanlight over the door glowed yellow but Patrick knew that the light in the hallway was on a time switch.

Patrick grimaced. Sodding dentist. Bloody bus. And the rain falling more heavily than ever, splashing through the bare branches of the sheltering tree.

The door of the surgery swung open. Mrs Oliphant's huge bulk filled the lighted doorway. From his earliest childhood, on one of the rare occasions his mother had taken him there, Patrick had taken his father's receptionist's name to be Mrs Elephant. It was impossible not to smile in the presence of Mrs Oliphant. Your smile was begun by the flabby roundness of her huge body and the smaller roundness of her head; your smile lingered in the warmth of Mrs Oliphant's kindness and good humour.

Her round head was covered in a white see-through rainhat tied under her multiple chins, like a football encased in a plastic bag. Patrick watched her turn her head to the dark skies. He imagined her nostrils twitching, her small eyes twinkling. He smiled as she took a firm grip on the red shopping bag and raised the big black umbrella in her other hand.

Mrs Oliphant squealed in delight when Patrick dashed up the path.

'Patrick! Dear, dear, you're drenched!' She stepped back into the surgery hallway, furled her umbrella and regarded Patrick with a kind of bemusement.

'You'll catch your death, whatever will your father say?'

'Is my father still here, Mrs Oliphant?'

She went on tut-tutting about his wet hair, about the threat of pneumonia. He had to assure her that it wasn't necessary to fetch a towel for him. He had to ask again if his father were still there.

Mrs Oliphant's round head bobbed up and down. 'Poor man, he's with his last patient, Mrs Stafford. I told him I'd wait but he insisted that I go – it's my bridge night, you know. We were running on time until Mrs Cole's appointment, she had twins last month, you know, and you know what your father is like, forever helpful, forgetful of the clock when he's with his patients . . .'

Patrick had grown used to Mrs Oliphant's songs of praise of his godlike father. He tuned out. To Patrick his father was a remote figure who wore bow ties and only rarely used his pair of season tickets to Wolverhampton Wanderers. Which was good news for Patrick and his pals.

Mrs Oliphant finally reminded herself again of her bridge night and said that she must go. She didn't think that Dr Miller would be much longer with Mrs Stafford and anyway Patrick knew his way around the place and if he liked he could make himself a nice cup of tea, it would warm him up while he was waiting.

Mrs Oliphant drew the door shut behind her with surprising softness. Dr Roger Miller's surgery premises seemed tomblike after her departure, as though she had taken with her into the wet night all trace of energy, of vitality.

Patrick stood for a minute in the darkness of Mrs Oliphant's reception room, the walls filled with shelves of manila folders, the curling edges of ancient pages peeping like dry leaves from broken mouths. He ran his finger along a line of files and they crackled like dead foliage. His father's history was typed in these files, he knew, each page signed off with his father's indecipherable scrawl. So many hours, so many days. So many weeks and years spent in the rooms upstairs where his father treated his women patients. He wondered how his father could endure it.

He looked in the small kitchen at the back of the ground floor. Mrs Oliphant's advice about a hot cup of tea came back to him but Patrick thought he couldn't be bothered. He wondered how much longer his father would be with Mrs Whatever-her-name-was.

There was no sound from upstairs. The house seemed settled in its own silence. He looked into Waiting Room No. 1, then Waiting Room No. 2 on the other side of the hallway. Both rooms were identical: flower-print curtains, beige carpet, stiff-backed dining-room chairs ranged along the walls. No copies of *Reveille* or *Titbits* here: *Country Life, Horse & Hound* and other assorted glossies were neatly arranged on the mahogany tables in Dr Roger Miller's non-National Health waiting rooms. Two such rooms were required, Patrick had heard his father explain, because his patients sometimes wished to wait alone, in the privacy they were paying for.

Patrick peeped between the window curtains, saw the sheen of his father's Jaguar at the side of the house. He watched the rain bounce off the polished bodywork like useless pellets.

The house seemed to creak and yaw in the rain. What could be keeping his father? Maybe Mrs What's-her-name had left quietly while he had been daydreaming in the kitchen. Maybe his father was merely scrawling his spidery notes on more pages for Mrs Oliphant to file away on her crowded shelves.

At the foot of the staircase in the hallway he stood listening. Only the whispering silence of the house came down to him. He climbed three steps, four, and stopped to listen. Still silence. He went higher until he could just see over the edge of the landing. Between the carved railings of the balustrade he could see that a sliver of light shone from the edge of the door to his father's room.

Light but no sound. Surely his father was just scrawling away at his notes.

Afterwards he would never be able to explain to himself why he tiptoed up the carpeted staircase. He would remember only that his heart was pounding, as if in his teenage heart he already knew that what awaited him at the top of the darkened stairs would forever change his life.

He stood listening on the landing. A low moaning of someone in pain came from the consulting room. He edged closer to the door. The door was barely ajar but the knife edge of light was enough for him to see inside.

Mrs What's-her-name, beehive hair a collapsed mess, was propped up against the raised head of the doctor's consulting couch. Naked from the waist up, her small white breasts seemed to stare accusingly at Patrick. Dr Roger Miller stood beside the couch, one hand cradling Mrs What's-her-name's left breast. His other hand was stroking the woman's inner thigh. Her thighs were marble pillars of whiteness framed between her brown stocking tops and her white skirt pushed up around her waist.

Patrick could barely breathe.

He saw his father's hand push upwards between the white thighs towards the brown mossy thatch. The white thighs stirred, spread themselves.

The woman moaned.

This is not real. Move.

But his feet refused to budge. In a moment, he knew, he would scream.

He didn't. He watched the woman's hand fumble, saw the white hand emerge from his father's trousers, heard his father moan.

Move. Or vomit and then faint into your own sick.

He moved, somehow without sound.

The moaning was louder, more hurried as he picked up his schoolbag at the bottom of the stairs and let himself out quietly into the night. Fear and panic drove him at full tilt through the blinding rain. Or maybe his own tears were what blinded him.

He could hear the music playing even before he opened the door of the big house on Compton Avenue. Donald Peers, 'The Longest Mile Is the Last Mile Home'. Sometimes he thought his mother did nothing else all day except load records on the spindle of the mahogany-cased radiogram.

She was waltzing between the coffee tables in the sitting room, singing along with the radiogram, a lighted cigarette replacing a partner in her left hand.

She ceased her singing when she saw Patrick, dripping, soaked in the hallway.

'Your father's not home yet, Patrick.'

He let his schoolbag fall on the carpeted floor.

His mother came and stood beside him. He could smell the alcohol on her breath.

'I don't suppose you've seen him, Patrick, have you? No, of course you haven't, silly me.'

He hadn't hugged his mother for years but he put his arms around her and held her small, thin body tight.

'Patrick, you're soaking! You'll destroy my lovely frock – I put it on specially for your father this evening.' She tried to draw away from him but he tightened his embrace. 'Please, dear, you must get out of those wet things – and I must check on your father's dinner, he should be home soon. I never know what keeps him so late.'

Something clicked in his sodden brain. *She knows. But she doesn't want to know.*

He let her go then, stood looking at her, at the stains of wetness on the pale blue flowered dress, the necklace of pearls, the permed hair.

He knew he would say nothing. To say anything would be to disturb, most likely destroy, her whole existence, her routine, her home, all of it as carefully crafted as her perm.

He told his mother that he wouldn't eat, his mouth was still sore after the dentist and anyway he wasn't hungry.

Later he was in bed, lying awake in the darkness, when he heard the hall door opening, his mother's words of welcome. He imagined the cheeks kissed, how was your day, you must be famished.

He wondered if Mrs What's-her-name was exchanging the same civilities with Mr What's-his-name. Did she manipulate *his* penis in the same way she handled Dr Roger Miller's?

He didn't want to think about his own parents lying together in bed. He didn't want to be connected to them in any way. He could see that, somehow, he'd have to look out for his mother but he knew that from now on he would have as little as possible to do with Dr Roger Miller. It did not seem possible that he was even related to Dr Roger Miller, Obstetrician/Gynaecologist.

Patrick Miller, aged fourteen, wondered if he might even be a foundling.

Eleven

September 1989
East Berlin
German Democratic Republic

General Reder will organize it.

Rosa's confident words came back to Miller when the contact was made on Monday. For all their sakes – especially his own – he hoped that the glaring unsuitability of the approach was not typical of how General Reder conducted his affairs: a young fellow bumping into him in an uncrowded street, a muttered apology, the folded note pressed into Miller's palm while the delivery man hurried away. It had about as much finesse as that of the bull in the proverbial china shop.

Miller wondered if it was merely a ludicrous pretence, specially designed to be noticed by observing eyes. He'd been in East Berlin now since 1980, was accepted as a contributing member of the working class, yet he never doubted that he was watched. Even for a believer like himself, it was the price of living in a society under siege.

And the longer you went on living under the unseen, watchful eyes, the harder it was to cling to your belief. It wasn't just the TV images. Even the dogs in the street could smell the rotten carcass of the regime. And that was it, Miller told himself: the regime, not the system. *You gave what you could, you accepted only as much as you needed* – this was a truth forgotten by the old men at the top, the grey faces in their grey suits and uniforms. *But you, Patrick Miller, sometime Englishman, cannot forget: you've come too far to forget.*

He pocketed the piece of paper, swung his briefcase briskly. The typescript of a collection of workers' poems inside the briefcase wouldn't take too long to read that night. Why a small company in the north-east of England had contracted to publish an English edition was yet another puzzle to Miller. Miller's guess – never spoken, never written – was that East German (i.e. Soviet) money went into the funding of the radical publishing house in the north-east of England.

In approved East German literary journals the English publication would be trumpeted as another success for proletarian art, for the superiority of the East German state. And, no doubt, fellow-travellers in England would applaud and praise the work. *If you were still there, yours would be one of the voices raised in praise.*

For a moment Miller wondered if the folded paper in his pocket might not in fact be from Axel. But only for a moment. Axel's material would never come in so amateurish a fashion as a bump-and-handover by a youngster in torn jeans and a silver stud in his left ear.

Miller hurried homeward. Having an unread note from an uncertain source in your pocket was not a healthy idea.

His flat was on the top floor of a peeling block near the Hackescher Market. It was a noisy location, opposite the railway station, but Miller enjoyed his view of the trains rattling along the elevated tracks. In the September evening the peeling pillars of the station platform caught the fading light of the sun and shone as though sheened with new life.

He watched a train pull in, its windows mirrored with light.

He watched the waiting passengers stand back to allow passengers to alight; he watched how those waiting boarded without fuss or pushing. No matter what he saw or heard – or feared – this worker's republic was still admirable: it was still a society that valued good manners.

He waited at his window until the train clanked away eastwards.

Unfolded, the note was no bigger than a matchbox. The message was blunt: *Ostbahnhof Currywurst 20.15.*

The writing was small, tidy. There was no signature. He wondered if it was Rosa's hand. He hoped not. No matter how you disguised your writing, the graphology experts at Normannenstrasse could always unpick the disguise. And if for any reason they couldn't, the Stasi HQ did not lack for less sophisticated interrogators who would simply beat the admission out of you.

Miller tore the scrap of paper into even tinier pieces which he flushed down the lavatory.

He left his apartment just after 6.30. The evening was darkening, the lights on in the small *Kneipe* beside the arches under the railway track. He sat at the window in the bar reading that day's *Neues Deutschland.* The Party newspaper was full of the usual platitudes about quotas filled and targets achieved by the national economy but Miller held a sneaking regard for it. He just wouldn't like to be writing a column for it, always attempting to second-guess the censor who would measure your words against the Party's own orthodox template.

He turned the pages, glanced through the window at the stragglers heading home. None delayed, studied him through the glass. *As if you'd be able to tell.*

Nor could he tell on the platform, waiting for his train. He stood reading his folded newspaper, remembering to turn over the pages. Around him rose the murmur of low conversation. A gaggle of teenagers with spiked hair and a couple of shared bottles of beer. A courting couple holding hands. A mascaraed older woman with her dyed yellow hair peeking from a scarf and a near-hairless little dog straining on a lead. At the far end of the platform a tall fellow in an overcoat patrolled like a sentry, cigarette glowing like a warning light in the gathering gloom. *As if you could tell.*

The train had more empty seats than passengers. Miller wondered about the wisdom of a meeting in such exposed circumstances. Especially when you didn't know if you were on a wild-goose chase. Axel would never set up such a meet.

Still, you had to suppose General Reder knew what he was doing. You didn't survive the Battle of Kirovograd and a Soviet POW camp without a modicum of cunning.

Miller almost smiled as the train shuttled high above the streets, snaking its way between the upper floors of peeling apartment blocks and rundown government buildings. In his years in the GDR he had grown his own skin of cunning. He just hadn't figured out why he had been forced to come here. Maybe the messages he delivered from Axel to his drop points in the West were no more than Marxist horoscopes or last week's football results from Saxony. All these years in these down-at-heel streets and he still didn't know what the hell he was supposed to be doing here. He might be no more than a 'sometime Englishman' but, even after all these years, it still went against the grain to find himself lined up against Shakespeare's 'other Eden'. So, Miller told himself, trust your instinct; what you ferry across the Wall is as lethal as a Dresden *Hausfrau*'s grocery wish list.

The Ostbahnhof, Miller had to admit, wasn't such a bad choice. It was, after all, East Berlin's main station. Passengers on long-distance trains and suburban trains interchanged here. Even after eight o'clock the platforms were busy with arrivals and departures under the vaulted roof.

Miller made his way to the southern exit. Just inside the tall doors stood one of the city's best-known kiosks, Georg's Currywurst. The stall had been raised amid the rubble of the city after the Second World War. Somehow Georg, now seventy years old and surveying his aromatic domain from a high stool, had managed to source potatoes and horsemeat to serve up to Russian soldiers who – mostly – paid for their newspaper-wrapped snacks with occupation Marks. Although a woman in the Western half of the city claimed to have 'created' currywurst – slices of sausage doused in a thick and tangy curry sauce – the leaders of East Berlin always claimed the dish had been invented by the now-elderly Georg. In a society where most shops were identified by number and category, Georg's Currywurst had been allowed to hang on to its individual name in its new station home. And the city's guardians, who were known to dispatch their personal drivers to collect their *grosse Portionen*, ensured that any food shortages did not affect the supplies of *Wurst* to Georg's Currywurst. Miller avoided Georg's eyes as he accepted his cardboard dish of currywurst from the young blonde assistant and left his coins on the high wooden counter. Not that it made much difference. A fellow like Georg, with his connections and supplies, just *had* to be a Stasi informant. Fat, suited and powdered, he sat on his high stool like a squat spider who spun webs with his searching eyes.

Miller took his food to one of the half-dozen high tables that stood outside the serving counter. The other tables were occupied: all men, intent on their food and newspapers, brief-cases and bags on the stone floor nestling against their shins. He had his back turned to Georg and the blonde girl. He laid his own paper on the wooden table beside his cardboard dish. He started to eat. *What now?*

Neues Deutschland no longer interested him but he folded the newspaper into a small shape and pretended to read an article which spouted the usual condemnation of Hungary for opening its socialist border with Austria. It could have been Hartheim come to roost on the zinc-topped high table in the Ostbahnhof. As ever, Miller's own feelings on the flight of East Germans from their homeland were complex. He wasn't even sure where his sympathies lay. Not to mention the activities he found himself mixed up in. He had lived and worked in the GDR for long enough to know its pitfalls: the need for strategic silence – even lies; the fear of the midnight hammering on the door; the ever-present menace of the anonymous letter of denunciation. And yet, in spite of – perhaps even because of – these undeniable failings, Miller was still in love with this half-crippled country that limped onwards towards its own notion of a worker's paradise.

Cue scornful laughter, he told himself. These tired-looking commuters dragging themselves across the station concourse were no different from their opposite numbers scurrying through the tiled halls of Waterloo or Liverpool Street towards their dormitory towns in Surrey or Essex. And if the Wall were breached, as the candle-lighting demonstrators in Leipzig were praying and demanding, the commuter trek to and from the outer reaches of Hamburg or Munich or wherever would prove no less unpalatable.

It was hard, Miller told himself, for an honest man to know what to think. Safer to belt up. Maybe his mother was right: shut your nose to the smell and your ears to the lies and busy yourself with polishing your mausoleum. Maybe you'd be dead by the time it came tumbling down around you.

Maybe that's what General Reder was at – presenting an innocuous memoir, devoid of insight into a life lived with danger and violence, a bland memoir that could serve as an equally bland epitaph for his tombstone.

Where the hell was the general's messenger?

Another train clanked in overhead. A fresh stream of disembarking passengers descended the stone staircase. A pair of men moved resolutely towards Georg's Currywurst. They sat at a table next to Miller's, two middle-aged fellows in shiny suits, conversing in low tones. They didn't look much like couriers or messengers.

The high tables were emptying. Miller's currywurst was eaten, the orange grease congealing on the empty dish. Time to go: too many trains had come and gone to allow him to linger longer.

The young blonde assistant was moving between the empty tables with a cardboard box in one hand and a wet cloth in the other. Miller watched her at work: a circular sweep of her folded rag swept crumbs and debris into the brown box, a second swipe gave the table a perfunctory cleaning. The girl worked with a tight-lipped concentration: wipe and swipe, wipe and swipe. The zinc tables gleamed wet and empty in her wake. She barely looked at Miller as she pushed his plate aside and wiped the table clean. Her heavy nylon coat seemed to creak as she took her box back behind the counter.

Miller was left staring at the tiny piece of paper sticking to the curry grease on his box. He palmed it as he picked up the paper dish and dumped it in the bin beside the counter. Georg said, *'Danke schön'*, without lifting his great head from his magazine. The blonde girl went on cleaning.

Miller could feel the stickness of the paper in his clenched fist as he made his way to the basement toilet. In the ill-lit cubicle he unrolled the paper. *Exit No. 3*. He flushed the lavatory, watched the greasy scrap disappear in the swirling water.

He washed his hands quickly, hurried up the stairs. *Take it easy, slow down.*

Exit No. 3 led out into a lane which seemed to contain only the service entrances of shops. Rubbish bins gleamed darkly under the pale light of the single street lamp at the far end of the street. He made his way softly along the cobbles but his footsteps echoed loudly in the narrow street.

An engine growled into life. He saw it at the end of the street: a dark motorbike, its helmeted rider clad in equally dark trousers and tight jerkin.

The rider looked at Miller from under his helmet but said nothing.

'I am . . .' Miller hesitated. 'Are you from . . .'

The rider gestured towards the pillion seat with a gloved hand.

Miller climbed on board. He wrapped his arms around the rider, felt the engine throb between his thighs. The rider pushed off and the night and wind cut into his eyes and Miller bent his head against the wide, dark-jacketed shoulders in front.

The watcher behind the rubbish bins straightened gratefully and flexed his shoulders. Pity he couldn't flex his knees: it continued to amaze him that artificial joints of metal or silicon – or whatever the knees were made of – could be a source of pain.

Bionic man indeed.

Those TV clowns should try walking – or crouching – with a set of metal inserts inside you on a chilly Berlin night. Only September and the city already felt like winter. 'Six-million-dollar man!' More like six-million-dollar rubbish.

He lit a cigarette, drew the hot smoke and the cold air into greedy lungs. Three pulls, no more, that was his concession to the doctor's warnings about emphysema. Fucking doctors – and none worse than the agency quacks. Did they think that laboratory conditions applied on the streets where he operated? Like this shithouse alley at the rear of a rundown station in East Berlin?

He trod on the cigarette, ground it into the cobbles until it was no more than a flaky mess in the darkness. Carelessness could kill you quicker than nicotine. It was carelessness that had cost him his knees in that squabble in Chile. Fucking Communists.

He cleared his throat, hawked a mouthful of phlegm on to the ground. Almost half an hour he'd crouched behind the reeking rubbish bins, waiting to see who came out of the station to join the motorcycle rider. He'd tailed the motorcycle for fifteen minutes through the night-time streets, driven past him at the mouth of the alley before parking the Lada at the other side of the Ostbahnhof.

How predictable was it, a meet at the back end of a railway station? You'd expect more from a seasoned old bird like General Reder.

Only one thing puzzled him: the guy who climbed on to the pillion seat. A new face.

They'd have him figured tomorrow. Baister was waiting at the general's villa, crouched somewhere with his night-work camera. He didn't like Baister much better than the desk guys back in Washington. Just another Kraut, no matter what side he was on. He hoped his nuts were freezing behind some garbage bins outside General Reder's villa.

He pulled his collar closer around his neck. Even his birthmark seemed to hurt in the cold. But the ponytail had had to go so he could become Walter Buchner, electrician, resident of East Berlin. He missed it, the comfort of it, lying against his neck. The desk fliers at the agency didn't really know what it meant, this fucking cold war.

He headed back to the waiting Lada.

Twelve

Monday, 18 September 1989
East Berlin
German Democratic Republic

The crumpled little fellow in the leather button-backed armchair didn't look much like the General Reder that Miller had seen take the salute on May Day on Unter den Linden. That general stood erect among the line of ribboned and medalled commanders of the GDR on the garlanded podium, hands raised in salute as the massed ranks of soldiers marched past and fighter planes screamed overhead.

This general was small, shrivelled, bundled in a brown cardigan that seemed several sizes too large for him.

And yet he had to believe Rosa's words.

'My father, General Reder,' she was saying, and then, 'Papa, this is Patrick Miller.'

There was nothing shrivelled or crumpled about the manner in which the general came to his feet. He was wearing soft grey house shoes but Miller could have sworn he heard leather heels click as General Reder bowed and extended his hand. This was, after all, a soldier who had been a decorated hero of the Panzer Korps in the Third Reich and, later, a hero of the GDR. Age might have withered the general but he had not lost the edge of command.

'Thank you for coming, Herr Miller.' A hoarseness in the voice but there, too, the tone of authority.

'Thank you for inviting me, General.' Despite himself, Miller found himself bowing slightly to the smaller man. 'I'm sorry I could not give more specific information about your book, General. Our Director will be in touch—'

The general waved a dismissive hand, motioned for Miller to take a seat.

'My book?' The general snorted. 'It's something I dictated some time ago for,' an ironic raising of eyebrows, a shake of the bald head, 'shall we say for the "official" record.'

Miller sat, shifted in the armchair, said nothing. *Keep out, dangerous landmines*. Even generals – *especially* generals – could lead you beyond the perimeters of safe roadways.

The general smiled, pale puffy features stretched into a hint of the lean-jawed tank commander who had survived both the eastern front and a Red Army POW camp.

'Your silence commends you, Herr Miller. When you lived in England you shouted your beliefs in the pages of newspapers but here,' the bald head nodded, 'here in the GDR you have learned the virtue of discretion and silence.'

'General, I'm not sure what you mean.'

'And you have learned how to utter words that themselves have no meaning.'

'General—'

'Please, Herr Miller.' General Reder raised his hand, palm out. 'I do not mock you. It is for your discretion that I sought you out and asked my daughter to invite you here.' General Reder reached a liver-spotted hand for his daughter's, standing beside his chair. 'In your years among us, Herr Miller, you have learned that some things are sometimes best not spoken about.'

Such as the cloak-and-dagger arrangements for getting me here.

Rosa had been waiting inside the wicket gate at the back of the large garden surrounding the house. Miller had wondered how she'd known of their approach: the rider had coasted the last stretch of their journey, the motorbike's engine killed. No word had been exchanged between the rider, still helmeted, and the general's daughter, as she led Miller through the darkened garden to the house.

Miller knew they were somewhere in Pankow, the northern district of the city favoured by Party elite. Further north, in Wandlitz, the members of the Politburo were housed in a heavily guarded compound. He knew that Hartheim lived in the area although he had never been invited to the Director's house.

Now, seated in what he took to be General Reder's study, he could only wish that he had never been invited to his house either. The general's elliptical words signified nothing good, and the way his fingers were wrapped around Rosa's didn't augur well for any notions Miller might harbour about his daughter. *Down, boy, and pay attention.*

The general's silence seemed to demand a reply.

Miller said, 'Thank you, General.'

And waited.

The general smiled as though gratified.

He turned to Rosa. 'Would you mind bringing us some coffee, Rosa?'

Both men watched her as she glided across the room. Without her, a sweetness was absent. Now the study was a man's room, peopled by books and brown walls and furniture.

'Sometimes,' General Reder said, 'ignorance is another word for safety.'

Miller knew he was talking about Rosa.

'We both know, General,' he said, 'that nothing so far spoken here demands any need for ignorance or secrecy.'

'I haven't brought you here to exchange platitudes, Herr Miller.'

'I'm a guest here in this country, General, I do my work as best I can, I keep my head down, I . . .' Miller shrugged.

'You keep your arse clean, Herr Miller.'

Miller spread his hands. 'I suppose so.'

'And you are fearful that I might say something improper – me, a decorated general of the National Volksarmee?'

'General, I'm not sure what—'

'You're afraid you'll have your ears exposed to something improper, yes?' The dark eyes in the weathered face bored into Miller's. 'Have you become so German, Herr Miller, that you are afflicted by our national virus? Yes, it's our national *virus*, our national *disease*, to close our eyes and our ears and even our noses to every smell or lie or crime that is in our midst. Can you close your eyes and your ears, Herr Miller? Can you cover your nose against the stench?'

The general got to his feet.

'You see this?' The general was brandishing a framed black-and-white photo of a family group. 'My father – a small farmer in West Prussia.' A finger stabbed. 'My mother – a farmer's wife.' More finger-stabbing. 'And my sister, Heidi, and – and me.' Miller stared at the solemn-faced dark-haired boy, the pigtailed girl, the unsmiling parents. General Reder seemed to take hold of himself, laid the photo gently back on his desk. 'I was the only one alive at the end of the war, even if I was in a prisoner-of-war camp. I never learned how they died, my parents and my sister.' A silence. 'Never even found their bodies.'

He sat again, heavily, and Miller watched him draw a hand across his brow. *For pity's sake, Rosa, come with the coffee.*

'They didn't have to die, Herr Miller. They were just little people caught up in events they didn't understand. They knew nothing about the camps, the killings, the confiscations. But a great many people *did* know the truth, Herr Miller, knew it from the beginning, but they did nothing, just kept their heads down and allowed the criminals to destroy their country.' His breathing was harder, the voice harder. He lifted his head wearily, almost whispered the words: 'Just like now, Herr Miller, just like now. Those of us who know the truth must speak and act, otherwise the deviants at home and,' he swallowed, 'our enemies abroad will destroy this country.'

I should be somewhere else, Miller thought, anywhere but here. I have my mother to protect from her own miseries, General Reder isn't the only guy with a family. If Rosa comes with the coffee, that will shut him up – but Rosa's not coming, not for a while, she's been told to wait, to give General Reder time to fuck me up, involve me in some fuckology with the dissenters and the candle-wavers in the church in Leipzig.

Time to nail your ambiguous colours to your wobbly mast, Patrick Miller.

'I fear you have misjudged me, General Reder,' he said. 'I'm happy to have been allowed to stay in this country and I simply want to do the best I can at the job I have been given.' The general's amused smile was unnerving, made him swallow before continuing. 'I have no involvement with any dissenting groups and I don't wish to have any involvement with these groups. Of course,' Miller raised a hand, 'I have heard nothing unorthodox here and, if you'll forgive my saying so, General, I'd like to keep it that way.' Miller swallowed again. It was, he felt, the longest speech he had spoken in his years in East Germany. And the most dangerous.

The general leaned back in the armchair. A wide grin spread across his face.

'You're good, Herr Miller,' he said.

'Pardon?'

'Herr Miller, I am a general of the army of the German Democratic Republic. Do you think I have no intelligence sources? Do you think I would have invited you here if I didn't know about you and your activities?'

The general was silent, Miller transfixed.

'My activities are an open book – my employment—'

'Oh, fuck your employment, Herr Miller!' The obscenity, harshly delivered, was a reminder of General Reder's battlefield beginnings. 'D'you think I don't know what you get up to on your little trips to the other side of our divided city? Yes, you buy your English newspapers and American magazines, you sip your espresso in the best cafes but we both know that you have other chores to perform, Herr Miller, don't we? A note dropped here, a paper left there, isn't that so, Herr Miller?'

Miller's tongue seemed swollen, his mouth dry.

'Little notes, Herr Miller, left in safe places for the personal information of one Warwick Redgrave, yes?'

The shadow of Normannenstrasse seemed to darken the brown study where the two men sat staring at each other.

In the German Democratic Republic you had to recognize when protest or denial was futile.

'General,' Miller said, 'what do you want from me?'

The general nodded. 'No denials, no admissions – very wise, Herr Miller. Let me ask you this.' He paused, steepled his fingers. 'Do you think our country is endangered by these protests and processions?'

Another shadow: in his mind Miller heard the plane swoop over the waving crowds in the embassy in Warsaw, saw the frightened look of the fellow being questioned on the island in the centre of Unter den Linden, watched hundreds of flickering candles in St Katherine's in Leipzig.

'I think,' Miller said, 'that attention should be paid to these developments.'

The general laughed. '"Attention should be paid."' He shook his head. 'Forgive me, Herr Miller. You really have been too long among us. *Attention should be paid!* Would you have written such bullshit in your *Guardian* newspaper days? If you produced such crap now, would the *Guardian* print it?'

The art of listening, of hearing the truth unspoken between the words, was a necessary skill for prospering, sometimes for surviving, in the GDR.

'General,' Miller asked, 'do you want me to write a piece for the *Guardian*?' The paper printed occasional pieces about his daily life in East Germany; the last piece he'd submitted had been politely declined on the grounds that it was 'too innocuous'.

'Maybe,' the general said.

'But the paper is generally sympathetic to the demands of the protesters.'

'Why do you say "but", Herr Miller?'

'I thought . . .' Miller shrugged.

'You thought I wanted a piece of propaganda criticizing these protesters?'

'I'm sorry—'

'The *Guardian* is a paper of socialist inclination?'

'Yes.'

'And the newspaper has a strong anti-American, anti-imperialist streak?'

Miller nodded.

He waited for the general to continue, watched the older man almost curl in the armchair, saw the spasm of pain flash across his features.

'General Reder.' Miller half rose from his chair.

'It's OK.' The liver-spotted hand waved Miller away, reached for a small brass bell on the desk. The bell was still tinkling when Rosa hurried into the room.

'Papa!'

The general tried to smile, pointed at the small bottle of pills on the desk, waited until Rosa shook a couple of the white pills in his hand. Miller and Rosa watched in silence as the general swallowed the pills dry, head bobbing, Adam's apple working.

'Papa.' Rosa shook her head. 'The doctor told you to take the tablets *before* the pain gets to you.'

'What's a little pain, daughter? We used to say in the war that if you could feel the pain then at least you knew you were still alive.'

'This isn't a war, Papa.'

'Isn't it, Rosa?' The general's voice was so hoarse as to be little more than a whisper. 'Are you sure it's not?'

'Papa!' Miller could hear the alarm in Rosa's voice. 'We have a guest, what will Herr Miller think?'

The general closed his eyes, gathering himself.

'Herr Miller,' he said, 'knows where we stand.'

'That's not quite true, General. I'm actually pretty confused.'

'Then let me explain.'

'No, Papa, that's enough explaining for tonight.'

General Reder laughed, turned to face Miller. 'I'd never have won a battle in the war, Herr Miller, if the enemy had been led by my daughter.' He squeezed Rosa's hand and Miller thought of his own father, squeezing other flesh.

'I'll get your coat, Herr Miller,' Rosa said.

'We'll meet again, very soon,' the general said when they were alone.

Miller nodded wearily. 'If you wish.' What I wish doesn't matter.

'I mean you no harm, Herr Miller. And remember that your Director knows nothing of our meeting. I was banking on Hartheim giving you my manuscript to read – that old fraud knows exactly when to duck his head.'

'And my head, General?'

'As safe as any head can be in these troubled times, Herr Miller.' The general stood and they shook hands. 'Remember also, Herr Miller, that we know all about you.'

Miller could find no comfort in the general's smile.

Thirteen

19 September 1989
East Berlin
German Democratic Republic

Work was a welcome relief for Miller next morning at the office. Although not employed by the publishing company housed next door, much of the foreign rights transactions for the publishers crossed his desk. It was begun, Miller figured, simply as a series of chores that could be entrusted to him: he was still the only native speaker of English, the lingua franca of business, in the two buildings. Over the years, as his proficiency and his masters' trust in him had grown, Miller's desk had become the recognized transit point for most foreign business, although all final decisions had to be approved by Hartheim or his opposite number in the publishing house next door.

Most such work concerned the sale of rights for foreign language editions of East German books. For Miller, book publishing was one of the glories of the East German state. When you got past the turgid collections of politicians' speeches and impenetrable economic plans and surveys, you discovered a treasury of fabulous art books, reference works and scientific treatises that were the equal of anything produced in the so-called free world. It seemed to Miller like a kind of heaven: you liked a book, thought it deserved publication, and a few thousand copies of the book were published at a non-market, affordable price. The 'market' did not apply here; it was doubtful if any book earned back its production cost.

Foreign business was where East Germany bared its fangs. The country's currency – the Ostmark – was a so-called 'soft' currency and universally rejected in Western countries. The official rate was one to one with the West German Mark but, to find a citizen of Hamburg or Munich who'd trade you a hundred of his precious Marks for a like number of Ostmarks, you'd first have to find a fellow who believed that Santa Claus was alive and well – and living on a moon that was made of blue cheese.

Western publishers who thought they could offer a pittance, measured in sterling or dollars, were sharply disabused of their notions. A letter from one such operator – this time a UK distributor rather than a publisher of schoolbooks – now lay on Miller's desk. The fellow, based in Welwyn Garden City and signing himself T. J. Whitacre, wanted to buy five thousand copies of a hardback German–English dictionary for a few coppers each. Mr T. J. Whitacre concluded:

> We are major educational suppliers in the United Kingdom and it is our expectation that this substantial first order is but the beginning of a long and profitable association between our two companies.

The seas, Miller reflected, were full of sharks that spouted shit.

He took extended pleasure in composing a lengthy reply couched in abstruse and long-winded language which, in effect, thanked Mr T. J. Whitacre for his derisory offer and advised him to shove it.

No matter how long-winded he made it, the letter was soon

done and Miller was forced again to consider his strange encounter with General Reder.

Whether by design or the pain which had seized the general, the purpose of the meeting had been left undisclosed. The pointers to what it was about were, at best, vague. The general wanted Miller to write something; his former newspaper's left-wing slant had been mentioned. And General Reder had made it clear that he was aware of Miller's message-carrying to Redgrave and Co.

All of which added up to what? That the general could accuse Miller of spying activities whenever he wished? That he could produce evidence to back up the accusation? That Patrick Miller, in short, hadn't a leg to stand on and could soon be enjoying the hospitality of the Stasi?

That Patrick Miller, if he had an ounce of sense, should use both legs right now to take himself to the Western half of this divided city and stay there?

Redgrave had explained in unnecessary detail what the consequences of flight would be.

And anyway, in his own peculiar confused way, Miller had grown fond of East Berlin. *And, admit it, you hardly know her but staying in East Berlin is your only chance of becoming better acquainted with Rosa Rossman.*

Miller got to his feet and scanned the corner of Unter den Linden visible from his window. People and cars passed in and out of the short stretch of window, short-lived figures in a foreshortened landscape. People like himself, who had learned to live with queues and shortages and cardboard dashboards and shirts and blouses and dresses that chafed your skin like over-used blades. People, unlike himself, who did not enjoy the luxury of free access to the consumer delights on the forbidden side of the Berlin Wall.

They were, Miller realized, people he had learned to love.

He turned from the window, went back to his desk and his letter to T. J. Whitacre, Esq. Hartheim would have to clear it but the Director wouldn't give this kind of stuff much more than a nod.

He fantasized with the notion of addressing the same letter to Redgrave. Telling the smarmy bastard where to shove it would make any day sweeter.

Oddly enough, he harboured no such fantasies about General Reder, whatever the general's plans for him might be. He just wished he knew what the general wanted from him.

Rosa Rossman was wrapping up a tutorial on *Room at the Top*.

John Braine's novel of English provincial life in the 1950s would, she'd felt, inspire some engaging debate among her small group of Third Years. She'd managed to get her hands on half a dozen battered-looking paperback copies and had enthusiastically doled them out to the group as a first 'discussion book' of the new semester. *Room at the Top*, she felt, was an ideal choice: a good yarn, good pace, engaging – if not very likeable – characters. Best of all was its candid portrayal of an ambitious young man's climb to the top of Britain's class system. Along his way to the pinnacle of the rotten heap, Joe Lampton betrayed the older woman he loved and the younger, richer woman he impregnated.

Her eager group of twenty-year-olds, raised in class-free East Germany, would make short work of Mr Joe Lampton.

Except it hadn't turned out that way. Yes, her students agreed, they'd enjoyed the novel, the pacy story-telling, the simple language. But Mr Joe Lampton's slimy climb to the top was hardly reprehensible; in fact, it was completely understandable.

'And his betrayal of the woman he loved?'

Four female faces, all bespectacled, stared questioningly back at her. In the two male faces, both bearded, Rosa could read the same uncomprehending question.

'He betrayed her,' Rosa said. 'He caused her death.'

'Nobody *made* her get pissed.' Antonia with the granny glasses looked amused. 'Nobody *made* her take the wheel while she was pissed.'

The half-dozen heads around the table nodded in agreement.

'And the girl he got pregnant – facing a loveless marriage with a fellow whose only interest is her father's money?'

Silence in the small room. The ticking of the clock on the back wall seemed louder.

'It's her choice too, Frau Rossman.' Antonia's wire-rimmed glasses seemed even more granny-like. 'That's the way it works.'

The circle of heads nodded again.

'And this "it",' Rosa said. 'Could this "it" which makes these people behave in such self-destructive ways be the class system itself? A dog-eat-dog system which gives citizens no option except to cheat and lie and destroy themselves and others? Is *Room at the Top* an indictment of the entire class system of the capitalist world?'

No gaze met hers. Everybody stared resolutely at the table, fingered the paperback.

'Nobody has an opinion?' This group wasn't usually reticent, opinions usually shot out of them almost without thought.

'We have a class system here too, Frau Rossman.' The words barely audible. Monika. Large Monika with the tiny voice, this time tinier than ever.

'Pardon?'

Still no gaze met hers. The silence in the room seemed to crackle, like ice getting ready to break. She looked from one bent head to the next, wondering where these students had spent their summer.

'That's quite a statement, Monika. Would you like to enlarge on it a little?'

Monika lifted her head, her round face red, her small mouth pursed. For a moment her eyes met Rosa's and then she bent again over the table.

'We have our own class system.'

Rosa looked at David: small, muscular, T-shirt and multi-patched jeans, the recognized brains of the group. She nodded encouragement.

David shrugged. 'It's no secret. There's one law for most of us and no rules at all for a few people at the top. Joe Lampton would have to dish a lot more dirt to get to the top in this society.' His look was almost apologetic. 'No offence, Frau Rossman.'

No offence. Everybody knew about General Reder.

'None taken.' And yet something shrivelled inside her. The beast being born on the streets was nosing its way into the classroom. You couldn't ignore the growl of menace, the hunger for a fairer share of the cake. *But I fear for my father: General Reder took me in, he and his wife made me their daughter. This country gave me back my life*. Maybe the beast could be tamed with kindness.

'Let's leave it there for today,' she said.

They gathered their books and pads with unaccustomed quietness. Nobody stayed behind, nobody had a question, a smile. Their farewells were nodded, sheepish. She'd thought they might continue their discussion over coffee in ZERO but nobody had asked if she'd be there.

A line had been crossed, however faint the line, however hesitant the crossing.

She'd missed something, she realized, some hint, some indication of this crossing of the line. Or the line had moved, had been moved: Rosa herself was now seen as one of *them*. There was always a *them*. The *them* who were beyond reach, beyond sanction. There were, as David had said, no rules at all for *them*. And now, somehow, she was numbered among *them*.

The idea angered her. Her anger pushed her at speed along the college corridors. A colleague passed, said hello, frowned at her haste, her glum silence. *Slow down. It's just a bunch of students, maybe you're mistaken.*

And yet she knew she wasn't.

It was unfair. She had come to this country as a refugee, spirited out of her own land with nothing except her fear, her sense of loss, her nightmares. She'd become part of this country that had rescued her, had learned to love its friends and to be wary of its enemies. Her students were not her enemies. Nor were they the enemies of the GDR. They were not so different from her. They recognized injustice not only in the pages of a book but on the streets of their country. As she herself did.

General Reder would listen to her, he always did.

The porter at the main door of the institute called out goodbye to her, '*Bis morgen*,' a half-smile, a small wave of his uniformed arm.

'*Bis Morgen*,' she said. Until tomorrow. Did he, too, see her as one of them, the daughter of a general of the GDR?

It was unfair.

At the top of the steps outside the institute she stopped, almost frightened by the demonstration below. It was a small affair. Five or six young people walking in a circle at the foot of the stone steps, placards in their hands. *Wir sind nicht frei!* We are not free! *Hallo, Mein Bruder in West Berlin*. Hello, my brother in West Berlin.

And yet solemnity was not something students could sustain. The smallest of the group carried a bright red placard emblazoned in white: VIVA COCA-COLA!

She smiled but she felt the weight in her heart. She couldn't be even ten years older than these demonstrators, but she felt like their mother. She could understand their frustration – anyone could see that the system was corrupted – but this wasn't the way to set about it. Joe Lampton didn't set out to destroy the system. Greedy bastard that he was, he married into it, became a part of it. Maybe, in his life beyond the book, he might even set about improving it.

A pair of Vopos were making their way towards the demonstration. They walked without haste, sure of themselves, pistols holstered. The small crowd of onlookers took off at speed. The demonstrators offered no resistance. Their placards thrown to the ground, they waited, faces ashen, until the police van arrived and they were herded into its cramped interior, placards chucked in behind them.

She wanted to run after the van, shout at both policemen and students: *it's not the way, the general has another way, a better way . . .*

And part of her wanted only to weep. These people who had sought her out under the warplanes over Chile were tearing themselves apart, destroying one another. Maybe they'd listen to her father. Maybe General Reder wouldn't even get the chance to speak to them. The Party Secretariat would offer him no platform. The Americans would happily have the general dead.

Her stepfather was an old man with cancer of the thyroid. What chance did he have? And maybe it was foolish even to think that a maverick Englishman like Patrick Miller could help.

She remembered the way Miller's dark hair fell across his

forehead, the curiously old-fashioned right-hand parting. She remembered the height of him, how his maleness seemed to shelter her when he stooped to take her hand.

Standing on the steps of the Institute of English Studies, Rosa Rossman shivered in the September sun. She wished she were on her way to Cafe ZERO, not to meet her students, but to sit beside Patrick Miller.

Fourteen

September 1989
Checkpoint Charlie
Berlin

It was a ritual, a kind of waltz they danced every few weeks to silent music that they both could hear.

First, Miller acknowledged Hartheim's directorial eminence by explaining that he, Miller, would like to pick up a few journals 'on the other side' and would therefore be grateful for the Director's permission to leave the office early.

Then Hartheim also displayed, firstly, his personal eminence by inquiring if Miller's assignments were up to speed and, secondly, his personal magnanimity, by graciously granting Herr Miller permission to finish work early.

Neither man smiled during this exchange. To do so would be to recognize the element of farce.

Anyway, Miller reminded himself on his way down the marble staircase of 64A, there wasn't much to smile about in his life right now. And there was much to be serious about. Not least of which was, what did General Reder want from him?

Wait. The general would be in touch.

Wait. He'd been waiting for eight years for an explanation as to what exactly he was doing in East Berlin and he was no wiser now than on the day he'd passed through Checkpoint Charlie with his suitcase and rucksack. Yes, pick up the messages from Axel and get them to one of Redgrave's collection points in West Berlin – but for what?

You know what for. You've looked at the messages, puzzled over the groups of figures and letters. Maybe codes, times, page numbers of popular books, references to psalms or verses of the bible – the staple fare of thrillers and spy novels.

And finally, on this afternoon, leaving Hartheim's corner office in 64A Wilhelmstrasse, you have to face the truth: the scraps of paper you carry with such fear and such care have no meaning whatever. They contain neither codes nor times nor technical information; they are no more than distractions, meaningless curlicues and flourishes in a dance composed and choreographed by Redgrave. A waltz as ritualized and meaningless as the *pas de deux* between you and Hartheim. You're a decoy. You draw the watching eyes, Patrick Miller, while the real action, whatever it is, is conducted on another stage, unlit, unobserved.

A decoy. The realization triggered in him both relief and anger.

And something more: the realization that this was a truth he'd known for some time but one that he'd refused to countenance. *The truth will set you free*. Maybe. But free to do what? To round on Redgrave and thus bring ignominy upon his mother's ageing head? His mother had her own reasons for hiding from herself the truth about her gynaecologist husband.

He signed out of the building under the unsmiling gaze of the two male receptionists. When he'd first started work at 64A he'd tried smiling at them, a touch of banter. He soon gave up trying.

The afternoon was sullen, sticky, a hint of thunder in the dark, rolling sky. He shouldered his rucksack, turned off Wilhelmstrasse in the direction of Checkpoint Charlie. At least he didn't have to worry today about the contents of his pockets or his rucksack. On his evening jog the night before, there had been neither a plastic bag pushed between the black railings at the back of the red-brick Lutheran church nor a cigarette packet casually impaled on the gate spears of the same church. So, no need to pick up from the hole in the old chestnut tree in the middle of the park nor from behind the moss-covered brick in the wall at the southern edge of the park. Just march confidently towards the checkpoint on Zimmerstrasse. Head up, carefree. You've been in and out through Checkpoint Charlie at least a hundred times since you arrived in East Berlin.

It was after four o'clock; already there was a line of day trippers returning to West Berlin. Conspiratorial whispers seemed to hang like cigarette smoke above the line: *Ich bin ein Berliner!* We have bearded the evil dragon in his den and we have the useless Ostmarks in our pockets to prove it.

Miller had given up using English whenever he was accosted by one of these day trippers. His English accent was invitation enough for a conspiracy of criticism, a licence to censure this grey city with its multiple deficiencies – no bananas, or Levi's or Wranglers. *And no freedom*. Their implicit sense of superiority, displayed like a badge along with their loud labels and brand names, had aroused in Miller a resentment that had surprised even himself.

The checkpoint police were solemn-faced as they surveyed the queue, slow-moving, whispers punctuated by an occasional nervous laugh. Not too nervous: the American soldiers were just a few metres away on the Western side of the checkpoint. A small group of youths got into the line behind Miller, all anoraks and rucksacks and American accents.

The burly border policeman at the head of the line turned to look at the newcomers. He took his time walking towards them, his gaze never wavering. He stood next to Miller, his eyes fixed upon the Americans, intimidated now into silence. He nodded as if trying to decide something, then turned slightly and pointed at Miller.

'You,' the accent heavy, guttural, 'come with me. Now!'

The collective intake of breath from the bunch of Americans was audible.

Miller stepped out of the line, followed the sergeant to the head of the queue.

He kept a straight face until they were both inside the checkpoint hut.

'Heinz-Peter,' he spoke quietly – the captain of the guard was smoking beside the window – 'you scared the shit out of those kids.' Miller recognized the captain from previous crossings. His face looked thinner than he remembered, cheeks sucking with desperation at the untipped cigarette.

'*Ja.*' The sergeant grinned. 'It'll give them a story to tell back in America.'

One of their goons hauled this guy out of the line at Checkpoint Charlie . . .

'It's a pity,' Miller said, 'they'll be able to see me walking to the other side all in one piece.'

'Maybe I should give you a few thumps outside, Herr Miller, just for the benefit of our American visitors.' The sergeant's voice was low. 'But then we might have an international incident and the captain has enough to worry about already.'

'Nobody needs an international incident now, Heinz-Peter.' He looked around at the tables spread with handbags, tote bags, rucksacks and their varied, spread-out contents under the poking hands of the border guards. 'You're all under pressure?'

Sergeant Heinz-Peter Reibert nodded slowly. 'All leave cancelled, everyone confined to barracks – I haven't seen my family for days.'

Heinz-Peter, Miller knew from their encounters over the years, had a wife and two children – a boy and a girl, if he remembered correctly. And – rightly or wrongly in this secretive society – they had dared to trust each other in a superficial way. He leaned closer to Heinz-Peter. 'You need anything?' He'd opened his rucksack on the table; the sergeant made a show of searching it.

'The usual, Herr Miller.' The words muttered into the rucksack as he drew it tight. 'Toothpaste, shampoo, maybe a toothbrush.'

'Done.' Miller took his bag. 'What time d'you knock off?'

'Midnight.'

Miller nodded, headed for the door. Outside he looked back at the group of Americans, closer now to the front of the queue. He saw the recognition in their faces, the flash of fear.

He turned away from them. They'd never understand, images burned on their minds of their murdered President spouting facile rhetoric at the Wall, and youngsters bleeding in the killing zone of no-man's-land. They'd never quite grasp that folk lived on this side of the city and, for all the shortages and difficulties, some of them wanted to go on living on this side. Maybe he himself did.

He shouldered his bag and walked towards the waiting American soldiers.

None of the policemen on the Western side of Zimmerstrasse looked familiar. Nor any of the American soldiers. They stood casual, confident, as though Berlin were theirs, the strident sign at the mouth of the street loud as an American flag: YOU ARE NOW ENTERING THE AMERICAN SECTOR. Also, just to make sure you got the message, in Russian, French and German.

One of the soldiers stepped away from the US army half-track near the sign and whispered something to the German policeman.

Miller was holding out his ID card even before the policeman summoned him.

The flimsy East German ID card was examined as though the policeman had never seen one before.

'*Warum kommen Sie nach West Berlin?*' Why are you coming to West Berlin?

Miller shrugged, gave the same answer as always: just for a look.

The American soldier stood closer. Miller could smell from the fellow a cloying mix of deodorant and sweat and cigarette smoke.

'What d'you want to look at, fella?'

Miller had underestimated this broad-shouldered American who, unusually, could understand at least a few words of German.

There was no point in pretending he didn't speak English. 'Toiletries,' he said. 'Shaving cream, soap, that kind of stuff.' He met the American's gaze. 'Maybe some newspapers and magazines.'

'You're English?'

Miller nodded.

'So what the hell are you doing with East German ID?'

'I live there.' Miller looked at the German policeman. '*Kann ich jetzt gehen?*' Can I go now?

He pocketed his ID, moved away among the crowd. Behind him he could hear the American, astonishment in the loud voice: 'Fucking Commies!'

Miller walked towards the Tiergarten, then changed his mind: he wasn't in the mood for parkland, trees, babies in prams. He wasn't quite sure what he was in the mood for. The years in Berlin had made him introspective: the price of constant vigilance over what you said taught you to say less. Not knowing why you were where you were made you wonder if there was *anywhere* you belonged.

Meeting Rosa had rattled him. Even more so his meeting with her stepfather. He'd tried to keep his head down all these years, get on with the routine of work, the collection and delivery of bits of paper. Truth to tell, he'd learned to like the life he'd been ordered to live, like easing your feet into new shoes that pinched at first.

A bus pulled in just as he was passing a bus stop. *Zoogarten*. Miller got on. There might be recent newspapers at the station. A girl reading a paperback made room for him in a seat near the back of the bus. When she turned a page he stole a glance at the cover. In English, an old Len Deighton book: *Funeral In Berlin*.

Whose funeral?

Increasingly Miller felt that he had much to lose. And, in some odd way that he could not articulate even to himself, he was beginning to learn something new about himself: that he might be prepared to risk losing it. Whatever the fuck 'it' might be.

The bus reached the Zoogarten. West Berlin's busiest station was, as usual, busy.

You're really on song today with these useful observations. Even the editor of the *Wolverhampton Express & Star* would be embarrassed by their poverty.

Miller shook himself, piled into the station with the end-of-work crowds.

The newsagent's was crowded. He scanned the papers, found a day-old London *Times*, the previous week's *Sunday Express*. He took his place in the line, paid, looked across at the paperback stand, changed his mind.

You don't know what you want.

Back on the street he went into a pharmacy, bought toiletries for Heinz-Peter, more for himself. *You never knew: the American might still be there later, might inquire if he'd bought his toothpaste.*

He found a small sweet shop, bought some toffees and jelly babies for Heinz-Peter's kids. He'd never met Heinz-Peter's children but, well, it felt good to have some kind of connection that was *real* in this divided city.

The demonstrators on the streets at night were real.

The Wall was real.

The pictures on TV of hundreds of refugees from the GDR spilling into Munich from crowded Austrian trains were real.

You had to ask: was the threat to the GDR real? At least, Miller figured, if he was right about the stuff he carried across the Wall, he was not a direct part of the threat.

He was walking aimlessly on a side street off Savigny Platz when a car pulled in alongside him. A small car, blue, some kind of Citroen. What Miller noticed were the peculiar rucked curtains on the back windscreen and the rear side windows.

The driver's door swung open, across the pavement, blocking Miller's way.

'Herr Miller.' A small face in tinted spectacles looked at Miller. 'Get in the back, please.' The driver reached behind, swung the rear door open over the pavement.

Miller stooped, glanced into the interior of the car, saw the balding figure leaning against the opposite door.

He looked again at the street, heard the S-Bahn rumbling on the bridge overhead, watched the cars and pedestrians pass by, utterly heedless. It's not like *Funeral in Berlin* at all, he thought, it's just a car stopping in a daytime street and you know you have no choice.

'Please, Herr Miller,' the hoarse voice said, 'get in or people will notice.'

Miller nodded, got in beside General Reder, and the blue Citroen moved smoothly off.

Fifteen

September 1989
West Berlin

Say nothing, Miller told himself as the driver nosed the small car along the commuter-time streets. Let the general explain what this is all about.

The general seemed to have the same idea. They sat in silence in the back seat, stared straight ahead at the busy streets, at the driver's shaven neck, the black beret clamped on his small round head. The wire arms of his spectacles seemed to disappear into the flesh behind his tight ears.

Once Miller made as if to move the rucked curtain but he sensed the general's forbidding eyes and he dropped his hand.

They were moving slowly enough for Miller to realize that they were circling and criss-crossing their own tracks. The same shops slid by, the same intersections, the same traffic policemen on point duty. The driver's bereted head swung from side to side, from wing mirror to wing mirror. In the rear-view mirror his eyes caught Miller's, coins of pale blue behind the wire-framed lenses. *At this speed we could be in a funeral: a fucking funeral in Berlin.*

The car leapt forward in the gathering gloom. The driver raced through the gears. The engine growled like a beast unleashed. A powerful engine, not the pedestrian gadget the manufacturer had fitted. The street ahead was suddenly clear of traffic, even empty of street lights.

Miller was no longer sure of where they were, in which direction they were racing. Not that you could go far in any direction in West Berlin. Every road in this isolated city led quickly enough to the closed frontiers of the GDR: north or south, east or west, you soon ran into the walls and fences of enemy country, the dammed waterways, the checkpoints, the patrol boats. You could cycle along country lanes to the north and west and imagine yourself in the great unfettered outdoors – but only for a little way. Only until you met the high walls, the spiked fences, the steel nets in the lakes and rivers.

Miller was pretty sure they weren't heading back to East Berlin.

He caught a glimpse of a familiar shopfront, realized they were racing through Charlottenburg. Heard the rumble of the S-Bahn overhead, knew he was right. He tried to keep track of their umpteen turns but the driver was too good – *how does he not confuse himself with so many turns?* – and Miller gave up.

They were in a dark street. No lights, no pavements, just cobblestones gleaming under the dimmed lights of the Citroen.

The driver killed the lights. The engine idled, so faint that Miller had to strain to hear its whispering. When the driver's door eased open, Miller was not surprised that no courtesy interior light came on. Everything about this souped-up version of a foolish-looking little car said the same thing: *Stasi or Redgrave or some such entity. Maybe even the Americans.*

The driver pressed a recessed button, head high, beside a steel shutter. The shutter began to rise, the driver got behind the wheel again, drove the car into an unlighted space.

Behind them the steel shutter closed silently.

In the dark silence the general's breathing sounded coarse,

laboured. When the lights came on suddenly, the general's face was flushed, a fleck of spittle at the corner of his mouth. He pulled his dark tie down, opened the neck button of his white shirt.

'I'll be OK,' he said to Miller. 'I just need to get out of this fucking little French box.'

Miller got out, circled the car. He held the door open and helped the general out. For a small, almost shrunken man his grip was strong.

All this in the confined darkness. To Miller's ears even his own breathing seemed loud, an echo of the general's panting. The driver seemed like a study in still life, motionless behind the Citroen's steering wheel. The car gave off its own cooling, petrolly hum.

The general moved, swore as he bumped into something in the blackness.

'Fucking lazy idiots!' The voice of the barracks, no longer the politeness of an officer at home with his daughter. 'How many times do these bastards have to be told!'

Which bastards? Miller thought. Whose? Yours or ours? *And which side is ours anyway?*

The general still had his finger on the wall switch, an empty carton upended beside him. White walls, white ceiling, stone floor. Empty of furniture. A series of steel rings bolted to a corner of the stone floor. The kind of rings you could moor a small boat to. Or a man, a man who needed to be moored. The stone floor was black, the kind of black that probably absorbed red stains.

'Come.' The general beckoned Miller to follow.

The door in the end wall swung open. A smaller space inside, a mixture of kitchen-cum-living space-cum-office. No windows here either, just a silence so deep that you couldn't tell where the front of the building was. You could be anywhere or nowhere. Here was neither east nor west, neither checkpoint nor border.

'Nobody can hear anything we say in here.'

The general's words reminded you that there *was* a border, that in every corner of this broken city ears were straining to hear every word whispered, every breath drawn.

Miller sat on a metal-legged chair at the small table.

'You have nothing to say, Herr Miller?' The general was pouring coffee into two mugs from a silver flask that was ready on the worktop.

'I think I'm here to listen, General Reder.'

'I like a man who knows how to keep his trap shut, Herr Miller.' The general handed him a mug of black coffee. 'I've seen men die because they spoke out of turn.'

'I haven't.' Miller shrugged. 'I guess I've led a sheltered life.'

'You make a kind of joke of it,' the general said, 'but this is not a joking matter.'

Miller looked at the smaller man seated opposite. 'You forget, General,' he said, 'that I'm on the same side as you – at least I think I am. We're both visiting in West Berlin and shortly we're both going back home to the German Democratic Republic. At least,' Miller paused, 'I am.'

The general laughed. The years seemed to fall from his face as his features crinkled into laughter and Miller felt he caught a glimpse of the dashing young tank commander who had become a legend among his men.

'And where d'you think *I* might be going, Herr Miller? D'you think I'd walk away from Rosa, or from the country I helped to build?'

Which was one of the unfathomable puzzles: how did a legendary soldier of the Wehrmacht become a faithful servant of the Soviet command that had overrun his own country?

Miller spread his hands in the universal gesture of submission. 'Like I said, General, I'm listening. I don't know what you want from me but I'm all ears.'

'Good.'

'But,' Miller looked around at the walls, at the ceiling, 'are you quite sure these walls don't have ears?'

A chuckle from the general, another crinkling of laughter lines in the withered face.

'We're in West Berlin, Herr Miller, West Berlin, where the alleged agents couldn't tail you across a pedestrian crossing in broad daylight. I think we know more about their intelligence operations than they do themselves. And to crown it all,' the old eyes twinkled, 'we're in the so-called French sector. What a joke – the *French* sector! But it's more than a joke, it's an obscenity. The French had fuck all to do with defeating the Wehrmacht – that was mainly the work of the Red Army – and it was an insult to put them in charge of even a side street in our beloved Berlin.'

Nothing was simple in this city: a general condones the capture of his capital by one army while he parades his contempt for another invader.

The general clamped his lips, seemed to swallow his anger.

'Anyway, these same incompetent Frogs make our job easier here.'

Miller nodded.

'Only myself and a trusted few know of the existence of this safe house, Herr Miller, but, just to be sure, the premises are swept regularly for surveillance equipment. And don't forget that,' the pale eyes narrowed, 'in the matter of espionage and counter-espionage equipment the GDR is what the Americans call the "market leader".'

'I don't think,' Miller said, 'that's what you want me to tell the *Guardian*.'

General Reder sat back in his chair, looked wryly at Miller. 'I should remember my own advice about shooting my mouth off, Herr Miller.'

Miller felt that he was, finally, about to hear what this strange business was all about: from the way General Reder straightened himself in his chair, the way the pale eyes blinked, the way the scrawny Adam's apple bobbed in its turkey neck as the general swallowed, caught his breath, prepared to speak.

'These demonstrations that are tearing our country apart at the seams – the principal agitators behind it all are the Americans.'

Miller stared, tried not to smile. *The candle-lighting thousands were being organized by the Americans?*

'I can see that you are sceptical, Herr Miller, but nevertheless it's true, the Americans are trying to undermine the GDR.'

'But, General,' – *careful what you say to this general, maybe the old boy is losing it* – 'the Americans have been trying to get rid of the GDR for the last forty years.'

'Do you take me for a simpleton, Herr Miller?' The pale eyes flashed – with amusement, with anger? 'What's happening on our streets now is different. Comrade Honecker is vulnerable, the entire Party leadership is indecisive, many of them are cowed by the crowds in the streets and the flood of people streaming through the open border with Hungary and on to Austria. No one knows if even the army would obey orders.'

The general's words posed a picture: rifles trained on demonstrators, the barked command to 'Fire!'

Miller was uneasy. 'General Reder, I'm a pen-pushing civil servant, I'm not sure I should be—'

The general's closed fist pounded on the table. The table shook. The mugs wobbled. The coffee spilled. Miller wondered if the general would be needing his little bottle of pills.

'Do you think I'm an idiot?' The voice low – and this time the general was using '*du*', not the formal '*Sie*'. It was the term you used to address intimates and children – and inferiors. 'I've already told you that I know about your fucking pissant operations for Redgrave, your bits of paper, your silly drops and pickups. I don't treat you as a clown, Miller, so kindly allow me the same courtesy.'

Now the general produced his little bottle of tablets, swallowed two of them with a mouthful of cold coffee. 'Fucking doctors,' he said. 'Fucking tablets.' He glared at Miller. 'I've got cancer of the fucking thyroid.' The glare turned to a grin. 'And don't tell me you're fucking sorry.'

'I wasn't fucking going to.'

Laughter, shared. A bridge, crossed.

'Tell me, General, about these American agitators and what it is you think I can do.'

For over half an hour General Reder talked and Patrick Miller listened. And the more he listened, the more puzzled Miller became.

The more General Reder spoke, the less he seemed to say.

There were American agitators at work in all the cities of the GDR, especially in Leipzig and Berlin, in Rostock and Karl-Marx Stadt. The Americans and the British were intent on the destruction of the East German state. The West Germans in their toytown capital of Bonn were waiting and watching to pounce, to swallow the GDR into their capitalist craw.

None of which – apart from the claim about American agitators – was news to Miller.

'The Americans aren't that stupid or provocative, General.'

'Three nights ago a demonstrator in Leipzig was picked up by the police. A hospital porter, his papers said, a resident of Zwickau, name of Kurt Kellerman. His papers looked good but it took only a few minutes and a couple of phone calls for the police in Zwickau to establish that the real Kurt Kellerman was at home watching television with his wife and kids.'

Miller said nothing.

'The fellow's bluffing didn't last long.' The general shrugged. 'The Stasi have their ways. The fellow was an American agent.'

Miller wanted to say it's the way of the world – *what else would you expect?* – but it would be unwise to speak in this way to a GDR general, even a retired one like General Reder.

The general went on, 'There are at least seven such American agitators in different police cells across the country. All of them here illegally with false papers. All of them have admitted that.'

'Stasi methods?'

The general sipped his cold coffee, made a face. '*Clever* methods,' he said. 'Not a finger was laid on any of them – orders from the very top. None of these Americans will have grounds for any complaint if . . .' He shrugged. 'You know what I mean.'

It took Miller a moment to work it out: *if Stasi officers are answerable to the West Germans and their American paymasters in the near future.*

'It hardly seems possible,' Miller said. 'We're sitting here with cold coffee somewhere in West Berlin and – you said it yourself, General – the Wessies don't even know we're here. It's hard to believe that – that—'

'You don't even want to say it, Herr Miller – that our country might disappear, just get wiped off the map as if it never existed.' General Reder stood up, busied himself with the coffee-maker. 'Rosa and the doctors tell me I drink too much coffee but who gives a fuck about coffee when this is where we are?'

Miller stood, rinsed out their mugs, dried them for the fresh coffee. Where would he stand if this unthinkable new world came to pass? How could a decoy – a *dupe* – survive in such a world? And why would he want to?

The general seemed to read his mind.

'You no longer have a British passport, Herr Miller?'

'You know I don't.'

'Be wise, get one.'

'Easier said than done.' When his passport had run out, Hartheim had wondered aloud why a loyal servant of the GDR would not choose to apply for citizenship; Redgrave had not wondered, just ordered him to get GDR papers.

The general was still inside his head. 'Tell Redgrave to go fuck himself.'

'Easier said than done,' Miller said again.

'Redgrave fucks a fifteen-year-old once a week in a flat in North London.' The general paused. 'A fifteen-year-old *boy*.' Another pause. 'I can give you photos.'

How much does General Reder know about Redgrave and me? About the gloomy, shining house on the edge of Wolverhampton?

'General Reder,' he said. 'I'd prefer to be able to go on using my GDR passport.'

'Then help us, write something for your *Guardian* newspaper.'

'You overestimate my importance, General, I've told you that. Once upon a time my byline meant something; now I'm just the weirdo who went to live in East Berlin and writes occasional pieces from behind the Wall.'

'So write one of your occasional pieces, that's all I'm asking.'

Miller poured fresh coffee for them both, glanced towards the closed door: 'A cup for the driver?'

'He has his own flask.' There are times, the general's look

seemed to say, when it's good for a man to sit in the dark in a curtained car, waiting.

'Look, General, if I write that seven American spies are in custody and have confessed to spying, then you'll see it on the front page of most newspapers in Britain and elsewhere. But how did I come by this information? I work for the Secretariat for Socialist Correctness, remember? And what's my Director going to say about one of his staff producing stuff like that?'

General Reder snorted. 'Hartheim is an idiot,' he said, 'but that's not what I want you to do.'

Once more the general seemed to gather himself.

Once more Miller thought: now we're getting to the point.

'In the next twelve months,' the general began, 'maybe even sooner, the GDR is going to come under almost unbearable pressure, from within and without. Reagan and his American warmongers want to see the back of us; Gorbachev in Moscow has lost his balls and wants to lie down like a castrated tomcat with his new American partners. And inside, here at home, we have these idiots demonstrating for what they see as future independence.' He paused, sipped his coffee. 'Independence is what we need. Independence to be ourselves, to govern ourselves.'

Miller thought: I don't want to hear this stuff, this treason. And yet . . .

Aloud he said, 'Maybe if the demonstrators were to hear these words . . .' He shrugged, wondered if he had gone too far.

'You think they'd listen? These insufferable zealots with their slogans and their candles? They want to sell their country for a few bunches of bananas and a pair of American jeans.'

'But,' Miller hesitated, 'if the Council of Ministers were to promise them elections and independence . . .' He left it there, sure he had overstepped a boundary.

'Our leaders, Herr Miller, don't want true independence. To

stand on our own two feet would be too demanding for them, too painful. Maybe even too poverty-stricken. Our leaders will sign our own death warrant because they're the same as the crowds fleeing through Hungary and parading on the streets. Our leaders are also seduced by the bananas, Herr Miller.'

'Erich Honecker has declared that the Wall will last for a hundred years.'

'Maybe he believes it but Honecker is too old and he no longer has the backing of Moscow.'

This is madness: the Wall is solid in the near darkness, the soldiers and border guards stand ready at the checkpoints.

The general pushed on. 'The GDR will live on for a year or so but we need to be ready for independence when it comes. Otherwise this country will disappear. We are a socialist state, a socialist people – it's the way we've lived since the war. But we can make it a *better* socialist state, a truly *democratic* state, if the Americans and the Russkis leave us alone. *And* the Wessis. Otherwise they'll gut us, carve us up like a corpse and steal the bits they want.'

'Steal what?'

'This is a rich country, Herr Miller.' Anger now in the hoarse voice. 'We have natural resources, great industries, magnificent buildings. The vultures will come in and feast on it all, steal it all. And,' a shake of the hairless head, 'many of our leaders want to get their own snouts in this trough of plenty.'

'You're saying,' Miller's voice almost a whisper, 'that some of our leaders want to see the collapse of the GDR?'

'That's what I'm saying, Herr Miller.'

Madness.

But Miller believed him. Eight years in this crazy country taught you that anything was possible. 'I'd be on my way to Sachsenhausen if I wrote stuff like that, General.'

'I don't want you to write that. Write a piece pleading for the GDR to be allowed to go its own way if change comes. What we need to do is start a debate, mobilize public opinion. Your paper carries no torch for Moscow but it's a good place to promote the idea of real freedom, of the right of a people to shape their own destiny.' He stopped, looked questioningly at Miller. 'You find this amusing?'

'Not at all, General, I was just thinking that there's a lot more to you than a wartime commander and a leader of soldiers.'

'I came up the hard way, Herr Miller,' another pause, eyes staring into Miller's, 'unlike some people.'

Their separate pasts hung between them like another wall above the small table.

'Whatever our past,' Miller said, 'right now we're both on the same side.'

A dismissive raised eyebrow. 'That's why you're here, Herr Miller.'

'And,' Miller had delayed asking the question, 'the Wall, General, and Honecker's "hundred years"?'

'Herr Miller,' the voice weary, 'surely you realize that what we've been talking about is a GDR without a Wall, a GDR that people are happy to stay in because it's free and democratic?'

It was tantalizing, this image of just another country with ordinary borders and ordinary crossing points.

'I'll write all this up as best I can, General, but the byline will have to be "A Special Correspondent". Even then . . .' Miller shrugged.

'Never mind that,' the general said. 'I'll fix a trail that leads to one of the hacks in Bonn.'

The general stood up. 'Time to go, Herr Miller. We'll drop you at a station.' He shook his head at Miller. 'Just leave the coffee things.' *Somebody else takes care of such things.*

The darkness met them when Miller opened the door. He could just make out the driver, sitting motionless in the small unlighted car. Beyond the heavy, steel shutter the city waited in its own bisected space of light and dark. *Waiting for what?*

'Twenty-four hours,' General Reder said. 'We'll get in touch about picking up your article.'

'You're setting a lot of store by one little article, General.'

The general's shrug said it all: *a campaign of attack and/or defence is organized on many fronts; NCOs need knowledge only of their own little bit of the front.*

Once more Miller sat in the back between the rucked, almost feminine curtains; this time the driver turned towards him with a blindfold in his hands.

'It's for your own safety,' General Reder said.

Miller took the blindfold, tied it behind his head. Behind the cloth he blinked in the enveloping blindness. He felt hands positioning the blindfold around his eyes and nose. Heard the rasp of the ignition key, the cough of the engine, the hum of the steel shutter rising.

They backed out into the cobbled alley and he heard the sounds of the city, at once near and still distant. He could smell the city through his blindfold: sweaty and sour, sweet and perfumed, fresh and petrolly. The blindfold didn't matter: Miller could see in his mind this scattered city that he loved. He breathed it in, the horns and blares and music of the street as the driver went through his circling routine.

He waited for his blindfold to be removed when they stopped.

He blinked, focused, failed to recognize the narrow street, the shuttered windows, locked down.

'Turn left at the corner,' the general said, 'then a couple of rights and you'll see Savigny Platz station.'

Miller nodded, shook the general's proferred hand.

On the pavement he stretched, breathed in the night. He smiled to himself, tapped at the passenger side window before the car could pull away.

General Reder's lined, tired face looked up at him from the open window.

'Yes?'

'You really have photographs of Redgrave with a young fellow?'

'Of course.' A smile, almost beatific, on the weathered features. 'You know that in the GDR we can manufacture *any* kind of photographs.'

Miller flinched.

General Reder winked.

'Only joking, Herr Miller.'

The window went up.

Miller stared after the departing car. *This city*. You loved it, thought you understood it. And then you couldn't even tell whether or not it was joking.

In the darkness he couldn't help smiling. He moved quickly now towards the station. You have promises to keep, an article to write, words to plead for the life of a country on the edge. *And toothpaste for Heinz-Peter at Checkpoint Charlie*. As for Redgrave, Miller told himself – not without satisfaction – that buying toothpaste for a border guard would have been the last thing on Warwick Redgrave's mind all those years ago in the King's Arms in Putney.

Sixteen

January 1980
Putney
London

Miller knew what they were as soon as they stepped inside the pub. They stood in the open doorway for a moment, scanning the quiet midday clientele, and he knew – *just knew* – that they were looking for him. He'd never seen either of them before but he'd been confronted often enough by their clones in his pre-*Guardian* days. Lend your name to a piece in *Marxist News* or *Fighting Fist* and you learned to expect the occasional visit from the guardians of state security and the morals of society.

He looked up from his notes on the pad as they approached his table. Their shoes clicked out a counterpoint rhythm on the pub's wooden floor, the man's shiny brogues squeaking in an odd falsetto against the female's medium-height, clacking heels.

Miller didn't invite them to join him; he knew they'd sit at his table anyway.

'Patrick Miller?' The words clipped, the voice as sure of itself as you'd expect from the crombie coat and pinstripe suit, the gleaming brogues.

'Who wants to know?'

'Redgrave.' A flash of an ID card in a leather folder. 'Office of European Cooperation.'

Miller laughed. 'That's a new one on me. Let me see.'

Redgrave shrugged, handed over the ID. *Warwick Redgrave, Office of European Cooperation*.

Miller looked at the mugshot, at the ginger-haired owner of the card.

'Like to show me a driving licence, Mr Redgrave, or would that be in a different name?'

Redgrave ignored that. 'This is my colleague Dr Shearing.'

The woman nodded but said nothing. *A Thatcher clone, down to the blue suit, the helmet-like perm, handbag chastely guarding her middle-aged lap*.

'These days,' Miller said, 'I'm a respectable *Guardian* columnist. You can't lock me up overnight like some freelancer from *Fighting Fist* – well, you can, but if you do you'll find yourself on the front page of a national newspaper.'

'People don't just get "locked up" here, Miller.' Redgrave pocketed his ID. 'This is not the Soviet Union or,' eyes narrowing, 'the German Democratic Republic.'

'What d'you people want?' *What does Sophie want? And whose is that voice answering her phone?* Miller took a long drink from his beer, tried to keep the exasperation out of his voice. 'Just tell me what you want and then leave me alone to do my work.' *To remember her smell, her taste, her touch*.

'We're here to help you, Miller.'

Patrick Miller laughed out loud. He saw Bernie, the barmaid, glance over at him; she winked, then went back to polishing glasses. 'You're going to *help* me? At what? Winning votes for Thatcher and harassing students?'

'We want to help you, Mr Miller.' The woman had a surprisingly deep voice. 'You and your family, Mr Miller.'

Miller's interest was piqued. Over the Christmas and New Year break he'd stayed away from Wolverhampton and his mother's needy voice, had clung to the bedsit in Putney with its imagined nearness to Sophie. In a way he almost envied Sophie: he knew that he could never leave his mother behind. Her face was stamped on his heart like the words on a stick of rock from the seaside. He just didn't want to be reminded of the detached house in Compton, least of all by this hatchet-faced woman with the ramrod in her back and the sensible handbag in her lap.

'What about my family? What are you saying to me?'

'We're saying,' Dr Shearing went on, 'that your parents are experiencing some difficulties at present and that we are in a position to relieve their problems.'

'What the fuck are you on about?' From the corner of his eye he saw the sharp look Bernie gave him, knew he was almost shouting.

'Why don't we calm down, Miller?' Redgrave's voice smooth. 'Why don't we order drinks and take things more slowly, yes?' In the King's Arms you ordered at the counter but Redgrave's raised finger brought Bernie to the table in an instant. Even in his anger and irritation Miller could see how the barmaid, usually brassy and offhand with customers, bent herself to Redgrave's tone of authority. In the exchange between master and mastered he saw much of what he detested about England. He simmered while she took the order, brought the two dry sherries – in his sullenness he refused a drink – and almost curtsied as she accepted payment and her tip.

When she was back behind the counter, he glared at Redgrave and Shearing.

'So?'

Redgrave raised his glass. 'Cheers.' He sipped, smacked his lips. 'Not bad.'

Miller pushed his chair back. 'Fuck you, I'm getting out of here.'

'Sir Roger and Lady Miller might not appreciate that, Miller.'

'What?' Miller thought he must be hearing things. 'What's my mother got to do with anything?'

'She's married to your father—'

'Of course she's married to my father.'

'Who was knighted by Her Maj.'

Through the window of the pub Miller could see cars idling on the High Street, bundled-up pedestrians waiting at a pedestrian crossing. The street had the usual limbo-like look that follows the consumer frenzy of Christmas and the New Year: it looked dull, bland, uninteresting.

And Patrick Miller wished he were part of it.

'So?' Even to himself his voice sounded unsteady. 'My father is a gynaecologist.' He spread his hands, waiting. He couldn't bring himself to mention his father's title.

'We could put this delicately.' Shearing paused.

'But it's better to call a spade a spade,' Redgrave continued. 'Charges of sexual assault have been laid against your father by a number of his patients and of course the British Medical Association is also getting ready to conduct its own inquiry into these allegations of professional misconduct. We've seen the evidence, Miller, and it's very likely that your father, Dr Sir Roger Miller, will be found guilty in the courts and will be struck off by the BMA.'

Miller watched Redgrave sip his drink. Watched Redgrave watching him. He picked up his own drink, tilted the glass to his lips. Anything to hide his face, to hide the memory of that open doorway. He drained the glass, felt the colour drain from his face. The only surprise was that he hadn't heard such an accusation before.

'Bullshit,' he said.

Redgrave laid some coins on the table, pointed at the phone in the corner. 'So call your father.'

'Or talk to your mother.' Shearing's expression was waspish. 'Ask her if your father is taking a break from the surgery for a while.'

'Of course, she doesn't know the real reason why her husband is taking some time off from his practice,' Redgrave said, 'and that's the way we'd like to keep it.'

Miller felt the shiver begin in him, hated himself for allowing his tormentors to see how he trembled.

'I think you could use a drink now, Miller.' Redgrave stood, went to the counter.

Miller avoided the woman's eyes, sought instead the safety of life – *boring life* – on the street outside the window.

'Here.'

He took the bumper of whisky from Redgrave, swallowed half of it.

'Everything we've told you,' Redgrave said, 'is the truth.'

'Fuck you.'

'Obscenities won't help.' Primness in Shearing's voice. 'Not you, not your mother.'

'I thought your accusations were against my father.'

'So they are, Miller, but your mother is going to be the real victim here. You know that better than we do.'

He knew from Redgrave's expression that they knew it all: the drinking, the depression, the insane bouts of housework. Long ago Miller had concluded that his mother willingly turned a blind eye to her husband's extra-curricular activities; now he wondered if this pair in the bar also knew that his mother knew. They don't know, he thought, that my mother has known for years – knows but hides that truth from herself. Take away the much-prized title of Lady Miller and there would be more pills strewn on the table in Wolverhampton.

'The scandal would destroy your mother, Mr Miller.'

Redgrave nodded. 'It would,' he said, 'if all of this were to get out.'

If: that one word said it all. Miller didn't doubt the story these two had told; now and again, over the years, he had wondered how such accusations against his father had never surfaced.

'What,' he asked, 'has all this got to do with your – what did you call it? – your Office of European Cooperation? And why haven't I read or heard anything about these serious accusations?'

'You can thank our little organization for keeping a lid on this,' Redgrave said. 'We had a word with the West Midlands constabulary, persuaded them to keep mum about it. The BMA was a little easier, vested interests always are – doctors can't see any benefit in having one of their own being caught with his,' he paused, looked at Shearing, 'well, shall we say with his hand in the till.'

'But why should the . . .' Miller swallowed, 'the "doings" of a doctor in a provincial town like Wolverhampton come to the attention of a bunch of security spooks?'

Redgrave tut-tutted, shook his head. 'Naughty, Miller! After all, we're here to help you.'

'And your mother, Mr Miller.'

Fuck you, Miller thought, looking at Shearing. 'So,' he said, 'why?'

'The Queen's peace, Miller.' Redgrave had decided to play the reluctantly stern schoolmaster. 'And of course the security of Her Majesty's realm.'

'What the fuck has a provincial doctor to do with the security of the realm?'

'You,' Redgrave said. 'You, Patrick Miller, scourge of Mrs Thatcher's capitalist society, left-wing columnist, our socialist star of chat shows on TV and radio.' Eyebrows raised, large head nodding sagely. 'Just your little self, Miller, that's your father's connection with the security of this United Kingdom.'

He got it, could see it coming – *but fuck them*.

'Why don't I just write up this cosy little meeting in my next column in the *Guardian*?'

'You do that, Miller,' all irony gone now from Redgrave's tone, 'and next day your father's name will be splashed across every newspaper in the land.'

'And see what that does to Lady Miller.' Shearing's voice as dry as her sherry.

He wanted to walk outside, feel the bitter wind of January on his face. He wanted Sophie to hold him, hold him tighter than she'd ever held him. He wanted to tell Redgrave and Shearing to leave him alone, to go fuck themselves or each other.

What he wanted didn't count. All his adult life Miller had despised his father for the way he had emotionally abandoned his mother; Miller himself would be no better if he now walked away from Shearing and Redgrave.

'What d'you want from me?' he asked.

It was Shearing who laid it out for him. 'We can continue to keep this unfortunate story out of the news, Mr Miller. There will be no court case, although I expect there will have to be out-of-court settlements with at least some of your father's patients, in exchange for binding, non-disclosure agreements. As regards the professional misconduct charges, the BMA will hold neither an inquiry nor a hearing and your father's reputation will remain untarnished. In other words, you will not have to fear for your mother's well-being.' She paused but Miller said nothing: the quid pro quo was coming. 'In return, you will go to live in East Berlin.'

For moments he was speechless.

'Live in East Berlin? What the fuck for?'

'Because that, Mr Miller, is our condition for protecting your family.'

'But why? Why go to live in East Berlin?'

'Because we could use somebody trustworthy there,' Redgrave said. 'And somebody that the East Germans will also trust, somebody just like you, Miller, somebody who's forever sounding off about the injustice of the capitalist system and the glories of socialism. The pinkos will love you, Miller. And look on the bright side: for you it will seem just like going home.'

'You're both out of your minds.'

'On the contrary, Mr Miller, we are offering you a simple arrangement whereby Sir Roger and Lady Miller will be protected.'

Miller looked at Bernie, pulling a pint for a lunchtime customer. He looked at his notepad on the table, felt the draught of cold wind from the street as a customer left. These were the simple touchstones of his daily life but now they eluded his grasp, pushed away from him by the crazy talk of East Berlin.

'It's madness,' he said, 'madness.'

'It's a simple business arrangement, Miller.'

'You expect me to be a fucking spy.' Miller was whispering. 'A fucking spy!'

'Don't flatter yourself, Miller.' Redgrave, too, had lowered his voice. 'From time to time we'd ask you to do us some little service, that's all.'

'You people – you and your "little services"!'

'What we are doing for you,' Shearing said, 'is no little service – just remember that.'

'So I just toddle across the border at Checkpoint Charlie and tell Erich Mielke, "Here I am, Herr Mielke, the boys and girls at the Office of European Cooperation would like me to spy on your country for a while." Just like that, yes?'

'Miller,' Redgrave's tone was softer, menacing, 'I'm getting just a little tired of your attitude. Either you take our proposal seriously or you can hear about your father's antics on the six o'clock news this evening. Do I make myself clear?'

In his *Fighting Fist* days Miller had twice spent a night in the cells and had once been slapped around by a zealous uniform; looking at Redgrave now, hearing his intense words, Miller knew that he was in the presence of a darker, angrier power.

'I'm a freelance columnist,' he said. 'You think the *Guardian* is just going to ship me off to East Berlin as their local correspondent?'

Shearing and Redgrave looked at each other.

'I'm afraid you're finished with the *Guardian*,' Shearing said.

'You're going to resign in a great glare of publicity,' Redgrave went on. '"Left-wing journalist despairs of capitalist lifestyle", that sort of thing. "Seeks just society in East Berlin".' Orange eyebrows raised. 'You know the sort of piffle newspapers like to produce. Our friends in the GDR embassy will have a field day, they'll roll out the red carpet to welcome you into their workers' paradise.'

'And for that,' Miller said, 'you expect me to spy on them. You're a shit, Redgrave.'

'Sometimes you have to be.' Redgrave sounded as if he were enjoying himself. 'England demands.'

Shearing looked at her watch, draped her handbag on her arm. 'We'll be in touch, Mr Miller. For now you should say nothing of these arrangements to anybody. And we have your agreement, yes?'

'I need to check a couple of things—'

'That's not good enough, Miller,' Redgrave said.

'No, let him do his checking.' Shearing adjusted the handbag on her arm. 'You have until noon the day after tomorrow. We'll phone you at your flat and I will expect your answer to be yes. If it's not, you know the consequences.'

He watched them cross the wooden floor of the pub, heard in the squeak of Redgrave's brogues and the clack-clack of Shearing's heels the funeral dirge for the life he had made for himself. The life and work he loved. *Unfair*. He should let his abusive father drown in his own disgrace but what then of his mother? She drank too much, smoked too much, hid herself from reality in that mausoleum in Wolverhampton, and yet she had been, with all her weaknesses, the only rock he could cling to in the years after that rainy night at the surgery. She was pitiable and he pitied her and he would protect her as best he could. Lady Miller she had become and, if he had anyting to do with it, Lady Miller she would remain.

Even if it meant going to fucking East Berlin. Redgrave and Shearing had been vague about what they would demand of him but he knew he could expect specifics when the phone call came in forty-eight hours. He'd been once, years before, on a day trip to East Berlin; he could remember only half-filled shop windows and limited menus and once elegant facades with peeling paint. And yet he admired the GDR's attempt to build a way of life that was different from Thatcher's adoration of the dollar and the divine rights of property.

Yes, he would call his contacts, do his checking. And yes, he didn't doubt that he would find the story told across the table in the King's Arms to be true.

The dregs of his whisky were sour with the taste of abandonment. Sophie had abandoned him, the voice on the phone was proof of that, a new keeper for the key of her flat door. Yet the prospect of a new beginning, even in a divided city, was not altogether unwelcome; Miller wasn't sure if he was deluding himself about protecting his mother – maybe he just wanted to put more distance between himself and Sophie and the new keeper of the key. More than once he'd written about the divided city of Berlin. Now the opportunity (or order) to live there – *on the wrong side* – would allow him to see and write from behind the lines. His mother would not understand but she'd open another bottle and forgive him. Dr Sir Roger Miller would neither forgive nor try to understand; best of all, his only son's highly publicized departure for East Germany would be a source of heartfelt shame for the ennobled gynaecologist. Which alone was cause enough, Miller reasoned, for another drink.

Checking out Redgrave and Shearing's story didn't take long.

Mrs Oliphant's voice on the answering machine at his father's surgery told him that Dr Miller was away from the office and that the caller should leave a message, etc., etc.

He could call a barrister contact who had defended more than one doctor in malpractice cases and ask him to make discreet inquiries at the British Medical Association.

He could call the crime correspondent at the *Guardian* and ask if he'd heard anything about a doctor in trouble in the West Midlands.

Miller did neither of these things. *Make the calls and you'll raise hares, the very hares that Redgrave and Shearing say they've killed off.*

He could call home but he'd have to listen to his mother. You might go to East Berlin to keep the truth from her but you won't listen to her smoky voice for an hour: *what kind of love was that?*

He called Sophie's number.

The new male voice said hello.

Miller swallowed, said nothing.

The new holder of the key said hello again.

Miller was silent.

The male voice said, 'I think I know who this is. You're not here any more, so don't call here again – just fuck off.'

Miller heard the click on the line but he went on holding the receiver, not hearing even the static in his ear.

A squall of winter rain lashing on the window brought him back to the small flat, his books, the disarray where there had been filed neatness. *Fuck it.* He slid a sheet of paper into the typewriter and typed his letter of resignation.

It was Shearing who phoned next day. She didn't seem surprised when he told her he'd do it. She gave him an address to meet in Finchley, spelled it out for him. What they call a 'safe house', Miller thought.

When he climbed up the steps out of Finchley Central next morning, Miller thought that all the houses looked safe, blandly so: this was the constituency of Margaret Thatcher. His brain reminded him that he was a chronicler of sorts, that he should commit these suburban streetscapes to memory. His heart couldn't listen.

The safe house had had its small front garden concreted over; blinds slatted shut on the windows. Inside, it smelled like a place not often occupied; the heavy old furniture seemed less designed for comfort than to fill up space. He sat with Redgrave and Shearing at an elderly dining table in a back room.

He was surprised that the instructions seemed so few, so banal. They knew – he no longer even wondered how – that he had about a thousand pounds in savings; he should withdraw most of it to take with him, a new account would be opened in his name with an initial deposit of two thousand pounds. He signed the papers set before him on the mahogany dining table.

After he'd sent in his letter of resignation, he should write a farewell article, setting out his disillusionment with Thatcher's Britain and his hopes for a better life in the GDR. Miller said the features editor might be pissed off with him, might reject such an article. Redgrave laughed, Shearing smiled: like Miller himself, they knew the features editor would lap it up.

And don't worry about your stuff, put it in boxes, we'll take care of it. Redgrave handed him a card for a storage company near Heathrow. The remaining three months on his flat would be paid up.

Miller knew he was taking it in. He also knew that he didn't care very much. These were no more than motions to be gone through, like the hounds chasing the fox in the hunting prints on the walls of this anonymous room in Finchley. Unlike the fox in the frame, at this moment Miller didn't care about the outcome of the chase.

'Do you understand all this, Miller?' Redgrave's voice was sharp.

'Yes.'

'You don't look very interested.'

Miller said nothing. He half turned in his chair but the blinds on the window were fully closed.

'You don't look very well,' Shearing said. 'I think, after your going-away piece is published, you should turn down any chat-show offers. Robin Day and the other TV vultures will be mad to have you but I'm not sure how you'd handle the kind of grilling you'd get.'

Redgrave nodded. 'Good idea – talk to us if the radio or TV people want you.'

Miller said OK.

* * *

Disposing of a life was easier than Miller could have imagined.

Rudiger, the affable press officer at the East German embassy in Belgrave Square, welcomed him with coffee and open arms, told him he'd loved his piece in the *Guardian*. No promises about work in East Berlin – not even about getting permission to live there – but he winked jovially, said he felt sure there'd be a terrific reception for such a distinguished writer as Patrick Miller!

Even Patrick Miller had to follow procedures. At the East German travel agency, Berolina, in Conduit Street, he applied for a month-long visitor's visa, signed forms, handed over his sterling.

'Sprechen Sie Deutsch, Herr Miller?' The middle-aged woman handling his papers was looking keenly at him.

'Ein bisschen,' he said. 'A-levels.'

'Good, it will make your time among us more enjoyable.' The woman beamed.

She knows me, she's read about me or maybe Rudiger told her to expect me.

Miller thanked her, walked back towards Regent Street. On an impulse he turned towards Oxford Circus, hurried east among the crowds, swung left on to Charing Cross Road. In Foyle's bookshop he sought out the schoolbooks section, found a German grammar and dictionary. *Time to snap out of it, time to start brushing up on his A-level German.*

He wasn't surprised that weeks passed before his visa came: even sympathetic souls knew that paperwork weighed heavily, moved slowly, behind the Iron Curtain. In the meantime he opened his grammar book for an hour every morning, another hour at night. The habit of study returned to him; his improving grasp of the language energized him. Rudiger invited him for a drink one evening; he tried out his Deutsch, was pleased with himself, with Rudiger's compliments. He enjoyed Rudiger's company but he knew also that he was being pumped, observed. He had no doubt that others at the embassy would be digging into his past.

For himself, he wished that the past could be buried somewhere very deep. All the same, a few days before his departure he travelled north from Euston, took a taxi from Wolverhampton station to the house in Compton. His father was on the driveway, getting into his car, when Miller arrived. They shook hands, avoided eye contact. His father explained, smoothly, that he had a meeting at the local hospital which he simply *couldn't* miss, he was sure Patrick would understand. He watched his father drive away and Patrick Miller registered his own surprise that he'd felt no urge at all to strike him.

His mother wept, drank too much wine over lunch in the Swan restaurant, fell asleep in the taxi back to the house. She woke up when the taxi stopped, began to weep again when they were once more inside the dark and polished house. Miller promised to write, that he'd phone if he could. He hoped he could keep his promise. His mother was asleep on the long brown sofa when he left to catch the train back to London.

His last meeting with Redgrave in London was two days before he left. A house in Manor Park this time, in London's East End. An artisan's house in an artisan's street, rubbish bins and bags beside front doors. Redgrave made tea with tea bags in beakers, milk poured from a bottle. *Who's fooling who, play-acting on a working-class stage?* Redgrave had little to say: they'd make contact in a few days, meantime do some sightseeing, make inquiries at the Ministry for Social Cooperation about work. You'll be watched all the time, trust nobody in the Hotel Adria – a half-smile – and maybe not the hotel food either.

Miller nodded. He'd heard it all more than once.

He didn't look back when he stepped out past the rubbish bins, in the direction of Ilford station.

Two days later Miller landed on a British Airways flight at Tegel Airport in West Berlin. That afternoon he passed through Checkpoint Charlie into the Eastern half of the city.

Seventeen

October 1989
East Berlin

It was almost a relief when the phone rang. His mind refused to focus on the manuscript on his desk: he could see only that wide full mouth, her shoulder-length black hair, the deeps of her black eyes. *Concentrate: you've got to write that piece for General Reder*. He picked up the phone.

'Miller.'

'Herr Miller, somebody is phoning from England.' The operator sounded angry. 'He insists on talking to you.'

Correspondence with the English-speaking world was one thing; phone calls from that world were rare – and they *never* came to Patrick Miller.

'Who is it?'

'I've told him that he should speak with Herr Direktor Hartheim but he keeps repeating your name. He says it's most important and urgent.' The operator's voice still tetchy, as if she'd been arguing with the caller.

'What's his name?'

'Whit-acre.' Two long drawn-out syllables, spoken slowly. 'He says you have written to him.'

Whitacre. No bell rang. He looked out of the window but he could still see her face in the patch of October sky.

'What did I write to him about?'

In his ear he could hear a phone ringing.

'Herr Miller, please hold, the other line—' She was gone, static in his ear. But no Whitacre or even Whit-acre.

'Herr Miller, sorry.' Exasperation in the operator's voice now. *You should get a different job*. 'Herr Whit-acre said he wishes to speak to you about our dictionaries.'

Dictionaries. Alphabets. R is for Rosa, Rosa Rossman.

'He wants to speak to me about dictionaries?'

'Herr Miller, shall I tell Herr Whit-acre you are engaged?'

Whitacre. He remembered now. Welwyn Garden City. Offering pennies for first-class dictionaries.

'Put him through.'

'Herr Miller? This is T. J. Whitacre in Welwyn Garden City.' The plummy polish of a public school education. 'I wrote to you about buying a lot of dictionaries from you.'

'And I explained in my letter that your offer was rather wide of the mark, Mr Whitacre.'

'I think you'll find what I have to offer now is very interesting indeed, Herr Miller.'

Another copper or two per book. 'I'm all ears.'

'I'd like to make you an offer for world rights in your entire nonfiction list.'

'Our *entire* nonfiction list?'

'Indeed – dictionaries, science books, atlases, the whole shootin' match.'

'But,' was T. J. Whitacre out of his mind? 'we publish hundreds of such books.'

'As I know full well.'

'And how many copies of these books are you proposing to buy?'

'Not *copies*, Herr Miller, *rights*. We're proposing to acquire publishing *rights*, worldwide, in your entire nonfiction list.'

'Mr Whitacre, this may be your idea of a joke,' *either that or you're plain fucking insane*, 'but these books are published by one of our state publishing houses and I can assure you that there is no plan – nor any reason – to sell off rights in the list.'

'That's not what I'm hearing, Herr Miller.' Was the fellow *chuckling* on the line? 'Not at all what I'm hearing.'

'Mr Whitacre, I have no idea what you're talking about. What exactly are you hearing?'

'Herr Miller,' the fellow *was* chuckling, 'you know how it is: a nod and a wink, rumours, remarks overheard at book fairs and conferences. As we understand it, your list may be for sale and we're prepared to make you a good offer.' No chuckling now, more like a gulped swallow down the line. 'A *damned* good offer, Herr Miller.'

'Mr Whitacre, I'm sure there has been some misunderstanding,' *and all phone calls here are automatically recorded*, 'and I'm afraid I cannot help you.'

'We're serious about this offer, Herr Miller.'

'I'm sure you are,' and I'm serious about not wanting to be part of a recorded phone conversation that could be considered treasonable, 'but I can assure you that you have been misinformed.'

'I thought I might fly over with one of my colleagues to discuss the matter.'

'There really is no point, Mr Whitacre.'

'We could be there tomorrow or the day after.' T. J. Whitacre was nothing if not persistent. 'We think you'll like what we have to tell you.'

'In three days' time,' Miller said, 'we celebrate our fortieth anniversary – not much of anything will happen here until after that.'

'Anniversary?'

'Yes, Mr Whitacre, our anniversary.' *If you want our books, you might at least learn something about us*. 'It's forty years since the GDR was established, way back in nineteen forty-nine.'

'Ah, of course!' An intake of breath, a more sombre tone, like words of sympathy offered to bereaved survivors. 'A great national occasion, I'm sure, but the world moves on.' Another pause. 'When you get the chance, Herr Miller, before or after your "anniversary", you might be good enough to call me back.'

'If you wish but I'm a very small cog in a very large and complicated machine.'

'But you're English, Herr Miller—'

'Nowadays I have an East German passport.'

'And we can remember your writings in the *Guardian*.'

'All in the past, Mr Whitacre.' And I don't need a reminder in the present, especially in phone recordings. 'I'll take your number.'

He jotted down the number, assured T. J. Whitacre that he would discuss the matter with his colleagues, and hung up with relief. *What on earth was all that about?*

And what did Whitacre mean by 'the world moves on'? Mikhail Gorbachev would lend the support of the Soviet Union to the celebrations, along with other leaders from the Soviet bloc; even the PLO's Yasser Arafat would turn up. What was Whitacre chuckling about?

At the very least, Miller figured, he might as well take a look at one or two publishing contracts.

He phoned Frau Siedel to ask if Herr Direktor Hartheim was available. She reminded him that the Herr Direktor was at Normannenstrasse, presenting copies of the jubilee celebration brochure to General Erich Mielke. Miller hadn't forgotten; he wanted it recorded by Hartheim's secretary that he'd *asked*. And it would seem perfectly natural, in light of Whitacre's call, for Miller to take a look at the publishing contracts for their dictionaries.

The Registry of Contracts and Agreements was housed in the basement. Frau Marta Tischler, tall, big-boned and almost sixty years old, guarded her domain of shelves and filing cabinets with the fierce vigilance of Cerberus at the gates of the Underworld. Someone had once remarked of Frau Tischler that, although she had only one head compared to Cerberus's three, she could observe more with her two eyes than the mythical dog with six. Patrick Miller had always felt that Frau Tischler's powerful jaws could also do as much damage as Cerberus with his three heads.

She watched Miller fill in the request form on the metal counter at the entrance to her territory.

'Our dictionaries?' Her white hair seemed even whiter under the basement strip lighting. 'You too?'

Miller looked at her, said nothing. He'd learned over the years.

Sometimes Frau Tischler gave you nothing even if you *didn't* ask.

Miller also knew that, for Frau Tischler, his Englishness was a plus. In April 1945, as the combined Allies had made their final push into Western Germany, the then fifteen-year-old Marta Tischler had been gang-raped by North African soldiers of the French forces; as they were finishing, buttoning their flies, a couple of American privates who chanced on the scene decided that they too were in need of relief. The young British lieutenant who was driving by the bombed-out building promptly stopped his jeep, pistol-whipped the American who was *in flagrante* while his accomplice waited impatiently, and scattered the entire assembly with a shot over their heads. He delivered the stricken girl to the nearest field hospital, ordered the medics to take care of her, and for the next week brought her chocolates, chewing gum, cigarettes and canned food to take home. Marta Tischler's home no longer existed; neither did any member of her family. In the ruins of her home city, she could not stomach the conquerors who had defiled her. Against the westward-fleeing tide of refugees she headed east to Berlin. The young British lieutenant helped her with papers of safe passage through the occupied country, gave her money and sweets for the journey. In the Soviet zone of Berlin she felt unexpectedly safe and, although never letting go of a deep fear and hatred of all things French and American, she cherished her affection for the young British officer who had saved her.

All of which Miller had heard, in dribs and drabs, from different colleagues who had a healthy fear of Frau Tischler's disapproval.

So Miller waited. *Our dictionaries? You too?*

'I've never known so many requests to examine my contracts for dictionaries and the like.'

Miller nodded, raised his eyebrows in silent question.

But Frau Tischler obviously felt that she had passed enough information across the registry counter.

'I suppose,' she said, 'I'm just *imagining* all the requests.'

'Very likely, Frau Tischler,' Miller said. *Except that you have a perfectly real grasp of everything that goes on in this registry*. 'Maybe I could just take a look at some of the contracts now, as I'm here.'

'*Some* of them?'

'Whatever you suggest.'

'And,' Frau Tischler brandished the single completed form, 'the request docket?'

'I could take a quick look here at the counter.' Miller gave her what he hoped was his best smile. 'No need to take the files away.'

The hush in the basement registry seemed to deepen. Under Frau Tischler's quizzical gaze Miller felt he could imagine even the pages in the assembled files holding their papery breath. *Life and business in the GDR*.

'Of course, Herr Miller.' Something like a smile on that lantern jaw. 'You can certainly have a quick look at some of the contracts here at the counter.'

The pile of manila folders that Frau Tischler laid on the counter held contracts for publications spanning more than two decades. A two-volume large-format German–English–German dictionary from the early 1970s. A single-volume paperback compilation. An atlas of the world. Various German grammars. A lavishly illustrated history of European art.

Miller was conscious of Frau Tischler's nearness as he turned the stapled pages of each contract and glanced at some of the accompanying letters in each folder. Everything was signed, every page initialled. All of the books had been produced by teams put together from various universities, copyright vested in the GDR. He shrugged, only partly for Frau Tischler's benefit.

'Thank you, Frau Tischler.' He pushed the stack of folders across the counter.

She nodded, left one more folder in front of Miller.

What now? He looked at her but she ignored him, eyes downcast.

He knew this book: a handsome catalogue of Renaissance paintings at the Hermitage Museum in Leningrad, widely admired for the quality of its illustrations, the scholarship of its commentary. No expense had been spared in this production, from the quality of its slip case to the heavy art paper pages. Not a year passed without at least one request for foreign language rights landing on Miller's desk. No request was ever granted. It was a jewel in the crown, worth even more than the welcome hard currency earned in international sales.

And Miller could see why Frau Tischler had handed him the file for this book.

The book had been published as long ago as 1969, the contract obviously typed on the oldest typewriters. The pages were yellowing, the top corners browned with the rust marks of an ancient staple. But the staple that now held the pages together was shining bright. Perhaps just replaced – maybe Frau Tischler was in the habit of replacing elderly staples in her beloved files.

Although standing opposite him, Frau Tischler was still too busy rearranging files to meet Miller's eyes.

Miller fingered the top page of the stapled contract. Someone had managed to find an ageing page of the same vintage as the rest of the contract but, to Miller's fingers, the page was of the wrong weight. The top page felt thinner, lighter – the GDR in money-saving mode.

Read it. With care.

It didn't take too much care: the alteration to the opening clause of the agreement was casual, blatant. The agreement began in the usual way, stating that it was made

> . . . between the Compilers of the Catalogue all of whom are public servants of the German Democratic Republic, of the one part, and Publishing House No. 1, hereinafter called 'the Publishers', which expression to include any publishing imprint subsidiary or associate or any nominee nominated by the legally appointed Director of the Publishers . . .

It was that seemingly innocuous phrase, 'any nominee

nominated by the legally appointed Director of the Publishers' that made him blink, look up at Frau Tischler. She met his gaze but without expression.

Without a word she handed back to him the files she held in her arms. It took only a minute to see that all of the contracts had been similarly doctored. *Any nominee nominated by the legally appointed Director of the Publishers*: meaning that Hartheim could hand control to anybody, from Mickey Mouse to Yuri Gagarin. Hartheim had the publishing operation where he wanted it – in his pocket.

You had to be careful with your phrasing of a question; ask it in the wrong way and it might not be answered at all.

Miller said, 'Do I need to look at the rest of the contracts?'

Frau Tischler shook her head.

Fine, but there was ambiguity in that shake of the head; perhaps it meant that only these contracts had been changed.

Miller said, 'All changed?'

Frau Tischler nodded. Without a word she gathered up the manila folders in her meaty arms and Miller watched as she began to replace the files in the grey cabinets. *So now you know more than Whitacre, what can you do about it?*

Frau Tischler didn't reply when Miller said thank you but she gave him the briefest of nods to acknowledge his presence and his going.

It's her country and yet all she can do is surreptitiously point out to a foreigner the possibility of a set-up and a sell-off.

Except that Patrick Miller didn't feel like a foreigner; he just didn't know what, if anything, he should do with this dangerous knowledge.

* * *

Almost 12.30. He signed out under the smile-free attention of the duty porters and stepped out into the day. October, but with the heat of an Indian summer day. He set off at a brisk walk through the noontime streets.

In the lobby of the university he checked with yet another unsmiling porter. Yes, Frau Rossman was teaching, her class would end in a few minutes.

They smiled when they saw each other. He longed to embrace her but he didn't know how she'd react. Or how the uniformed porter would record such a display. They shook hands and Miller kissed Rosa Rossman chastely on the cheek.

Yes, she was free for lunch but the day was too fine to sit indoors, shouldn't they make the most of what might be the last of summer? They could share her sandwiches, she always made too much, she'd have to get a smaller lunch box. She smiled at him, dimples blinking in the creamy skin under the black eyes.

He took her rucksack and they walked towards the river. A kind of tension hung over the streets, as though the late blast of summer might darken into a roll of thunder. Armed Vopos stood on corners, patrolled in pairs. On the previous Monday night hundreds of demonstrators had spilled out of St Nicholas's Church on to the streets of Leipzig in silent, candle-carrying protest; no shots had been fired but Honecker and the Politburo had made it clear that no demonstration would be allowed to jeopardize the jubilee celebrations.

Others had had the same idea about making the most of the weather but Miller found an empty patch of grass on the crowded bank. He spread his jacket on the grass, Rosa took the packet of sandwiches from her rucksack.

It seems almost normal, Miller thought, as they chewed in a companionable silence. There is no Wall, no armed policemen on the streets. No doctored contracts in Frau Tischler's registry, no preparations in hand to sell off a country's assets.

He leaned close to Rosa's ear to tell her.

'So it's happening,' she whispered.

'About a year, the general said.'

The river streamed below them, oblivious. The Vopos patrolled the streets, the border guards manned the crossing points of the Wall. *Like the river, they know nothing.*

'I don't know what to do,' Miller said. 'But I feel I must do *something*.'

'I'll speak to my father.'

Miller looked at the river, at other couples on the grass.

'And I'd like to see you, Rosa. I mean soon.'

'After the jubilee parade,' Rosa said. 'My father will be on the reviewing stand but somebody will drive him home after – we could meet then.'

'Yes.' He didn't want to think about contracts now. 'Yes,' he said again.

The nearness of her was almost overwhelming. He felt her eyes on him, he knew he could happily drown in those huge black eyes; he thought, we could go somewhere else, maybe London, forget all this shit, just be together. Then again, Miller thought, maybe I don't want to be elsewhere.

Rosa Rossman, it seemed, could read his mind.

'Patrick,' she said, 'I have no wish to live anywhere else.'

Miller laughed. 'How did you know I was thinking about that?'

'Maybe it's because I'm beginning to feel close to you.' She poured tea from her flask for both of them. 'Sometimes I can tell what my father is going to say before he says it.' The eyes twinkling like dark diamonds. 'You'd better think only nice things about me, Herr Patrick Miller.'

She drank some tea, smiled.

'You're blushing, Herr Miller!'

'But only because you make me feel good.' Miller looked at the sky, at the still river. 'I've always liked this city but now,' he glanced at her, wished he wasn't blushing, 'well, it's different now.'

'Different *good* or different *bad*?'

'Rosa . . .' He felt her nearness on the grass, wanted to touch her, could find no words.

'I know,' she said.

'You do?'

'Yes, Patrick, I know.'

He felt her hand on his, resting on his jacket. She leaned closer and kissed him on the mouth. When they drew apart, Miller knew that Berlin – his life – was changed forever. He looked at Rosa in wonder. 'Coming here,' he said, 'was worthwhile just to meet you.' She touched his face with her hand. Her voice was no more than a whisper.

'I could say that too, Patrick.'

'Maybe,' he said, 'it's because we're outsiders thrown together in a great city.' He knew he was leaving much unsaid but knew too that everything didn't have to be spelled out, that she could hear his song in the spaces between his words. 'You and me, even you and General Reder.'

'You're curious about my father, aren't you?'

'Forgive me,' Miller said. 'Maybe it's because he's your father and he obviously loves you. My own father . . .' Miller shrugged. 'I've read General Reder's "official" autobiography, the stuff you brought to the office. I have a feeling there's a great story there somewhere, a life lived close to the edge, but General Reder has done a great job of concealing it.'

'You have to be careful, Patrick, when you're a general,' Rosa said. '*Especially* when you're a general. And you're right, I helped my father to make it as bland as possible.'

'I understand,' Miller said, 'and anyway it's not my business.'

She looked around, her eyes measuring the nearness of the others on the river bank. Miller had to lean closer to hear her.

'My father fought in the war on the eastern front, Patrick. I'm certain that he fought honourably and bravely. He saw terrible things done but I can be sure that he took no part in such – such *things*. He was a tank commander in the Ukraine and you know what was done there.' Rosa paused, leaned even closer. 'You know the stories – the *truth*. My father saw the Einsatzgruppen in action.' Her face paled as if the horror of the SS special action groups were unloosed again on their Jew-hunts across eastern Europe. Miller saw her shiver, took her hand in his. 'My father knew what they were doing but there was nothing he could do about it. As a tank commander his duty was to keep himself and his men alive.'

She saw the question in Miller's eyes, met his gaze.

'General Reder,' she said, 'was a German soldier but he was never a Nazi.'

Now it was Miller's turn to shiver, as if the mere words, Nazi, Einsatzgruppen, could chill the midday sun.

'And now . . .' Miller hesitated. He needed to know but he didn't know how to ask without offence; he feared losing her in the very moment of finding her.

'You're wondering,' Rosa said, 'if you can trust a man who fought against the Red Army and then took their side. You're wondering if he's just a turncoat who only ever wants to save his own skin.'

Miller was silent. *She's doing it again, reading my mind.*

'My father saw what was right and what was wrong,' Rosa said. 'He chose the *right*, that's all.'

Something like a song swelled in Miller. *This woman, these people, this divided city, this tortured country riven by doubt and protest*: it's my truth, my here-and-now, my tomorrow.

'Say something, Patrick.'

Miller was smiling, 'Your father chose the right.'

'Yes,' Rosa said, 'he did.' She pressed his hand on the jacket. 'I don't want to have secrets from you.'

She drew closer to Miller and started to tell him.

PART 3

REDER'S STORY

Eighteen

January 1944
Kirovograd
Ukraine

'We move at 0600 hours.' General Bayerlein looked at the tired faces gathered in front of him. 'From that moment all radio contact with HQ will cease. It is,' the faintest of smiles on the general's weathered features, 'for our own safety.'

At the back of the crowded cellar someone laughed nervously. General Bayerlein didn't laugh. Watching his men burn to death in their own tanks wasn't much of a laughing matter. He'd seen enough charred corpses in North Africa and here on the snows of the Ukraine. So for their own safety, no radio communication after the 3rd Panzer Division begins its attempt at escape from encirclement in Kirovograd.

Like the other group commanders in the packed room, Major Hans Reder understood the real reason for the radio blackout. In Berlin the Führer had, as usual, vetoed any attempt at break-out and escape; like the soldiers at Stalingrad, the men in Kirovograd should fight to their last bullet and the last drop of their rich, unyielding German blood. German honour – and the Führer – demanded and deserved nothing less.

At nineteen, Reder was the youngest man in the gathering. Hans Reder didn't feel nineteen. Mostly he just felt exhausted.

'Major Reder?' It took him a few seconds to realize that *Major* Reder was *Hans* Reder. *Him*: the boy from West Prussia.

'Sir?'

'Your group will lead off, along with Major Kolf's group and,' General Bayerlein nodded to the two men standing beside Hans, 'Captain Schmidt.'

'Sir!' A chorused response, cigarettes cupped in hand, heels clicked. The Panzer Korps was less formal, less interested in spit'n'polish than much of the military but when General Bayerlein gave an order, even in his casual way, you remembered your place and clicked your military heels.

The general went on outlining his breakout formation. There were no questions. There was no need: General Bayerlein's orders were clear, delivered as simply as Hans's teacher's half-time instructions to the village football team on a Sunday morning. *Another life, another world.*

A huge explosion shook the packed cellar. The lights went out on the low ceiling. Matches were struck, cigarette lighters flared, the waiting candles caught flame. In the candlelight the faces seemed even greyer, more weary. The general lit a cigarette. The assembled men spoke softly in pairs and groups.

They waited for the next explosion.

The barrage that followed seemed to be moving away, east, towards the city centre. But again the cellar shook as the blast waves ripped through the earth. The candles flickered. *Fucking Ivan. You never knew when he'd decide to send a few shells over. You just knew that he was out there, beyond the city, waiting for the chance to gut you. Slowly.*

The barrage ended as abruptly as it had begun. The lights came on in the cellar.

Hans Reder nodded to the men beside him, the men who would lead the groups on either side of him, Major Kolf and

Captain Schmidt. Like himself, short, jockeys for the metal monsters that could so easily – and so often – become flaming metal tombs. So better not to know them too well. You never knew which shell had anybody's name on it.

The men waited.

'Any second now.' A stage whisper from the back of the group. The men laughed nervously. Ivan had, for the last few days, lobbed over a few extra shells just when you thought it was all over.

On cue, it came, a brief salvo that reverberated through the earth. The lights flickered but did not go out. The cellar seemed to settle back on its haunches. The tank commanders doused the candles. Outside, they knew, it was a starless night under the winter sky of the Ukraine. Outside, too, they'd be sorting the freshly dead from the freshly wounded: like every man in the cellar, Hans Reder had no wish ever to be numbered among the wounded, waiting your turn for the surgeon's knife in the abattoir confines of the field hospital. The bleary-eyed doctors did their best to stem an impossible tide of guts and blood – and Ivan was no respecter of Red Cross ethics.

'Any questions, gentlemen?'

Nobody had any questions for General Bayerlein. Least of all about the wounded and dying who would be left behind in the breakout attempt.

'So, good luck, gentlemen.' General Bayerlein's words broke up the meeting. The men dispersed slowly. Why hurry towards the dark dawn over the filthy snows of the Ukraine? Soon enough their great beasts would growl into life and push on across the churned landscape towards the Russian guns. Soon enough, blood would be spilled.

Only the broken walls of Kirovograd Town Hall remained standing above the cellar. With the others Reder picked his way among the rubble towards a gap in the walls. He skirted the tangled remains of a once-elegant staircase. Overhead the dark sky seemed to threaten snow. Falling snow would help to hide their advance; drifts would mire their caterpillar tracks. Six of one, half a dozen of the other.

Reder said goodnight to Kolf and Schmidt, the men with whom he would spearhead the dawn breakout. Both men seemed equally unwilling to linger amid the rubble. All of them had seen enough of battle – of death – to know the pointlessness of conjecture, the uselessness of trying to anticipate the nature of the battle to come. You couldn't write the script for the battlefield. Death came where and when it wished.

Less than two years ago Hans Reder had begun learning his trade as a mechanic in a garage in Danzig that had once specialized in German and Czech motorbikes; by the time Hans arrived, in the summer of 1942, the entire workforce had been dragooned into military support. Lorries, cars, motorcycles, all in military grey or green, passed through the garage on the narrow street above Danzig harbour. The men who taught Hans Reder his trade were old or infirm or both. They wheezed over engine blocks, coughed into the entrails of trucks and cars. They taught Reder what they knew and looked at him with unenvying eyes. They were men who had been rousted from retirement; they were men who had survived the war of 1914–18. They had watched the younger workforce of the garage march off to restage the madness. They shook Hans Reder's hand when he was called up in the summer of 1943 but they did not look him in the eye.

His training was brief and on the job. It seemed inevitable that his knowledge of engines would lead him to the Panzer Korps. And he was small, wiry, the right size and shape for the cramped belly of a tank. With the 3rd Panzer Division he fought his way into the Ukraine. He learned how to catnap, how to keep alert while he napped. He learned that the distance between life and death could not be measured. He was the assistant gunner in his first tank when death came for the chief gunner, pierced through the eye by a stray bullet in the push towards Kirovograd; the following day, he and the assistant driver were the only ones to scramble free when their tank took a direct hit and burst into flames. Trained men were scarce; they made him a sergeant.

He was hardly used to being called 'Sergeant' when a field commission followed and he was Lieutenant Reder. He couldn't remember exactly why or how he had won the Iron Cross. He remembered the long barrel of the Soviet tank poking between the walls of the ruined farmhouse, the thud of the shell on his Panther, the loss of power, the great tank grinding to a halt. A sitting duck. He was the tank commander, he roared at his crew to get out. When he tumbled through the hatch he saw his men bleeding in the snow. In an unremembered madness he ran towards the advancing Soviet tank. He heard the ping and thud of bullets in the dirty snow, wondered why he was still alive, rolled the grenade between the tracks, raised his pistol and fired, saw the Red commander slump in the open turret. Two numbed Soviet tank men exited the crippled tank, their hands in the air. He marched them back to base, handed them over for interrogation. An hour later he saw them lying face down on the ground, skulls blasted open. He remembered their frightened faces as they'd come up out of the tank turret, country fellows with flat faces, not so unlike some of the boys in his own village outside Danzig.

No, you couldn't write the script for the battlefield. Now he was *Major* Hans Reder, promoted by General Bayerlein himself, waiting to lead the 3rd Panzer Division into a dawn battle. His mother, milking her cows in the early morning in West Prussia, surely wouldn't believe it. Hans Reder did believe it. Believing it was part of his job – the job of keeping his men alive.

And keeping himself alive.

The tanks rolled in the darkness. Under the steel tracks of a hundred Panthers the earth shook. Standing in his turret, Reder could sense rather than see the tanks on either side. And he could hear them, a rolling rumble that seemed to come from deep in the frozen belly of the earth.

Ivan could hear the growling earth too; he'd be listening, preparing, priming his artillery. Waiting for them.

On cue, the barrage started.

The shells fell further back, in the ruined city.

Ivan hasn't got it yet, doesn't realize we're all making a hell-for-leather dash for it, thinks it's just a bit of reorganization behind our lines.

Reder ducked below to check his crew.

'Everyone OK?' He had to shout above the engine noise. Nods, thumbs up. Like him, they wouldn't have slept much. Like him, they were hungry. Like him, they wanted to get out of this godforsaken wasteland.

'Springtime in Paris, lads!' The men smiled at his rally. No one in the tank had ever been to Paris but everybody knew about French women.

Reder hadn't told his group that their job, along with Schmidt's group, was to swing north, away from the main advance, in an attempt to mislead the Russians. It was a strategy he had agreed on with Schmidt: each tank commander had to be told but there was little to be gained by letting the men know that they ran the risk of being cut off.

He shivered, drew his field cap lower, pulled his leather

gloves tighter. The gloves were a necessary encumbrance: lay your naked fingers against the hull of the tank and you'd leave a patch of your skin on the frozen metal. It was minus 20 degrees, too cold to snow. The sky was lightening.

Reder could see the tanks on either side now, grey monsters growling through the grey darkness. The exhausts of the tanks pumped their fog-like fumes into the frozen air.

No radio contact. Schmidt was waiting for his signal, saw his wave. Schmidt's group of four – one tank was frozen solid – swung right, followed by Reder's group of five. Ahead lay the unending snow, dark and dirty in the breaking dawn. Ahead lay Ivan.

As the sky lightened further in the January dawn, Reder could see that they had pulled away from the main body of the advance.

Now. He bawled instructions at his gunner, distance and elevation, saw the long barrel move and find its direction and level, heard his own command: 'Fire!'

The Panther shook as the gun roared. Even with the ear-covers he was almost deafened. It was still too dark to see the explosion in Ivan's quarters but he heard the boom, thought he heard cries but maybe he imagined that. The other tanks fired at intervals. You had to husband shells, playing the decoy left you exposed.

The response was fierce. Salvo after salvo falling in front, then behind, then stepping towards them, finding the range.

Time to beat it. Together with Schmidt he'd decided their best prospect of survival was to make for a small forest – under this barrage, did it still exist? – and somehow try to loop round the Russian lines to join up with the main advance.

Daylight had arrived. Dark, dirty light under a dark, dirty sky. A sky that flared with the orange track of artillery shells. A sky that boomed with the roar of guns, the screaming of men and beasts.

Through the smoke and exploding earth he signalled to Schmidt. He watched the small convoy of tanks make for the questionable shelter of a forest that might no longer exist. At least all nine tanks were still moving.

And then, disaster.

In the split second before the shell hit them, Reder knew: *the one that had your name on it.* He ducked, felt the shell hit, heard screams, the huge bang as metal met metal. He felt the Panther lift, tilt, thump sideways on the ground. And then nothing, blackness.

He came to on the scorched snow. The stricken Panther lay on its side, its tracks shattered, hanging like metal guts from the smoking undercarriage. Somehow he'd been thrown clear. He levered himself into a sitting position, cautiously swung each arm, each leg. All intact, unharmed except for the blood leaking from a gash on his forehead. Intact, but alone and too close to the Russian lines. A hundred metres away another Panther belched smoke and flames. The rest were gone, hidden in the mix of murky light and the fog of battle. *Move.* An early-morning encounter with Ivan was best left for another day.

Reder got to his feet, shook the snow from his leather greatcoat. If Ivan didn't get him, the icy cold would.

He heard faint moaning from the belly of the tank. Through his gloved hands he could feel the throbbing heat of the metal. The cockpit of the tank was a pit of darkness.

'Who is it?' He kept his voice low: sound could carry for miles across the frozen space.

Only groaning answered him. He focused his eyes, saw the hand move slightly in the dark interior. Reder levered himself through the hatch. The smell hit him, blood and shit and piss.

But the driver was alive: Muller, the lad from outside Munich who liked to show photos of his girlfriend, a blonde with a gap between her teeth and a pair of large, well-upholstered breasts. Muller didn't look to Reder like somebody who'd be taking any interest in any kind of breasts for a long time. He manoeuvred Muller through the hatch, lowered him to the ground.

Blood was leaking from the fellow's mouth. Reder moved him, saw the huge dark stain on the snow where Muller lay. His shirt and tunic were seared to his back and buttocks; it was hard to know where flesh ended and clothing began. It was obvious that Muller's groaning wouldn't last long. But he couldn't be left like this, haemorrhaging in the snow, waiting for the Russians.

Waiting no longer.

Reder saw the Soviet truck breasting the low rise in front, soldiers spread out on either side of the slow-moving vehicle. No tanks, just a small truck, unguarded except for infantrymen. A small group on a sweep for prisoners and wounded – and you knew what Ivan did to the wounded.

Reder drew his pistol, the dark Walther P38, and put Muller out of his pain.

The shot seemed to galvanize the approaching Russians. Reder saw the soldiers break into a run, heard the barked command to drop his weapon. Reder knew what awaited him, wondered for just a second if he should turn the Walther on himself. *But you never know: where there's life . . .*

He dropped the weapon and stood waiting with his hands in the air.

The officer in the truck waited until Reder had been given the customary bruising and kicking before ordering the soldiers to stop. On his knees, Reder found himself looking at a pair of knee-high, fur-topped boots. He heard the Russian order him to stand up – Reder had some grasp of the language: it was vaguely akin to the Polish spoken by the kids back home in West Prussia – but he looked up blankly into the round Slav face. For his troubles he got a kick in the face from one of the fur-topped boots. A pair of Ivans dragged him to his feet to stand facing an angry-looking officer in a fur hat drawn down over his ears.

More snarled instructions. *My coat,* Reder thought, the bastard wants my coat. The soldiers unbuckled his belt, began to undo the buttons of the leather overcoat. Reder snarled at them, swung his arms free and unbuttoned the coat. He heard the officer shout at the soldiers not to strike him, saw the glimmer of a smile cross the Slav features as Reder shook the snow from the coat, folded it neatly, and handed it to the Russian.

'*Danke.*' The Russian nodded the single word of German.

'*Bitte schön.*' You're welcome. And you can leave me to freeze but you'll not have the satisfaction of hearing me cry out in protest or in pain.

One of the soldiers took the folded overcoat from the officer. For a moment Reder met the officer's gaze, then lowered his eyes. *It doesn't look like you're going to get out of this but don't antagonize the bastard.* Behind the Russian he saw the endless sweep of snow, the clouds of smoke rising over the enemy lines in the near distance. He was wondering if General Bayerlein had managed to break through the Russians when the rifle butt struck him on the head and he collapsed into the darkness of the snow.

The small one-room farmhouse seemed chaotic. A huddle of Red Army officers bent over a map. Three radio operators shouted into field telephones. Two fellows in the corner were smoking, drinking from tin mugs. The smell of burning dung from the fireplace carried on the smoke that blew back through the open doorway.

Reder was at the front of the line of German prisoners outside the door. Coatless, he tried not to shiver. Smell or no smell, the glimpse of the fire inside was tantalizing. But getting near to it had its own price. The young army lieutenant who was being interrogated was paying that price now. Reder couldn't hear the questions but he could see and hear the blows struck. Blood trickled from the lieutenant's nose and mouth; one of his eyes was closed.

The Russian wearing Reder's coat sat at the interrogators' table but it was the fellow in the insignia-free grey greatcoat who did most of the talking. *Political, commissar*. Reder had heard about these commissars, the thought police who told their soldiers what to think, what to love and hate. *Like our fucking Gestapo*. He watched the German prisoner's mouth move, knew that he was reciting the prisoner's permitted litany of name, rank and number. The commissar shrugged, nodded to the NCO standing beside the table. This time the NCO's kick in the balls brought the prisoner to his knees.

Reder, watching through the open doorway, shivered despite himself. The Russian guarding the line of prisoners caught the shiver, chuckled, stamped on the frozen snow more enthusiastically. A pair of Russians dragged the lieutenant outside and dumped him, groaning, on the ground.

A smack of the guard's rifle butt on his shoulder told Reder it was his turn. He felt the eyes of his fellow prisoners follow him as he was shoved into the makeshift HQ.

He did his best to stand upright before the commissar. He was a lean fellow, clean shaven, his fair hair close-cropped. And he asked his questions in the kind of upper-class German that was spoken only by the doctor and the pastor and the schoolmaster in Reder's home village.

Reder declared his name and military serial number.

The commissar shook his head, lit a cigarette.

The officer wearing Reder's leather greatcoat whispered something to the commissar, fingered the lapel of the coat, laughed.

The commissar said something sharp and the laugh died.

'I am Captain Nikolai Kulakov,' the commissar went on in German, 'Commissar to Captain Bukanin's company.' He nodded in the direction of the leather greatcoat. 'I am told that you kindly gave your coat as a gift to Captain Bukanin. The good captain,' a faint curl of the commissar's lip, 'is impressed by his booty. Personally, I have no interest in such plunder. As a fluent German speaker I have been entrusted with the task of obtaining essential intelligence from all prisoners in this sector. I intend to obtain whatever information our prisoners have – even if they don't know they have it. Now, Major,' a glance at his notes, 'Major Reder, there are many prisoners to be interrogated and I don't have a lot of time. Do we understand each other?'

Reder clicked his heels, bowed.

'So, a small detachment of your Panzer Division broke away from the main group – what was the plan?'

Reder repeated his name, rank and number.

The commissar nodded. The NCO's clenched fist smashed into Reder's jaw.

'I'm not impressed by your bowing and heel-clicking, Major Reder.' The commissar drew deeply on his cigarette, tossed the butt into the smoking fire. 'You have information about your Third Panzer Division which is crucial to us and I mean to have that information. If *you* don't give it to me, somebody else will.' Kulakov picked a shred of tobacco from between his thin lips, studied the tiny black flake for a moment before flicking it from his fingers on to the earthen floor. 'The choice is yours, Major Reder.'

You can have your bullet in the back of your head right now – or talk and buy some time.

'You are wondering,' Kulakov said, 'if you will be executed anyway, even if you do answer my questions.' Reder said nothing. 'We are not all uncivilized beasts like this fellow here,' a sideways glance at Bukanin, 'and I give you my word that, as long as you are within my reach, no harm will befall you. So I say again, the choice is yours, Major Reder.'

He saw it all in a blurred rush. The smoke-filled cellar, your comrades-in-arms around you. The Iron Cross at your throat, the swell of pride in your heart, General Bayerlein's salute. He saw his mother in the milking stall, the full tits in her fingers, the fresh milk steaming into the waiting pail. He felt the motorbike throb between his thighs along the country lanes near home, the wind against his goggled eyes. And he saw his own prisoners lying in the snow, the dark blood pooling around their shattered skulls. The murder of unarmed prisoners did not sit easily on Hans Reder's young shoulders. Nor on his conscience. Yes, he fought under a flag, for the Fatherland, but he fought also for his comrades. As had those soldiers of the Red Army who now lay murdered in the dirty snow.

'What d'you want to know?' he said to Nikolai Kulakov.

Kulakov shrugged. 'Everything,' he said.

There was something hypnotic about the commissar. The pale eyes, Reder thought, they bored into you with all the fervour of that old idiot woman back home who assured you that the delft figure on the village chapel cross had leaked red blood from its side. And the commissar's voice, musical, unthreatening, and yet full of its own certainty, the voice of a man who only ever spoke the truth and who expected his listeners to recognize that truth.

'I need this information,' Kulakov was saying, 'because it

might help to shorten this conflict, even if only by a single day. There's been too much dying, too much killing. The Red Army does not come to destroy your homeland but to give new life to your diseased country. We bring you the gift of socialism, a fair and just system where all men and women are equal.' Those eyes once more reaching into Reder's heart – or what remained of his heart. 'Where we are all equal *in life*, Major.'

And Reder knew that Kulakov was reminding him that the only equality to be shared on this filthy battlefield was in death.

'I want to hear everything,' Kulakov said again.

Later, it seemed to Reder that everything was just what he had told Kulakov. Starting was the hard part; once he'd opened up about General Bayerlein's disposition of his forces, the rest spilled out more easily. Or maybe it was the skill with which Kulakov probed him, taking him from his village in West Prussia through his brief training in Danzig to the campaign on the eastern front.

When Kulakov offered him a cigarette, the commissar saw the nervous way that Reder glanced back at the line of prisoners outside the open doorway. A look and a word from Kulakov saw the NCO hurry outside and snarl something at the guard. The unlucky prisoner nearest to the guard got a rifle butt to the chest as the prisoners were herded from view.

'So, Major Reder, you have decided to help us, yes?'

I want to see home again, sit in my mother's kitchen. 'I've told you what I know, Captain,' he said.

'Sit down, Major.' Kulakov nodded to the NCO, pointed at a wooden box which seemed to be waiting for the fire. He waited until Reder was perched on the unsteady box before continuing.

'You should know, Major Reder,' he began, 'that the Soviet army is an unstoppable machine. We have defeated the fascist forces at Stalingrad, at Leningrad – and your comrades will die here also at Kirovograd. All across the eastern front our armies are advancing towards Germany. In a year or so the Soviet armies will be in Berlin. Make no mistake about it, Major, we will cross your borders and exact the most awful revenge upon your people for the crimes that have been committed against the Russian people.' He stared at Reder. 'You understand this, Major?'

Reder nodded.

'I need to *hear* your answer, Major Reder.' Steel in the voice.

Reder swallowed. 'Yes, Captain.' *Barbarians let loose in our streets and fields, and yet this man speaks Hochdeutsch, the language of educated Germans*. 'I hear you.'

'Hear this also, Major. We are a just people and our armies will bring to your country the true justice of the proletariat. We will bring you the justice of socialism and work with the German people to build a new socialist democracy. For this great work, Major Reder, we are going to need the cooperation of Germans who understand and appreciate the true meaning of socialist justice.' Another pause, another stare. 'You understand my meaning, Major?'

Only too well, Captain: I have no wish to lie dead in the snow.

Reder said, 'I understand, Captain.'

'You speak Russian, Major?'

'Only a little – I speak Polish.'

'The Poles! At least you Germans know how to put up a fight.' Kulakov snorted. 'Take my advice, Major, learn Russian. And stay alive, wherever you are. From now on you're out of my hands, in the care of animals like this,' a thin smile at the NCO, who grinned back, 'as a guest in one of our prisoner-of-war camps. You'll be half starved and half frozen to death. We both know that life is cheap out here in the snow. If you're lucky, you'll live to see the end of this fucking war. If you're wise you'll cooperate with the authorities wherever you're sent. You understand me?'

Once more Reder nodded. This time it didn't seem so difficult.

'This,' Kulakov looked around the smoky farmhouse, 'this is the future, these uneducated, honest members of the proletariat. I was a lecturer in German literature at Moscow University but some of our officers can't even read, they need pictures on a map. You're in the middle, Major Reder, you can read and write, you're the son of peasants but you have mastered modern machinery, the very heart of today's proletariat.' He took the half-full packet of cigarettes from his pocket, passed them across the table to Reder. 'I'll see that you are given something to eat here – the cigarettes are a token of my good intent. You impress me, Major Reder, as someone who is not afraid to make a decision, someone who is not afraid to survive – unlike some of your comrades.'

Again, Kulakov looked around at his companions. 'Survive, Major, and join with us in a great understanding when this war is finally won. You know my name – Captain Nikolai Kulakov of the Fifty-second Guards. Remember it. I can't help you once you are taken to a camp but, if we both survive, maybe we can do great things together in Berlin.'

Kulakov was no more than a few years older than himself, Reder guessed, but there was something in him that inspired obedience, the desire to please. Or maybe the desire to close your eyes to your betrayal of your country, of the Iron Cross that was hung round your neck. It was for his comrades, not for a bunch of Nazis, that he had gambled with death.

The commissar got to his feet. 'Like I said, Major, your first duty is to survive.'

Reder looked at him. 'I've been in here a long time, Captain

Kulakov.' He shrugged. 'I have to try to survive when I join the other prisoners outside so maybe,' he made a face, 'maybe your sergeant should rough me up a bit.'

'We can do better than that, Major Reder.' Kulakov spoke rapidly to the NCO. Reder watched the sergeant blink, open his mouth as if to speak, then march quickly outside.

From outside came the bark of commands, then the rat-tat-tat of machine-gun fire.

'Go now,' Kulakov said, 'your secret is safe.'

Instinctively Reder clicked his heels and bowed before marching out into the day. Gun smoke hung in the air but it could not hide the dozen or so bodies that lay dead in the snow.

'Du! Für du!' The sergeant grinned, impressed by his own command of German. He was holding out to Reder a German greatcoat. He pointed at the nearest corpse, coatless, blood leaking through the tank man's field blouse. *'Für du,'* the sergeant said again.

Reder forced himself to look at the corpses lying in the bloody snow. *For you indeed.*

He fell to his knees, his hands clawing at the stained snow.

He heard the metallic cocking of a weapon and looked up into the barrel of the sergeant's rifle.

'Get up, Major.' Kulakov was standing beside the sergeant. 'There's nothing under the snow except more blood and dirt.'

Reder got to his feet. He wiped his face with the back of his hand, tried to come to attention. *You're a prisoner but you're still a soldier.*

He tried to speak but no words came. *Shoot me too,* he wanted to say.

'You're alive, Major Reder,' he heard Kulakov say, 'and maybe you and I will both survive to work together in the future. I hope so anyway.' Kulakov took a thin paperback book from his pocket, handed it to Reder. 'It's a gift, Major.'

It was strange, a book put into your hands while you stood among corpses. *Socialism: The Solution*. In German, the title printed in black on coarse brown cardboard, the inside pages only a little less brown. Reder had heard of the practice of such books and pamphlets being handed to selected German prisoners.

'Stay alive, Major.' Kulakov turned away. There was neither power nor malice in the sergeant's kick that sent Reder on his way.

In his long captivity *Socialism: The Solution* became Reder's companion. He read it in snatched moments, always fearful that it might be taken from him by one of the illiterate guards. Over time the words and ideas in the book became part of him – an idea, in the midst of hell, to cling to with hope.

Sometimes, too exhausted to read, Reder's eyes would linger on the dedication printed in the book: *In Memory of Rosa Luxembourg and Karl Liebknecht*. Reder could remember the names being mentioned by his mother and father in a not-in-front-of-the-children whisper: two Berlin Communists murdered by the Nazis. The names on the rough paper became friends on Reder's journey west with the Red Army.

The Soviet advance westward was inexorable. Long before his country's surrender, it was clear to Reder that the war was lost. What was less clear was whether he would survive to see its end. Life with the Red Army meant you were always hungry, always lice-ridden. And always living on the edge. As the Red Army pushed west, prisoners came and went. Mostly they went.

Some of them went in goods wagons, destined, according to their guards, for Siberian camps where they would be worked until they dropped. Some succumbed to hunger, wounds that would not heal, illnesses that were beyond recovery. For these, a bullet seemed a merciful end; the alternative was to be clubbed and kicked to death or simply to be abandoned in the frozen wasteland.

Hans Reder survived through cunning and luck. He laid railway tracks, fixed broken machinery, coaxed reluctant engines back to life. He took his kicks and bruises without complaint, worked fast at whatever tasks he was assigned. He listened to his captors, engaged his guards in brief exchanges of conversation, gained a basic command of the Russian language. This, and his skills as a mechanic, won him the confidence of the transport boss attached to the attacking forces.

In October 1944 Reder was a tiny cog in the support machine of the huge Soviet army encamped on the eastern bank of the Vistula River, opposite the city of Warsaw. The eastern districts of the city, Praga and Mokotow, were in Soviet hands, taken without too much difficulty from the retreating Germans. Across the river, in the doomed Polish capital, the doomed Polish army of resistance fought against the superior German forces. Hans Reder wondered, along with the rest of the Red Army, why they did not attack across the river. He was still a prisoner, still on starvation rations, but now trusted enough to be thrown extra scraps of food along with scraps of information. The accepted rumour was that Stalin had forbidden any assault on Warsaw until the Polish resistance was already crushed by the Germans. *You can see the shape of things to come*: thus, the softly spoken words of another prisoner, a Luftwaffe pilot who had survived a crash-landing east of Minsk and who, like Reder, owed his survival to his skill with engines. 'Stalin wants rid of the Polish leadership,' Captain Pillnitz said between spoonfuls of the watery potato soup. 'After the war Poland will be just one of many Soviet satellites.' Captain Pillnitz seemed undismayed by his own prophecy: like Hans Reder, he had accepted the need to cooperate actively with his Soviet captors.

The Red Army sat and waited while the Poles surrendered and the still-retreating Germans systematically destroyed the city, street by street, block by block, house by house. In January 1945 the Red Army marched into a devastated place of rubble and smoke. By then Reder, along with Captain Pillnitz and hundreds of other 'lucky' prisoners, was wearing on the sleeve of his German greatcoat the identifying armband of the Free German Army of the Soviet war machine. His armband didn't put a gun in his hands but it confirmed his trusty status, made survival perhaps a little more possible.

Reder hoped that their advance might take them north, that he might learn something of his family. It seemed almost too much to hope that they would all survive the Russian onslaught – and yet what else was there to hang on to except hope?

Instead, Reder's division swung south, towards Krakow, sometime seat of the kings of Poland. Reder never got to see the city of Krakow. Their advance across the flat Polish countryside was swift; resistance was light, as if the German army were prepared to surrender this monotonous countryside without a fight. *They'll make a stand in Krakow,* was the agreed wisdom of the advancing troops. Reder looked at the Slav and Mongol faces around him and wondered what they'd make of the fabled city of kings. He overheard only guffaw-laden exchanges about watches and jewellery and women waiting to be fucked. *Savages,* Reder thought.

Next day, as part of a detachment diverted to a place called Birkenau, Reder found a new savagery that was beyond his ken. The smell reached them long before their handful of trucks got there: a sickly stench that made some of the men vomit over the side rails of the lorries. Rotting animals, decayed corpses. The smell of death had become familiar but this was different – heavier, danker, choking the sky, defiling the very earth. The stench intensified as they drew closer to the compound: a series of barrack-like huts surrounded by fences of barbed wire. The guards had fled, the gates hung open. Stick-like creatures with shaven heads and sunken eyes stood listlessly behind the open gates, watching without interest as the trucks drove inside and the Russian soldiers jumped down on to the stinking, frozen earth.

'Jews,' Pillnitz whispered in Reder's ear.

Reder had never quite believed the stories of mass murders, of crematoria specially built in the depths of Germany and Poland, of death squads, Einsatzgruppen, whose sworn aim was to rid the world of the scourge of *Juden*.

He believed now. The smell forced you to believe. The still-breathing ragged skeletons. The fly-blown piles of tangled corpses that had never made it to the fires. And the tall chimney stacks rising like sentinels of death above the whole rotten structure. Reder looked again at the Soviet soldiers from the cities of Russia and the central plains of Mongolia and thought: *who are the savages now?*

He bent beside the fence and vomited on to the wire.

When he stood upright again, Reder knew that he no longer served under a flag of convenience, a banner of survival. In the year since he had been captured, through all the beatings and kickings and humiliations, he had asked himself: can you truly fight against your own? Is your own skin more precious than the survival of your own homeland?

Reder wiped the traces of vomit from around his mouth and knew his answer: the perpetrators of this obscenity in the Polish countryside were not his people. The flag they flew was not his.

The state they fought for was no longer his homeland. The Führer could go fuck himself.

The words of Commissar Nikolai Kulakov came back to him: *we will bring you the justice of socialism and work with the German people to build a new socialist democracy.*

He hadn't seen Kulakov since that day outside Kirovograd. Other commissars had come and gone, lectured the prisoners on the vices of fascism and the virtues of Communism, but it was Kulakov's simple words that had stayed with him. Maybe, just maybe, they would meet again.

He was lost in his own thoughts when he realized that one of the walking skeletons was standing in front of him. There were sores on the fellow's scalp and face; only toothless gums were visible when he opened his stinking mouth.

He strained to understand the words croaking from the toothless mouth.

'Food,' the skeleton in rags said in Polish. 'Have you anything to eat?'

'Leider nicht,' Reder said. *'Es tut mir leid, aber ich habe Zigaretten.'* Unfortunately no, I'm sorry but I have cigarettes.

He saw the fear, the horror, in the wasted features, realized that he had answered in German.

He saw the skeleton step back then move towards him again, raise its skinny arm, and swing at him with a puny fist.

It was like being tapped on the face with a withered daisy. He could have pushed the skeleton away but he stood there being beaten with feeble slaps; he saw the toothless mouth purse itself and he waited for the spit to come. The slaps ended and Reder put his arms around the falling skeleton and realized that his face was wet with more than spittle; that he, too, like the ragged bundle he was holding upright, was weeping silently.

Nineteen

June 1945
Jaworzno Labour Camp
Poland

Colonel Solomon Karel, square-jawed, heavyset, took the salute of the departing Russians almost casually. The steel in Karel's eyes had nothing casual about it. Karel had things to do, scores to settle. The sooner these Reds were out of *his* labour camp, the sooner he could dole out the kind of punishment these inmates deserved.

He looked at the lines of prisoners in the central square of Jaworzno Central Labour Camp: ragged, scabrous creatures, eyes downcast, afraid to look at their new camp commandant. *They don't realize yet how much they have to fear.*

Karel had ordered this assembly so that the prisoners might witness the formal transfer of power from the Soviet forces to Poland's Ministry of Public Security. The war was over, the fucking Führer was dead and Stalin and Churchill and Roosevelt would soon meet in Berlin to decide how to rule the world.

They wouldn't be ruling Jaworzno Labour Camp. The small detachment of the Red Army that had taken charge of the camp was finally pulling out. From now on, it was a Polish camp run by Poles. And mostly a camp *for* Poles: collaborators, Nazis, fascists. The local so-called 'ethnic' Germans could take what was coming to them also: Karel would personally make sure of that.

He shook hands with the young Russian captain who was handing over to him. Too young, too easy on the vermin within these barbed-wire fences. Fucking Russkis had even deloused and cleaned up the camp after releasing the small group of inmates who had escaped the gas chambers at nearby Auschwitz. Cleaned it up for the scum who now stood under the burning sun waiting for Colonel Karel's dismissal. *Let them wait: the burning sun was nothing to what the future held.*

'All yours, Colonel Karel.' Captain Zhivkov had had enough of Poland. The stories coming back from Berlin meant he'd been missing all the entertainment, stuck in a Polish backwater.

He dismissed his men, could see their eagerness to be gone in the way they hurried to the two waiting trucks. Their kitbags had already been stowed, the drivers had the engines humming.

'One moment, Captain.'

The Russian turned, saw the hatred in Karel's eyes. *This fucker was bad news.* Pity the poor bastards lined up on the baked mud of the square, waiting for Karel to take charge of their existence. Even Karel's own uniformed men looked apprehensive.

'Yes, Colonel?'

'I want those two Germans, Captain.'

'What?'

'Those two Germans wearing Freie Deutsch armbands – they're mine.'

'What the fuck are you talking about, Colonel?' The captain glanced over at the waiting trucks, saw Reder and Pillnitz waiting to climb aboard. *They knew their place, last for everything, but they were good men, knew which side they were on.* 'Those two are my men.'

'They're Germans, Captain, the fucking enemy.' Karel's grin was menacing. 'And they're from Poland, *ethnic* fucking Germans. They're mine.'

Captain Zhivkov sighed, exasperated. What the fuck was an 'ethnic' German? 'Those men have served under me for months, Colonel,' he said.

'And now they're going to serve under me.' Karel looked across at the Russians settling themselves in the trucks. 'They're mine, Captain, make no mistake about that.'

Fucking Poles, we liberate them and all they do is make trouble for us. But the captain was in no mood for a confrontation, the June sun was too high and too hot; his men were as anxious as he was to be gone from this evil, stinking hole.

'Reder! Pillnitz! Over here!'

The two men jogged over, their expressions an odd mix of anxiety and an eagerness to please.

'Sir? They stood to attention in front of their captain.

'Colonel Karel here claims you are ethnic Germans from Poland.'

Neither of the two men looked at Karel.

'Well?' The captain's impatience was evident.

'I'm from Hamburg, sir,' Pillnitz said.

'And you, Private Reder?'

'I'm from Steinplatz, sir.'

'Which is Poland, Captain.' Under the beetle brows, Karel's eyes narrowed. 'This one is mine, Captain.'

'Sir,' Reder swallowed, looked only at his Russian captain, 'Sir, Steinplatz is in West Prussia, in Germany.'

'Fuck you!' Karel spat. 'Steinplatz was part of the land you fucking Germans stole from us.'

Reder licked his lips. Had he come this far, survived this long, to face certain death in a stinking camp run by a Pole? 'Sir,' he said to the captain, 'I'm a soldier in the Free German Army—'

'You're a fucking Kraut!' Karel turned to the Russian captain. 'I tell you, Captain, at least one of these fuckers is mine.'

Captain Zhivkov looked at his men, seated on the benches in the trucks, smoking, laughing, some of them looking back, the question written on their faces: why aren't we out of this fucking place? He looked at Karel's own men, saw in their weary expressions how much they distrusted the Russians who had set them free. And in the rows of ragged prisoners he saw despair, the despair of men who knew that from now on their lives would hang by a thread.

And then there was Pillnitz. And Reder. Two men who had given whatever he had demanded but whose lives, like the prisoners', now hung by the same flimsy thread.

Fuck it, Berlin was waiting and he'd had enough.

'Pillnitz,' he said, 'get in the truck.'

He didn't look at Reder as Pillnitz hurried to the lorry. He couldn't look at Reder.

'Sir—'

'Shut it!' Karel roared.

'This man is still under my command, Colonel.' Zhivkov still couldn't look Reder in the eye. 'What is it, Reder?'

'My kit, sir, it's in the truck.'

'Your kit won't be much help to you here, Fritz.' Karel laughed.

'Come with me, Reder.' Zhivkov turned on his heel, followed by Reder.

'Don't forget to come back!' Karel's taunt followed them to the truck.

One of the soldiers threw down Reder's stuff, rolled up in the greatcoat that had been taken from one of the prisoners executed outside Kirovograd. *How long ago? A year, a grisly lifetime?*

'We have to get moving, Reder.' Captain Zhivkov could not say what he truly felt. How could a Red Army captain say sorry to someone who was, after all, just a German prisoner-of-war? But the fucker had served him well and willingly. Impulsively he took a packet of cigarettes from his tunic pocket and held it out to Reder.

'Take them,' he said.

Reder shook his head. 'Thanks, Captain, but we both know they'll just be taken from me.'

Zhivkov shrugged, nodded.

'I have a favour to ask, Captain,' Reder went on. 'In Berlin, or wherever you serve, you might come across Commissar Captain Nikolai Kulakov of the Fifty-second Guards. He and I met at Kirovograd. It was Captain Kulakov who,' Reder hesitated, 'who showed me the way to socialism. He once said to me that he and I might work together to build a new socialist Germany.'

Captain Zhivkov saw Reder with new eyes: *you just never fucking knew.*

'Captain Nikolai Kulakov of the Fifty-second Guards?'

Reder nodded.

'And you want me to tell him where you are?'

'Yes, Captain.'

Zhivkov looked over at Karel, waiting with hands clasped behind his back.

'Stay alive, Reder,' Zhivkov said.

He couldn't stand it any more. Abruptly he swung on his heel, got into the cabin of the truck. As the two lorries pulled away he looked back and saw, through the rising dust, Karel beating Reder about the head with clenched fists. Staying alive, Zhivkov said to himself, is easier said than done.

* * *

The best that could be said for Colonel Solomon Karel's reign over Jaworzno Labour Camp was that he ensured that all his prisoners suffered equally: nobody escaped his brutality.

You took your turn in the forest, sawing and hauling, eaten alive by insects. Or on a whim you were dispatched to the nearby coal mines, hacking at the brown coal hundreds of metres below the earth, the sweat running in black rivulets down your scarred skin.

And sometimes, just for the hell of it, you were ordered to dig a trench that was long and deep and straight. You learned quickly that, when you had finished, you'd be ordered to fill it in again.

Letters and parcels brought with them their own particular pain. Once a week, before work, Karel read out the names of the prisoners who had mail.

A corporal stood beside Karel, in his hands a small box of letters and parcels; there were never many. Karel held each letter and package above his head as he called out the name of each fortunate inmate.

Or not so fortunate. Often Karel would explain that because of some misdemeanour prisoner so-and-so had forfeited his right to his letter. The pain of deprival was deep as hunger, sharper than the cold. One dwarf-like fellow – a farm labourer, he'd told Reder – couldn't take it. Driven to madness by the sight of a letter denied to him, he'd hurled his small, squat body at the camp commander and tried to grab the letter from Karel's hand. 'My wife!' he'd screamed. 'My wife!' Two guards held the little man while Karel kicked him into unconsciousness. The battered body still lay on the ground when the prisoners returned at the end of the day. Reder and two other inmates were detailed to bury the remains in a corner of the camp near the latrines. Don't let that bastard Karel ever know what you're thinking, Reder told himself as they filled in the shallow grave.

Reder had never seen a parcel handed over to an inmate: some infraction always meant confiscation. The inmate was, however, always made aware of what he was losing: a loaf, a length of Polish sausage, a pair of thick, knitted socks – Karel waved each item in their faces, then tossed it into the corporal's box.

Sometimes a book came and suffered the same fate as the bread or the sausage.

Once the book was for Reder, the only package – or letter – ever directed to him in Jaworzno Labour Camp.

Karel shouted Reder's name as he waved the book almost jauntily in the air.

'*The True Meaning of Communism*, Reder!' Karel came closer, stood in front of Reder. 'Tell us the "true meaning of Communism", Comrade Reder.'

Reder was silent. Speak and you'd be kicked.

'Answer me!' Silence also earned a kick or two.

'I don't know, Colonel.' Reder stared straight ahead, past Karel's shoulder.

'And you're not going to learn from this shit, Reder.' Reder risked a quick look as Karel tore the book in two, saw the red hammer and sickle on the paper cover.

'We think this might be seditious material, Reder, sent to you by a traitor.' Karel had a single sheet of paper in his hand; Reder caught a glimpse of a few handwritten words on it.

'Who is "K", Reder? Who is this writer without a name, someone who signs himself only "K" and says "I have found you, stay alive"? Who is this "K", Reder?'

'I don't know, sir.'

Karel nodded. It was the corporal's turn to kick Reder.

'Who is "K"?'

'I don't know, sir.'

Karel punched him in the stomach. Reder stayed upright, waiting for more but Karel had tired of his sport. Reder watched as Karel tore the note into small pieces and threw them into the corporal's box.

The pain didn't bother Reder. Elation welled in him. K, he thought. *Kulakov hasn't forgotten me*.

You couldn't look to Karel's underlings for any easing of the ferocity. When, at noon on a scorching day in August, an unwary Polish corporal bent to help a Polish prisoner who had fallen under the weight of a heavy and cumbersome log, Karel seemed to materialize from nowhere and laid the corporal on the ground beside the prisoner with a blow from a wrist-thick cudgel.

'Let me catch you doing that again,' Karel told the fallen corporal, 'and you'll find yourself on the wrong side of the fence here.' He poked a toe into the bare back of the prisoner on the ground. 'Move,' he said, and then kicked him savagely in the base of his spine.

The prisoner died a few days later.

Reder kept his own tally of the deaths. As summer eased into autumn and then into winter, he calculated the deaths at about one a week. In winter, he knew, more would die: the cold, the starvation diet and their flimsy clothing would combine to make sure of that. And if you were strong enough physically to cope with all of that, you still ran the risk of disease in the cramped, overcrowded prisoners' huts.

The snow fell on Jaworzno in the second week of November. As the cold intensified, Reder realized that he faced a brutally stark choice: escape or die. He was emaciated from the daily ration of bread and cabbage or potato soup, his hands were raw and blistered, and his greatcoat, although cared for and guarded zealously even at night in the freezing hut, was too worn to get him through a winter in Jaworzno. A run for it in the forest, maybe when he was permitted to go for a shit, was the best Reder could think of. It wasn't much of a plan but a bullet in the back was at least a quick exit. *But fuck it, he'd come so far, survived so long.* He'd given up hope of Kulakov: too much time had passed since Karel had destroyed the book and the accompanying letter. Reder knew now that he was on his own.

Yes, you're on your own, Hans Reder. Ask for permission to go for a crap when that fat corporal is in charge of the forest detail, the slow-witted one who smokes a lot and puffs and pants between drags on the cigarette. Wait for the next fall of snow, the falling snow will hinder you on your run through the forest but it will also slow the pursuers down.

The corporal was on duty in the first week of December. The prisoners were marching back to the camp at the end of the twelve-hour shift when the snow came: big soft flakes swirling so heavily that you could hardly see the man in front of you.

'No slacking!' The corporal panted. 'Pick it up – we're almost there.'

Tomorrow, Reder thought. Let it go on snowing, it's this fat fuck's last day on this roster. *Tomorrow.*

Inside the camp they had to line up in the square for evening roll-call. The snow went on falling. The group from the coal mine wasn't back yet. Even the lousy soup seemed desirable as they stood waiting in the thickening snow. You picked up your can of soup at the cook hut and took it with you to your hut.

The waiting prisoners seemed to heave a collective sigh of relief when they saw the coal-mine group come looming out of the snow. The main gate opened, the prisoners hurried through, lined up for roll-call. Names were quickly called, answers shouted even more speedily.

Colonel Karel came striding through the thickening snow before the prisoners could be dismissed. Over his leather coat a rubber cape lay draped across his shoulders; a grey, Russian-style fur hat covered his head and ears.

The men groaned. But silently. They looked only at the snow-covered ground.

'Everything in order?' Karel demanded.

'Sir!' The fat corporal sounded wheezier than ever.

'All present and correct?'

'Sir!' Another wheezing shout.

Karel adjusted his cape on his shoulders as he surveyed his prisoners: sodden, frozen, starving.

He seemed about to say more when a black car came through the falling snow like a dark ghost. It drew to a halt outside the gates, engine humming, windscreen wipers clacking, steam rising from its long bonnet, snowflakes floating in the headlights.

Karel seemed as transfixed as the prisoners: visiting cars were infrequent at Jaworzno Labour Camp.

A long, impatient blast on the horn came from the car.

'Open the fucking gates!' Karel's angry outburst set the sentry fumbling at the lock, hauling the long bolt back.

The long black German car drew to a halt beside Karel.

The heavyset figure who got out on the passenger side had NKVD written all over the long raincoat and the felt hat pulled low: Reder had seen enough of the Russian Gestapo in his time with the Red Army.

'Colonel Karel?'

Karel's salute was perfunctory: Russian secret police or not, this was Polish turf.

The Russian clicked his fingers and the driver, a uniformed Red Army corporal, was out of the car, unfolding a black umbrella over the NKVD man.

'My credentials.' The Russian handed an ID card to Karel.

The prisoners watched in silence. Maybe the Russians were taking over the Jaworzno camp again: a change couldn't be worse – and just might be less brutal than Karel's regime.

'What can I do for you?' Karel's tone had become respectful: whatever your rank, you didn't fuck around with the Soviet secret police.

Reder, in the front row of the assembled prisoners, could hear only the words 'fucking snow' and 'vodka' in the Russian's reply. He saw Karel nod, heard him order the corporals to dismiss the prisoners. In silence the prisoners hurried to the cook hut for the daily round of soup and a slice of bread. For once the bread was not green with mould; there was even half a potato in Reder's mug. Like everyone else, he wolfed his food down. In seconds his tin mug was empty; there was nothing to chew on except the arrival of the thuggish Russian in the falling snow. Tomorrow, he reminded himself.

'Prisoner Reder!' Karel's adjutant, a skinny fellow with glasses, was standing in the open doorway of the hut, shouting. 'Prisoner Reder!'

He felt the prisoners' eyes upon him as he pushed between them, sensed their relief: *someone else was in the firing line.*

'Move, Reder!' The kick in the arse from the bespectacled adjutant was routine, the kind of reminder that you learned to expect. 'Colonel Karel's office, now!'

Reder wondered what offence he'd committed. He knew the other prisoners would be wondering what punishment he was in for – the nature of any offence was unimportant.

He ran shivering through the falling snow, stood shivering, waiting outside Karel's office for the adjutant.

Karel's voice barked in answer to the adjutant's knock.

Inside, the office was baked in heat from the pot-bellied

stove in the centre. Reder stood just outside the door, head bowed, waiting for Karel to speak.

'You are Hans Reder of the Free German Forces of the Soviet Army?' Not Karel but the newcomer, in the accent that Reder had learned was from Moscow.

Reder straightened, lifted his head, looked from the Russian to Karel.

'Answer the officer, you German pig!' Karel was sprawled in the captain's chair behind the desk, his eyes dark.

'Yes, sir.' No bowing, no clicking of heels. 'I am Hans Reder.'

'You stink, Reder.' The Russian snorted. 'I can smell you across the room.'

'Yes, sir.' Always agree, to do otherwise could earn you an extra beating.

'All Germans stink.' Karel spat at the stove; for a second they all watched the thick phlegm sizzling on the hot metal. 'They stink like pigs.'

The Russian laughed. 'Maybe we should put you in the boot, Reder, rather than inside the car.'

The car. Inside the car. Reder said the words to himself, couldn't stop his lips moving silently. He heard Karel tell the Russian to sign here, saw the Russian bend over the desk, scrawl on the bottom of a foolscap page. Karel signed another page, the pen scratching like the spit still sizzling on the stove. Reder could hardly breathe. They wouldn't take him in the car if they were going to shoot him, would they? *You never knew with the NKVD*.

But by then everybody was on their feet and Karel was saying something to the Russian that Reder couldn't hear. The Russian was putting on his coat, his hat, and the driver – Reder hadn't noticed him until now – was opening the door of Karel's office. The sudden rush of swirling snow and freezing air woke Reder up, opened his ears.

'Reder!'

Reder turned in the doorway to face Karel.

'I should've killed you when I had the chance.'

Reder waited, silent.

'Fuck this,' the Russian said, 'let's get in the car.'

Reder went back to hardly daring to breathe. Yet the car was real, the rear leather seat was real. He touched the side window, fearful least it melt and he should find himself again in the falling snow, waiting for Karel to decide if he should live or die. As in a dream he saw the guard open the gates and the car swung outside into the night. He stared back through the rear windscreen and already Jaworzno Central Labour Camp was hidden in the dark and the snow. He started to shiver.

'Here.' The Russian turned in the front seat, handed him a bottle of vodka. Reder hesitated but the Russian nodded his encouragement. 'Drink up, Reder. Colonel Kulakov sent word that we're to take good care of you.'

Colonel: so Kulakov had done more than survive, he'd climbed the ranks.

'I just wonder,' the Russian said, 'if the colonel realizes what kind of stinking package we're going to deliver to him in Berlin.' He laughed at his own joke. 'You'd better wash, Reder, or stay downwind of Colonel Kulakov.' The driver joined in the laughter.

Reder didn't heed the laughter. He pushed his finger inside the lining of his coat, felt the comforting coarseness of the book. Somehow they had both survived, Reder himself and *Socialism: The Solution*. Through everything, the little book had seemed like a lifeline to Reder, to the hope of a tomorrow.

The NKVD officer had turned in his seat and was watching Reder.

'Let's see what you've got there,' he said.

Reder took the book out slowly, handed it over.

The Russian grinned at the title. 'Good stuff, this – obviously Colonel Kulakov has been educating you,'

Reder nodded. He took the book, held it close as he curled up in the luxury of the leather seat. He knew he wouldn't sleep. He didn't want to. He wanted to savour every moment of this journey of liberation.

They drove through the night. Progress was slow, hindered by the thickening snow. In some Polish town, grey, silent, the driver kicked at the door of a bakery and an elderly Pole, frightened, brought them thick slices of Polish bread covered with dark lard and gave them mugs of steaming black tea. When they had finished, they stood and pissed in the middle of the deserted street.

The NKVD officer, nameless, slept and snored. Reder dozed and woke, wondering if he was dreaming. The snow stopped as dirty grey light filled the sky. They skirted a small town and Reder sensed they were in Germany. Another stop, at a farmhouse this time, its windows boarded up, and a toothless crone gave them dry bread and a hot black drink that might have been brewed from leaves or berries or grain. The old woman curtsied as they drove out of the mucky farmyard.

They stopped to fill the tank from a pair of jerrycans stored in the boot of the BMW. Spoils of war, Reder thought, liberated from the BMW factory in Bavaria. The entire country was the spoils of war. We brought it on ourselves. He remembered Kulakov's words: *we have to build a better, socialist country*. Daylight now and Reder tried to focus on the remembered words, but exhaustion took him and he fell asleep in the hot interior of the car.

A poke in the shoulder woke him.

'Berlin,' the Russian said.

Reder had never been to the city. What he saw through the windows of the car were the leftovers of civilization. Jagged broken walls. Mounds of rubble. A single tram carriage crawling through the ruins. Old men and children and women in crocodile lines collecting bricks and stones and slates. And everywhere dust, like stony snow, thickening the winter air.

'You can thank your fucking Führer,' the Russian said.

Reder looked at the gaunt, ragged creatures working on the ruined streets and kept his silence. They looked like ghosts wrapped in rags. And he looked worse, knew he smelled worse.

He coughed. 'Sir?'

The Russian turned in the front seat, looked at Reder.

'Could I please wash, sir, before meeting Colonel Kulakov?'

The Russian stroked his stubbly chin, wrinkled his broad nose, shook his head. 'Let's show the good colonel what we've put up with all the way from fucking Poland.' The driver yawned, spat out through the open window. He looked at the NKVD officer but said nothing.

They left the rubbled streets behind. A Russian officer waved them down at a roadblock, waved them on after he'd inspected their papers. A wider thoroughfare now, stumps of trees on either side that had once guarded a gracious boulevard. Wide, spear-tipped gates ahead, pulled open; papers examined once more; waved forward once more on a curving drive that opened on to a baroque *Schloss* with yellow walls and carved pediments over the windows and the tall door.

The NKVD agent got out, signalled to Reder.

The Russian tipped his hat to the sergeant inside the door but presented no papers. Reder followed him along a narrow corridor to the left of the sweeping staircase. Doors were open along the corridor, a telephone rang, typewriters clacked. A blonde woman in Red Army uniform looked up from her typewriter as he passed and he saw what he looked like in the expression of horror on her round face: a stinking bundle of rags clattering along the tiled floor in wooden clogs.

The Russian knocked at the last door, turned the brass knob.

Kulakov looked up from his desk. His hair was thinner, his jaw more lantern-like. He sat upright behind the leather-topped desk, his uniform buttoned up to the neck.

'The prisoner Reder, Colonel,' the NKVD agent said, laying a folded piece of paper on the desk.

Kulakov nodded. 'Thank you.'

He waited until he was alone with Reder before he spoke.

'So we both made it to Berlin, Reder.'

Reder tried to forget his rags, tried to stand to attention.

'I have to thank you, sir.'

Kulakov took his glasses off, put them on again. 'You look awful, Reder, and you smell even worse.'

'I'm sorry, Colonel Kulakov.'

'My sergeant will show you where to wash and shave and get you some clean clothes,' a half-smile around the thin lips, 'unless you're terribly attached to those for sentimental reasons.'

'No, sir, thank you, sir.'

'And the sergeant will get you something to eat.' Kulakov stood up. 'After that we have work to do, Reder, that's what I've brought you here for. Are you ready for that?'

'Yes, sir.'

'I'm putting a team of trusted men together to run the city, to wipe out the criminal elements that would prevent us restoring this city to some kind of normality. I need men I can trust, men who are not afraid to make decisions and not afraid to take decisive action. You were able to do all that in the war, weren't you, Reder?'

'Yes, sir.' Gunfire in his ears, fire and gun smoke in his nostrils, mixed with the tang of blood.

'Think you can still do it, Reder?'

'Yes, sir.' But a whisper, so he said it again, more loudly. 'Yes, sir, I can.'

'We have a country to build here, Reder,' the colonel said, 'a socialist democratic country and we need good socialist Germans to build it with us.'

Reder tried to stand more erect in the heavy, ill-fitting clogs. He was sick of war but the faint echo of a bugle seemed to rouse him.

'Yes, sir, I want to serve.'

Kulakov nodded. He smiled, more fully now, before he shouted for the sergeant.

PART 4

DUNKELFELD

Twenty

October 1989
East Berlin

Whatever reservations the candle-lighters and the kohl-eyed punks might have about their walled-in city, Unter den Linden was thronged for the march-past by the Volksarmee of East Germany. Even the sun came out for the GDR's celebration of its forty years of existence.

The army's brass band played a marching tune. Hundreds of boots beat time as the soldiers marched past. The massed crowds waved familiar flags, the black-red-yellow horizontal fields with the divided compass in the centre. Some waved the flag of the Soviet Union. Maybe in honour of Prime Minister Gorbachev, Miller thought. Or maybe in fear of him. The Soviets had sent their tanks into the streets of Budapest in 1956; they'd descended upon Prague in the spring of 1968. Maybe if you showed them you loved them, the Russians might keep their tanks at home.

Gorbachev had come to share in the celebrations but nobody was quite sure what his presence meant. He'd let the Hungarians open their border with Austria. He'd been quoted as saying that countries in the Eastern bloc must decide their own future. Or so Miller had read in the *International Herald Tribune;* such pronouncements tended to be overlooked in the GDR's own *Neues Deutschland*.

Now Gorbachev stood in the centre of the reviewing platform, taking the salute of the marching soldiers alongside the leader of the GDR, Erich Honecker. Between the marching rows of the Volksarmee Miller caught interrupted glimpses of the two leaders. Gorbachev looked as if he was enjoying himself; Honecker looked like somebody who'd just been given bad news by his doctor. Or maybe somebody who was expecting bad news from his doctor. *The Wall will last a hundred years*: this pronouncement by Honecker had not been overlooked by *Neues Deutschland*.

Honecker himself looked as if he might not last even one hundred days. There had been rumours that he was suffering from cancer. Beside the burly Gorbachev, surrounded by his generals in uniform, Erich Honecker looked small, frail.

He looked even frailer when he stood – or tried to stand – to attention, hat over heart, as the band played the national anthem of the GDR. Miller wasn't sure why this unmartial, almost mournful, melody always moved him. The composer, Hans Eisler, had fled Nazi Germany; years later, although a successful, Oscar-nominated, Hollywood-based composer of film music, Eisler had been deported from the USA for his Communist sympathies. Eisler made his way to East Berlin, collaborated with his friend, the dramatist Bertolt Brecht. Now Eisler's composition swelled over Unter den Linden to mark the fortieth anniversary of the founding of the GDR.

So maybe you like his music because he, too, was forced to come here. At least Eisler did something, left a legacy of music that will not die, while you play useless games with useless scraps of paper in a country that is not your own.

He could just make out General Reder on the platform as the anthem ended, and the review party clapped, turned to one another to shake hands, chat, do whatever dignitaries did after reviewing a march-past. Some of the old faces smiled, most looked grim. It was the first time Miller had seen Reder in his uniform. He looked shrunken in his general's outfit. Like an old man with cancer. About a year, the general had said. The book contracts had been doctored. If plans were already underway to buy and sell a country's books, Miller reasoned, the faceless vultures were sure to be setting about the sell-off/rip-off of even more valuable assets.

You can't write music, memorable or not, but maybe you can at least make it less easy for a crime to be committed. Even if it's not your country.

The crowd was milling around him. He could hear people chatting about the parade, about getting home, about going for a beer. It was noisy, cheerful, shouting at kids, lighting cigarettes. Maybe the general was wrong: this march-past and these milling crowds did not seem like the elements of a country that might have only a year to live.

Miller moved slowly through the crowd. He hoped he'd be able to find Rosa.

Rosa found him.

He was drifting towards Friedrichstrasse when she seemed to step out of a wave of bodies rolling towards him on the wide pavement. Amid the swell of jeans and zipped-up jackets she was a vision in colour: knee-length woollen coat, wine-red, belted round a tiny waist, a glimpse of a plain dark dress, soft knee-high boots gleaming darkly.

A touch of hands, a brush of cheeks.

The formality didn't matter, he knew there was nothing formal about her smile.

'You look . . .' He shook his head. 'Stunning, yes, stunning.'

Rosa laughed. 'Papa expected this.' A grimace that was as

lovely as her smile. 'I couldn't very well turn up among all the dignitaries and the medals in a pair of jeans and a T-shirt, could I?'

'You could for me.'

'You're too easy to please.' She put her arm through his.

How did we get to this easy place? And who has ever told me I'm easy to please?

'So Gorby made eyes at you? Honecker gave you the once-over?'

'I saw them but I doubt if they even noticed me.'

'You were up close?' Miller stopped on the pavement. 'You *met* them?'

'Not likely.' A shake of her head, her hair swung like dark silk. 'I delivered Papa to the People's Palace, the army took over from there, they'll see he gets home OK.'

They turned on to Friedrichstrasse. The trams were running; the shops, though closed, had their windows lit up. *So it's not as bright as the Kudamm on the other side of the Wall and there's not a lot on display in the windows – who cares?*

Miller felt he had all he ever wanted, strolling with her arm in his on Friedrichstrasse.

'There's a place there.' She pointed to a cafe on a side street.

It wasn't much of a place, not much better than an *Imbiss*: half a dozen small tables, non-matching rail-back chairs, some kind of vinyl floor covering, a mix of blue and grey squares and triangles. The fare on offer seemed limited to tea, coffee, beer, sandwiches with cheese or what might be ham.

The thin-faced woman behind the counter finished her cigarette before she approached them but even that didn't matter. Miller smiled at the woman, didn't stop smiling when the woman's face refused to lose its scowl.

They ordered beer, touched glasses, said, *'Prost'*, to each other. And afterwards Miller couldn't remember very much of the rest of their conversation. He knew they'd each talked about themselves but was clearer about what he *hadn't* said to Rosa Rossman. His father was a doctor – the knighthood, the absurd title of *Sir*, had come in one of Thatcher's lists, a bauble tossed to one of her own. And what could he say about Lady Miller? She was his mother, that was all; to speak of her drinking, of her attempted suicide, would have seemed cruel, a betrayal. *Blood is thicker than alcohol*. Yet over two hours passed while they talked across the small table; outside, the October night came down, the lights came on, the woman behind the counter went on not smiling.

None of which mattered. The woman opposite him was listening to him, speaking to him, smiling at him. Which was about all that Miller could afterwards recall.

The little cafe was busy. Men came in for beers, couples came in for coffee. None stayed as long as Patrick Miller and Rosa Rossman.

'We should go.' She turned to look outside. 'My father will wait up, worrying as usual.'

Miller knew he was going to remember the rest of their conversation, as if Rosa's words had brought into the cafe the world outside, the night, the GDR.

'At least the whole parade thing went off peacefully.'

'Papa said the streets would be crawling with plain-clothes officers.'

'Stasi?' He whispered the word.

She nodded, shivered, drew her coat closer around her shoulders.

'At least nobody got hurt.'

'Not that we could see,' Rosa said.

'Maybe there was nothing to see.' He wanted to be positive,

to have this evening unsullied, unthreatened. 'Maybe most people were just happy to take part in the celebrations.'

'It's different for us,' Rosa said. 'I mean, for you and me. You came here of your own free will, to be part of something you believed in.'

He couldn't tell her. Yes, he'd come to this place with belief but, no, he couldn't tell her the rest of it.

'And you?' He didn't want the light shining on himself. 'How is being here different for you?'

'This country saved me, Patrick, gave me back my life.' He saw her shiver again, waited for her to go on. 'Not now, not on this special day, Patrick. I'll try to tell you another time.' She laid her hand on his, left it there for a moment. 'I really have to go now.'

'And,' Miller leaned closer to her, 'the contracts, what did the general think?'

He could read the nervousness in the black eyes.

'Only that it was earlier than expected.' She was whispering again. 'That's what he said, "earlier than I expected". He said that maybe they were trying it out on the small stuff first.'

'"They"?'

'Not here.' He felt his fingers gripped in hers. 'Not on this special day, Patrick.'

'The day is special because you're here with me.'

She blushed. 'It's special for me too.'

They stood together at the small counter while he paid. He left a couple of Marks as a tip but even that didn't raise a smile behind the counter.

'Thank you,' Rosa said. 'We enjoyed ourselves.'

Miller watched the woman's features relax, loosen from a sour grip; no smile but the eyes seemed to light a little.

'Goodnight,' the woman said. 'Come again.'

'You softened her,' Miller said when they were outside.

'She's just lonely,' Rosa said, and for a moment her eyes held his.

She slipped her hand into his as they walked towards Friedrichstrasse station.

The night was dark, moonless; Friedrichstrasse, lit only dimly by the street lamps, was almost deserted.

They were at the entrance to the S-Bahn station when they heard the shouts.

'Stop! Stop!' From inside the station.

And the sound of pounding, running, feet. Running towards them from within the station.

Miller didn't hesitate. He gathered Rosa into his arms, drew her into a recessed doorway beside the station entrance.

'Halt! Police!' Louder now, the footsteps hurtling closer.

Rosa gasped, turned in his arms when the bodies came tumbling down the station steps on to the pavement. Miller put his hand across her mouth, hushed her, tried to draw her deeper into the shallow recess of the doorway. The uniformed Vopo had eyes only for his captive on the ground. His gloved fist swung at the young man sprawled beside him; they heard the thump of fist on face, heard the young man's cry, the Vopo's grunted panting as his fist swung again.

'Get the fucker on his feet.' A second Vopo, older, paunchy, wheezing his way down the steps.

The two Vopos hauled their prisoner upright: dark jeans, dark sweater, in his twenties, close-shaven.

The elder Vopo studied him for a moment. From their hiding place Miller could hear the policeman's heavy breathing.

'When we tell you to stop,' the Vopo panted, 'you stop.' He punched his prisoner in the stomach, watched him double up, fall to his knees, puke on the pavement.

'Dirty fuckers, soiling our streets.' The Vopo's voice carried in the night. 'No respect for our streets.'

Rosa flinched in Miller's arms as the Vopo struck the kneeling figure across the face. Once, twice, three times, the blows loud in the night.

On the opposite pavement a young couple looked, hurried by. Two young women coming out of the station stopped on the steps, looked at the Vopos and the young man on his knees, then almost ran from the scene, their heels clacking in the darkness.

A new sound in the night: an engine growling towards them. The vehicle that pulled up was not the box-like Stasi van that took prisoners away; this was a two-door Polski Fiat, lights dimmed, doors swinging open. The driver almost jumped from the car; the passenger was slower, limping on the pavement.

A flash of ID cards, words too low to be overheard.

To Miller it was like a mime show. The newcomers pointing, first to the prisoner, then to the Polski Fiat, doors still open, engine idling. The older Vopo shook his head, the driver of the car raised his voice.

'You will do as I say, understood?' Even in German, Miller knew that voice. The fellow turned slowly and Miller saw him: no pinstriped suit now, just the ubiquitous grey windcheater zipped across the paunch, but that round, ruddy face with its thin ginger moustache was imprinted on Miller's brain. 'Now get out of here!'

The two Vopos hurried away into the darkness.

Miller shivered, quelled the gasp in his throat.

He felt Rosa tremble in his arms, push back against him. *Surely she couldn't know Redgrave?*

The prisoner was on his feet, wiping his face with a coloured handkerchief. There was blood under his nose, a swelling over his left eye.

'I just got unlucky.' *In English*. An American accent. 'We threw a few stones, yelled a few slogans.' The twangy words clear in the night. 'The others got away OK, I tripped over a fucking dog. Like I said, I was just unlucky, or those fucks would never have caught me.'

'You told them nothing?' Those clipped tones that sounded as if made for command.

'What do *you* think?'

'Course he told them nothing.' The driver's voice. American, even more of a drawl. 'Let's get the fuck out of here before the cavalry come charging over the hill.' For a moment, when he limped in front of the car, he was clearly visible in the headlights: lean, almost stringy; a high forehead that furrowed back into a skull that was almost hairless. And when the fellow turned his head, the spreading birthmark behind his ear glowed like dark blood in the light.

The car doors slammed.

Miller felt Rosa's body slacken against his own as the Polski Fiat pulled away.

Rosa turned to him, buried her face in his chest. He held her close, waited until the trembling stopped, until her body felt calm against his.

'You know him, don't you – Redgrave?'

'Is that his name?' She leaned back in his arms, looking into his face. 'Redgrave? The bald one with the birthmark?'

For a moment he didn't get it.

'You know the American with no hair?'

'He had a ponytail when I,' her voice cracked, 'when I met him. But I'd know him anywhere, that birthmark, that murdering voice.' He had to strain to hear her words. 'His name is Herbert Dover,' she said. 'A murderer.'

The night seemed to darken, grow colder.

'Tell me,' he said.

In the darkened doorway, clinging to him, she told him about Chile.

Twenty-one

October 1989
East Berlin

In his nine years in East Berlin, Miller had rarely asked for a meeting. He couldn't quite recall exactly why he had sought the meetings, just that he had done so twice in his first year, unsure of his ground, uncertain as to his role behind the Wall.

You won't forget *this* reason, he told himself the morning after Rosa spilled out the story of her flight out of Chile. In his mind he saw the ponytailed assassin, heard the scream of jets overhead as a government was toppled and a president died in a smoking palace. Through a teenage girl's eyes he saw her father's colleague murdered in cold blood, saw the ponytail swing, watched someone called Dieter blast both knees of the man who called himself Herbert Dover.

'I'll never forget that name.' Her body shivering against his in the darkness. 'He said wherever Dieter was, he'd find him – kill him.'

Time enough to ask who Dieter was.

Ponytail aka Herbert Dover was a killer.

And what on earth was city gent Warwick Redgrave doing in the company of a killer? Redgrave minus pinstripes, masquerading in a proletarian windcheater on the wrong side of the Berlin Wall? Apparently giving orders to a couple of Vopos?

He'd slept hardly at all. Rosa had insisted on taking the S-Bahn home alone, insisted she was OK, the general's batman would meet every train at Pankow, don't worry. How could you not worry? He'd given up even trying to sleep, sat beside the window overlooking the sleeping city, saw only the jeep careering through the streets of Santiago, felt her mother's blood leaking away on the stained brown seat. Saw the unmarked hole in the ground, the father of the twins with the spade in his hands.

He made coffee, shaved, checked his briefcase. He didn't taste the coffee, didn't know what he was checking in his briefcase.

Miller walked to work. He hoped the morning streets would revive him, get him through the day. Get him through the coming night and yet another day at the office.

On Universitätsstrasse he stopped to tie his lace. He propped his briefcase on the window sill beside curving bars, stooped to tie the errant lace. He took his time at it, felt pedestrians move around him, the swish of overcoats, the pad of hurrying feet. He made a show of flexing his shoulders in his coat when he straightened, tugged hurriedly at the lapels. A man on his way to the office. He took hold of the briefcase, swung it beside him as he went on his way.

He didn't look back at the red-and-black cigarette packet he'd wedged against the bottom of the window, behind the elegant, curving bars.

It took thirty-six hours for Redgrave to respond.

Hartheim sent for him that afternoon.

'Come,' Frau Siedel's metallic voice said after he knocked. The blond head raised, the blue eyes taking him in, the head bent again, fingers flying over the typewriter keys. Nobody important, the bent head said.

She finished the page, drew it from the machine, took time to study it before again looking up at Miller.

'The Director is expecting you.' Frau Siedel was busy again, rolling a new sheet into the typewriter. 'You may go in.'

He was unprepared for Hartheim's fulsome welcome.

'Herr Miller!' The Director was on his feet, chair pushed back, hand outstretched. 'Good of you to come – I know how busy you are.'

'Thank you, Herr Direktor.' Miller sat, waited, knew what this was about: he'd given Frau Siedel a memo about Whitacre's inquiry.

Hartheim took his time getting to it. First there had to be a review of the jubilee parade, Honecker's speech ('Inspiring!'), Gorbachev's contribution ('So supportive!'). Hartheim leaned back in his chair, rested his laced-together fingers on his ample stomach, beamed generously as he reviewed the weekend celebrations. In the pauses for breath Miller nodded, said, '*Ja*,' nodded again.

'Forty years, forty years!' The Director shook his head, patted his stomach. 'Imagine! This will show them!'

'And a hundred years,' Miller said.

'One hundred years?'

'The Wall,' Miller said. 'Herr Honecker told us the Wall will last for one hundred years.'

'Ah, *ja*, the Wall.' But Miller wondered if he'd gone too far, Hartheim was eyeing him warily. 'Yes, one hundred years.'

Hartheim settled himself in his seat, reached for a piece of paper on his otherwise empty desk. Miller recognized his own brief memo.

'So we've had an inquiry about rights in many of our publications?'

'More than half of the entire list, Herr Direktor.' Miller

opened his hands, helpless in the face of such nonsense.

'How very strange.' Pudgy fingers stroking the dog-chewed knuckle stub. 'Why would anybody make such an inquiry?'

'No idea.' *Look dumbfounded*. 'No idea, Herr Direktor.'

'Extraordinary.' More caressing of the finger stub. 'And what exactly did this fellow, Whitacre, have to say?'

As if you haven't listened to the tape of the phone call. 'That he wished to buy rights in all of our nonfiction and reference titles.'

'And you told him?'

'I was astonished.' Miller shrugged, hoped he looked puzzled. 'Well, I told him I'd speak to you, Herr Direktor.'

'Still, a strange offer. I wonder what prompted all this?'

Miller smiled. 'England is a strange country, Herr Direktor.'

'Kings and queens!' A laugh like a bark. 'Don't these people know that history has marched on!' The great stomach jellied with Hartheim's rumble of laughter. Miller watched, fascinated, the shirt straining over the expanding flesh, the white vest flashing between the button gaps. The stub of the missing finger nestling in the other hand.

'Herr Miller, you must forgive me making fun of your country.'

'Herr Direktor, this is my country now.'

'Truly?'

'Truly.' Miller thought: yes, truly.

'One more thing, Herr Miller. Why d'you think this publisher, Whitacre, contacted you and not the publishers themselves next door?'

'I suppose because I replied to the original letter.'

'Yes, the original letter.' Hartheim looked at his watch. 'Well, I'll deal with the matter now, Herr Miller. Thank you.'

Miller said thank you, rose to leave.

He was at the door when he heard Hartheim clearing his throat.

'You asked for a publishing agreement in the registry, Herr Miller.'

'Yes, Herr Direktor, the contract for the basic dictionary that Whitacre originally asked for.'

Hartheim said nothing.

'I just wondered – after the phone call – I thought I might as well take a look at the contract.' *Lame, so lame.*

'And?' Hartheim's gaze stony.

'A perfectly ordinary contract, Herr Direktor.'

'What else did you expect?'

'Nothing, Herr Direktor. It was foolish of me, wasting time like that.'

Hartheim stared at him for a long moment. 'Thank you, Herr Miller.'

Miller said thank you.

He didn't trust himself even to look at Frau Siedel as he passed through the outer office.

Back in his own office he could hear his heart racing, pounding. He sat at his desk, hunched, tensed. It took a while for his pounding heart to slow, for his breath to come easier. He stood at the window, looking out over Berlin.

Was it really his city?

Was this, as he had told Hartheim, really his country?

Next morning the tension was palpable. In the streets on the way to work, in the office.

Late-night West German TV news bulletins had carried no pictures of the astonishing sequence of events in Leipzig last night. Maybe, Miller thought, Western cameras had been forbidden for the by now usual Monday-night show of prayers and candlelight protest in St Katherine's. It didn't matter: pictures of previous demonstrations in Leipzig let you know what was going on. Watching the black-and-white images at midnight in his flat, Miller had a sense of the GDR, in cities and towns across the darkened land, looking in amazement at itself – at a version of itself that was strange and new. And just a little bit frightening in its strangeness and newness.

Over fifty thousand people, the reporter's voice told them, had marched in the streets of night-time Leipzig, candles alight, a murmur of expectation rising from the huge crowd. The awe in the voice of the reporter as he told of what had *not* happened: the soldiers facing the marchers had not fired. Instead of gunfire, something different had crackled in the darkness: a long breath held, a hint of hope, the forbidden apple dangling within reach. *Reisefreiheit*: the freedom to travel.

A hundred years, Honecker had said, the Wall would last for a hundred years.

The guns silent in Leipzig, the streets wreathed in candlelight and smiles.

In the Secretariat for Socialist Correctness in Publishing no word was spoken of the previous night's events – or non-events. The pair of porters in reception said nothing about it; neither did Frau Siedel. Nor did the balding fellow who stood at the neighbouring urinal midway through the morning. But in the bleak faces, in the studied silence of omission, even in the hiss of piss in the urinal, Miller could clearly hear the astonishment of an entire country.

He tried to concentrate on routine correspondence. Watched the street from his window. Wondered what it would be like to kiss that wide mouth, feel that firm body crushed against his own. Heard Redgrave silence the Vopo. Saw the birthmark like a stain on the night. You'll go mad, he told himself.

Hartheim summoned him before lunch.

The Director came straight to the point. 'I want you to prepare a promotional catalogue of certain titles that have international appeal. Our colleagues next door are preparing a new catalogue in German but we feel that our English edition should be an original offering,' Hartheim's version of a smile, 'and who better than yourself to compile it?' The Director moved two typed pages across the desk to Miller. 'We've been planning this initiative for some time, it's part of our celebration of forty years of our socialist state.'

Miller glanced quickly at the list of books.

'How much d'you want on each book?' He tried to keep the surprise out of his voice. *Whitacre's offer hadn't been a shot in the dark.*

'Nothing lengthy. A brief description, a word on the target market, a few bullet points on the strengths of each book.' You could be a capitalist anywhere, Miller thought, lining up your wares, setting out your spiel. 'The usual,' Hartheim said.

'There are,' Miller ran his finger down the list, 'about forty books here. How much time have I?'

'As soon as possible – shall we say a couple of days?'

'So it's urgent?'

Hartheim shifted on his chair. 'Do you need more than two days?'

'Two days is fine.' *The Wall will last one hundred years.*

'Good.' We have about a year, General Reder said.

Hartheim was pushing his chair back; the meeting was over.

'Thank you, Herr Direktor.'

'Thank you, Herr Miller.'

Not a word about Whitacre's offer, Miller thought. Not a hint about the doctored contracts.

Maybe General Reder had got it wrong. The idea was hardly credible but maybe the GDR didn't have a year.

At Checkpoint Charlie the border guards were edgy. They seemed in two minds, as if they were trying to be unusually courteous while at the same time applying extra vigilance to their inspection of bags and documents. There was no sign of Heinz-Peter; Miller wondered if guards from further afield had been brought in to possible flashpoints in Berlin.

Miller's briefcase held pens and pencils, a copy of that day's *Neues Deutschland* and a manila wallet folder packed with typed pages. His ID card as an official of the Secretariat for Socialist Correctness in Publishing was enough for the guards; they barely looked at the stack of typed pages in the manila folder. It would have taken a page-by-page search to uncover, scattered in random order throughout an English version of a Polish academic's thoughts on the responsibilities of socialist writers, Miller's own account of the pressures being heaped on the GDR from within its borders – and possibly from outside provocateurs. The article carried the byline *By Our Special Correspondent*; it could have been dictated by General Hans Reder.

He assured the guards that he would be returning before midnight and passed into the Western half of the city. In the kiosk across the street he bought a copy of *Berliner Zeitung*, quickly turning to the classifieds. The notice was halfway down the 'Items for Sale' column.

> Encyclopaedia Britannica, complete set.
> Unwanted gift, best price secures.
> Tempelhof area. Box No. A8934.

So, the Tempelhof rendezvous. He took the U-Bahn, climbed

up the steps to the street and made his way to the cafe on the other side of the little park near the airport.

Despite its name the Flughafen Cafe drew little business from airport passengers. Tucked away in a side street, it could not be seen by those leaving or arriving at Tempelhof. Which was, perhaps, why the cafe figured on Redgrave's list of movable meeting points in West Berlin.

Redgrave was already there, at a corner table, turning the pages of a magazine, a half-drunk beer on the table. The black rucksack on the chair beside him and the blue windcheater hanging from the back of the chair told you that this was just another worker having a beer on the way home after work.

He waved at Miller, stood up, shook hands. Two friends who perhaps hadn't met for some time. Or maybe since the football match on Sunday morning. Redgrave's German accent was pure Berliner.

'You're well?'

They went through the motions and sounds of meeting and greeting. Redgrave called for another beer. They raised their glasses, touched the bases, said, '*Prost*', with genial gusto. The few other patrons in the Flughafen Cafe had gone back to their own conversations and newspapers: nothing worth looking at or listening to at the corner table.

And Redgrave and Miller's voices had, imperceptibly, dropped a couple of levels.

'What's up?' Redgrave asked. 'I hope there's some good reason for dragging me all this way.'

All the way from Friedrichstrasse the night before last?

Miller bit his tongue, killed the flip response. Knowing something that Redgrave didn't gave him some advantage – if he could only figure out how to use it.

'There's something strange going on at the office.'

Redgrave waited, pale eyebrows raised.

'Umpteen contracts for backlist books have been doctored, all reference books, art books, that kind of thing.'

'So?'

'The rights in these books can now be sold by Hartheim – our Director – to whoever he pleases.'

'You brought me all this way to tell me about new clauses in some publishing contracts?'

All this way. Easy does it, Miller told himself.

'Don't play the idiot, Redgrave. You know as well as I do that tampering with state contracts over there,' Miller nodded vaguely in the direction of the East, 'can lead to a very sudden one-way trip to Moscow, Gorby or no Gorby.'

'It's your office,' Redgrave said. 'What d'you expect me to do about this?'

'We both know that nobody except the government of the GDR can dispose of these rights. Neither Hartheim nor anybody else can flog these rights as long as . . .' Miller paused; no matter what General Reder said, the idea was absurd.

'As long as *what*, Miller?'

'As long as the GDR exists.'

Redgrave sipped his beer, turned a page of his magazine. 'And you think that existence might be nearing its end?'

'It's what you want, it's what the Americans want.' Miller heard the frustration in his own voice. 'It seems to be what half the fucking world wants.'

Redgrave smiled. 'And you, Miller, is it what you want?'

'I want to know what's fucking going on!'

'You going all native on us, Miller? Turning into the Dean Reed of the pen?'

Miller had met Reed at a reception shortly after arriving in Berlin: a handsome rock'n'roll singer from Colorado who'd turned his back on the American dream and settled in East Berlin. Party bosses across the Communist bloc had loved him as much as the masses: their very own rock'n'roller.

'Poor Dean,' Miller said.

'Mind you don't finish up like him,' Redgrave said.

Poor Dean. Found dead in his car in a lake near Berlin in 1984. Suicide, they said. *But you could never be sure.*

They both drank, studied their beer. Nobody really knew how Dean finished up dead in a half-submerged car.

'Initially we had hopes they might parade you as a kind of journalistic Reed.' Redgrave shook his head. 'Patrick Miller, the caped crusader who dishes the dirt on capitalism, that sort of thing. Instead they stick you in an office reading manuscripts and contracts.'

'How terribly disappointing for you,' Miller said. 'I'll try to do better next time.'

'Fortunately you're not our only asset here, Miller.'

'Maybe your other "assets" could fill me in on what's going on.'

Redgrave sipped almost delicately from his glass. 'What's going on is that you've dragged me here on a fool's errand, Miller, with some tuppence-halfpenny tale of changes in a few contracts – which hardly justifies the time and effort of making this trip, does it?'

'A helluva trip.' Frustration got the better of him. 'All the way from Friedrichstrasse the other night.'

Miller could read the anger in Redgrave's expression.

'What are you talking about, Miller?'

'Stop pissing me about, Redgrave. I saw you there, in a Polski Fiat; you and some guy with a bad limp.'

Silence settled on the corner table. Redgrave looked at Miller, looked around the small cafe as if looking for an extra exit.

'Miller,' he said, 'take my advice – my *friendly* advice – and don't meddle in dangerous matters. Now,' voice descending almost to a whisper, 'tell me how and where you claim to have seen me.'

'After the parade you passed me, driving slowly.'

'What time?'

'After the parade, I was just having a stroll.'

'A stroll?'

Miller nodded. How had this turned into an interrogation?

'On your own?'

He heard the fear in Rosa's voice, saw the birthmark red in the lamplight on the passenger's neck.

'Yes, of course.'

'You said we were in a car.'

Miller nodded again.

'Why say the other fellow had a limp?'

'Did I?'

'You know you did.'

Miller laughed. 'It was a Polski Fiat, maybe he got out to push.'

'Miller—'

He raised a placatory hand. 'I was coming round the corner, heading for the S-Bahn, and there you were, the pair of you, getting into the old Fiat, I almost called out, then I thought I was mistaken.'

'And that's all you saw?'

'Did I miss something interesting?'

'You know, Miller, one of these days you'll shoot your mouth off to somebody who's less courteous than I am. Just do what you're supposed to be doing and keep your nose out of what doesn't concern you.'

'I've been here for years,' Miller said, 'and what I'm supposed to be doing still isn't clear to me.'

'I haven't time for this, Miller, and you're trying my patience.' Redgrave reached for his jacket.

You've learned nothing, Miller told himself.

'They know,' he said.

'Who? Who knows what?'

'They know I carry messages for you.'

Redgrave's jacket hung from one arm. 'What are you talking about? Who knows?'

'I can feel it, I'm sure they know.' *Don't give them Reder, don't lead them to Rosa.*

'You feel it? Has anybody done or said anything to you?'

Miller shook his head. Suppose Redgrave asks Birthmark to check on the general, suppose he connects him to Rosa? 'It's just a feeling,' he said, 'but I'm sure.'

Redgrave finished putting his jacket on. 'What you need is a holiday, Miller.'

He stood up, went to the counter to pay. When he came back to the table, he was smiling.

'A "feeling" indeed!'

'You're not going to tell me what you were doing on the other side?'

'You know how it is, Miller – honouring the fortieth anniversary celebrations.'

'That's it?'

'Affairs of state, my dear fellow.' Despite the windcheater and the rucksack, he spoke like a Whitehall mandarin. 'Need to know and all that.'

'And if they know what I'm doing?'

'Try not to use your imagination so much, Miller.' Redgrave hoisted the rucksack. 'Give me ten minutes.'

Miller watched him go, picked up the magazine Redgrave had been reading. *Der Spiegel*, Gorbachev on the cover, smiling under the banner, THE WALL IN HIS HANDS. Gorbachev looked surprised, happy but surprised, as if he hadn't been expecting the flash of a camera.

Redgrave hadn't looked surprised. He'd shrugged it off, tried to make a joke of it. But he hadn't looked surprised.

General Reder wasn't the only one who knew. *Redgrave knew that the East Germans knew*. And it didn't seem to bother him.

All of it bothered Patrick Miller. More than ever he felt like a marionette, pulled every which way by hands on both sides of the Wall.

In the late-night post office near the Zoogarten, Miller reassembled the pages of his article for the *Guardian*. The counter clerk looked only at the London address on the brown envelope as he handed Miller his change. There was no way to tell if he was being watched by other eyes; what was not in doubt, Miller reminded himself as he pushed the envelope into the Deutsche Post box, was that he was again behaving puppet-like on a string – he was doing exactly as General Reder had directed.

He was at his window again, looking out at the night. Outside, more shadow than light. Half-light over a half-city.

And his mind full of the same shadows, the same absence of light. He'd been over it and over it, always reaching the same conclusion – a conclusion which was no more than one more question: Redgrave knew that some of the East German establishment were aware of his message-carrying activities but was not at all bothered by this knowledge, and the question was, why not?

Were the messages he ferried across the Wall of no importance, in whatever direction he carried them?

Were they fragments of misinformation, designed to mislead? What else could it be?

He'd chewed upon it on the trek home, through Checkpoint Charlie, up the stairs to his flat, a dog with a bone that yielded no marrow, no answer.

And if Redgrave knew that he was rumbled, why did he allow it to continue?

The same question could be asked of General Reder. If the general knew, then others also knew.

But not everybody knew. Some did. Some did not. A faction. Or perhaps factions. Divisions in a divided city. Perhaps these divisions spanned the Wall that cut through the city.

Miller saw himself reflected in the window, the city a dark backdrop behind his own image.

No answers in the dark city.

And in his own reflection, answers he had no wish to discover. Eight years in East Berlin, written in the dark glass. Dark hair flecked with grey, the hairline receding. Was the jawline sagging? The eyes deeper, the face paler? Or was it all a distorted image in a distorted city?

He should take himself in hand, get jogging again, dust off the bike in the basement cage and take to the forest trails north of Pankow – where Rosa lived with the general. Rosa of the long dark hair and the black eyes: why would she ever look twice at a pen-pusher, a reader of contracts, a carrier of messages? At least Dean Reed had had a guitar to pluck, hips to rock, songs to sing.

Miller knew himself for what he was: a jumped-up clerk sitting alone in his fourth-floor flat looking at his own reflection at eleven o'clock at night. He hadn't touched a woman for almost two years: an editor on a business trip to Berlin who'd drunk too much and fumbled her way through hurried intercourse in her cramped hotel room before scuttling back, apologetically, to her husband and children in Leipzig. She'd left no phone number – nor had Miller asked for one.

Once upon a time you were a columnist with a name that people recognized. Now look at yourself.

Miller was sick of looking at himself.

He was turning away from the window when there was a knock on his door. Three taps, soft, almost intimate.

'*Ja, wer ist da?*' Who's there? His words little more than a whisper: you didn't welcome callers here at such an hour.

'It's me.' Her words also whispered but like music in his heart.

She slipped past him when he opened the door. He checked the corridor: darkness, all doors closed. He eased the door shut, saw the tension in her face as she looked at him.

She saw the question in his eyes.

'I waited until someone left the back door open.' A small smile. 'I was lucky, I didn't have to wait too long.'

He imagined her hidden in the shadows, maybe watching from the corner of the apartment block. It didn't surprise him that doors opened for her.

'And if nobody had left the door open?'

She shrugged. 'Why worry about the what-ifs?'

They were both whispering.

She pointed at the TV; while he switched it on she shut the blinds.

'May I?'

Miller watched as she turned the TV to the local channel. Late news from East Berlin: the East German Politburo has been in emergency session, the activities of reactionary hooligans had been discovered. Leader Erich Honecker looked tired, old, like a weak tree waiting for the storm. The hooligans, he said, would be firmly dealt with.

Even a small wind, Miller thought, would blow you away.

He turned to Rosa. 'Your coat . . .'

'I can't stay – Papa sent me.' But she gave him the leather coat anyway.

'The general sent you?' Miller tried to focus, but the nearness of her made it impossible to concentrate.

'He has to go to Leipzig in the morning – he sent me to warn you.'

'Why warn me about Leipzig?' He didn't care about distant Leipzig; he could taste her breath across the small space between them.

She shook her head. 'Papa will be in Leipzig so he couldn't warn you himself.' She bit her lip. 'It was cold out there.' She nodded in the direction of the rear entrance, the dustbins, the place where you crouched until somebody didn't close the door properly.

Miller wanted to touch her, hold her, warm her.

'I'll make you some tea,' he said.

'I can't stay – he just wanted me to warn you.'

Warn me about black eyes I could drown in, soft skin that would scorch me. Miller said, 'Warn me about what?'

'Papa said he thinks they'll come for you soon, maybe even tomorrow – he's afraid it's his fault, that he's exposed you to them.'

'Them? Who's coming for me?'

'The Stasi, Patrick.' Miller could barely hear her whispered words. 'The Stasi, Papa thinks they'll take you to Normannenstrasse.'

The Stasi. A bad dream made flesh. A cold breath from a place you didn't want to know about. But everybody knew about Normannenstrasse, the complex of tall buildings that everybody hoped never to be taken to.

'I don't understand.'

'Papa knows he's being watched.' She took his hand in hers.

'He tells me very little, says it's safer not to know too much. But he's hinted that there are factions in the state getting ready for what he calls the "endgame". And some of them, he thinks, are also from outside the state.'

She leaned into Miller and he felt her tremble against him. Miller drew back from her, hoped she hadn't felt his response.

Concentrate, he told himself. 'But why me?'

'Papa thinks they've come to you through him.'

Miller already knew that General Reder was being watched.

'But who spies on a general, a hero of the state?' he asked.

She didn't answer, came tight against him, wrapped in his arms.

There was no need to answer. Generals were watched by other generals, marshals, Politburo bosses, captains of multinational industries.

'I'm only small fry. What am I doing in the middle of all this – all these factions and endgames?'

She leaned back in his arms, smiled up at him. 'Are you sorry?'

'No.' A hoarseness in his voice, the deep pools of her eyes inviting. 'No,' he said, 'never.'

She drew his head down, kissed him fiercely. He felt her tongue, warm, sweet, filling his mouth. He drew her closer, pressed her to his groin.

'No, not now.' She drew away from him, her hand on his chest.

'I'm sorry.'

'Don't be, it's just that I really must go.' She kissed him quickly on the lips, smiled. 'It's not as if I'm leaving the country.'

'No, me neither.' He tried to smile, tried to forget his physical longing.

'But why? You never told me why you came here, why you stay.'

'It's a long story, Rosa.'

'So give me the shortened version, Herr Patrick Miller.'

'OK, I'll try,' he said.

He told her of London, of his studies, his left-wing articles for non-paying left-wing journals, his elevation to columnist with a national newspaper, his decision to 'experience life in a practising socialist society'.

She listened attentively to his whispered words, listened as if she didn't already know the story – the single page, marked CONFIDENTIAL, that General Reder, deliberately and wordlessly, had left lying on the table. She tried not to listen to the question thrown at her by her own heart: why do I dissemble so, act out a pretence, a lie, with this man?

'And that was it, Patrick? Just a decision to throw up a career and move to East Berlin?'

She caught the sharp look he gave her, hated herself for this charade.

'It was a bit more complicated than that, Rosa.' He sounded tired, uncomfortable.

'Can you tell me?'

And he knew he must. Part of him felt that he shouldn't, that to tell was just one more betrayal in a maze of falsehood. Yet to conceal the truth was to leave another wall between himself and Rosa. And Miller was growing tired of walls.

He told her about Redgrave, about the woman, Dr Shearing, how they had pressurized him to give up his life.

'But I don't understand, Patrick.' She hated herself but it was the missing link in the typed page. 'How could they force you?'

He turned away from her, went to stand by the windows, parted the blinds a little. She watched him staring out at the darkness, pitied him, hated herself for this act of betrayal.

'I've never told anyone about this.' He went on looking out

at the darkness as he spoke and she heard the darkness in his halting words. She saw the dark at the top of the stairs, felt the dark in a boy's heart, the dark in the dark house in a place called Wolverhampton.

She felt the dark in her own heart, in her pretence.

She went to him, touched his face. 'I'm sorry,' she said. 'Thank you for trusting me.'

'Trusting you with my sordid story.'

'It's not *your* sordid story, Patrick.'

'Maybe I should have told my mother.' He let the blinds fall, turned to her. 'I don't know what I'm doing any more.'

'You're here with me,' she said, 'and I'm here with you.'

He looked at her. 'You're here because General Reder sent you.'

'I should have left,' she said, 'but I didn't.' She kissed him. 'Papa said to remember that they don't know about the messages.'

'The messages I carry.'

'Yes.'

'Do you hate me for it?' He forced himself to meet her eyes. 'For the messages?'

She shook her head, smiled at him.

Then they clung to each other. Mouths, tongues, hands touching, exploring. Obscuring the ponytail and the birthmark; stilling the moaning behind the door at the top of the stairs.

This time Miller drew back, held her from him.

'Rosa, it's late, you should go.'

'I know.' Her voice husky. 'We'll have to be quick.'

'But—'

For a moment they stalled, caught in anticipation. Then a fumble with buttons, underwear on the floor, hands searching, the carpet hard and rough against their skin. And for a longer moment – the briefest moment – their bodies fused, lost in one another, moving together on the rough carpet.

You could hold the night and the world outside at bay for only so long.

He stood, helped her to her feet. She took the tiny underpants from his hands. 'Maybe I shouldn't bother – they're not exactly going to keep me warm, are they?' She laughed. 'Still, General Reder wouldn't approve, so . . .' She stepped into the knickers, drew them over her hips.

He wanted to tell her she was wonderful, that her irreverence made him giddy.

'I'm terrible, aren't I?' Rosa said. 'Those South American genes.' Laughter in her whispering.

'It's late, how will you get home?' White noise and flickering black and white from the TV.

'I parked the car a couple of streets away, just in case.'

'You have the general's car?'

She shook her head. 'My very own Trabi.' The smile left her face. 'I knew I shouldn't take it but Papa insisted.' For a moment she looked shamefaced. 'People wait half a lifetime to get one but for people like the general . . .' She shrugged.

Miller watched her button the overcoat, draw the collar around her throat. 'I'll walk with you to your car.'

'No, Patrick, it's not far, just a few streets.' She kissed him quickly. 'It's safer if I go alone.' Her words hung between them like a shadow of the world outside.

She came into his arms and he felt her heart beating against his own.

'Until tomorrow,' he said.

'But remember,' she touched his face, 'why I came here.'

Maybe they'll come for you tomorrow – the Stasi.

'I would've come anyway, Patrick.' Her words nuzzling in his ear with the tip of her tongue.

He opened the door quietly and she tiptoed past him into the dark, empty corridor. At the top of the stairs she turned, blew him a kiss, a smile. He waited with the door ajar but only the building's silence came back to him. He thought of her hurrying through the night-time streets of the sleeping city and he smiled to himself. *I'm still not sure why you forced me to come here, Redgrave, but I'm truly glad you did.*

Twenty-two

October 1989
East Berlin

'Reder's daughter was a long time in there.' Herbert Dover sipped at the hot coffee, fingered his birthmark with his other hand. 'Too goddamn long. When she parked the Trabi I tailed her on foot, watched her hide for damn near thirty minutes at the back entrance to an apartment block on Hermann Strasse until someone left the door open and then I had to sit in that shitty Polski Fiat for another couple of hours until she came back. The heater in that damned excuse-for-an-auto is pretty useless but I couldn't use it anyway – it sounds like a fucking tractor – and we don't want any more over-enthusiastic Vopos crossing our paths, do we, Redgrave?'

Redgrave nodded but said nothing. Like many of his foul-mouthed countrymen, Herbert Dover was a cross to be borne. Still, the Americans had their uses, especially their surveillance hardware and their dollars. It was their dollars that were financing this operation behind the Wall and their minuscule equipment that ensured that this safe house in Köpenick was bug-free.

The price you paid was the company of louts like Dover.

'I checked the names at the front door. None of them meant anything to me but there was one name that could be Kraut or

English – a P. Miller on the fourth floor.'

'He's English,' Redgrave said. 'Or used to be, he works at the censorship office, travels on an East German passport now.'

'A fucking Commie renegade!'

Redgrave smiled. The Americans had never learned to button their lip, play their cards close.

'We hear,' Redgrave said, 'that Miller has the task of checking General Reder's memoirs for orthodoxy in all things Marxist.'

'Jesus H! What a country – a goddamn limey gets the job of vetting a German general's life story.' Dover shook his head. 'So this guy Miller is ballin' the general's daughter to spice up the boring job of proof-reading – that about it?'

'It's a possibility,' Redgrave said. It was essential to give the Americans something – you didn't want them to pick up the football and piss off home in a sulk – but it was always advisable to keep some of your cards up your sleeve. Besides, maybe Miller *was* servicing the general's brat. It was something to find out, maybe something with which to rein in Master Miller, who seemed to be getting just a little frisky of late.

'You know this Miller guy?' Dover asked.

The sound of a car froze both men. It was almost 3 a.m.; even in daylight there was little traffic on this back street in Köpenick, not far from the Wall. The car chugged past – the unmistakable chugging of a Trabi – and both men relaxed. You could sweep a safe house daily for bugs, you could keep your neighbours at arm's length, you could try to be invisible, but in this city behind the Wall you never really knew when eyes were watching, when ears were listening. And you could never legislate for simple bad luck.

Redgrave switched off the light and crossed to the window. He edged the curtains apart, looked at the street below. The street was silent, unlit. He fixed the curtains carefully before sitting down.

'So, you know much about this Miller guy?'

Redgrave nodded. 'He used to be a rather well-known English journalist of the pink variety, took it into his head some years ago to move to the land of socialist milk-and-honey.'

'You Brits have a knack for producing guys like that – like Burgess and Maclean and Philby.'

Redgrave was nettled. 'Or even your dear Dean Reed,' he said.

'Oh, yeah, our Red Elvis.' Dover chuckled. 'I'm sure Dean took just *volumes* of intelligence across the Wall.' Americans, Redgrave thought, are not even ashamed of their own inadequacies. Any failure is interpreted and presented as 'a learning experience'. And for their dollars we have to kowtow to them.

'Is the funding in place for the next twelve months?' Redgrave asked.

'Yeah, old Uncle Sam has come through with the dollars,' Dover said. 'No expense spared in our struggle to share democracy with the downtrodden masses of Eastern Europe.'

'Do I detect a note of cynicism?'

'What you probably detect, Redgrave, is the pain in my knees. They trouble me in cold weather.'

'You hurt your knees playing football?'

'Some football.' Dover grimaced. 'A difference of opinion while we were taking out Allende back in seventy-three.'

'You were in Chile?' Redgrave looked at Dover with renewed interest. *You never knew where you were with these Americans.*

'I was there all right. Trouble is I came out of it on a stretcher with both kneecaps missing.'

'At least you came out of it – not like Allende.'

'Pinko fucker.'

'Bit of a coincidence though,' Redgrave said.

'What?'

'You helped bring down Allende and here you are tonight keeping a friendly eye on the general's daughter.'

Redgrave saw the puzzlement on Dover's face. 'You don't know?'

'What the fuck're you talking about?'

'General Reder's daughter – she's his stepdaughter, Rosa Rossman. Her father was a minister in Allende's government.'

'What did you say her name was?' Dover's voice was a whisper.

'Rossman. Her father—'

'Yeah, I know who he was. He died in the shootout.' Dover felt Redgrave's eyes on him. Time to be cool, give nothing away; you only worked with these Brits when you had no choice. 'Nice of you to let me know.' The sarcasm drooled around his words.

'Didn't seem important.' Redgrave shrugged. 'Is it?'

'Everything is important,' Dover said. Especially your two kneecaps exploding beside a Disney-style water well in a Communist courtyard. Was it possible that this well-stacked dame he'd tailed tonight was the same kid who'd gotten away with that Commie bastard Dieter? 'Everything is important,' he repeated.

'Anyway,' Redgrave said, 'everything is going to plan. Twelve months from now this pathetic little state will have disappeared from the map of the world. Our people are in place, protests going nicely and old Honecker himself is coming under pressure to step down.'

Dover said nothing. His own masters gave the GDR less than a year. Leave it to the Brits and East Germany would be there until the Second Coming. Meantime, Herbert Dover told himself, Dieter might be out of reach but this general's daughter could damn well take his place in his personal quest for righteous revenge.

Twenty-three

October 1989
East Berlin

It wasn't Miller they came for.

The morning was confused, confusing. The early morning radio news announced that hundreds of demonstrators who'd been arrested in previous weeks would be released throughout the GDR. So why come for me? Miller thought. I haven't even been demonstrating.

No, what you've been up to, the small voice reminded him as he made his way on foot to the office, is infinitely more serious. *Does treason have another name, a kinder one?*

The office, like the streets, felt edgy. At the reception desk the wall-faced porters showed a crack in their features. Frau Siedel, incredibly, delivered a cup of coffee, even offered a small smile when he thanked her. Hartheim sent for him in mid-morning and took time out from lamenting the activities of 'those bastards' in Hungary and Czechoslovakia to remark, looking out from his corner windows, that the sun was shining on the German Democratic Republic.

There was no mention of the doctored contracts in the bowels of the building.

Nor a sign of the Stasi who might be coming to pick Miller up.

Miller told Hartheim he would take an early lunch that day if that was OK.

The Director beamed: of course it was OK, Herr Miller should take an extended lunch break, it was a good idea to take advantage of the unexpected sunshine, so late in the year, likely the last they'd see before winter.

Miller reminded himself to stop staring at Hartheim. Maybe the Director knew he would be arrested as soon as he stepped out on to the street. But what could Hartheim know? The Director had no knowledge of Redgrave, of the guy with the birthmark, of General Reder's safe house in West Berlin – or had he?

Paranoid. But suppose – just suppose – they're all somehow connected? Or competing? And if they are in competition, what is the prize? A couple of dozen publishing contracts didn't seem, even to Miller, a prize worth demonstrating for. Factions, the general had said. Natural resources, he'd said. Land and property. *But how could you steal a country?*

Miller stepped briskly through the sunny streets. Even the people seemed sunny, prepared to apologize for bumping into you, to smile at you just because they were there, because you too were there.

Miller smiled because Rosa was there.

The porter at the university reception desk didn't smile when Miller asked for Frau Rossman's office. He looked almost horrified when Miller repeated the name.

'Einen Moment, bitte.'

Miller watched the balding porter step into a back office with a glass door. Through the door he could see the porter speaking to a sharp-faced, middle-aged woman seated at a desk. The woman looked out at him, turned again to the porter. More words, puzzlement on the porter's face: *what shall I tell him?*

Miller saw the impatience in the woman's expression, saw the impatience harden to anger.

The porter stood aside as the woman got up, came to stand behind the porter's desk.

'Who are you?'

'I'm a friend of Frau Rossman—'

'Who are you?'

Miller stated his name, his position at the Secretariat for Socialist Correctness in Publishing. He told himself not to worry but his stomach refused to listen. 'And Frau Rossman? If you would be kind enough to tell me where her office is, please?'

'Frau Rossman is not here.' The words were not unkindly spoken but they offered nothing, invited less.

'I see.' Miller tried to smile, to quieten the butterflies in his stomach. 'And has she a class this afternoon?'

He saw the struggle in the woman's face, was aware of students passing behind him in the corridor, felt himself the object of curious stares.

'Herr Miller.' The woman lowered her voice, leaned across the counter towards Miller. 'Please, it is better if you go now, please.'

'But—'

'Please, Herr Miller.' Almost a whisper now. 'Please go.'

Miller saw the kindness behind the icy eyes. And the fear.

He thanked her, stepped away from the desk, was aware of the balding porter staring out at him from the inner office.

He stumbled out of the building, stood at the bottom of the steps. What was going on? Why the shadow of fear in the woman's eyes?

'Herr Miller?' A young woman, a student, looking not at him but into a thick notebook spread open in her arms.

'Yes?'

'Don't look at me.' Whispered into the notebook. 'Follow me.'

Miller sauntered casually behind her. On another day he might have admired the athletic figure; now he saw only the darkening day, heard only the fear in the woman's voice behind the counter.

The student stopped outside a bookshop, stared at the display in the shop window. Miller stood beside her.

'You're looking for Rosa?' Whispered now into the window.

'Yes.'

'Don't look at me.'

'Yes, my name is Patrick Miller.' He saw the girl's reflection in the window, tall, blonde, an icon of German beauty.

'I saw you with her in ZERO, and again at the parade.'

'What's wrong? Has something happened to Rosa?'

'This morning in class.' A wobble in the voice, the notebook and books hugged closer to her chest. 'The secretary came into the class, called Rosa out. The door was open, we saw them in the corridor, two of them. They let her come back for her books but we saw them take her away.' Her reflection seemed to shiver in the window. 'Two of them,' she said again.

'Who?' Miller asked. 'Who took her away?'

She looked at him then. 'Who d'you think, Herr Miller? Who always takes you away?'

He heard her footsteps on the pavement and he knew he was alone.

Six of them, Rosa looking like one of them, seated in their midst. A small group, Fourth Years, the end in sight, another year and a bit and they'd be out of there, out to classrooms, offices, maybe newspapers. Nothing too stressful in this early-morning class with Rosa. *Rosa was cool, you could have a bit of a laugh, a joke, in this little group that gathered weekly in her office.*

Not just a joke, Rosa's class, a discussion group and you managed to have some grammar revision too: whatever cropped up.

So, the nature of power. Everybody chipped in. Mad King Lear. Murderous Macbeth. Murdered Julius Caesar. Words and ideas sparked more words, more ideas. The exercise of power in the factory, in the home. The notion of power seized, authority exercised. The refusal to bend the knee to unjust rule, back to Caesar on the steps, blood in the Senate.

A sudden silence over the seated circle. The students, five girls and one man, seemed to draw a collective breath. They looked at Rosa; knew, like her, that they were skirting the borders of the unspeakable. The unrest on the streets, on the TV screens, had infiltrated Rosa's office. They looked uneasily, sheepishly, at one another. Even here, in this small group that had coalesced from a bigger group four years previously, even here you never knew if your words were safe, if Judas sat on one of the chairs in the small circle.

Everyone knew that Rosa had most to lose. It was Georg – fat, slobby Georg, the only male among them – who punctured the moment. He stirred in his seat, seemed to spread not only his chubby arms but his substantial haunches, and burst into song:

'If I ruled the world, da-da-da-da-da-de-dum-dum-de-dum.'

They all laughed. Clapped. Some of them knew the song. Some of them even knew that Georg had the girth to match the English singer, Harry something, who had made the song famous in some London show.

And Rosa, too, was grateful for the diversion.

'Thank you, Georg, for reminding me that this might be a

good moment to take a quick look at the mechanics of the conditional mood.'

Mock groans all around.

'If I ruled the world, I'd make sure Georg wasn't allowed to try to sing ever again.' This from Hannah, beautiful Hannah, who turned every male head in the Institute of English but who seemed always to be in fat Georg's company.

More laughter.

A quick run through the conditional mood.

If you ruled the world . . .

If Rosa ruled the world . . .

If we ruled the world . . .

If Georg didn't rule the world . . .

You should go to warn Patrick that they might pick him up tomorrow. She tried to shut out the words, concentrate on the class. She could still taste him, still feel him inside her. Would the world be better if it were ruled by Patrick Miller? Or by the general?

'Unless Georg rules the world,' Rosa began . . .

The students were still laughing when the knock came on the door. A flustered-looking Frau Scholl, armoured in corsets and metallic perm, stood in the doorway.

'*Entschuldigung, Frau Rossman.*' Her nervous gesture signalled for Rosa to come.

Rosa felt the students' eyes follow her into the corridor.

'These gentlemen . . .' Frau Scholl's secretarial poise had deserted her; she gestured helplessly at the two men who stood behind her in the corridor. They were not in uniform but they didn't need to be.

'Frau Rossman, you must come with us now.' They were like twins, neckless, close-cropped, leather-coated.

Rosa looked at the two Stasi, at the students looking out at them.

'I have to finish my class.'

'Now, Frau Rossman.' The small mouth barely opened in the beefy face.

'But where? Why?'

Both men flashed IDs; Rosa had a glimpse of black-and-white mugshots.

'May I call my father, General Reder?'

She heard Frau Scholl make a gulping sound. From the class came the sound of chairs creaking.

'Enough, Frau Rossman.' This one's scalp stubble was darker than the other's. '*Now.*'

'May I get my books?'

'*Schnell, bitte!*'

The silence in her office was heavy as she gathered up her books, picked up her bag.

'Rosa – Frau Rossman . . .' Georg was whispering.

She shook her head, put her finger to her lips. There was no point in dragging any of the students into this.

'*Bitte kommen Sie,*' she heard from the corridor.

'Finish your discussion.' She tried to smile at the little group. 'When you're done, lock up and leave the key at the porter's desk.' She saw the alarm in their faces, broadened her smile. 'I'll see you all same time next week.'

She saw the fear, the doubt, in them as she went to face the waiting Stasi. She just hoped the same fear wasn't written across her own face.

At least they hadn't come for her in the hated – and feared – Trabi arrest van. And they didn't rough her up, getting into the back seat of the car. The older of the two men stood aside, tipped the passenger seat forward as she climbed into the cramped rear of the Trabi car.

Not a word exchanged between the pair as doors were slammed, gears were ground and the vehicle pulled noisily away from the kerb outside the Institute of English.

So far, not a finger laid on her. Not a harsh word thrown at her.

Silence settled inside the Trabi like a threat, burrowed its way into her innards. The familiar streets rolled by outside: pedestrians, shop windows, policemen. Now the streets looked like a foreign country, peopled by aliens who ignored the red Trabi that was taking her to Normannenstrasse. The smell of male sweat and cigarettes mixed with her own fear.

She wanted to pee.

'Please,' she said, 'I need a lavatory.'

The shaven cannonball heads in front went on staring straight ahead.

'Please, I need to go.'

The older one stirred in the passenger seat, turned towards her. 'Cross your legs,' he told her.

She realized there was a smell of piss in the car too.

'Please.'

'Shut it.'

She tried to draw her insides together, hold the flow back.

The streets slid by eastward towards the HQ of the Stasi. Like the entire population of the city, she knew the location of Normannenstrasse; like everybody, she'd hoped never to go there. Once, as a teenager, she'd asked the general what kind of place it was, if the rumours were true. He'd avoided her eyes – she knew that his military work sometimes took him there – and said, speaking to some point over her shoulder, 'It's not the sort of place I'd ever want any friend of mine to be taken to.'

She shivered on the plastic-covered seat, pressed her thighs more tightly together. *Forget these two toughs in front, remember how you opened your flesh to welcome him last night.*

Or maybe not. She wondered if Patrick was the reason they'd come for her. Or the general. She knew only very little of the secret meetings at the general's house, the nocturnal visitors, the cryptic, seemingly innocent remarks spoken by her father into the phone. If they quizzed her about the general or Patrick, she'd hold out as long as she could.

But in the end you'd let go.

The streets were thinning out. The city was falling behind them, the countryside spreading out ahead. An open road, secondary, a tractor crawling ahead of them, pulling over to let the Trabi pass.

'Where are you taking me?'

The smell of animal dung, the sickly smell of silage.

'Where are we? What's going on?' She knew she was shouting, felt the damp leakage in her underpants. 'I am General Reder's daughter!'

The stinging back-hander across the face brought her to her senses. *Don't give the bastards the satisfaction. And you* are *the general's daughter.*

'No more,' the one in the passenger seat said. She met his eyes, all blue shallows, told herself not to tremble.

They swung off the road, moved slowly along a rutted lane. The complex of farm buildings on the left was dilapidated, deserted. A pathway ran through knee-high weeds to an open space between barns. People had lived here once: a rusted harrow lay in one corner, the broken cutting shaft of an old plough in another. Now it seemed that even the birds shunned the place.

The Stasi got out, motioned for her to follow. One of the men looked at his watch.

'He's late,' she heard him say.

Don't ask. Whoever he is, you'll know soon enough. Or too soon.

'You can piss there.' It was the first time the driver had opened his mouth.

'What? Here?'

'Suit yourself.' The driver lit a cigarette, grinned at her through a mouthful of smoke.

The men watched her as she got down on her hunkers, pulled down her underpants.

She stared at them as she pissed, felt a small triumph as they looked away.

More than piss had bled into this abandoned earth. She wondered why the iron implements were left abandoned, unsalvaged. Some places kept within them the memory of pain, the aftertaste of evil. The Red Army would have come this way, raping and killing on their way to Berlin.

'What the fuck is keeping him?' The driver was edgy, as though he, too, wished to be gone from the lingering smell of evil.

She got to her feet, went on looking straight at them as she fixed her clothing. *You can look, you can hear, but you can't even begin to guess the joy I shared last night with Patrick.*

They heard it then, the coughing sound of a car coming through the flat, untenanted landscape.

'It must be him.' The driver trod on the cigarette end, ground it viciously into the dead earth.

The car came closer, gears changed, a metallic cry in the silent day. She waited, her heart thumping. Her heart sinking, watching the car nose towards them between the roofless buildings. She recognized the Polski Fiat, knew that shaven head even behind the dust-caked windscreen.

The car door opened, slammed shut and he stood facing

her – as close as when, long ago, Dieter had shattered both his kneecaps and left him bleeding in the courtyard in Santiago.

'Well, well!' Dover grinned. 'If it isn't the little lady herself, all the way from Santiago, Chile.' He moved closer to her, looked her up and down, whistled. 'And just look how you've filled out!'

She felt his hand on her face, flinched.

Dover winked.

His hand dropped to her breast. She swung her hand at him but he caught her wrist, twisted her arm suddenly and flung her to the ground.

Dover looked down at her, smiled. 'Manners, lady, manners!'

She felt the toe of his shoe on her knee, pushing her skirt up her thigh. Rosa half sat, reached with both hands for his ankle but he stepped away with surprising nimbleness.

'You should have let Dieter kill me back then.' He stood over her. 'But I'm glad you didn't, lady, as you and me are going to get to know each other a lot better in the very near future.' Dover smacked his lips, winked.

Her fingers scrabbled in the earth and she flung a handful of muddy earth at him. Dover swore, stepped back, rubbing his eyes with the back of his fingers. She saw the fury building in him.

'If you touch me,' Rosa said, 'General Reder will kill you.'

'That old dinosaur,' Dover said, 'couldn't kill a half-cooked hamburger.' He guffawed at his own wit. 'Anyway, where is the dear old general?'

In Leipzig, Rosa thought, and not due back until tomorrow.

'He'll find you,' she said, 'and he'll kill you.'

'Enough.' Dover turned to the two Stasi. 'Get her inside.'

They seized her, dragged her through an open doorway. Inside the wrecked building a secure windowless room had been built: wooden walls and a plank door which Dover opened with a key on a steel ring that jangled with many keys. He flipped a switch and the room flooded with light from the overhead fluorescent tubes. The room held everything necessary for a short stay in a safe house: a table, two chairs, a small refrigerator, a two-ring electric hob.

In the corner stood a single bed with an undressed striped mattress and some folded grey blankets.

'Put her down there.' Miller pointed at the bed.

She struggled but the Stasi pinned her to the mattress. Dover reached for her right wrist, forced her arm up and she felt the cable cut into her skin as he tied her wrist tightly to the iron bedstead.

She gathered the spit in her mouth and spat into his face.

Dover's hand swung, slapped her hard across the face. 'More bonus points, baby,' he said. He forced her other arm backwards, tied it to the other side of the bed.

Dover stood back from the bed, nodded down at her.

Then she felt his fingers behind her knee and she swung her body violently, lashing out with her legs.

Dover laughed again. The older of the two Stasi coughed. Dover looked at him.

'You have something to say?'

'They've seen us. This,' he looked at Rosa, at Dover, 'this isn't part of our agreement.'

'Get out of here.' Dover dug in his pocket, produced a thick wad of notes – from the bed Rosa could see it was a roll of dollars – and handed it to the Stasi.

'But they've seen us!' The other Stasi sounded frightened. 'They know what we look like!'

'Bullshit,' Dover said. 'Everybody in this sick fuck of a country is too scared to look at guys like you.'

'Call my father! He'll forgive you if you help me—' Another blow to the face from Dover cut her off.

'Now get out of here,' he told the Stasi officers, 'and give the little lady and myself some much-needed privacy.'

'Call my father!'

Dover punched her in the stomach and she gagged with pain.

When she got her breath back, gasping for air, she was alone with Dover.

Twenty-four

October 1989
East Berlin

The red Trabi's eastbound journey out of the city had not gone unnoticed. General Leon Krug noticed it. He noticed it because his own driver had to brake and swerve to avoid the oncoming car which had pulled out around a pair of workmen on bicycles.

The driver swore. So did Krug, flung against the armrest in the back of the Zil.

Krug grabbed at the armrest, threw an angry glance at the speeding car: two men in front, a woman in the back. Just a glimpse, the car disappearing behind them, Krug's driver pulling out into the road with apologies.

Just a glimpse, but enough for General Leon Krug to recognize both the driver and the woman in the back. What was the daughter of General Hans Reder doing in the back of an unmarked car driven by a Stasi sergeant who, even by Sicherheitsdienst standards, was a known thug? And why today? Today of all days?

Krug knew that retired general Hans Reder had let it be known that today he was visiting a few old comrades in Leipzig. Krug knew that this was a lie, the kind of lie you told to protect those closest to you. And Krug also knew that a couple of 'old comrades' would happily swear that Hans Reder had indeed spent that day reminiscing with them in Leipzig. Another lie, one known to Krug because he and Hans Reder had together arranged the cover for General Reder's clandestine rendezvous.

So why was Rosa Rossman being taken out of the city today by a Stasi sergeant who was certainly not privy to their plans? Coincidence? Neither General Reder nor Krug himself had climbed to the peak of the GDR military hierarchy by believing in coincidence. When you caught the whiff of danger, you had to trust in your nose.

As the car pushed on into the city, Krug rapidly turned his options over in his mind. Phoning Reder at the military airport base outside Dresden *might* be secure – the airbase commander was a trusted member of their group – but you never knew who might be listening in. It was too risky, could draw attention to the presence of the other senior officers from the southern battalions at Erfurt, Halle, Karl-Marx Stadt, even Leipzig itself – not to mention their visitor from Moscow.

No, they'd come too far to have their plans jeopardized by a rash phone call. They were too close to success – or to a bullet in the back of the head.

Rosa Rossman was too close to something unpleasant. Leon Krug had known her almost from the moment she'd arrived in the GDR with the small band of refugees who'd been delivered from Pinochet's coup in Chile. He'd watched her become part of Hans Reder's family, had seen how the Reder household had bloomed under her wide smile. A childless couple had found a new way of living, so had an orphan from a plundered country. *We've done wrong things in the GDR*, Krug thought, *but sometimes we did save lives. Dreams come true*. Krug almost laughed aloud. The GDR was going through a nightmare. If Reder and himself and the rest of their small group did not succeed, then their country would perish in that nightmare.

'Martin?'

'General?' The driver caught General Krug's eye in the rear-view mirror.

'That driver who almost put us into the ditch – you got a look at him?'

'Yes, sir. Stasi sergeant.'

'Name?'

'Baister, sir – I think.'

It was enough for General Krug. Martin had been his driver for over a decade, turning down promotion to sergeant to do so.

'Then Normannenstrasse, Martin.'

'Yes, sir.'

Driver and general exchanged a rear-view-mirror glance. They didn't say much, these two, but they could read each other's mind. Neither man relished a visit to the Stasi HQ but they both knew that some things couldn't be avoided. And Martin knew that General Leon Krug wasn't the kind of officer to report a subordinate for some driving misdemeanour.

'And afterwards, General, we're still going to the barracks?'

Krug nodded to the mirror. The northern officers – from Schwerin, Rostock, Greifswald – would be waiting for him, anxious, like himself, to know the news from Moscow and Hungary, maybe from Poland.

'This won't take long, Martin,' he said, as they swung into the Normannenstrasse complex.

A dozen tall buildings surrounded them. Hundreds of windows stared down at them.

General Leon Krug settled his cap firmly, smoothed his military leather coat. You are a general of the National Volksarmee, he reminded himself, and your rank carries weight here too, in this corrupt heart of our socialist country. All the same, he'd be glad to be done here. A quick word with this lout – Baister, Martin had called him – find out what's happening with Rosa Rossman, probably some simple explanation, and he'd be on his way.

Martin held the door for him and Krug stepped into the heart of the Stasi world.

The reception area of the Stasi HQ wasn't the sort of place where you expected to find a citizen, concerned or otherwise, attempting to conduct inquiries with one of the uniformed male receptionists. And yet the tall, dark-haired fellow facing one of the porters across the desk seemed not to have been dragged or pushed into Normannenstrasse. He was about Krug's own height, about six feet, brown eyes, hair thinning. And Krug could tell, stepping to the desk, that the fellow was not bothering to conceal his irritation with the way both porters snapped to attention in Krug's presence.

'*Guten Tag, Herr General.*' A duetted greeting for Krug who saluted brusquely.

'*Entschuldigung.*' The 'Excuse me' polite but Krug sensed an edge of impatience, even anger, in the other man's voice. '*Eine Frage—*' Whatever the caller's question or inquiry was, neither porter was interested in dealing with it.

'One moment.' The porter who spoke, the shorter, stouter one, cast a withering look at the caller. 'You have no business here.' He addressed Krug directly. 'How can we be of service, General?'

Leon Krug was intrigued; only a very unusual kind of citizen would voluntarily enter these premises. And he liked the fellow's protest, however politely expressed, at being so pointedly ignored. When Krug looked more closely at the man standing beside him, he could see the strain in the pale face, the tiny drops of sweat on the receding hairline.

'This gentleman needs your assistance first,' Krug said.

The two porters exchanged a glance.

'We've already told him,' the short one said, 'that we cannot help him.'

'Please, if you could just ask the . . .' stumbling for words, 'the officer of the day if there is any information about the lady – please.'

'We have no information.' Hostility in the porter's words, in his face. 'Make inquiries at the police station.'

'They told me to ask here.'

And you had the courage or foolhardiness to do so. General Leon Krug looked with closer interest at this citizen with a briefcase, this citizen who was prepared to trade words with the guardians at the gate of the Stasi stronghold.

'I am General Krug of the National Volksarmee,' he said. 'Perhaps you'd like to tell me what this is all about.'

'A friend of mine was asked to leave her class this morning by two members of the security services, General.' Words swallowed the drops of sweat sliding past his ear. 'I'm just trying to find out where she's being held.'

'Her *class*? What class?'

'At the university, General, the Institute of English Studies.'

It was Krug's turn to experience a pang of dismay.

'And your friend's name?'

'Frau Rossman – Frau Rosa Rossman.' Krug felt himself being measured. 'Frau Rossman is the daughter of General Hans Reder.'

'And your name?'

'Patrick Miller, General.'

Krug recognized the name, remembered Reder telling him of the transplanted Englishman who was vetting his 'memoirs', of how Reder thought his daughter was becoming attached to the fellow. And how Miller's newspaper contacts in the UK might be useful to their group.

Krug nodded, shook hands with Miller, looked at the pair of porters still standing at attention behind the chest-high desk.

'And you have no information to help Herr Miller?'

'No, General, we have not.'

You never knew with these bastards, they just might be telling the truth. Maybe they really didn't know that Rosa Rossman had been driven at speed out of the city by a thug called Baister.

Krug wasn't about to make them any the wiser.

'I wish to speak with Herr Miller,' Krug said to the porters. 'I shall require an interview room.'

'But . . .' The porters looked at each other, at Krug. He was a general, yes, but of the army and this was highly irregular. 'General Krug—'

'*Now,*' Krug said. He stared hard at them.

The porters bent together over their desk, consulted a diagram.

'Room 205, General, on the next floor. I'll take you.'

'No need.' Krug nodded, turned to Miller. 'Come with me.'

A curt nod to Martin sent the driver out to the car.

Miller looked dazed as he walked beside Krug up the broad marble staircase. He'd been scared coming here; now he wondered if he had made things worse for Rosa.

'Quickly,' Krug said, 'we don't have much time.'

He could hear the phone at the reception desk being picked up, the click of buttons being pressed. Before they even got inside Room 205, Erich Mielke, the head of Stasi, would know that a general of the army was on the premises and throwing his weight about.

Room 205 was a rectangular windowless room with a metal cupboard in one corner and a small table on which rested a black phone. Two straight-backed chairs with metal legs faced each other across the table.

Krug motioned Miller to one of the chairs while he tried the corner cupboard. Krug wasn't surprised that it was locked. Maybe it held the chamois cloths that interviewees were said to sit on, depositing their frightened sweat and body smell for future use with hunting dogs. More likely the cupboard housed the recording machines that automatically clicked into gear when an interrogation began.

Or maybe the recording device was in the light switch. Or the leg of the chair. Or hidden behind one of the walls. The location of the bug didn't matter. You just had to remember that every word spoken in the room was being recorded. Maybe even being listened to as you spoke.

So, proceed with caution. Ascertain if your friend's daughter is in any peril, if she needs help, if you can give that help. And speak no word that might endanger the group, the very work that Hans Reder is engaged upon right now at Dresden airbase.

He looked at Miller, tensed upright on the chair, overcoat still buttoned, gloves choked in his hands, briefcase on his knees.

'Would you like to take off your overcoat, Herr Miller?'

Miller shook his head. 'What does my coat matter? I want to know where Frau Rossman is, General Krug.'

So, the Englishman is enough in control of himself to remember my name. 'Tell me what happened,' Krug said. 'In your own words and,' he pointed at the walls, at the ceiling, then cupped his hands around both ears, 'with no unnecessary detail, just what happened, OK?'

Miller looked at the ceiling, at the general. He nodded at Krug. Krug nodded back. At least the Englishman was no fool.

It took only a few minutes, a few sentences, for Krug to get a picture of what had happened at the Institute of English. He picked up the phone and dialled the porter's desk.

'This is General Krug.' His voice gruff: *don't fuck with me*. 'You are sure General Reder's daughter is not being held here?'

Miller watched him listen, watched him put the phone down.

'They say she's not here,' Krug said.

'But maybe . . .' Miller stopped.

'I know,' Krug said. *Maybe they're lying*. Lies were part of the air that everyone breathed in Normannenstrasse.

He picked up the phone again. 'Is Corporal Baister on duty?'

Papers turning, crackling on the phone. Krug said thank you, put the phone down.

Baister was on duty at 4 p.m., in ten minutes. And Room 205, with all its unseen ears, was not the place to question him.

He stood up, motioned for Miller to come with him. Miller followed him down the stairs, stood beside him at the reception desk as Krug asked which building Baister worked out of.

'Block Nine,' he was told.

Krug touched his fingers to his general's cap while the two porters saluted and clicked their heels.

Martin had the Zil's engine running, held the rear door open for Krug.

'Get in,' he told Miller. To Martin he said, 'Block Nine, we haven't much time.'

None of it made sense, Krug thought, as Martin slammed the car door shut behind Miller. Maybe the Stasi didn't have Rosa Rossman, maybe Baister was playing some freelance game. If so, he was a fool who might not have long to live: by now news of Rosa Rossman and General Leon Krug – not to mention the Englishman, Miller – would definitely have reached the ears of

General Erich Mielke, boss of the Stasi, self-proclaimed 'sword and shield of the Party'.

'Pull over to the side of Block Nine,' Krug told his driver. Pathetic, he told himself: there was no place to hide from the hundreds of Normannenstrasse windows. 'We'll have to be quick, Martin,' Krug said. 'We have to get to Baister before anyone else does.'

'Don't worry, sir.' Martin drew the Zil to a halt at the corner of Block 9; they sat there waiting, the engine idling, watching the approaches to the complex.

'There.' They didn't need Martin's pointing finger, they could see and hear the red Trabi chugging towards them across the concrete concourse.

'Martin.' Krug laid a hand on the driver's shoulder. 'No fuss, nice and quiet.' The Trabi came to a halt at the rear of the building. There was another man beside Baister in the front. 'Tell them both that I wish to see them immediately.'

Krug and Miller watched Martin march smartly to the Trabi. The car door was open; they saw Baister look up at Martin, saw him look across at the Zil, saw him shake his head.

Krug lowered his window, his general's peaked cap and badge framed in the fading day.

Martin's lips moved again, his right hand pointed at the Zil.

Baister shrugged, turned in the car seat, said something to the other Stasi.

Miller watched, puzzled, frightened, as the two Stasi marched with Martin towards the Zil.

'I'll do the talking,' General Krug said.

Miller nodded. His throat was too dry to speak anyway.

Twenty-five

October 1989
East German countryside

She watched Dover watching her. He took an apple from his pocket, bit into it. Despite herself she flinched, as though it were her own flesh that had been sliced by the small white teeth.

Dover caught her movement on the mattress. His pale eyes seemed to dance above the green apple.

'Don't worry, baby.' He chewed noisily. 'You'll get your turn, just be patient.'

He moved closer to the bed, stood looking down at her. He'd taken her coat before tying her to the bed and she felt naked under the blue, watery eyes – as though the American could see through her sweater and skirt.

Dover poked a fingernail between his teeth, studied a shred of apple speared on the nail. His jaw worked, searching, chewing, and he spat on the floor.

'My manners are godawful.' He shook his head, spat again, between his teeth. 'You'd never think I'm an Ivy League graduate, would you, darlin'? Whatever I am, it's all down to you Commie bastards, not to my old high school in Purdue or the hallowed halls of Harvard – bet you've heard of Harvard, Fräulein Rosa, haven't you? Everybody's heard of Harvard.'

Dover raised his right boot on to the edge of the bed, leaned over her. She could smell him, his animal sweat; she could see a fleck of green apple skin wedged between his upper teeth. She stared up at him, straining against her bonds. *Don't flinch, look him in the eye.*

'My daddy was a career soldier, a *decorated* soldier. He survived the war over here,' Dover poked at her thigh with the toe of his boot, smiled to himself, 'but he didn't survive the Commie gooks in Korea. So it was just me and my mom trying to stay alive in Purdue, but I did my best, because that's what my daddy'd expect of me and what Uncle Sam'd expect of me and Uncle Sam took care of me, sent me off to Harvard on a scholarship and when he came looking for me, wantin' to know if I'd serve my country in special ops, I didn't have to think even once about it. 'Cos the man said ask not what your country can do for you and I was ready and willin' to do what I could for my country.' Dover sighed.

Rosa didn't look down but she felt her skirt being pushed upwards by his boot. She wanted to spit in his mock-sad face but she lay still on the bare mattress, her legs tight together. They were miles from anywhere, enclosed in what was little more than a sealed box in an abandoned farmhouse, but you never knew. Against all odds you survived your first encounter with this American monster on the other side of the world. Stay alive, Rosa told herself, while Dover rattled on in his affected folksy style.

'I was twenty-five, darlin', when I went into North Vietnam to do my duty for Uncle Sam – "special ops", they called it, but what it really meant was stopping Commies, gettin' rid of gooks. I was good at it, little Frau, and when they needed my help to remove your pinko Allende down there in Chile, I was happy to serve there too. In America we knew it was important to stop that Communist plague spreadin' north through South America.'

Dover paused, took another bite of the apple, went on talking with his mouth full. 'I had the bad fortune to get my knees busted down there,' he spat a chunk of half-chewed apple on to the earthen floor, 'and you were dumb enough to stop that Commie shit Dieter from killing me – and I told him, lady, you heard me tell him but you just wouldn't fuckin' listen, would you? Like all Commie bastards, you knew better, didn't you?'

Rosa watched in horror as Dover began to unbuckle the belt of his workman's trousers.

'Until then, Fräulein, it was never personal, it was just Herbert Dover against the forces of darkness, you could say. It got personal when my legs got busted – in fuckin' South America of all places – and that's why it's personal now, Fräulein Rossman.'

Dover chomped on the apple. 'It's personal with guys like your old man too, Fräulein. It was Commies like the old general who killed my daddy.' His spittle landed on Rosa's face and she blinked, turned away.

Dover laughed. 'You could make it easy on yourself, Fräulein Rossman. Tell me what you know about General Reder. We're hearing whispers that the old guy is up to something – you know anything about that?' He took her face between thumb and forefinger, pressed until her mouth opened. 'You able to tell me anything? Like I said, you could make it easy on yourself.'

Rosa swung her head violently and spat into Dover's face.

He laughed, wiped his face with his sleeve. 'Not a good idea, lady, not good at all.'

Dover had both legs planted firmly on the floor beside the bed; his belt hung loosely from the loops of his trousers. He winked at her. 'It's almost biblical, isn't it? You know, Adam and Eve and the apple.' He rubbed the core of the apple against her clenched lips, then dropped it beside her face on the striped mattress. 'And the forbidden fruit just waitin' for old Adam.'

She wanted to shut her eyes to it, pretend it wasn't happening, that it was happening to someone else.

Open your eyes. Watch him bend over the mattress – watch him, you never know.

He was standing on one leg, his left leg raised to climb on to the bed.

In that frozen moment she twisted on the mattress, drew her right foot and swung her boot with all the strength she could muster.

She felt her boot smash into his genitals, heard Dover roar, reach instinctively with both hands for his groin. And in that same frozen moment she pulled her right leg back, knee against her belly, and she stabbed hard against him. The heel of her boot crunched against Dover's balls, his bellow filled the room and she stabbed again but Dover was on the dirt floor by then, groaning now, whimpering below the bed.

She was panting. Spreadeagled on the mattress, her skirt was around her hips. *He'll kill you.* Fuck him, she told herself. He'll rape you anyway.

The groaning, the whimpering, diminished. She watched as Dover's hairless head raised itself beside the bed and she gathered the spit in her mouth and spat into the watery, blue eyes.

Dover grimaced, wiped the spittle from his eyes.

He laughed. 'Oh, baby, baby.' His head was close to hers; she could smell cigarettes on his breath. 'I like a woman with guts, I really do.'

He got to his feet, then lowered himself gingerly to the edge of the bed. She felt his buttock pushing against her hip and she tried to squirm away on the mattress.

Another laugh, the small teeth bared again.

She saw the fist coming, felt his knuckles smash into her

face. The pain had hardly begun when the fist hit her again. She felt his fingers in her hair, lifting her head, holding her head steady while he went on slapping her face with his other hand.

When he was done, breathless, he flung her back against the mattress.

She could taste her own blood and tears leaking into her mouth. *Fuck him. You're alive. You never know*. She stared at him and tried to force back the tears.

He slapped her face again, but then he moved away, and switched off the light. She heard the sound of the key turning in the lock. She was alone. She could taste blood in her mouth. Her hands were tied.

You're still alive, she repeated to herself. And it hadn't been such a long car ride in the Trabi, less than an hour. Berlin was not so distant and surely *somebody* – from her class, from the office – would get in touch with her father. Then she remembered that General Reder would not be back until next day and he had told her not to expect a call that night. She trembled, and not just from the cold air on her bare flesh: she didn't know when Dover would be back.

And there was Patrick. *Where* was Patrick?

He'd be thinking of her, looking out of his window at Berlin, in a country he'd been told to spy on. A country that, like her, he'd learned to love.

A country that Herbert Dover was plotting to bring down.

You're still alive. She said the words aloud: *Noch lebst du*. Fuck Dover. *You never knew*.

'So,' Krug said, 'you deal with me or with General Erich Mielke himself, your choice.'

A window on either side of the Zil was half lowered but the air inside the car stank with the odour of five male bodies and the dampness of winter clothing. General Krug had moved to sit up front beside Martin; Patrick Miller sat behind Krug, alongside Baister and the other Stasi.

'Make your mind up, I haven't all day.' Krug had removed his cap; Miller could see the stamp of the cap band furrowed deep into the general's wide forehead. 'So what have you done with Frau Rossman?'

Miller saw Baister exchange a glance with the other man, saw the fear in both faces.

'We were told to take her away just for a little while,' Baister swallowed, 'that we'd be taking her back to the institute in no time at all.'

And nobody would question a Stasi pick-up, Miller thought.

'So?' Krug's eyes narrowed above the seat back, the furrow in his forehead deepening to an angry red.

'He kept her there, ordered us to leave.' Baister's voice a whisper.

'He?'

'We were told to call him Herr Wander.' Baister was staring past Krug's shoulder, at the open space beyond the half-open window. 'Honest, that's all we know.'

'We didn't arrange it.' The other Stasi had found his voice. He hurried on, scrambling for forgiveness, for safety. 'He tied her to the bed . . .' He stopped, twisted his uniform cap in his hands. 'We told Herr Wander that wasn't the deal but he wouldn't listen . . .'

Miller was only half-listening. *He tied her to the bed.* He lunged across Baister in the rear seat, grabbed at the other man's coat. 'Where is she? What have you done to her?'

Baister pushed him back, Krug's hands pulled him off.

'Calm down.' Krug was looking at Miller. 'We'll get her. Remember where we are.'

Miller looked at Krug, at the pair of frightened Stasi beside him. At the Stasi buildings around them, looming in the dull afternoon light. He nodded at Krug, said nothing.

'Where is she now?' Krug asked.

'It's a place we sometimes use,' Baister said, 'about thirty kilometres east, an old farmhouse, nobody's lived there since the war.'

'Where the fuck is it?'

'They call it Dunkelfeld.' The dark field.

'I know it,' the driver said. 'We did some manoeuvres around there when I joined up.' He made a face. 'It's a fucking awful place, General.'

'Another thing,' Krug said, 'who ordered you to do this?'

'Major Reimann, sir.' Baister's voice eager now. 'He ordered us, we had no choice, General.'

Krug held his gaze until Baister looked down at his hands.

'How much?' Krug asked.

'Five hundred.'

'Marks?'

'Dollars, sir.'

'Give me the money.'

Krug took the roll of green notes, stared at the thick wad. *Dollars, so the Americans were probably in on it. But did this kidnapping have anything to do with the group? With their fears? With Rosa Rossman's father's secret meeting in Dresden?*

'Please, General, let's get going!'

Krug heard Miller's anxious words as if through a screen, his mind still engaged with his own subterfuge, the group's secret – and dangerous – plans to save their country.

'I know,' Krug said, 'I know.'

His attention was caught by a noise, a kind of low hum that seemed to come first from the main block and then, as Krug looked round, from all the other blocks.

'What's going on?' he said. You didn't expect noise from the Stasi HQ. Normannenstrasse kept its noises to itself, hugged the screams to its bowels. And why, Krug wondered, were small knots of Stasi, twos and threes, coming out of the buildings, gathering on doorsteps, cigarette tips glowing in the gloom, the hum of low conversation carrying into the Zil?

'You.' Krug glared at the second Stasi.

'Corporal Zimmerman, sir.'

'Go and find out what's going on.'

They watched the Stasi cross the concourse, edging between parked vehicles, to the small group gathered at the entrance to Block 9. And they watched him hurry back, a look of astonishment on his face. Zimmerman didn't speak until he was again inside the car.

'It's General Mielke, sir,' he said to Krug.

'What about him?'

'He's resigned, sir.'

'What?'

'That's what they told me, General. The Central Committee has accepted General Mielke's resignation as head of the Stasi.'

Astonishment on the Stasi face, in the Stasi voice. General Erich Mielke, who had controlled the fate of every citizen of the GDR, no longer held in his hands the power of life or death. Mielke was gone, resigned.

In other words, they sacked him. And we're all at risk, Krug told himself. All of us, north and south, Reder at the airbase in Dresden with his group.

'General Krug, please!'

He looked at Miller, turned his attention to Baister. 'This Herr Wander that you left Frau Rossman with, is he German?'

'He speaks like a German, sir, but I don't think so.' Baister hesitated; offering opinions could be fatal. 'It's hard to tell, sir, but he could be American.'

Was Mielke's removal part of the American plot?

Krug turned to Martin. 'You sure you can find this Dunkelfeld place?'

'I'm sure, General, it's not the kind of place you forget easily.'

'Both of you,' Krug said to the Stasi, 'get out and not a word to anybody about any of this, understood?' Both men nodded. 'And especially not to this Major Reimann, just tell him you did as you were ordered and left the woman with Wander.' Again, heads nodded. 'I'll deal with both of you later.' A last stare, a last reddening of the furrow across the wide forehead. 'People like you are not fit to serve our country – now get out.'

They mumbled, 'Thank you, sir.' The car door opened, a blast of cold air, the door slammed, the two men scurried off.

Krug looked back at Miller.

'We'll get her,' he said. He tried to keep the edge of fear out of his voice.

Krug nodded to Martin and the big Zil headed for the eastern edge of the city.

It was faint at first, the noise of the car. It came closer, louder, penetrating the stone walls of the farmhouse and the wooden walls of the room, ghosting into the darkness that enveloped her.

She was cold, her wrists sore from useless tugging against her bonds. Her left eye was half closed from Dover's fist.

She could hear the car clanking closer over the uneven ground. The engine cut. Doors opening, slamming. Voices, indistinct. More than one voice. Dover had brought company.

Well, they wouldn't have an easy way with her. She could bite, she could spit.

Footsteps. Voices.

She heard her name, twitched on the hard mattress, dared to hope.

Her name was called again, fists pounded on the metal door.

'In here!' Her voice broken, croaky. 'I'm in here!'

'Forget the fucking door, it's made of steel.' She didn't recognize the voice but it didn't matter. It couldn't be Dover.

'I'm here, in here! Hurry, please!' Hope lifting her voice but tearful now, daring to hope, allowing the tears.

'Kick the fucking wall down!' Anger in the voice, but authority too, a voice used to command.

She heard footsteps recede, screamed for them to come back.

'All together now!'

Something ramming at the wooden walls, once, twice, three times. The wall cracking, splintering. More shouting, the wall giving way, falling in, a huge length of rusted metal crashing after it, and torchlight found her and she screamed again.

'It's Patrick, Rosa.'

Another torch, the beam turned on Patrick's face now, a pair of uniforms beside him.

'It's OK, Rosa, it's OK.' The torch pointed at the uniforms, Patrick's voice soothing. 'They're friends, Rosa, they're friends.'

One of the uniforms cut the cords that bound her. She folded her arms across her breasts and began to whimper.

Patrick lifted her, folded his coat around her, whispered to her, kissed her hair, her forehead.

'You're safe now,' she heard him say, 'that's all that matters.'

'We'll get her to the hospital.' The voice was strange but the words kind, soothing.

She felt herself carried through the cold to the car, felt Patrick settle her on the wide back seat. He sat beside her, cradled her head in his lap. Doors slammed again, the car moved off. She pushed her head against Patrick's midriff, sucked in the smell of him, the strength of him.

'We have you now, *I* have you,' he was whispering. 'You're safe.'

And she was. She heard the spade clanging against stone where that unknown peasant put her mother in the ground and she knew the grave was not hers. Patrick was hers, her life was still hers. And the land beyond the car – that land was hers.

'You'll have to stop the car,' she said.

She saw the question in Patrick's face.

'I need to pee,' she said. 'Now.'

After the phone call there was silence in the basement planning room at Dresden airbase. Thirteen men looked at one another, at the low ceiling, the fluorescent lighting, the wall map of the GDR studded with pins of red and white and blue and yellow. Some of them sucked on cigarettes, on pencil tops. They chewed over the words they had exchanged throughout the afternoon and evening; looked back at the long road that had brought them together here, the months of hesitant planning, of trust and distrust, that had brought them to this pass.

The phone call to Hans Reder had shown them that, willingly or not, they stood at a crossroads. When Reder had put the phone down, he'd said simply, 'The Politburo has fired Mielke.'

His words filled the basement, hung beneath the low ceiling, shaded the map, moved the pins. The news impregnated the cigarettes and pens and pencils they sucked on and nobody was sure if they liked the new taste, if it was sweet or sour. What was certain was that it was different.

It was Reder who broke the silence.

'It's make-your-mind-up time, gentlemen,' he said. 'We either go on or we stop now.'

The others looked at the small man who was their acknowledged leader. It was Reder – the oldest among them – who had first put out feelers over a year ago. And it was Reder who had taken the risk of exposing himself, of showing his lack of faith in their country's leadership. Over the course of a year Reder had approached these individuals of varied ages and backgrounds, stationed throughout East Germany. He'd done his homework, studied the personnel files in HQ. Above all, he'd relied on his own judgement of men he'd personally encountered during his long military service. Sometimes Reder made his approach during an official inspection of his target's barracks; sometimes the approach was made on training courses in Berlin or further afield. He tried to cover all the bases – infantry, artillery, air power, navy, intelligence. What Reder looked for in each member of his chosen, secret group was sound military judgement coupled with coolness under pressure. And he gave his trust to nobody who did not share his own commitment to the ideals of the GDR, ideals which were no longer being honoured. Only Reder would have stuck his neck out, gambling against betrayal. And for that leap of faith he was their unelected but accepted leader. Hans Reder was also the only one among them who was retired. He could summon neither divisions nor tanks, neither planes nor ships. In a real sense, the ability to act was not his.

'The question is this: is the Stasi about to change?' The others looked at Rexin, saw the half-smile on his face. He was the youngster of the group, the commander of the base where they were gathered.

'We'll take that as a rhetorical question.' General Filmer from Erfurt was unsmiling as he spoke.

They batted it back and forth for no more than a few minutes. Mielke's departure changed nothing or, at best, not much.

They'd talked it through and thought it through for long enough. The country was falling apart; the scavengers were waiting, within and without, to rip it asunder and swallow it whole or in pieces.

Reder looked at Dieter Jessen.

'This will change nothing for Gorbachev,' Dieter said. 'You heard him yourselves – Moscow no longer decides the fate of Germany or other socialist states. The Soviet army in the GDR will not interfere.'

'But,' Filmer was lighting yet another cigarette, 'how can we be sure that Mielke's departure will not affect Gorbachev's attitude?'

'I think,' Reder said, 'that we can rely on Dieter's assessment of the situation in Moscow.' All of them knew that for almost two decades Dieter Jessen had worked at the heart of the KGB in Moscow, not only surviving but prospering through changes of leadership. For Reder, the connection was more intimate: it was Dieter who had first told Hans Reder and his wife of the remarkable teenager he had spirited to safety from the bombed ruins of Santiago.

'And Warsaw?' Reder asked.

All eyes turned to General Michal Jablonska of the Polish Army. Every man among them was aware of the deep underlying hatred nurtured in Polish hearts towards Germans and Germany.

Jablonska was a thin, humourless soldier with wiry blond hair and a famously short temper.

'I've told you,' he said. 'You have nothing to fear from Poland.'

'So.' Reder looked around the table at this circle of men who had decided to trust one another with their lives. The men looked strained, unkempt; tunics hung open or were draped on the backs of chairs; the tabletop was buried beneath paper, cigarette packets, cups and saucers, overflowing ashtrays. The men and the place hardly looked like the cradle of a movement that planned nothing less than the overthrow of a government, the restoration of a truly socialist state that recognized that there was no socialism without a people. And yet Reder could see beyond the apparent disarray. War was never neat and tidy – and neither were the men who made war.

'So,' he said again, 'what's our decision?'

'We go.' Rexin stubbed out his cigarette. 'There's no turning back.' He raised his hand and, one by one, every man around the table followed suit.

'We need to set a final date.' Again Reder's words drew them back to what they were about.

The timing had been discussed at length and in detail between them, but events were moving quicker than they thought and they had to move. Nothing could be done unless it was done together: the seizure of barracks across the land, of television and radio stations, of the national newspaper *Neues Deutschland*. Above all, the need to overpower and control the Stasi HQ in Berlin and the entire network of Stasi provincial stations. The need to avoid bloodshed had been agreed yet all of them knew that blood might have to be spilled – and some of it might be their own. Every man present knew that, at all levels from battalion through regimental to divisional, there was no shortage of officers whose loyalty to the Politburo was unshakeable, and these men would oppose any action that they saw as treasonable.

'Tomorrow,' Reder said, 'is November the first.'

'We need a week,' General Filmer said. 'Better still, ten days.'

'In ten days' time it will be November the eleventh.' They all looked at Rexin.

Another 11 November had been a day of shame for Germany, in 1918, when Allied troops had inflicted a humiliating peace on the German people.

There seemed a rightness about the date. Reder could sense it, watching the men round the table.

'We're agreed, then,' he said. 'We move on November the eleventh.'

Rexin spoke for all of them when he said, 'A new beginning on an old date.'

The meeting began to break up. They said their goodbyes with the solemnity of men on the eve of battle. They shook hands in the knowledge that they would not meet again until after the battle had been fought. And they slapped shoulders and casually saluted one another with the mock joshing of military men who knew that not all of them might live to meet another day.

They left the basement quietly. It was unlikely that their gathering on the airbase had gone completely unnoticed but, still, there was no point in drawing attention to themselves. Their cars were parked at different points around the base; they'd made their own sandwiches and coffee in the small kitchen off the planning room.

Each man's last farewell was to Reder. He'd picked them, drawn them together, inspired them with his vision of a socialism that set people free to serve themselves and others out of a sense of justice.

Reder watched each man go with both pride and foreboding. These were men who were ready to trade their own privilege and status for the sake of a common good. He imagined them in their cars, a couple of them with trusted drivers, journeying through the night-time land to homes and families, burdened with their secret, burdened too with the demands of final preparation for 11 November. He was glad that Dieter was hanging back to speak privately to him.

'Let's clean up,' Dieter said.

Reder smiled. Dieter couldn't have survived in the maw of the KGB without such attentiveness to detail.

Together they carried mugs and plates to the kitchen. Dieter washed, Reder dried.

'I wonder,' Dieter said, placing a mug on the draining board, 'if General Mielke will have to prepare his own breakfast now.'

They laughed together. Erich Mielke's meticulously presented breakfast tray was well-known in senior military circles: every item – cup, plate, pot, egg, bread, butter and jam – precisely positioned on the tray which must be perfectly aligned with the corner of his Stasi desk.

'Soon,' Reder said, 'no man will wait on another man in this country.'

'If only, Hans.' Dieter was putting the crockery away in the cupboard above the sink. 'If only.'

'I know, Dieter, but we have to try anyway.'

'Maybe this is a start – an East German general and a colonel of the KGB doing the washing-up.'

There was shared warmth in their laughter.

They put their coats on, checked one last time that the planning room held no trace of their meeting. Reder put the lights out, shut the door behind them. They climbed the stone steps, walked a corridor of locked-up offices and stepped out into the night.

Dresden military airfield was quiet. There was light in the control tower; windows were lit up too in the billets at the southern end of the base. But the hangar to the west was dark and only two twin-engined planes rested on the tarmac.

'Gorbachev has already ordered most of the air force back to Moscow,' Reder said.

'And more to follow.' Dieter held the cigarette pack out but Reder shook his head. 'This fucking cancer,' he said. 'And Rosa is like a fox, she'd smell it on me.'

Dieter's face was tired, lined, in the glow of the match. He laughed. 'You're scared of your daughter.'

'There's no harm in being scared of *somebody*.'

'Will you send Rosa away?' Dieter asked.

Reder shook his head. 'She'd refuse anyway.'

'But it might get bloody – these Stasi fuckers won't just lie down.'

'I know that but,' Reder shrugged, 'it's her country too.'

'Not for long if Kohl and the Brits and the Americans have their way.'

'Fuck them.' Reder took the lighted cigarette from Dieter's fingers and sucked heavily on it. He exhaled noisily, gratefully, the blue smoke drifting above their heads. 'Why can't they just leave people alone, let people try to find their own way of doing things?'

'Still, we can't blame folk for wanting the things they see on Wessie television every night – cars and shop windows full of jeans and gear and,' Dieter laughed, 'sex.'

'We need *time*,' Reder said. 'After the eleventh, we need time to show our people that it's possible to run our own country fairly, without the Stasi, without the informers.'

He reached for the cigarette again but Dieter laughed, pulled his hand away. 'C'mon,' he said, '*some* dangerous things make sense.'

'Doctors,' Reder growled, 'fucking thyroid glands.'

Dieter dropped the cigarette, stood on it. 'Think of Rosa.'

Reder nodded. 'You're right – and I'm going to drive back

now. I've been offered a bunk here but I want to get home.' He looked around him, at the starry sky, like a sailor considering the waves. 'What about you?'

'I'll go with you,' Dieter said, 'if you have no objections.'

'Of course not.'

'I'm not expected back in Moscow for a few days,' Dieter said. 'I hopped a number of military flights to get here, the last leg was from Prague this morning – but you know that.' He drew the collar of his leather coat tighter around his neck, stared past Reder into the night. 'I want to be here when it all happens, Hans. This once I want to be there when we make it go right for the side that is right.' He laid a hand on Reder's shoulder. 'They hunted us out of Chile as if we were the criminals, Hans. I've never forgotten that.'

'This isn't Chile, Dieter.' Reder spoke mildly. 'These are some of our own people we're trying to get rid of.'

'All we want to do is replace them, isn't that what we're planning, not to get rid of them? Moscow will let the Germans get on with it but we have to convince the Americans and the rest of them to let us try it our way.'

'I'm just an old soldier, Dieter,' Reder said. 'You're the thinker and the speech-maker.'

Dieter laughed.

'Just don't practise any speeches on the journey.' Hans turned away. 'C'mon, the car is around the corner.'

'One other thing, Hans.'

Something in Dieter's tone stopped him, made him turn round.

'Yes?'

'That fucking Wall has to come down.'

Reder nodded. 'I'll take a pick to it myself,' he said.

Twenty-six

October 1989
Charity Hospital
Mitte, East Berlin

The young doctor was having none of it. 'You'll have to wait your turn,' he said. 'Look around you.'

Even the floor in the cavernous waiting room of the emergency department was occupied by the broken and the bleeding. The drunks were there, of course, snoring, hawking, talking to themselves, but so were the ordinary damaged and bruised of East Berlin.

'You know there was a march,' the doctor was saying. He looked squarely at Krug, at his general's uniform, his braided insignia. 'But,' he shook his head, 'we've never had casualties like this after a protest march.'

Panic, Krug thought. Mielke's gone so the leaderless Stasi beat heads, smash limbs – and maybe the Vopos join in.

'I don't need to see a doctor, General Krug.' Rosa was leaning on Miller's shoulder, his coat buttoned across her torn clothing. 'Really, I'm OK, these people need help more than me.'

A grey-haired nurse pushed past, turned her head long enough to glare at the young doctor. 'Are you going to stitch that boy's head or just leave him in there dripping blood?'

'On my way.'

Krug reached out a restraining hand but the doctor was already gone.

'What's the trouble here?' Another doctor, older, balding, a trace of blood on the sleeve of his white coat.

Krug started to explain.

'Please.' Rosa laid a hand on Krug's arm. 'I just want to get home and – and clean myself.'

The doctor looked at her, tucked his tie between the buttons of his shirt front. 'You've been assaulted and – may I?' he opened the front of the coat, folded it again across her body. 'Come with me.' He took her elbow, looked back at Krug and Miller. 'It's not a good idea to wait there,' he said quietly. 'Uniforms aren't very popular in here.'

Miller was suddenly conscious of the space that had opened about them in the waiting room, of the hostile eyes watching them from all sides. He caught Krug's eye; they followed Rosa and the doctor along a corridor with green walls and matching floors and the smell of disinfectant.

They sat on stools with metal legs in a small room at the end of the corridor. From behind a curtain came the murmur of the doctor's voice, the higher pitch of Rosa's. A lot of 'Here?' from the doctor, 'Yes, yes, a little' from Rosa.

It didn't take long. The curtain swished, Rosa stood there still wrapped in Miller's coat. She thanked the doctor and he nodded stiffly before hurrying away in the direction of the waiting room.

'Let's go home now.' Rosa's voice seemed to come from a far distance.

'But are you OK?' Krug sounded sceptical.

'I'm bruised, a bit sore.' She took Miller's hand. 'I just need a bath and clean clothes and some coffee.'

'You're sure?' Miller put his arm around her.

'Patrick, look at these people.' They were edging their way

through the crowded waiting area. 'These are the people who need help.'

She didn't know if she really meant it but looking at the mass of sick and wounded and drunken helped to blot out the memory of Dover bending over her. Rosa knew that when they got home she'd have to tell General Krug what had happened. She didn't want to think about that either.

Martin had the car parked not far from the hospital entrance. They were almost there when a marked Vopo van drew to a screeching halt beside them.

Krug looked at the pair of uniformed Vopos who stepped out of the van. Watched them adjust their caps, their belts. Saw the nervousness in their white faces, in the way they twirled truncheons.

'You're going into the hospital?'

Instinctively they stood to attention before his general's uniform.

'Sir, there was trouble in the streets.' The taller one had sergeant's stripes but he was having trouble with his words. 'We're ordered to arrest any – any *troublemakers* who have gone into the hospital . . .' He tried to say more but no words issued.

'There are no troublemakers in the hospital,' Krug said.

The sergeant's Adam's apple bobbed a couple of times. 'But, sir.' He looked at the other Vopo, at Krug.

'Sergeant, go in there and both of you might get lynched.'

The sergeant's face grew whiter. 'Our orders, sir—'

'Sergeant, I'm not your commanding officer but suppose I confirm for you that there are no "troublemakers" taking refuge in the Charity Hospital, will that suffice? You heard it from General Leon Krug of the National Volksarmee, OK?' And for good measure Krug repeated his name slowly.

'Thank you, sir.'

Even Rosa smiled as the two Vopos got back into their van and drove off.

'That was kind, General Krug,' she said.

'Somehow,' Krug said, 'all of us in this country must learn how to be kind to one another again.' He looked at Rosa, at the way she leaned into Miller's shoulder. Maybe, he thought, for my generation it's too late to learn kindness but perhaps we can save these younger ones from repeating our mistakes. First, we have to save a country for them.

'Let's get you home,' Krug said.

'WILLKOMMEN' on the bristle-backed floormat was facing the apartment door so Dover knew it was safe to enter. He tapped gently, three times, so Redgrave wouldn't be tempted to do something stupid when he heard the key in the lock.

He didn't have to use his key. The door swung open and Redgrave stood there looking at him with a schoolmasterly frown on his thin features.

Dover breezed past him, pulled the door shut. He was in a hurry. He'd spent half the afternoon and much of the evening waiting for two contacts who had to be paid for their enthusiastic roles in protest demonstrations; he'd come back to the apartment in Köpenick only because he and Redgrave had agreed to compare activities every other evening. Herbert Dover wasn't in the mood for updates with Redgrave. He was in the mood to renew his acquaintance with little Miss Rosa.

Redgrave's cheap East German holdall was resting on a kitchen chair beside the table. The holdall was zipped shut.

'Going somewhere?'

'I should be gone. I waited only to warn you.' Redgrave was at his most imperious, his British inflexions most emphatically inflected. 'Heaven knows what you think you're doing, Dover.

You and your,' Redgrave made a face, '*appetites* have jeopardized our entire mission here.'

'Like to explain that?'

'You know perfectly well what I'm talking about. You had a couple of Vopos take that woman – General Reder's daughter! – out of her classroom in broad daylight and then you attempt to rape her in some godforsaken shed in the middle of nowhere.' Redgrave shook his head, almost speechless. 'Are you out of your mind, Dover? We're trying to find out what Reder is up to, not assault his daughter!'

'A little R'n'R is good for us all, Redgrave.' *So the broad must be gone, the bird flown.* 'This was on CBS News?'

'This is not a joke, Dover. Somebody spotted you on your little excursion and some army general got involved. It's all supposed to be hush-hush but I have my own sources.' *And even though I'm obliged to work with you, Dover, I'll be damned if I'm going to reveal all our British contacts in Normannenstrasse to a randy American.*

'Pity,' Dover said. He smiled bleakly. 'And now she owes me for more than two busted knees.'

'What're you talking about?'

'It's personal, Redgrave, intimately so.'

Redgrave glared at the American. 'Get your stuff – we can't be sure this place is safe any more.'

Dover clicked his heels, saluted. '*Jawohl, mein General.*'

The road north from Dresden seemed unfamiliar to General Reder. It was a road he'd travelled umpteen times, in wartime and in the years since; he'd even driven it that very morning, he reminded himself. Now, heading north through the night, he felt he was journeying in a foreign land. Even the darkness seemed edgy, as if it were waiting for a deeper darkness.

There was little traffic. They passed through villages shuttered into silence. Lights in distant farmhouses seen across the fields seemed lost, ghostly. They skirted Hoyerswerda, heard only silence from the town. Later, further north in the cloudless dark, they could see the factory smokestacks of Cottbus; even the factories seemed dead, the smokeless chimneys on strike.

'Jesus.' Dieter broke a silence that had lasted too long. 'You'd think the whole country was dead or asleep.'

Reder glanced at him, saw the pale face paler in the dashboard light.

'It's not dead,' Reder said, 'but we both know it's dying.'

Berlin was different. They could hear the city as soon as they caught sight of the city glow, like a pale canopy in the night. A kind of hum seemed to rise above the roads and buildings, a living sound that you couldn't break down into voices or shouts or traffic – just a mixed-together hum that was the growl of a city that was up past its bedtime but couldn't – or wouldn't – go to sleep.

Reder drove slowly through the streets of the city. Groups of men and women stood on street corners, anoraks zipped up against the night cold. Hooded heads bobbed in animated conversation. Cigarette ends glowed, pale knuckles bony in the red glow. Boots and shoes stomped on pavements. Someone laughed, a group joined in.

Heads turned to follow the progress of the big car.

They saw a hand raised, a bottle brandished. In the rear-view mirror Reder watched the beer bottle somersault through the night air, heard it smash on the road behind them.

A pair of Vopos on the opposite corner saw and heard it too. Reder watched them come charging along the street towards the group. He slammed on the brakes, squealed to a halt in front of the policemen. They would have run round the car but Reder put the heel of his palm on the horn, left it there, the siren noise braying in the street, almost forcing the policemen to halt.

Through the open window of the car they looked at Reder, faces angry.

'Leave it,' Reder said.

'Who the fuck—'

Dieter leaned forward in his seat, wagged a finger at the angry Vopo.

'This is General Reder,' Dieter said.

Reder flashed his ID.

'Leave it,' Reder said again. 'We don't need trouble on the streets.'

'There's plenty of trouble on the streets tonight, sir.' The Vopo was stooped, his countryman's face almost pushed into the car. 'All over the city.'

'Well, let's not make more.' Reder was feeling his years; home was what he needed now.

'Be careful, sir, nobody knows what to expect after the resignation.'

Reder wanted to be gone; the Vopo's breath, foul with stale garlic, was filling the car.

'Yes,' Reder said, 'but General Mielke's successor will soon take charge.'

The Vopo's rough face grew darker. He drew back from the car as if to study Reder, then leaned closer again.

'Not General Mielke, sir.' The Vopo almost stuck his head in the car. 'Herr Honecker, sir. The Party accepted Herr Honecker's resignation as leader a couple of hours ago, sir.'

'What?'

'Erich Honecker is gone, General, the Central Committee told him it was time to go.' The Vopo straightened, nodded to his waiting partner. 'Goodnight, sir.'

It was Dieter who broke the silence in the car.

'Honecker gone.' He shook his head. 'I can hardly believe it.'

'Me neither.' Reder was staring at his own reflection in the windscreen: *like a ghost, you look like a ghost that is even older than Honecker*. 'I know we agreed on ten days,' he said without looking at Dieter, 'but it's possible that none of us will last ten days.'

'So we need to move,' Dieter said.

Reder nodded. He put his foot on the accelerator pedal and the big car moved north towards his home in Pankow.

PART 5

ENDGAME

NOVEMBER 1989

Twenty-seven

Wednesday, 1 November 1989
East Berlin

Miller was up and dressed by six o'clock but when he opened the bedroom door he could hear the murmur of voices from the kitchen.

General Reder and the man who'd been introduced the night before as Dieter Jessen were seated at the small kitchen table with coffee mugs in their hands. Dieter – was he German, Russian or some kind of blend? – looked almost as tired as the general, who must be a good ten years older.

'Couldn't sleep?' Dieter was smiling.

Miller said good morning. He waited until General Reder told him to help himself to coffee and cereal and whatever he could find in the cupboards. The general's daughter had been assaulted and hospital waiting rooms were full of bloodied heads and broken limbs but good manners never went amiss – or so his mother would remember to remind him, even if she were drunk. Especially if she were drunk.

General Reder's expression had been a mix of puzzlement bordering on outraged fatherhood when he'd arrived home with the German/Russian long after midnight and found Patrick Miller in his kitchen only a few paces from his sleeping daughter.

Miller had put General Reder in the picture as quickly and as succinctly as he could. And as gently. How do you tell a father that his daughter had been kidnapped and sexually assaulted? Miller emphasized General Krug's intervention and the doctor's assurance that Rosa was OK but it was Dieter's presence that stopped Reder from driving immediately to Normannenstrasse to the Stasi kidnappers, and demanding a manhunt for this fellow with the birthmark who'd tried to rape Rosa.

'Wait, Hans.' Dieter had stood close to Reder, laid his hand on his sleeve. 'Wait until the morning when Rosa is awake.' Miller had noticed the narrow-eyed look he'd given Reder. 'And General Krug will be in touch – we need to be as sure of our ground as possible.'

Something was going on. *And maybe it's better you don't know what.*

Miller finished his breakfast. He felt the eyes of the other men watching him as he washed his cup and plate.

'I have to go to work,' he said.

'Please.' Reder shook his head. 'I'm sure it would be helpful to Rosa if you were here when she wakes up.'

'I'm expected at the office.'

'Please,' Reder said again. 'I'll phone and clear it with your boss – Hartheim, isn't it?'

'Of course.' The things you could do when you were a general in the GDR.

Miller didn't say that. You've earned your East German passport, he told himself; you're better than most of them at keeping your mouth shut.

He told Reder he'd spend a little time in the garden, if that was OK.

The garden was a wide, rectangular space. It faced south-west; at this hour of the morning the grass was rimed with a frost. It's the first day of November, Miller reminded himself; in less than two months it will be Christmas. The way things were going, it might be the last Christmas in the life of the GDR; still, it might be a Christmas – a *first* Christmas – that he could spend with Rosa. A religious Christmas was actively discouraged in East Germany but the workers took their break and decorated trees in their flats; carols were sung as only German voices can sing them; some even went to church.

And there was, on this frosty November morning, birdsong in the garden. Tall trees, still half-dressed with yellowing leaves, were ranged inside the high back-garden wall; the warbling song from the winter trees seemed like a whistling act of defiance.

Miller walked through the frosted garden and stood under the trees. Overhead, the defiant song trilled on.

Christmas with Rosa: who d'you think you're kidding? The general is going to smile cheerfully while you stroll into a yuletide dreamland with his only daughter? Have you forgotten the scowl on his face when he walked into his house last night and saw you sitting there within reach of his daughter? Don't you remember the way his liver-spotted fist clenched when you started to speak of the assault on Rosa – how it seemed, for just a moment, as if that pensioner-fist was about to explode in your face because yours was the only face within fisting range?

Fuck it, Miller thought. You've survived worse, come this far, to this garden north of Pankow in a country that surrounds itself with walls and invents new ways to fuel its own paranoia. You just might have to include General Reder in your Christmas plans.

It made him smile, the thought of an East German general sitting down to Christmas dinner in the mausoleum in Wolverhampton.

He was still smiling when he heard his name called.

Rosa wasn't smiling, waving to him from an upstairs window, but Miller sensed that she was at least trying to.

He stood beneath the window, felt his heart melt as he looked up at her: a pale-blue towelling dressing gown buttoned up to her neck, the thick, dark hair falling across her bruised face.

'You OK?' *Great line, some Romeo.*

And yet she didn't seem to mind his inadequacy in their personal balcony scene: her face flowered into a full smile.

'It's a lovely morning.'

You make it lovely. But he said, 'There's even a bird singing.'

Her face grew serious. 'Is General Krug still here?' Almost a whisper.

'He left as soon as we got you to bed.' That didn't sound right – but too late now. 'Your father got back after midnight.'

She pushed the hair away from her face and he could see the half-closed eye, the stain of purple on her skin. 'My father is here?'

'He's in the kitchen.' Now they were both whispering. 'A friend is with him – German or Russian, I'm not sure. Dieter – Dieter Jessen, I think.'

Was that sorrow or joy that flashed across her face? Excitement? Or just a cascading jumble of emotions?

'Dieter is here?' No doubting the excitement now. 'Oh, Dieter . . .' Inexplicably, she was crying.

And then smiling.

She closed the window and was gone.

Something of her smile hung in the frosty air above him. And the bird was still singing.

She was in Dieter's embrace when Miller got to the kitchen. She was laughing, crying, leaning back in Dieter's arms, holding his face between her hands. She reached a hand for her father's, turned again to Dieter, kissed his face.

It dawned upon Miller that this was the Dieter who had spirited her to safety from Santiago. This was the Dieter who had failed to save her father, who had comforted her when her mother died in a jeep in the Andes. There was something of the medieval ascetic about him – the pale skin almost translucent, stretched tight over the sharp Slav cheekbones; the face, hollow-eyed, almost cadaverous. And yet, when Dieter laughed, holding Rosa, his features lit up with an infectious warmth. Even a KGB spymaster, Miller thought, can show his heart when he is among people he cares about.

General Reder broke it up.

'Rosa.' He handed her a cup of coffee, spoke gently. 'Can you tell me what happened to you?'

She sipped her coffee. When she lowered the cup the purple stain around her eye seemed to have been made uglier by the heat.

Miller watched her watching him, the other two men.

'I can go, Rosa,' he hesitated, 'if it makes it easier for you.'

He was glad when she shook her head. She touched his hand briefly, motioned for him to sit beside Dieter and her father. Opposite them, alone, she seemed small, fragile.

There was nothing small or fragile about her voice. She told her story simply, without hysterics or exaggeration – almost, Miller thought, as if she were reading an academic paper to a gathering of academic peers. Distance, he told himself, it's a way of putting distance between herself and what she had survived.

Only when she was done did Rosa lower her gaze from the spot above the cooker that she had studied while she told her tale. Only then did she look into Miller's eyes, into the faces of Dieter and her father.

'I know him.' She was trembling now.

'The man who attacked you?'

She ignored her father's question. She was looking directly at Dieter.

'I know him,' she said again. 'That purple mark on his neck – I'll never forget him. Anyway, he took pleasure in reminding me of his name.'

Dieter leaned across the kitchen table, took her hand in his.

'Dover.' His voice a whisper.

Rosa nodded.

'I should have killed him then.'

Rosa shook her head, wiped her eyes.

'We've all had enough killing,' she said.

Miller was remembering the tale she'd told him, how she'd begged this Dieter for Dover's life. *Have we really had enough killing when this maniac is still walking around?*

'There's something else,' Miller said.

The others looked at him, waited.

'This man, Dover – Rosa and I saw him with an Englishman on the night of the jubilee parade. The two of them seemed to be giving orders to a couple of Vopos.' He stopped. Rosa nodded: go ahead.

'An Englishman?' Dieter asked. 'They were speaking English to a pair of Vopos?'

Miller shook his head. 'They were speaking German. I know he's English because—' *what did it matter? He'd told Rosa and the general already knew*. Still, it was difficult to come out with it – 'because I deliver messages for him.' He looked at Rosa. 'In West Berlin.' He looked at Dieter. 'His name is Redgrave.'

Dieter's fine, almost invisible eyebrows arched above the hollow eyes. 'Herr Miller, what an interesting fellow you are turning out to be! An Englishman in the home of General Reder – and you deliver messages for a certain Mr Redgrave, who is not unknown to me and my colleagues.' The words spoken lightly but Miller thought he could detect an edge of menace to Dieter's voice.

'It's nothing, Dieter.' General Reder sounded hoarse. 'Herr Miller is also probably known to you—' a bout of wheezy coughing, 'it's low-key stuff but the papers must have crossed your desk somewhere along the line although you might know Herr Miller under the name of Janus.'

Dieter nodded, warmth in the smile now. 'I have seen the name,' he said. 'It is good to know you, Janus.'

Miller glared at the Russian. *Janus*: so that's what he was called east of the Wall. Janus, the two-headed god of Roman gates and doorways, one head facing east while the other looks west. *It's how you are seen, a fool who's so busy looking both ways that he observes nothing – someone who doesn't know if he's coming or going.*

Miller was angry. He could imagine the jokes made about him and the meaningless messages he carried. He told himself that at least he'd had his suspicions confirmed, that all along he'd been no more than a decoy, a diversion from others on both sides who waged their cold – and deadly – war.

'This amuses you?' he asked Dieter.

Dieter shrugged. 'War is not amusing, not even a cold war, Janus.'

'Patrick!' Fury in Miller's voice.

'I apologize, Herr Miller.'

'Patrick!' Miller took a deep breath. 'Patrick is fine.'

'Patrick.' Dieter held out his hand. 'Shall we shake on that?'

Why not, Miller thought, at least now you know. Dieter's hand in his was warm and strong.

Miller felt Rosa's eyes on them, saw her shake her head.

'Men,' she said. 'Children!'

'I'm inclined to agree with my daughter,' General Reder said.

'Herr Miller, you are owed an explanation and you shall have it – at least as much as I and,' he waited for Dieter's nod of assent, 'Dieter here are able to give you. But first we have other pressing matters to consider, agreed? We have work to do.'

'Agreed, Hans,' Dieter said, 'but we should ask Patrick if he wishes to be here. What we are about is dangerous and it is up to Patrick to decide if he wishes to be part of it.'

'I'm here,' Miller said, 'and,' he looked at Rosa, 'I don't want to be anywhere else.'

His words silenced them. From the garden came the sound of birds, or maybe just the same optimistic fellow warbling away against the arrival of November. For a moment all four of them in the kitchen listened to the winter song. Then, drowning the song, came the rumble of heavy machinery on the road beyond the garden. The rumbling rolled on, trucks, maybe caterpillar tracks, growling their way north.

'They must be sending reinforcements to Wandlitz.' Dieter's voice a whisper. 'With Mielke and Honecker gone, the rest of them will be shivering up there in their luxury villas.'

Wandlitz. Like the rest of the GDR, Miller knew of the fabled compound where the members of the Politburo and the rest of the Party elite were said to live in Western luxury with guards at the gates; like most of the GDR, Miller had never been inside those guarded gates.

'They *should* be scared,' General Reder said, 'locking themselves away behind fences, away from the people.' He shook his head. 'Is it any wonder our country is fighting for its life?'

Rosa tut-tutted loudly, theatrically. 'Papa!' Her voice mocking. 'So much talk!' Her words softened by her smile. 'And they say women . . .'

She left the rest unsaid, got up from the table.

'I'm going to get dressed,' she went on. 'In the meantime

maybe one of my trio of heroes,' another dazzling smile, 'could manage to make a fresh pot of coffee.'

The men looked at one another, listening to Rosa's footsteps padding on the stairs.

'Rosa is right.' General Reder drew a tired hand across his furrowed forehead. 'The time for talking is past.'

'It was past long before now,' Dieter said.

'Not quite.' General Reder and Dieter looked quizzically at Miller. 'Could somebody,' Miller went on, 'please explain to me what's going on and what the hell I'm doing here.'

Dieter stood up, nodded to the general. 'I'll make the coffee, as your daughter commanded,' the faintest of smiles on the ascetic face, 'while you fill Herr Miller in.'

Twenty-eight

Wednesday, 1 November 1989
East Berlin

General Reder began by reminding Miller – and possibly himself – that the German Democratic Republic had just celebrated its fortieth birthday.

'Which was no small achievement, Herr Miller.' A hint of fire in the old soldier's voice, in the faded blue eyes. 'This was a country born out of the ruins of war, and it wasn't even a Germany created by Germans. Nobody dared to say so – even now it's unwise to say so – but this country, this *Germany*, was the creation of our enemy, of the very people who conquered us.'

The general was staring out of the kitchen window but Miller was certain that Reder's eyes saw nothing of the winter garden, that his gaze was fixed upon another time, another place.

'They conquered us and raped us and robbed us of anything of value that was left in this ruined land of ours.' The voice mild, as though Reder were describing how a neighbour had borrowed some garden tools. 'And when they had left us with nothing, they taught us a better way.' The pale blue eyes shifted, blinked, saw Miller sitting in the kitchen. 'There are flaws and weaknesses in a people's democracy, Herr Miller, corruption too, but it's still a better way than the way that gave us fascism, brutes like

Hitler, thugs like Thatcher and Reagan and all the rest of them in their palaces while ordinary people are deluded into thinking that their miserable lives are somehow founded upon personal freedom.' The general laughed.

'Listen to me, I sound like some puffed-up politician! And yet I believe in our country. Of course the Soviets wanted a bulwark here as a buffer against the Americans and their satellites but they did give us a different plan, another way of doing things – another kind of country.' General Reder shook his head, snorted like a horse.

'And we fucked it up, Herr Miller, which is why it's pretty doubtful that this country of ours will be around for another forty years. We have hospitals and schools and universities that are the equal of any in the world, we have jobs for everybody, we,' he licked his thin lips, 'we had it all and those bastards in the Politburo . . .' The mildness had gone: *he'll have a heart attack*, Miller thought. Rosa will come back into the kitchen and hate me for causing her father's death. 'They're no better than the scum who run the capitalist countries of the West.' General Reder was striving for calm. 'They steal from the people, set themselves apart, force our people to spy on one another—'

'Hans.'

Miller had forgotten that Dieter was still in the room.

Dieter smiled at Reder. 'Perhaps Herr Miller does not need to hear all this political philosophy.'

'It's OK.' Miller looked at Dieter. 'You *can* trust me.'

'And who can our people trust now?' Reder's voice was quiet again, his anger faded like the blue eyes. 'Mielke is gone, Honecker is gone and both of them no loss. Who can the people turn to? They're still looking West, hankering for the trinkets of the West – and who can blame them?' He looked at Miller as though expecting an answer.

A time not to answer, Miller thought.

'We have to show the people that there *is* another way.' Reder spread his hands in a gesture of helplessness. 'But why should they believe us if we tell them that a people's republic – a people's *democracy* – can work if we stick to the principles of socialism? There isn't much principle on display in Wandlitz – a compound hidden behind barbed wire and guarded by soldiers with rifles.'

Dieter stood up, went round the table to stand beside Reder's chair.

'Hans.' He laid a hand on Reder's shoulder. 'Have a care.'

'I told you.' Miller could hear the tension in his own voice. 'You don't have to worry about me.'

'Herr Miller knows anyway, Dieter.' Reder smiled. 'Don't you, Herr Miller?'

Miller nodded. *A coup, you're planning a coup. And God help me, I don't condemn you.*

He said nothing.

'See?' Reder looked up at Dieter. 'Herr Miller is no fool. He knows but he says nothing.' He smiled now at Miller. 'Yes?'

'Yes,' Miller said. *And so much for my* Guardian-*fed principles: a fucking coup.*

'When?' Miller asked.

'When the time is right,' Reder said.

Miller nodded. *Soon.*

'What can I do, General?'

'What you *can* do, Herr Miller: write. As I asked you to before.'

Miller almost blushed at the implicit accusation: you haven't written what I asked.

'Use your contacts in your old newspaper. Tell the world that this country is under siege, that Thatcher and the rest of her gang are set upon bringing us to our knees, on wiping out our way of life. And they're in it for what they can steal from us – our streets, our old palaces, our universities, even our trains and our factories. They'll take them over, charge us for using what is ours to begin with – and there are plenty of thieves right here ready to help them with the stealing.'

'Like Hartheim fiddling with our book contracts,' Miller said.

Reder snorted. 'Hartheim is just a petty thief! Who cares about stealing a few books? You have to think big, Herr Miller. Beyond our borders there are capitalists ready to seize our railroads, our harbours, our airports. They'll seize our streets, our hospitals, our apartment blocks.' Reder seemed to slump in his chair. 'It's all about money, Herr Miller, and some of our own people want to get their snouts in the trough along with the capitalist pigs. They're everywhere, in the army, in the police, in the Politburo.' He paused. 'Even in the Stasi.'

Silence settled over the kitchen table. The three men avoided looking at one another, as though afraid they might see in the other faces the carcass of a country dismembered.

Miller broke the silence. 'I'll write as best I can but I don't see how my words can help much. I mean, words in a newspaper?'

'We have to use whatever weapons are to hand.' Dieter's ascetic features seemed more monk-like than ever. 'Sometimes the pen is mightier than the AK47.'

'And it's not just *your* words, Herr Miller.' The general drew himself upright in his chair. 'We have friends in France, in Bonn, in Italy and Spain, friends in newspapers, on radio and television. When the time is right, they will plead our case, ask the people of their own countries to leave us alone while we sort out our affairs.'

'And the Soviet Union? Gorbachev?'

'Gorbachev,' Dieter said, 'has washed his hands of us. Which means the Soviet army will stay in their German barracks.'

'I have to ask,' Miller bit his lip, 'who are "we"?'

Reder and Dieter looked at each other.

'We are a small group from many fields,' Reder said. 'Small but not without influence. We have access to weapons and to power and we love this country.'

'And we have a plan,' Dieter added.

Miller looked into the garden, saw the winter trees, heard the song of the tireless bird. He looked at Reder, at Dieter, saw the marks of war in their furrowed faces, caught the whiff of gun smoke above the kitchen table. *This is your life now: that garden, this kitchen, these men. This country.*

'Why are you telling me all this?' he asked.

'I've known you since before you set foot in East Berlin.' Reder was staring at Miller. 'I was still serving then, heading up army intelligence. I knew you were on your way to Berlin even before the Stasi did.'

'You *knew* I was being sent here?' For a moment Miller was listening to Redgrave and Shearing laying out his future in that lunchtime pub in Putney, their voices rich with the menace of power. 'But how?'

'It was our business to know what British intelligence was up to, Herr Miller. And where Redgrave was concerned,' Reder made a face, 'well, it was never too difficult to find out what he was planning.' He turned to Dieter. 'Was it, Dieter?'

'Redgrave is not a serious opponent.' Dieter waved a dismissive hand. 'Sometimes we knew what Redgrave was going to do even before he knew himself.'

Miller looked at the two men, listened to their shared chuckling.

'I'm glad you find it amusing, gentlemen,' he said. 'Having a giggle at my life.'

'Not you,' Reder said. 'Redgrave. It's hard not to be amused by his so-called intelligence activities.'

'In which I played – am playing – some part that I still don't understand.' Miller was not amused. 'Maybe you can enlighten me.'

'Redgrave thought he was pulling off a great coup by sending you into East Germany,' Reder began. 'An avowed socialist-leaning journalist heads into the badlands behind the Iron Curtain and is welcomed, even celebrated, like others before him. Like the American singer, Dean Reed. Like Paul Robeson, the star of *Porgy and Bess* and a real black Othello, choosing life in our socialist country over the riches of the capitalist West. The trouble was,' Reder's smile was rueful, 'the bureaucrats got hold of you and slung you into an office.'

'I still don't see what Redgrave hoped to get out of it all.'

'As General Reder said, Redgrave is an amateur.' Dieter shrugged. 'An *incompetent* amateur. Maybe he planned to have you renounce socialism after some years and parade you in the media like some born-again capitalist.'

Even Miller smiled. 'You know I was carrying messages – still am.'

'Yes, Herr Miller, we have always known that.'

Miller looked at Reder, at Dieter. He shook his head, let the smile come. '*You* write those messages – I mean, your people do.'

Reder nodded.

'So what's it all about?' Miller couldn't hide his exasperation. 'Why have I spent all these years here?'

The coffee was burbling, popping against the glass dome of the percolator like questions in Miller's brain.

He saw Dieter nod to Reder.

'Redgrave had an important source in East Berlin who was

getting information out to the West. The idea was that you would be a cover for his source – you'd be more obvious, easily identified. And Redgrave had arranged for a more expendable source to feed you with unimportant material from the GDR. Redgrave calculated that we'd harm nobody, just let you and your source get on with carrying your low-grade information since we'd be able to keep an eye on everything.'

Miller stared hard at Reder. 'Redgrave leaked the information that he was sending me to East Germany?'

'Let's say he made it easy for us to find out.'

'But why was I never questioned?'

'Simple, Herr Miller,' Reder said. 'You couldn't give away any answers that we didn't already know. And your commitment to this country was evident. At first, we wondered if your brand of socialism was just a badge of convenience but,' the general shrugged, 'it became clear very soon that you believed in this country, even though you had been forced to come here by the British.'

'You belonged to this country, Herr Miller.' Dieter was pouring cups of coffee; he spoke over his shoulder. 'It was clear that you were one of our own.'

'It was never clear to me where I belonged.' Miller couldn't keep the bitterness out of his voice. 'Yours, Redgrave's. I wanted to be my own man. And yet all these years . . .'

Overhead a door opened and closed. Light footsteps came tripping down the stairs.

'You think your years in the GDR have been a waste of time, Herr Miller?' Reder asked.

The kitchen door opened and Rosa came in. Miller looked at her, at the jet-black hair, still wet from the shower, framing the face he loved.

'No,' he said, 'the years haven't been a waste at all.'

Rosa took the cup of fresh coffee that Dieter offered her and she sat beside Miller. Her smile made him forget about Redgrave.

Almost.

'One other thing,' he said.

'Ask.' Reder patted his daughter's hand.

'Redgrave's "important source".' Miller shut his eyes. It was hard to concentrate with Rosa's thigh next to his own. 'What became of him?'

'I'm still compiling important information for Warwick Redgrave.' It was Dieter's voice that Miller heard.

When he opened his eyes, he saw that Dieter was smiling his monk's smile.

Miller felt Rosa's fingers briefly, furtively, touch his own.

A twisted, twisting road of deceit and manipulation had brought him to a place of warmth, among people who cared for him. People he felt at home with. In that moment Miller felt the absence of his mother. Lady Miller took what comfort she could find in her title, her shining house, her bottles and sparkling crystal; she'd find little to impress in these untitled citizens of a workers' state but maybe, just maybe, she might respond to their natural grace. Wishful thinking, he told himself. Yet the truth was, he missed her.

He was glad when Rosa again put her hand in his – and this time she left it there.

Twenty-nine

Thursday, 2 November 1989
West Berlin

Redgrave took the stool at the counter beside Miller and ordered a beer. He took a long, almost angry pull at his drink, shook his newspaper open on the counter with a kind of violence.

'What on earth are you playing at?' He didn't look at Miller as he spoke.

And good evening to you too, Mr Redgrave.

'Got up on the wrong side of the Wall this morning, did we?'

'I'm not in the mood, Miller.' The African documentary on the TV was being ignored by everyone in the bar but the animal roaring and loud commentary covered their voices. 'You were sent in to do a job but you've apparently decided to join the inmates in the asylum.'

'Maybe I've seen the light.' Miller was puzzled by Redgrave's apparent anger. He wasn't in the mood for Redgrave and his posturing. Rosa had driven him to Pankow station and they'd promised to meet that night.

Which isn't going to work out, Miller thought, unless Redgrave gets a move on and lets me know why he's summoned me to the Zoogarten Bar this evening. He'd been taken aback – although it was no more than normal procedure – when he'd spotted the empty tin on the *Imbiss* window sill on his way to work that morning. The torn strip of newspaper stuffed with artful carelessness into the tin had carried an advertisement offering special weekend prices for Berlin Zoo; the figure 'seven' had been scrawled across the open jaws of a lion.

So, the Zoogarten Bar at seven.

It appeared Redgrave had demanded his presence to deliver some kind of reprimand – but for what? When – if – his apologia for an imperilled GDR appeared in the *Guardian*, Redgrave would go positively apoplectic.

Redgrave was in bureaucratic garb this evening: sober grey suit, restrained silver tie, a flash of double cuff. Miller watched warily as Redgrave snapped open his bureaucrat's attaché case. He had to lean closer as Redgrave began to read, quietly, from the sheet of paper he took from the case.

> Russian President Gorbachev's stated policy is to leave his sometime Soviet satellite states to their own devices. In other words, Gorbachev has made clear that the Soviet Union will not interfere while members of the Eastern bloc establish their own policy and work out their own political future.
>
> This is a remarkable development, one that could not have been foreseen even a few months ago. States such as Hungary and Poland, Czechoslovakia and East Germany may now decide their own future – perhaps not immediately but, barring opposition from within the Soviet Union, at least in the not too distant future.

Miller tried to hide his confusion. On the television behind the bar a bunch of chimpanzees were flailing their arms and screaming excitedly as if they shared Miller's confusion: he'd handed over his article to General Reder only the previous evening, since when – as was perfectly normal – Miller had received neither acknowledgement nor acceptance from the newspaper. So how in God's name was Redgrave now reading – whispering – from the article in the Zoogarten Bar twenty-four hours later?

> Nature, we were told at school, abhors a vacuum. Other forces rush in to occupy the unguarded space. Which is what appears to be happening already in the German Democratic Republic. While the citizens of East Germany are trying to work out their own social and political salvation – witness the church-based demonstrations in Leipzig and other cities; witness also the astonishing dismissals by the East German Politburo of the Head of State, Erich Honecker, and of the head of the much-feared secret police, the Stasi, General Erich Mielke – there are signs that the Western powers are already interfering in the internal democratic procedures of this country. An unknown number of foreign agents provocateurs are said to have been arrested by police at otherwise peaceful protests in East Germany. And rumours are rife that Western powers are funnelling funds to anti-regime groups with the sole purpose of destabilizing the country and shaping East Germany's future government.

'And blah-blah-blah.' Redgrave folded the page, replaced it in his attaché case. 'Have you gone stark raving mad, Miller?'

'Some things need saying.' Even to Miller's own ears it sounded lame.

'And some things do *not* need saying by a foreigner employed at a senior level in an important government agency.'

'Who's to say I wrote it?' You're spouting gibberish, Miller told himself, just like the chimps who were still jumping up and down and squawking on the TV. 'I have a feeling the byline above that piece is "Our Special Correspondent in East Germany".'

'You're pathetic, Miller.' Redgrave glared at him. 'Even if I didn't know it was yours, I can see your fingerprints all over the piece – anybody could.'

'It's called a recognizable style, Redgrave.'

'Everything about you is recognizable, Miller.' Redgrave nodded at the television. 'You're like those chimps. Dangle a banana in front of your "liberal" eyes and you'll scream and shout and cry capitalist mayhem. At least the chimp has the good sense to take the banana and eat it. We gave you a chance when we sent you here, Miller, the chance to make something of yourself. We offered you a big, juicy banana, and you don't have the wit to take it.'

'Maybe I don't like bananas.' *And what the fuck does that mean?*

'Miller, I'm losing patience with you – and so are my superiors. You were sent here to do a job. It's more important than ever right now, when the situation is more . . .' Redgrave paused, searched for a precise word, 'more fluid than it's been for forty years. It's precisely now that you need to remember why you were sent here.'

Miller gestured at the screen. 'What am I, a fucking chimpanzee?'

'You are a man under orders, Miller, always have been.'

'Such orders to be always obeyed? Even when I don't understand them?'

'Especially,' Redgrave said, 'when you don't understand them.'

'What d'you think I am? A fucking Communist?'

'A poor joke, Miller, and a dangerous one.' Redgrave sipped his drink thoughtfully. 'Your UK passport is out of date and you've opted for East German citizenship, right?'

'You should know, Redgrave, it was your idea.'

'Just suppose,' Redgrave said, 'that there is a regime change on the other side of the Wall. Suppose that new regime might not be Eastward-looking, might even be hostile to whatever kind of Soviet Union survives under friend Gorbachev, where d'you think you'd stand with your GDR passport then?'

'Exactly where I'm standing now.' Miller tried to affect a jauntiness he didn't feel. 'Why should anything change?'

'Because,' Redgrave said, 'the new zookeepers might not like their old chimpanzees, they might think their bad habits were too deeply ingrained.'

'I did no more and no less than what I was ordered to do – ordered by you.'

'You're a fool, Miller, just like all the rest of you leftie clowns.' Redgrave was still whispering into the pages of his newspaper but his voice was animated with an edge of enjoyment. 'Let me explain it to you like the *Telegraph* or the *Mail* would. You moved to East Berlin with a touch of fanfare. The authorities didn't exactly greet you with a similar fanfare but they took you to their socialist bosom and gave you important work at the heart of their intellectual apparatus. You repaid them by spying on them, betraying them.' Redgrave turned a page of his newspaper. 'Nobody likes a traitor, Miller.'

'I wrote an account of my so-called recruitment,' Miller said. 'Word for word, all that guff from you and Dr What's-her-name. It's in a safe place. I can tell the truth. My newspaper will publish it.'

'Like they're going to publish this piece of propaganda?' Redgrave tapped the briefcase on the floor with his toe.

'How—' Miller stopped. *Don't give him the satisfaction of asking.*

Redgrave didn't need to hear the question.

'Your girlfriend's father is a leftover dinosaur, Miller, and his communication methods are prehistoric. It's not difficult to intercept whatever he sends out.'

Miller didn't buy it. General Reder, for all his years, was a most modern conspirator, the sort of conspirator whose secret communications were intercepted only when he wished them to be. *So there's someone else beating our drum in the English media; once more I am the decoy.*

He smiled at Redgrave; it didn't feel so bad to be the distraction in a cause you believed in.

The TV chimps were gone. On the small screen a perfectly shaped model was demonstrating how a new cream concealed the non-existent lines in her improbably perfect face.

'Have your friends developed new agencies to hide their preparations for thieving, their looting?' Miller said.

'You can't control an avalanche.' Redgrave shrugged. 'You're talking about those book contracts, right? A few books – nobody gives a damn, Miller.'

'And what about looting the assets of a country? Should anybody give a damn about that?'

On the TV a fellow in a suit was preening himself while he luxuriated in the new car he was cruising in on the autobahn. It wasn't a Trabi.

'Has the old general been telling you fairy tales?' Redgrave had turned on his stool to look directly at Miller. 'What's important is that the country belongs to people who are friends of ours.'

The fellow in the TV car smiled as he shifted the gear lever, his manicured fingers tantalizingly close to the shapely leg of the smiling blonde in the passenger seat.

Miller blinked and the blonde was gone; he saw Rosa's wounded face, her bruised eye. 'Are these "friends of ours" allowed a little attempted rape now and again, just to keep their hand in?'

The look of disgust on Redgrave's face was enough. *He knows*.

'Ask your "associate" with the purple birthmark about his assault on Rosa Rossman,' Miller went on. 'Dover – isn't that his name? Next time you meet up with him to play supervisor with the Vopos, tell him that if he's picked up on the other side of the Wall he's going to face charges of kidnap and attempted rape.'

Redgrave's shoulders drooped. 'Obviously I do not condone such behaviour. You know that.'

'What I know is that you cultivate some strange bedfellows, Redgrave.' Miller looked beyond Redgrave, saw the light rain falling outside, tiny drops glowing like white pearls in the street lights. Berlin was on its way home, on both sides of the Wall. 'These are just people living their lives, Redgrave, or trying to, and it doesn't matter much which side they live on.' He knew from Redgrave's wooden expression that he might as well be talking to the Wall.

Redgrave buttoned his overcoat, picked up his briefcase. 'Do what you're supposed to do, Miller, and we'll make sure that any record of your activities is snow-white. Persil-clean, in fact, as the Yanks used to say about the Germans they'd cleansed of a Nazi past after the last little disagreement. Are you clear?'

'You're scum,' Miller said, 'just like Dover.'

'Remember which side you're on,' Redgrave said. 'And don't forget,' eyebrows raised, 'we have a situation in Wolverhampton also. I'll be in touch.'

Miller watched him pass by the window, an overcoated bureaucrat on his way to the station, maybe a visiting businessman hurrying through the rain to his hotel. He wondered who it was that looked back at him from the mirror under the television. A journalist whose career had been hijacked by grey functionaries of what was called 'British intelligence'? The only offspring of a lecherous father and a drunken mother? Or just someone trying to live his life?

Miller paid, turned up the collar of his anorak as he stepped out into the rain.

Whatever else he was, he was Rosa Rossman's lover and he didn't want to lose her; nor did he want to lose his place, his own place, in this divided city.

Redgrave didn't know it all. *Soon*, General Reder had said in the kitchen of the house in Pankow. This world, this city of softly falling rain, might change in ways that Redgrave and Dover and the forces beyond the night could not imagine.

The rain felt clean on his face and there was a spring in Miller's step. He was heading for the Wall. For home. For Rosa.

Thirty

Friday, 3 November 1989
East Berlin

November in Berlin. Not yet five o'clock but the evening already drawing in under the lowering sky. Collars upturned against the cold in the queue on the East side of the crossing point. Gloved fingers clenching, unclenching. Shoes and boots stomping against the cold.

But quietly.

The border guards looked edgy, their barked commands sharper in the November air. *Grepos,* the Berliners called the border police, to distinguish them from the regular force of Vopos.

Something more than winter in the air, Miller thought. At the front of the queue a backpacker's rucksack was upended on the tarmac and Miller watched as the bag's owner, his pimpled adolescent face reddened by what Miller took to be a mix of indignation, anger and fear, retrieved his scattered belongings while the Grepo urged him to get a fucking move on.

For a moment or two the foot-stomping stopped entirely.

Four Grepos were checking IDs, passports, one-day visas. The windows of the prefab control hut were lit. Although he strained to see, Miller couldn't tell if Heinz-Peter was among the uniforms moving behind the Venetian blinds. Not that it mattered, no messages to carry today. And yet a friendly face – or at least a face that was not unfriendly – would be welcome. Miller couldn't have explained even to himself how he was feeling. When he'd stepped out after work on to Wilhelmstrasse he'd felt suddenly overwhelmed by a sense of unbelonging. Faces of passers-by were alien. Snatches of overheard conversation were hostile. *You know these people, you speak their language like your own*.

And yet he felt suddenly lost, frightened.

He wanted Rosa but Rosa was busy with a postgrad student's thesis consultation.

On the spur of the moment he had decided to go into the West of the city. He needed his old touchstones. There was a small cafe behind the Zoogarten station which occasionally produced baked beans and chips; if you wanted to go the whole hog, the elderly English expat owner might serve you up a fried egg and even a slice of fried bread. It was the kind of dish Miller had been glad to leave behind in the greasy spoons of London; once or twice, in the cafe behind the Zoogarten, he'd watched in fascination as half-cut Brits tucked into the greasy offerings. And yet on the Wilhelmstrasse pavement, outside the offices of the Secretariat for Socialist Correctness in Publishing, while East Berliners eddied around him, Miller had recognized, admitted, his own longing for the greasy taste of home. Maybe tomato ketchup was thicker than socialist water.

So here he was, waiting in the queue, his GDR ID – his *Personalausweis* – ready for inspection by the Grepo. The line was moving again, shuffling slowly forward. He'd have yesterday's *Guardian*, or maybe a two-day-old paper, with his great English repast. He might even find a *Telegraph* in the station kiosk; its homage to all things Tory would remind him why he hadn't resisted Redgrave's blackmail too strongly.

Then he was beside the Grepo, the fellow's hand outstretched for his ID.

The Grepo was of medium height, blue-jawed, keen-eyed. You had to be keen-eyed to be selected for membership of the border police, with its higher pay and better conditions.

Now those keen eyes looked from Miller's ID to Miller himself. The usual, Miller told himself, although the pages of his ID were being examined with seemingly extra care. *Thank Christ I'm not carrying anything*. He concentrated on the hands holding his ID, short stubby fingers, nails gnawed to the quick.

The Grepo folded Miller's ID shut but held on to it. Miller felt himself being scrutinized by those narrowing brown eyes, as though the guard were wondering if he knew Miller, had met him somewhere.

Something seemed to click in the Grepo's mind; Miller saw the pupils grow in the brown eyes, watched – with the first inklings of alarm – as the guard drew from the pocket of his greatcoat a grubby, much-thumbed sheet of paper. The guard unfolded it and half turned from Miller for a better look at the page under the crossing-point floodlights. Over the guard's shoulder Miller got a glimpse of typed names and serial numbers.

A kind of grunt, perhaps of satisfaction, from the Grepo. The stubby fingers refolded the paper, stowed it again in the overcoat pocket. The brown eyes more alert now, their stare hostile.

The Grepo pointed at the control hut with Miller's ID.

'*Bitte?*' Miller tried to sound confident, his hand held out for his identity card.

The guard was having none of it. He nodded towards the hut. '*Jetzt. Schnell!*' Now. Quickly.

The Grepo's hand on his shoulder was firm.

The air in the control hut was clammy with the smell of

paraffin heaters. Naked fluorescent tubes on the low ceiling buzzed like tireless flies.

'Shut the fucking door.' The shirt-sleeved guard at the desk nearest to the door barely looked up from his typewriter.

The corporal at the facing desk laughed. 'You're in Germany, Michi, not in fucking Greece, put your fucking tunic on.'

The guard called Michi grunted but went on tapping slowly at the keys.

The corporal looked at Miller, went back to the handwritten pages of the book on his desk, some kind of ledger, maybe a log.

A finger in the back prodded Miller towards the captain standing beside an untidy desk in the corner. The captain's tunic hung unbuttoned, a cigarette smoked in one hand, his other hand held a sheaf of papers. Between his chin and shoulder was clenched a telephone into which he was talking quietly.

'Right,' he said. The captain looked at Miller over the shoulder-held phone. 'Right. Goodbye.' He replaced the phone amid the shoals of paper on the overwhelmed desk.

'What have you got for me, Sergeant?'

He handed Miller's ID to the captain.

Once more Miller felt himself inspected, his face compared to the mugshot on the ID card. He felt the sweat trickle between his shoulder blades, knew it wasn't just from the clammy heat in the hut. Smoke trailed from the cigarette hanging from the captain's lips; he stifled a cough as he trawled with both hands in the sea of paper on his desk.

'Gotcha.' He sounded almost amused as he flourished a single typed page. 'Today's list.' A glance at the list, another at Miller's ID. 'Thank you, Sergeant, you can go.'

Another 'Fuck' from Michi as the door was opened and the bitter November evening burst in.

'Oh, shut it, Michi.' The captain laughed.

Miller didn't feel like laughing. The sweat between his shoulder blades felt like ice.

'You are Herr Patrick Miller?'

Miller nodded.

The captain waved the ID card. *'Haben Sie auch einen Reisepass?'* Do you have a passport as well?

Relief flooded Miller: an extra check on those – not so many – who hold not only an ID card but also a passport. He fumbled with gloves, with the zip of his anorak, drew out the black-covered *Reisepass* from an inside pocket.

Another mugshot, another comparison.

The captain laid the passport sideways against the overflowing ashtray on his desk. 'I am instructed, Herr Miller, to retain your passport.' He handed Miller his ID card, nodded. 'You are free to go.'

'But what – why . . .' Miller looked at the captain, at his passport propped uncertainly beside the cigarette butts. 'I need my passport, Captain.'

'You have your ID card, Herr Miller, like every other citizen.' No humour in the voice now. 'It is all you need for travel within the German Democratic Republic.' The captain drew on his cigarette. His next words came veiled in breathy smoke. 'Today you are not permitted to enter West Berlin.'

You learned quickly how fruitless it was to argue, to plead.

'And my passport?'

'You will be contacted, Herr Miller, in due course.' The captain hooked his foot round a chair leg and dragged it closer.

Miller watched him flop into the chair and pick up the phone.

You learned also when you no longer existed.

He felt the eyes following him as he stepped out of the hut

into the Berlin night. He waited until he heard Michi spluttering about 'the fucking door' before he drew it shut behind him. It was, he knew, a petty, meaningless gesture.

The Grepos gave him only a cursory look as they went on with their inspection of identity cards, visas, backpacks. Those waiting in line looked at him more keenly as he made his way back into East Berlin.

Fucking Redgrave. Or was it Dover?

Thirty-one

Saturday, 4 November 1989
East Berlin

Rosa phoned at about nine on Saturday morning. 'Please come,' she said to Miller. 'Papa wants you to.' A tinkling laugh. 'So do I.'

General Reder had already left by the time Miller got to the house in Pankow. The general had left a note, written in a neat hand, the envelope formally addressed to Herr Patrick Miller:

> Dear Herr Miller,
>
> I have to be away for a short while, possibly for longer than the weekend. In view of my daughter's recent experience I'd appreciate it if you could stay at my house during my absence.
>
> With thanks,
> Yours faithfully,
> Hans Reder (General, Retd.)

'My father is a bit of a Prussian,' Rosa said when Miller handed her the note. 'But he's also sharp and he's also kind. He's telling us both that you don't have to sneak around here while he's away.'

They were in the kitchen again, the room bright with watery

November sun. Miller touched the yellowing bruise around her eye.

'He trusts me to take care of you,' Miller said. 'I hope I don't let him down.'

'I can take care of myself, Patrick.'

He heard the anger in her voice, saw the honeyed South American skin darken.

'I know, I didn't mean . . .' Miller stopped. *Who am I to protect you from Dover and his like?*

They were sitting side by side at the kitchen table. She laid her hand on his.

'What's wrong?' she said. 'Tell me.'

He told her how they'd taken his passport from him the day before.

'They were waiting for me, my name was on a list.' Miller was whispering. He reached behind him, turned the radio on loud, turned the dial until military music almost drowned his words. It was the general's house but you never knew. 'They were waiting for me,' he said again.

Rosa took his hand, led him out into the winter garden.

'Papa could sort it,' Rosa said, 'or—'

'Or Dieter,' Miller said. 'The creator of Janus.' He looked at Rosa, longed to ask, knew he mustn't.

She could read him anyway. 'Papa didn't tell me where he was going and Dieter hasn't been here for days.' She leaned closer to Miller. 'But he's been on the phone to Papa, I'm sure he's still in Germany.'

Still in Germany. Miller didn't know what the general and Dieter were up to. And yet he *did* know. Assignations inside or outside barracks. Instructions to or from men in uniform, men with braid on their collars, insignia on their epaulettes. Maps to be consulted, timetables checked. And weapons too.

Whatever dream the general and Dieter and their unknown conspirators harboured, Miller knew it would not be born without weeping. And of weeping he'd had enough. The house in Compton had shed enough tears for a lifetime.

But still, what could you do but dream? How could you not dream when Rosa took your hand and said, 'Dance with me, Patrick Miller'? The military march had finished, the strains of the 'Blue Danube' floated through the morning air from the kitchen. He took her in his arms and they giggled as they waltzed inexpertly on the grass.

The ground beneath their feet began to shake violently and they both knew it wasn't from the rhythm of Strauss's music. They stopped their spinning, stood staring at each other, listening to the rumble of heavy machinery on the road beyond the garden. They knew it for what it was: military on the move, trucks, maybe tanks, heading for the Politburo compound at Wandlitz again.

Rosa shivered. She led him inside without speaking.

No bird sang in the winter garden.

Sunday, 5 November 1989
East Berlin

Sunday morning, the trees bare under the low winter sky. Somewhere in the leafless branches over their heads a rook cawed.

'He sounds lonely,' Miller said.

Rosa looked at him, said nothing. Miller saw the way she walked with arms folded under her breasts, the way her body seemed to lean forward into the chill air, searching for purchase.

She'd barely spoken since they'd left the house, walking along the winding road. Miller knew that her mind was wandering some other road where he couldn't reach her. He sensed that he shouldn't try to reach her but his own loneliness was too hungry.

The bird cawed again, hoarse, yearning.

'Maybe it's a she,' Miller said.

She didn't smile at his attempted joke, just half turned her face to him, half raised the dark eyebrows.

'Sorry,' she said.

'No,' Miller said. 'I'm just happy to be with you.'

All morning she'd seemed absent, withdrawn into some shadowed corner of herself. When he'd reached for her in her narrow bed in the early morning, he'd felt her go rigid under his touch, sensed the way she'd seemed to shrivel into the mattress. 'Please, Patrick.' The words gulped into his shoulder and he'd sensed the terror of that windowless, stinking room, Dover's breath on her uncovered body. Delayed shock, he told himself, but what did he know? Have you forgotten the smell – the *taste* – of shame in the private surgery of Dr Roger Miller? *The deed another's, the shame yours?*

He'd held her close in the early-morning gloom. Even in the silence he knew that her terror was still awake beside him in the narrow bed.

The coffee that he brought her was left untouched on the locker beside the bed.

When she came downstairs, her skin innocent from the shower, her dark hair shining and lustrous, he wanted to tell her she looked more beautiful than ever but he held his tongue. He fried some boiled potatoes he'd found in the fridge, cooked an omelette, coaxed her to eat a little.

A walk, he'd said, when she moved back from the barely touched food, a walk might do them good. He might have said more, might have dribbled on like his mother, but he saw the emptiness in her bruised face and told himself to shut up. As in a trance she put on a duffel coat, a red woollen scarf; she sat on the bottom step of the staircase and drew on the black knee-high boots that closed around the black trousers, flexed her fingers in the leather gloves. There had been a sadness in the smile she gave him, standing in the hallway inside the front door, waiting for him to tell her it was time to go. *You have to give her space but you have to let her know she's not alone, that no wall divides you.*

'Baked beans and chips,' Miller said now.

A pause in her stride, a small frown.

'I just got a longing for them – that's why I was going to West Berlin when they took my passport.'

'Baked beans?' She stopped, arms still folded, staring at him.

'You know, beans in a tin, lathered in tomato sauce, sweet as sugar, haute cuisine for the English working classes.'

'Yuk.' But she was smiling.

'Best enjoyed in one of England's greasiest greasy spoons.'

'A greasy spoon?'

'A superior London caff. Fatty food obligatory. Uncleaned tables normal. Crumbs and slops from previous customers supplied free of charge.' Her face wreathed in a smile now. 'Tea poured from huge, swan-necked kettles, too bad if you don't like milk in your tea.'

Rosa laughed. 'And this is what you yearned for?'

'I can't explain it. A sort of beans-and-chips longing just seemed to overwhelm me.' He stood close to her in the middle of the road. 'All these years I've been here I've hardly missed the place, I came to think of here as home and,' he swallowed, 'since I met you it feels more like home than ever. But,' he looked at Rosa, at the winter trees, 'it was a very real feeling. Imagine, chips and baked beans!'

Something unfroze in her. She unfolded her arms, reached her hand for his.

'It's all this uncertainty, this not knowing. It's natural to reach out for what we know best.'

They walked on, closer now, hips touching.

He figured the question wouldn't bother her, took a chance on asking. 'D'you ever think about home – I mean, the home where you were a little girl?'

'Santiago is always with me.' He felt the pressure of her hand, was glad he'd asked. 'Always, but this is home now and,' she hesitated, 'I'm worried about my father, he hasn't phoned.'

'He doesn't trust the phones,' Miller said, 'and he did say he might be away for longer than the weekend.'

'He's not young any more,' Rosa said, 'and we both know that wherever he is, whatever he's doing—'

'Yes,' Miller said. They both knew that General Reder was playing a dangerous game. 'We just have to accept that he knows what he's doing, he's a soldier who has lived through dangerous times.'

Ahead of them a small convoy came round the bend in the road, led by a military jeep. The jeep slowed, then stopped as it came abreast of them. Behind the jeep a grey military lorry and a Stasi van came to a halt.

The army captain in the passenger seat of the jeep eyed Miller and Rosa warily.

'What are you doing out here?'

Miller could hear the unspoken words: *in the vicinity of Wandlitz.*

It was Rosa who answered. 'I live nearby.'

The captain glanced at the ID she handed him.

'Frau Rossman.' A hint of a smile on the captain's face as he read out Rosa's name. 'And you live nearby with . . .' A questioning look at Miller.

'With my father, General Reder,' Rosa cut in.

'Ah, General Reder.' The captain's face inscrutable, he might have been saying what the time was. He returned the ID card to Rosa, turned to Miller. 'And you are?'

'Patrick Miller.'

'Ah, Herr Miller.' The captain barely looked at Miller's ID. As though my name is not unknown to him, Miller thought.

'My advice to you,' the captain said, 'is to find another road for your Sunday-morning stroll.'

The dark eyes, almost hidden beneath the captain's cap, gave away as little as the bland, speaking-clock voice. A gloved finger to his cap, a nod to the driver, and the jeep pulled away.

Rosa put her hand in Miller's as the lorry followed, then the familiar Stasi van. She looked at Miller when the convoy had passed out of sight round the next bend.

'You noticed?'

'He recognized both our names,' Miller said.

'You'd expect him to know Papa's name.'

'But you'd wonder how and why he knows the name of Patrick Miller.' He looked at the bend round which the convoy had disappeared. 'I'm on a list, Rosa.'

'Maybe it's a friendly list, Patrick.'

'And maybe not.

'We just don't know,' Rosa said. She tried to smile. 'At least we know where we are.'

'Yes,' Miller said, 'where we were told not to be.'

He put his arm round her and they began to retrace their steps along the twisting road.

Monday seemed to Miller like a day spent in no-man's-land. He was glad to be with Rosa but he missed the familiar touchstones of his own flat. There was nowhere else he wished to be yet he felt literally stateless without the comfort of his passport.

'Don't worry, Papa will know what to do,' Rosa said.

There was no word from General Reder. Nor from Dieter. Their absence, their continuing silence, seemed to fill the house. Rosa was looking out of the sitting-room window but Miller felt sure that she was seeing little of the winter garden. She touched her swollen face, gingerly.

'They both know what they're doing,' Miller said. We speak now only in whispers, he thought; we are afraid not only of what others might hear but of what we ourselves may hear from our own tongues.

Rosa said nothing, nodded to him from the window.

Soon, the general had said. But 'soon' was not enough now. Miller needed more than 'soon'; for good or ill he had thrown in his lot with General Reder and he was entitled to know how and where and when his ass might be on the line.

The ugly American phrase reminded him of Dover and the assault on Rosa. He reached for her hand, saw how the discoloured skin darkened when she smiled tentatively at him.

'We should go to the hospital,' Miller said, 'and let the doctor take a look at you again.'

She shook her head. He knew it was pointless to ask again.

'Then come with me to the office,' he went on, 'I need to check a couple of things.'

He knew that she could guess that there was nothing that needed checking at the office – she'd heard him phoning Hartheim to say that he'd been asked by General Reder to keep an eye on his property for a few days – but she nodded again. Maybe, Miller thought, she needs to get out of the house too.

Rosa drove. It was lunch hour, the streets of East Berlin seemed almost deserted. The car put-putted along to its usual Trabi soundtrack. The low sky seemed to hang close above them, heavy with the promise of snow. For all the quietness of the roads, what traffic there was seemed slow-moving, as though the drivers were on edge, fearful of making a hasty or unexpected move.

It seemed to Miller that the whole city – drivers, pedestrians, traffic police – was waiting, as if the changes in the Politburo, especially the departures of Honecker and Mielke, had left Berliners holding their breath. Snow was not the only threat in the air.

They were close to Wilhelmstrasse when he felt Rosa's hand rest lightly on his thigh.

'Do you *really* want to go to your office, Patrick?' Her touch was electric; they'd held each other in the night but they hadn't made love. 'Or would you prefer just to have a coffee together?'

He loved this street of tall, gracious houses but the thought of further explanations to Hartheim was not appealing.

He laughed. 'As you wish,' he said and she took the next left and he knew where they were heading. ZERO seemed unchanged. The same black decor, the same punkish students sucking on cigarettes, clouds of tobacco smoke clinging to the low ceiling. The same loud music and insistent rhythm, the turning of heads, the frank examination of Rosa and himself as they entered the premises. And yet, within minutes of sitting at a cigarette-scarred table, Miller knew that ZERO too had changed. A couple of students stopped Rosa as she was returning from the counter with two beakers of coffee; he saw the animation in their faces as they spoke to her; he thought he saw apprehension in their expressions as they turned to stare at himself.

'Everyone's nervous,' Rosa said as she sat beside Miller.

Was there an edge of tension in the mixed jumble of competing conversations? Miller felt it, said so to Rosa.

'Everyone's waiting,' Rosa said.

'We're all waiting, Rosa.'

'Yes.' The word hung in the cigarette smoke.

'Yes,' Miller said, 'but for what?'

Thirty-two

Tuesday, 7 November 1989
East Berlin

Darkness was falling on Tuesday evening when, unannounced, General Reder came home. To Miller the little general seemed shrunken; he looked, in Rosa's embrace, like a child that she might carry off to an early bed.

'Thank you, Herr Miller.' The general shook hands with Miller in the most formal of German manners. 'Thank you for helping as I asked.'

'*Bitte schön.*' Miller was equally formal. 'I'm glad I was able to help you and Rosa.'

'Thank you again.'

They were in the sitting room. General Reder lowered himself, almost painfully, on to the dark leather sofa and Rosa fussed, picking up his overcoat, kneeling beside him to remove his shoes and slip a pair of house shoes on his small feet. The general accepted her attentions as a patient might a nurse's. Yes, he told her, a cup of tea would be good.

'I'll make it.' Miller went to the kitchen, prepared the tea, set the tray. He saw himself reflected in the darkening window, the tray in his hands: *and this old man with the years carved in his face is going to lead this country to a new tomorrow?*

'You look tired, Papa.' Rosa was sitting on the carpet at the general's feet; she smiled at Miller as he entered with the tray. 'You've been travelling all these days?'

'I've been travelling, Rosa.' The voice tired, as if the voice itself were still on a long journey.

'To . . .' Rosa hesitated, looked at Miller. 'To many places, Papa?'

A tired smile, an inclining of the balding head.

Once more Rosa caught Miller's eye: they both knew that it was pointless to pry further.

'Oh, Papa!' Exasperation in Rosa's words, but fear too: all day the nearby road had rumbled under the wheels of trucks and jeeps and tanks.

Reder leaned forward on the sofa, stroked his daughter's long, dark hair.

'Everything will be OK,' he said.

Miller put the tray down on a low coffee table. 'And everything will be *soon*, General?' His words whispered but urgent too.

The noise of the key turning in the hall door stalled any reply; all three waited, listening to the footsteps approaching in the hallway.

The door opened quietly and Dieter stood there, dark coat unbuttoned, black gloves in his hands, his face pale, gaunt. Reder rose from the sofa, suddenly energetic, and Miller and Rosa watched as the two men embraced in the open doorway.

'All is well?' Reder asked.

The monkish head nodded, something like a smile on the thin lips. 'And with you?'

'All is well,' the general answered.

Rosa crossed the room. Dieter touched her face with his long, thin fingers. 'And with you, Rosa?' His fingers close to her bruised face. 'You are strong again?'

Rosa shrugged. 'I'll live.'

'Good. In any case,' Dieter's voice low, looking at the general, 'your father and I need to talk now.' He shrugged, half smiled. 'Privately.'

'Please, Dieter.' Rosa took his hand, her voice as low as Dieter's. 'If we could talk to you now – we need your help, Patrick and I. Maybe you can help us – I mean you and Papa.'

Miller watched the two older men exchange a glance.

'I know nothing,' General Reder said. 'I just got here.'

'Not here,' Dieter whispered. 'You never know – we're too close now.' He pointed at the window, smiled. 'Coats, outside.'

Miller hurried to get coats in the hallway. Rosa helped the general back into his leather greatcoat.

Almost sheepishly, all of them trooped out of the back door into the darkened garden. In the light spilling through the kitchen window their faces looked pale, tense.

'What is it, Rosa?' The general was standing beside Rosa; he took her hand in his.

'Will you . . . ?' Rosa looked at Miller.

Miller shook his head. 'You tell it.'

In the end they told it together. It didn't take long: a few words to describe the scene at the Wall crossing point, the confiscation of Miller's passport.

'I'm sure it was Redgrave's doing,' Miller said. 'He'd already threatened me, warned me what my life would be like in a different world if certain files were exposed.'

'Not just his own files on you,' Dieter said. 'The danger to you, Patrick, lies in the Stasi files in Normannenstrasse and in how they might be used against you by Redgrave – by your own side. If I were Redgrave, I'd have already compromised you in some way. All it would take is a note or memo in the Stasi files showing that you've delivered some information, however unimportant, to the regime here in East Germany – that you destroyed the country of your birth as well as your adopted country.'

Miller was stunned. 'But how – why?'

'The *how* is easy. You think Redgrave is without a conduit to Normannenstrasse? And putting something in there is not as difficult as getting something out.' Again the thin smile. 'As to the *why*, it's what we do in my world, Patrick, the way we control our assets.'

Words failed Miller. This glimpse into Dieter's world – Redgrave's world – revealed a corrupt darkness deeper than any at the top of the surgery stairs. But he also knew he should have expected it.

'If the Americans and the British succeed in toppling the GDR,' Dieter went on, 'one of their prime targets will be the huge cache of files in Normannenstrasse. For two reasons, first to protect their own assets identified by the Stasi – these assets may need protection, they may even have continuing value so it's going to be important that their identities are not exposed.' Dieter paused, looked around the darkening garden as if listening.

'And the second reason?' Miller prompted.

'People like you,' Dieter said. 'Any so-called traitors exposed in the files will be at risk. We all know,' he looked quickly at Rosa, 'that the Americans like to punish those they see as their enemies. It's not always obvious – sometimes a traffic accident, a sudden heart attack, a fatal dose of food poisoning. If the Americans ever get on your case, Patrick, the best you can expect is to be allowed to go on living while you do what you're told. And Redgrave will simply follow American instructions. Can you see yourself as a convert who has seen through the very heart of socialism and now writes propaganda for the right-wing press?'

'And that's what *you* would do, Dieter?'

'I'm sorry, Patrick. I'm just telling you the truth about my world.'

Miller shivered; the darkness had grown icy cold.

'Can you help us, Dieter? Patrick and I . . .' Rosa didn't finish but Dieter and her father both knew that she was speaking of a life she might share with Miller. 'What are we going to do?'

The Slav cheekbones seemed to sharpen, the thin lips almost formed a smile. 'We're going to steal those files,' Dieter said.

General Reder broke the silence that fell upon the circle.

'Dieter, we haven't time for this. It's the seventh of November, our plans—'

'We have time, Hans,' Dieter said. 'I have contacts inside Normannenstrasse who may be able to lift the files for us.'

Miller was watching them closely. *Soon*, the general had told him: the sound of marching feet, of growling tanks, of gunfire in the German air.

'So "soon" is almost here, General?' Miller asked.

General Reder nodded.

'But we have time to do just this first,' Dieter said. 'We'll have to lift those files tomorrow night or the night after.'

On Wednesday Dieter said there was a slight problem. He had three 'live' contacts in Normannenstrasse but one was in hospital, one was on honeymoon and the third had decided to join the throng in the West German embassy in Budapest. The usual thin smile, his hand on Miller's shoulder. 'Don't worry, it's on for tomorrow night, the ninth. I know someone who will open a door. He'll open it because he has no choice.'

Dieter had been gone all day; so had General Reder. They'd left separately, returned separately, then closeted themselves in the general's study for an hour. Only silence issued from behind the closed study door.

The TV carried news of further resignations from the Politburo. New appointments followed, fresh promises, new plans to keep the citizens of the GDR happy. From Leipzig came the promise of more candle-lit vigils. Like predators circling a wounded animal, the protesters were growing more daring. Concerned citizens across the land promised more candles, more marches.

Miller wondered about Redgrave's plans, Herbert Dover's plans – for Berlin, for the rest of the German Democratic Republic.

Soon, General Reder had said.

Tomorrow night, a break-in at Normannenstrasse, Dieter had told him when he'd surfaced from General Reder's study. And he knew someone who'd open a door in Normannenstrasse because 'he has no choice'.

His own choices, Miller knew, had also run out.

Thirty-three

Thursday, 9 November 1989
West Berlin

'It's for you, Herr Redgrave.'

Redgrave looked with distaste at the large-chested German woman who handed him the phone. *Herr* Redgrave indeed. In these Wilmersdorf offices of the service – in the *British* sector of Berlin – one might reasonably expect not to be addressed in the German style.

'Yes?' He couldn't quite keep the irritation out of his voice. Three rooms, a middle-aged civil servant on secondment from Whitehall and a pair of well-padded German matrons in twinsets didn't constitute much of a secretariat for Redgrave's organization in Berlin.

'Yes?' he said again into the phone.

'It's me.'

'Ah.' His conversations with Dr Pamela Shearing were often satisfyingly monosyllabic; they were never more than brief and to the point.

'Something you should know and probably act upon.'

'Yes?'

'Our cousins are said to be arranging to collect some excess paper tonight from Norman's storage facility and you might like to pop along and pick up our own material.'

'You're sure of this?' Redgrave turned his back to Brunhilde – it was his generic name for all large-busted, blond-helmeted German women of a certain age – and inwardly cursed again the failure of Her Majesty's Government to supply the Berlin secretariat with sufficient accommodation to ensure privacy.

'As sure as we can be,' Dr Shearing said.

If Dr Pamela Shearing said it was so, then it was so: the Yanks were going to try to spirit some files out of Normannenstrasse tonight.

'Our friend from the white cliffs?'

'The very same,' Dr Shearing said.

'Thank you,' Redgrave said.

He heard the click of the receiver being replaced in London, handed his own phone to Brunhilde: at least make the Frauen work for the generous salaries paid to them by Mrs Thatcher and Her Majesty.

So Herbert 'white cliffs' Dover was planning an excursion to Normannenstrasse. The American was a loose cannon: one moment he's attempting to rape a general's daughter, the next he's raiding Stasi HQ. All the same, Redgrave reflected, the fellow could be devastatingly effective.

Redgrave crossed the landing, looked into the tiny office where the Whitehall secondee was, as usual, engrossed in the records of the costs of running the secretariat.

'We solvent today, Percy?'

Percy Palmer, low-grade Whitehall secondee, gave Redgrave his usual frightened look. 'Yes, sir.'

'Good show. You couldn't locate some extra legal tender for us to hire more space and more bodies to keep the show on the road?' *Like the blasted Yanks, a whole army of personnel – even cooks! – over at their intelligence HQ in Tempelhof.* 'Even a few tenners might help.'

'No, sir.' Percy smiled sheepishly.

'Carry on.'

Truth was, Redgrave didn't dislike Percy Palmer. He wasn't a *complete* liability, and the overseas allowance helped pay to keep Percy's eight-year-old boy at some prep school that nobody had ever heard of.

'Any calls for me,' Redgrave said, 'you take them.'

'Sir.'

Salt-of-the-earth, Redgrave thought, not like that prig Miller he'd sent into East Berlin all those years ago. Fellow seemed to have gone completely native over there. He'd be cooling his heels for a while now, without his passport, with crossing restrictions against his name.

Redgrave dismissed Miller from his thoughts, started down the flights of stairs. One of the unintended benefits of the under-funding of Her Majesty's service in Berlin was that one couldn't afford an office with a lift; the high and narrow stairs in the Wilmersdorf building helped keep you in shape.

Redgrave's mind was also in shape. If the Yanks were set on raiding the files in Normannenstrasse, then things were close to breaking point in East Berlin. The Yanks weren't the only ones who needed to remove files, protect sources – and conceal evidence of collusion with a Politburo that was being rapidly dismantled.

In the event of the collapse of the GDR, God alone knew what chaos might ensue. Gorby might sulk on the sidelines but Kohl, Chancellor of West Germany, might decide to take matters into his own hands. Or Thatcher might decide to pull another Falklands stunt. The only certainty you could entertain was that, as usual, the French didn't count.

One *could* count on Herbert Dover: an excursion to Normannenstrasse meant that something was brewing. Herbert

Dover didn't know it but Redgrave intended to be there to share in the brew.

Redgrave stepped out into the street of tall, imperial houses. The air was chill, the Berlin sky low and heavy but snow had not fallen yet. Redgrave checked his watch. Ten minutes after noon, time to grab a bite before presenting himself to Dover. He was looking forward to seeing the expression on the American's face.

Dieter Jessen thought General Hans Reder's idea was simply too risky. Rosa was frightened by the general's suggestion.

'Please, Hans.' Dieter spoke softly, almost plaintively. 'Getting involved in this could jeopardize our plans completely. Suppose something goes wrong and both of us get picked up – who's going to coordinate our larger plans?'

It was mid-afternoon; the house in Pankow had been electronically swept that morning so they were speaking indoors.

'And it's too dangerous for you, Papa.' Even Rosa didn't dare tell General Reder that he was too old, too feeble, to play a part in Dieter's break in to Normannenstrasse.

'I can be useful,' General Reder said. 'I can keep lookout. If we're questioned, I can speak with the authority of a general of the People's Army.'

'And if a general of the army is arrested in the course of a treasonable raid . . .' Dieter left the rest unsaid. Even Patrick Miller, listening, saying little, stateless Englishman at large, knew that the penalty for treason would be death – and what Gorbachev or Kohl or any other foreigner might say would count for nothing.

'I have cancer,' Reder said, 'or have you all forgotten? Another month, another year – I want to do what I can while I can.'

'But without you, Hans—'

'Without me, Dieter, our group will go on and can still succeed. You saw our leaders the other night in Dresden – d'you think such men need an old man to lead them?'

'Even so, Hans—'

'I'm going with you, Dieter.' In Reder's easy, determined words Miller felt he could hear the voice of the tank commander who had fought – and survived – against impossible Soviet odds on the eastern front. 'Nobody expects us,' Reder went on. 'Surprise is on our side. We'll be in and out with Herr Miller's files,' he glanced at Miller, at Rosa, 'and those crooked bastards in Normannenstrasse won't even know we've been there.'

His words produced silence. The four of them were seated around the kitchen table: somehow this small, functional room with its domestic machines and cooking utensils had become their war chamber.

'Then I'm going with you, Papa.'

Rosa's words seemed to galvanize the three men into a flurry of speech.

'No.' The protest simultaneously voiced by General Reder and Miller.

Rosa turned to Dieter. 'Tell them,' she said.

Miller saw the look they exchanged, knew that Rosa was reminding the Russian of their flight from Santiago, their journey across the Andes, her mother's stony grave in the mountains. *I survived that,* she was telling Dieter, *I can help in this.*

'We don't need to doubt Rosa,' Dieter said. 'She and her father stay in the car to keep watch. Two pairs of eyes, after all, are better than one. We,' he looked at Miller, 'will go in together. If my information on Patrick's file is not accurate, then both of us may have to do some searching in the stacks.'

Dieter had gone out at dawn and returned by noon with the information that Miller's file was stored in the British section, in the basement of Block 5; Dieter's 'associate' – a Stasi quartermaster – would be on duty by 4 p.m. The quartermaster would himself open the door – or have the door left open – to the basement at 6 p.m.

'Agreed, Hans?'

'Agreed, Dieter.' You had to know when the negotiating was over, Reder thought. Colonel Kulakov had taught him that in the wastes of the Ukraine, in the ruins of Berlin in 1945.

'We leave at five.' Dieter, they all knew, had assumed command. 'And no weapons.' He was looking at Reder.

The general nodded. The Walther pistol would go unnoticed in the pocket of his greatcoat. 'No need for guns,' he said.

'None whatever.' Except for my Makarov, Dieter thought: *the best-laid plans . . .*

Miller was scared but elated. He had the sense that he was in the presence of some defining moment in the life of this embattled, fucked-up country. He sensed that across East Germany men and women would be watching clocks, checking weapons, holding their breath. Something was about to happen and though neither Reder nor Dieter had offered anything more concrete than 'soon', Miller was certain now that whatever was going to happen would do so in the next few days.

'Lunch!' Rosa, deliberately breezy, broke the tension. 'We need to eat.'

'Five o'clock,' Dieter reminded them. 'We leave for Normannenstrasse at five.'

Dover pulled the door open as far as the chain would allow. He saw Redgrave outside, said, 'Fuck,' closed the door again.

He left it closed. It was Dover's idea of a joke.

He waited until Redgrave tapped urgently on the door – twice, a third time – before he unloosed the chain and opened the door. Redgrave's face was white with anger.

'Leaving me standing like that – anyone might see me.' Redgrave stepped past Dover, surveyed the American's new bolt-hole. The one-room flat in Marzahn was like any other worker's flat in East Berlin.

'I don't want to see you,' Dover said. 'What the fuck are you doing here?'

Redgrave took his time, took stock of the flat. A kitchenette area with a two-ring cooker, a table and two kitchen chairs, a sofa that opened out into a bed. *It wasn't fair, the way the Yanks could source and pay for god knows how many places on both sides of the Wall.*

'You should have told me,' Redgrave said. He pulled out one of the chairs, sat at the small table. 'I'm going with you.'

'Told you *what*? Going *where*?'

'You know what and you know where.' Redgrave pushed with a dainty finger at the empty greasy container of currywurst on the table. 'Your housekeeping skills leave something to be desired.'

'Fuck the housekeeping skills.' But for all his bluster, Dover couldn't conceal his dismay. *Redgrave knew*. Once in a while the lame-duck Brits actually managed to find out something; it was Dover's bad luck that somehow they'd found out – or been told of – his plan to liberate a truckload of files from Normannenstrasse that very night.

'OK,' Dover said.

'OK, what?'

'You can tag along, just don't get in my way.'

'You know perfectly well that it's not my habit to get in

anybody's way.' Redgrave sniffed. 'I ought to be offended by the mere suggestion of such behaviour.'

Dover allowed himself a smile. Redgrave sometimes sounded like a goddamn poof but he could take care of himself.

Radio music came from the adjoining flat: loud, sentimental *Schlagermusik*. Redgrave cocked his head, listening.

'It's no problem.' Dover shook his head. 'Just a middle-aged factory hand feeling sorry for himself 'cos he hasn't been laid for too long.'

'Your neighbour has seen you?'

'What does it matter? When I leave here, I'm not coming back again.'

Next door the music got louder.

'And when do we leave?'

'About six. I have to pick up some transport.' Dover looked sharply at Redgrave. 'How did you get here?'

'I crossed at Bornholmerstrasse and caught a bus. The guards were edgy – lots of shouting and pushing.'

'This whole country is edgy,' Dover said. 'The old guard are being knocked down like ninepins – not that changing the faces in the Politburo is going to change much. This pinko shithole of a country is going down the pan in the not so distant future.'

'How elegantly you put it.'

'In our business,' Dover said, 'it's not elegance that counts but results.'

'Quite.' Redgrave poked the greasy food container to the furthest edge of the little table. Best not to irritate Dover; it was important to get his hands on those Stasi files and he needed the American for that.

'Results,' Dover said again, 'that's the name of our game.'

'So we leave at six.' It's only three o'clock, Redgrave was thinking; three hours in *this*.

'Pretty grim, Redgrave, putting up with this set-up for a few hours, isn't it?' Dover gave a dry laugh. 'We'll go pick up our wheels and then head for the Alamo – we're expected there at eight p.m.'

'We're expected?'

'We sure are,' Dover said. 'At eight o'clock my reliable and well-paid Stasi associate will be rolling out the red carpet for old Herbert Dover – all the way to the secrets of Block Five of Normannenstrasse.'

They were sitting in the kitchen in Pankow – edgy, silent, coats folded on their laps – when the phone rang. They looked at one another, startled.

The phone went on ringing.

General Reder picked it up. He held the phone to his ear, waited silently.

'Wolfgang?' The voice on the line sounded breathy, hurried.

Reder knew the name for an occasional alias of Dieter's. Without speaking he handed the phone to Dieter.

'Yes?' Dieter glanced at the plastic-cased clock on the kitchen wall: seven minutes to five.

'Wolfgang?'

'Yes.' The wheezing voice of Klaus Kneesestrecker. *What the hell was the fellow phoning at this late hour for?*

'A small problem about the collection, I'm afraid.'

'Go on.'

'The goods won't be ready as planned.' Kneesestrecker paused, gulped in air. 'But you can have them an hour later.'

'That's not convenient.' Dieter felt the eyes of Reder, Miller and Rosa upon him, saw the concern on their faces, wondering, puzzling. 'And it's not what we agreed.'

'I'm sorry, Wolfgang, but you'll have to collect them an hour later than planned.'

In his mind's eye Dieter could see the blubbery face, the blubbery neck pushed into the Stasi NCO's tunic; he could see the small eyes blinking, calculating the odds. *Fuck*.

'OK, one hour later.'

'Yes. About twenty minutes, you said?'

'Twenty-five, thirty, at most.'

'OK, *bis dann*.'

'There'd better be no fuck-ups,' Dieter said.

There was no reply. Dieter heard static on the line. He put the phone down, looked at the others.

'You heard that,' he said. 'Nothing to worry about. Pick-up is at seven.'

'You think it's still OK?' Rosa couldn't quite quell the tremor in her voice.

General Reder smiled. 'I've learned to accept Dieter's word – if he says it's OK, then it's OK.'

'We have an hour to kill,' Dieter said.

The good life. Quartermaster Klaus Kneesestrecker felt he'd at last grasped it as he replaced the phone on Claudia's bedside locker.

He hauled himself, puffing, a little more upright against the mound of pillows on the double bed. He'd ordered Claudia to wait in the kitchen while he made his phone call – 'an important, confidential call'. He could almost see the greed reflected in her pale blue eyes: perfume, scented soaps, Western shampoos on their way to nourish her generous body.

The telephone exchange with the so-called 'Wolfgang' unnerved him. 'Wolfgang' indeed: Klaus could smell Moscow off the fellow at a hundred paces. High-handed, the cold Russian eyes even colder when he smiled – or tried to – and offered you two hundred US dollars to 'leave the door to Block Five's cellar ajar for just a few minutes'. In the brief and unexpected exchange at the railway station *Stehcafe* Klaus had been tempted to ask for more but something in the icy eyes had silenced him.

Still, he'd shown 'Wolfgang' on the phone. What else could he do when Claudia had called to say her husband – *why had she left the fucker's trousers and shoes with dirty socks balled inside on display in the bedroom?* – was detained at work and she'd be free at four for an hour or so.

'Claudia!' he called.

Odd. Block 5 and its basement seemed the city's most sought-after destination this evening. Still, shouldn't be any traffic jam in the basement. 'Wolfgang' was due at seven, should be gone by seven thirty at the latest, plenty of time before that thug with the birthmark turned up at eight. Klaus couldn't figure the fellow – he might be a Berliner but there was a whiff of the West about him. And he paid more, twice as much as 'Wolfgang'.

A cloud of perfume wafted towards him. The bed sank as Claudia climbed aboard. Her hands worked, lifting him. He felt her mouth on him.

Oh.

It was almost half an hour since they'd left General Reder's house but they'd covered not much more than a mile. In twenty minutes they'd hardly moved, stuck in a short line of traffic outside Pankow Rathaus – so short that they could see the traffic police at the checkpoint. Less than a hundred metres, less than twenty vehicles in the line.

'They're searching everything with a fine-tooth comb,' Dieter said. 'Look.'

All of them could see the driver at the head of the queue standing beside his Trabant: a young man, long-haired, in dark overalls, his face pale under the street lights. He had his hands in the air while he was patted down by a Vopo; another Vopo, rifle at the ready, stood close by.

'Something's up.' General Reder was in the front seat beside Dieter.

Dieter looked back at Rosa and Miller.

'It's OK,' he said. 'Just remember that we're on our way to a family dinner.'

And you've probably taken the precaution of booking all four of us into some restaurant, Miller thought. The last weeks seemed to him like a crash course in the ways and means of a half-legal underworld. Stuff happened, explanations were not offered, as in the four-door Volvo saloon they were travelling in. When Miller and Rosa had looked questioningly at the unfamiliar car waiting for them in the yard of the house in Pankow, Dieter's only comment had been simply, 'We need something that can't be traced to us.' The key to the car was in Dieter's hand. The Volvo was the chosen car of the Party elite; questioning the occupants of one could be bad for your health.

'I'll do the talking at the checkpoint.' General Reder sounded hoarser than usual; the others could hear the gulping noises as he sucked on a lozenge.

'It might not be necessary, Papa.' Rosa leaned forward between the front seats, her hand on Miller's knee. 'Look!'

In the lights of the checkpoint they could see the driver of the Trabant drop his arms, try to protect himself from the swinging fists of the Vopo. The second Vopo joined in. They saw him raise his weapon, saw the rifle stock move through the light, saw it connect with the Trabi driver's head. For a second the driver was erect, motionless; they watched the blood spout above his ear, saw him crumple to the ground, out of sight.

The Trabant was pushed to the side of the road. A whistle shrilled, the queue of vehicles crawled forward. Heads turned, quickly, fearfully, to snatch a glimpse of the victim being flung into the police van. And heads turned quickly away – the last thing anybody wanted was eye contact with one of the Vopos.

'Poor bastard.' Miller was surprised to hear his own voice.

'Still feel this is your kind of country, Patrick?' Dieter caught Miller's eye in the rear-view mirror.

Miller said nothing. He felt Rosa's hand on his, her thigh warm against his own.

'Right now he has no country, remember?' General Reder's voice was low. 'That's why we're doing this, to make sure he can get himself a passport.'

The general's face was worn, waxy, in the light from the dashboard. His wrist looked small, stick-like, when he raised it to look at his watch.

'I hope we don't run into problems,' he said. 'It's almost six thirty.'

'Fucking checkpoint.' Herbert Dover checked his watch. It was 7.30. 'We're late.'

'We should have left earlier,' Redgrave said. 'Schonefeld is a long way out.'

'Gee, I'm glad you told me that.' Dover was thinking exactly the same thought but he wasn't about to let Redgrave know that. 'But Schonefeld was where the van was stashed.'

Redgrave held his tongue, looked at the line of traffic ahead. There was nothing to be gained by antagonizing the American.

The line of cars inched forward.

Dover checked his watch again. Two minutes had passed. He figured they were ten, maybe fifteen, minutes from Normannenstrasse. Kneesestrecker wouldn't be going anywhere; the fat slob was on until 4 a.m.

'Our friend in the back,' Redgrave nodded towards the rear of the van, 'his papers will hold up at the checkpoint?'

In the cabin of the van Dover stared at Redgrave. 'What d'you think?' *I'm heading for Stasi HQ to liberate a van-load of files and my paperwork is going to let me down?*

'Just checking,' Redgrave said.

'Plumber's mate,' Dover said. 'And I'm the plumber, returning from an urgent job at Schonefeld airfield.' Like Redgrave and the man in the rear of the van, propped among plumber's tools, Dover was wearing overalls. 'Trouble with you,' he told Redgrave, 'is you worry too much.'

'Only sometimes,' Redgrave said. *Only when I'm on a job with a self-confessed killer with a sideline in attempted rape.*

At the checkpoint another car was released, waved forward. Another look at the watch: three minutes had passed. Once more the line of cars moved forward; only three ahead of them now. Under the street lights the cars gleamed like giant beetles, steam rising from their bonnets, smoke belching from their exhaust pipes. An armed Vopo stood guard; a pair of traffic policemen stooped at the car windows, stood upright to scrutinize ID cards under the light.

'What d'you think they're looking for?' Redgrave tried to keep the concern out of his voice.

'Any kind of future.' Dover's chuckle was dry, mirthless. 'And this fucking country hasn't got one.' He looked at Redgrave, wondered for a moment how this stuffed-shirt Brit ever got mixed up in this business.

Dover put the car into gear, edged the van forward. He could see the faces of the traffic cops now, young guys, but tiredness etched on their faces.

Within minutes it was their turn. IDs were checked, given a perfunctory once-over. You guys wouldn't be on my team, Dover thought.

The van was waved forward in the night.

Another look at his watch. 'Almost eight,' Dover said.

Thirty-four

Thursday, 9 November 1989, 8.00 p.m.
East Berlin

Dieter doused the lights, killed the engine, coasted the Volvo close to the rear of Block 4. The building was dark, silent.

'Mainly storage,' Dieter said. 'Not even a night watchman.' *Who'd be fool enough to break into the Stasi HQ? Especially when you're an hour behind schedule, delayed at too many checkpoints across the city.*

A single light showed over the entrance to the rear of Block 5. Dieter turned to Reder, spoke over his shoulder to Rosa.

'Patrick and I will knock, walk in.' He didn't tell them that Kneesestrecker would have his hand out for the balance of his dollars. 'If we're not out in twenty minutes, drive off.' He shushed Rosa's protests, the general's shake of his head, with a raised palm. 'I mean it, if we're delayed, leave. Patrick and I can find our own way back. Agreed?'

Nobody answered.

'You must do as Dieter says.' Miller half believed what he was saying. 'Promise me, Rosa.'

She nodded, leaned towards him, kissed him quickly.

'Another thing.' Dieter was staring straight ahead. 'It's quiet here, our Volvo might be left undisturbed for a while, but if you see anybody – any car, whatever – moving towards you, start the engine and move off *slowly*, as though you're just another car on official business.' Dieter reached under his seat, straightened with a military peaked cap in his hand. He handed it to Rosa.

'Put your hair up, Rosa, and sit up here. In the dark you'll just about get away with it.'

'And if she doesn't?' Miller asked.

'I'll pull rank.' Nobody laughed at General Reder's words. If it came to it, even a general's rank wouldn't pull high enough or hard enough.

'Time to move,' Dieter said.

Miller felt Rosa's lips brush his again, saw her fingers touch Dieter's face.

'Come back safe,' she whispered.

They eased the doors of the car open, the interior remained dark. He's taken the courtesy light out, Miller thought.

The cold hit them, sandwiched between the Volvo and the dark rear of Block 4. The sky was starless, black as the building.

Rosa got into the driver's seat and Miller fixed her in his mind, her face pale in the dark interior, the military cap covering the rich hair he loved. In the dark cold he shivered, wondered if he would see her again. He saw her lips mouth the words, '*Ich liebe dich*,' and then he turned away, following Dieter, hugging the shadow of Block 4.

Stasi HQ operated around the clock. After 6 p.m., however, the registry in the basement of Block 5 could be accessed only through the small, rear entrance. It wasn't a cellar in any complete sense. Four shallow steps led down to the black door; the low-ceilinged basement was about half below and half above street level.

Dieter and Miller stood on the bottom step. Dieter tapped

gently on the door. From within came the sound of footsteps; they knew they were being studied through the brass-ringed eyehole. Inside, a bolt was drawn back, a key turned.

The door opened a fraction. Miller followed Dieter through the narrow opening of light. Behind them the door closed, the bolt slid home. A radio was playing pop.

In front of them a steel-barred gate, to their left an unvarnished door that opened on to a cramped office that held the usual desk, chair, directories on the window sill, phone and crank-up switchboard. A kettle and mugs fought for space on the small government-issue desk.

The office seemed even tinier when Kneesestrecker followed Miller and Dieter inside.

Kneesestrecker looked at Miller, at Dieter.

'You didn't say there'd be two of you,' he said.

'So? I forgot to tell you.' Dieter handed the quartermaster two fifty-dollar bills.

'That's not what we agreed.'

'Another hundred when we're done.'

'Ten minutes – no more.'

I can smell a woman on you. Miller noticed the girly magazine on the desk, half covered by a copy of *Neues Deutschland*, the grainy image of naked thighs and breasts entirely appropriate in this cellar of secrets and lies. Cigarettes and garlic and the smell of sex filled the room like obscene incense.

'We'll be quick,' Dieter said.

'Ten minutes, no more.' Kneesestrecker's belly shook, his open tunic flapped. 'You're late, we agreed on seven o'clock.' Come back another day, he wanted to say, but he was frightened of the monk-like Russian. 'Please,' he wheezed, 'ten minutes, no more.'

'When we're fucking ready.' Dieter seemed almost waif-like

beside the Stasi NCO but Miller watched Kneesestrecker swallow, blink, before the steel in Dieter's words.

'And turn that fucking radio down – keep your eyes and ears open.'

Kneesestrecker reached for the small transistor on the desk, lowered the volume. A DJ was spouting his spiel between records. Even here, Miller thought, they listen to West Berlin stations.

They followed Kneesestrecker out of the office, watched him unlock the steel gate that led to the registry. Ahead of them lay the filing stacks: rows of steel shelves crammed with manila folders and foolscap envelopes. Even Dieter paused to gaze in a kind of awe: an assembly of lives, a compendium of a country's hopes and secrets and betrayals.

'It takes two archivists,' Kneesestrecker wheezed with a hint of pride, 'full-time, to keep the files up to date.' He pointed to the steel gate at the opposite end of the aisle, at the main entrance. 'Their office is there, beside reception.'

'If the filing system is that good,' Dieter said, 'we'll be out of here in a few minutes.'

Kneesestrecker began to swing the gate shut behind Dieter and Miller.

'Leave it open.' Dieter's voice as steely as the gate. 'You wait inside the office.'

Kneesestrecker shrugged; they watched him shuffle into the small office.

Dieter turned to Miller. 'That prick doesn't have to know which stacks we're looking in.'

They moved further along the aisle. The music from Kneesestrecker's transistor radio followed them between the shelves of files. Under the muted strip lights the files looked like rows of cardboard tombstones.

They stood together at the front end of the stacks. The filing system was basic, moving from A on the left to Z on the extreme right.

Dieter pointed, led Miller along the M stack. *Mi* seemed to begin on the top shelf. Dieter hauled a stepladder along the aisle, climbed until he could thumb his way through the ranks of files. Miller worked through the middle and lower shelves.

'Nothing.'

Miller didn't question Dieter's thoroughness. 'And nothing here,' he said.

Both were silent.

'Bloody music,' Miller said, looking towards Kneesestrecker's office.

'Fuck the music,' Dieter said. 'We need to find your file. *Think!*'

I think of Rosa and her hair piled up under a peaked cap, sitting in the Volvo beside General Reder—

'Reder,' he said. 'Maybe they've put me into a file along with Rosa and the general.'

He ran between the stacks. It almost seemed benign, welcome, to be coupled with Rosa.

Dieter hurried after him, and together their fingers flew through the manila tombstones.

They found the Reder file, a fat folder tied together with a brown lace with steel ends. They flicked through dozens of pages, carbon copies, yellowed pages, flimsies. Even the most cursory of examinations showed that Patrick Miller, sometime UK resident, occasional and reluctant UK/GDR intelligence agent, must be interred elsewhere.

Dieter and Miller looked at each other in dismay. More than fifteen minutes had passed without profit. The stacks of files presented an unintelligible labyrinth. And Rosa and her father would be sitting in the dark, counting the passing minutes. *And the fucking music went on creaking tinnily from the smelly office.*

Dieter shook his head. 'I'm an idiot,' he said.

'What?'

'Janus,' Dieter said. 'And take the Reder file.'

It took them seconds to get to the J aisle, seconds more to locate the file marked 'Janus'. The first page of the file had a photograph of Miller attached.

'Wait here,' Dieter said. He was gone for two, maybe three minutes. When he came back, he had three fresh files in his hand.

'These are others who also need protecting,' he said to Miller. 'Now let's go.'

They were hurrying towards the exit when they heard the knocking on the door.

Kneesestrecker swore when he heard the knocking. *Why was the fucking Westerner here already?* Why was 'Wolfgang' *still* here?

Kneesestrecker hauled himself to his feet, puffed his way to the door. Through the peephole he could see the Westerner, black knitted cap pulled down to his thin eyebrows, beside an older fellow in a padded anorak; behind them Kneesestrecker could see a small, dark van.

'Moment, bitte.'

The quartermaster switched off the light outside, heard the muttered 'Fuck!' outside as he turned back to the registry.

Dieter and Miller stood beside the steel gate, staring at him.

'It's just a couple of fellows to collect files.'

Dieter snorted. 'Tell them you're busy, to come back in five minutes.'

Kneesestrecker spread his pudgy hands, turned back to the door.

'Come back in five minutes,' he wheezed.

'Open the fucking door – now!'

Kneesestrecker faced Dieter and Miller again, spread his hands again: *what can I do?*

'Who is it? Miller was whispering. 'Stasi?'

A shake of the quartermaster's head, a wobbling of the blancmange gut.

'Just somebody who wants a file,' Kneesestrecker said.

Dieter looked at Miller, at Kneesestrecker.

'A lot of private enterprise in the workers' democracy,' Dieter said. He wasn't smiling. Neither was Miller.

Kneesestrecker was sweating.

'I told you, open the fucking door now!' Anger in the words piercing the door.

'We'll go into your office.' Dieter signalled to Miller. 'Take them, whoever they are, straight through to the registry. While they're at the stacks, we'll slip out. Just make sure you leave that door unlocked.'

Kneesestrecker nodded, watched as 'Wolfgang' and Miller tiptoed into his office. The office door was left ajar, the radio was turned up louder. *The good life was still safe, more dollars just waiting to drop into his welcoming palm*. Anyway, these fuckers don't know each other, so what's the problem?

'Coming!' Klaus Kneesestrecker was smiling as he drew the bolt back on the door. *Dollars equals Claudia*. What more could a man desire?

Herbert Dover wasn't smiling as he pushed open the door.

'What the fuck are you playing at? Anybody could've seen us out there!' Dover was uneasy: the black Volvo outside the rear of Block 4 seemed to be empty but why would anybody park there?

Kneesestrecker managed to position himself between Dover and the door to the office.

'Sorry, sorry!' He ushered Dover and the anoraked fellow – *doesn't look German either* – towards the registry. 'I was getting the gate open for you.'

Kneesestrecker wanted his money but was afraid to ask for it before 'Wolfgang' and the other fellow had left.

Dover was hurrying past Kneesestrecker towards the registry stacks when he stopped, his hand raised, his head cocked, listening to Kneesestrecker's transistor radio.

The DJ had given way to a news reporter.

> *. . . at a press conference which has just ended, Herr Günter Schabowski, a member of the Politburo and Socialist Party chief for Berlin, capital of the German Democratic Republic, made this amazing announcement concerning travel arrangements within the city . . .*

Time seemed to stand still in the basement of Block 5. Kneesestrecker and Redgrave were looking at each other. In the office Miller and Dieter were listening, holding their breath.

The radio voice changed to Party boss Günter Schabowski's measured tones, as though reading from a prepared statement:

> *Permanent emigration is henceforth allowed across all border crossing points between East Germany and West Germany and West Berlin.*

'What the fuck?' Dover was bounding towards the office, towards the radio.

Miller was staring at the transistor: *the border was open?*

Kneesestrecker was wondering if this announcement might interfere with his access to dollars and to Claudia.

Dieter was thinking that you never know. *And why was the office door being shoved open so roughly?*

Those seconds of indecision cost him the advantage.

Dover was standing in the doorway, staring at Dieter and Miller. Faster, smoother, the Colt pistol was in his hands.

'I'll be damned!' Elation in Dover's voice. 'This is my lucky day!'

The small office was crowded, Dieter and Miller looking across the desk at Dover.

'What on earth is going on?' Miller was staring past Dover's shoulder.

'I might ask the same of you.' Redgrave was equally astonished by Miller's presence.

Dover kept his gaze fixed on Dieter. 'This your tame Brit in Berlin? The guy who's giving it to Reder's daughter?'

'And you're the bastard who tried to rape her,' said Dieter.

'Shut it.' Dover didn't bother to look at Miller: any danger lay with the guy from Moscow. 'Changes at Checkpoint Charlie or anywhere else won't make any difference to you, pal.' He grinned. 'I told you all those years ago in Chile, you should've finished me off when you had the chance.'

'We can't just—'

'We can and we will.' Dover cut off Redgrave's objection. 'But not here. We'll take them outside the city, someplace quiet.'

'For God's sake, Miller is a British subject!'

Dover laughed. 'He has a British passport?'

Dover levelled the pistol at Dieter. 'Time to move,' he said. 'Any tricks and I'll kill you right here.'

Minutes earlier General Reder had seen the black van in the Volvo's rear-view mirror. He touched Rosa's hand, quickly stooped out of sight. They held their breath as the van passed by. Cautiously, peering above the dashboard, they watched the van pull in at the entrance to Block 5. Two men got out of the van, looked furtively about as they stood under the door light; one of them, it seemed to Reder, paid particular attention to the Volvo parked a block away. The same individual knocked on the door of Block 5. Moments later the light above the door went out.

In the Volvo, Reder blinked, trying to focus on the darkened doorway. He saw the crack of light, saw the men go inside.

He felt Rosa's hand on his, saw the fear in her eyes. Rosa looked at her watch.

'They've been inside almost twenty minutes,' she said.

'Start the engine,' Reder said.

'But we're not—'

'You think I'd leave anyone behind?' *Not alive anyway*. 'Trust me, I'll get inside. Move the car up there, quiet as you can – and keep the engine running.' He opened the door of the Volvo.

'Papa . . .'

Reder looked at her in the dark interior of the car, thought of all the joy that this orphaned girl from another world had brought into his life. He smiled, patted her hand.

'Trust me, Rosa.' The door of the car closed behind him.

Reder edged his way forward, keeping to the shadows. From one pocket of his coat he drew the Walther, felt the pistol cold and heavy in his palm. *You're too old for this*. From his other pocket he took the silencer, twisted the dark, stubby cylinder in his fingers. He had no need to stop, to look, as he fitted the coil to the mouth of the Walther. *You should be at home, preparing to die from cancer*.

He put his ear to the door of Block 5. Voices, indistinct. Reder's mind saw the line of German prisoners outside Captain Nikolai Kulakov's farmhouse HQ, heard the rat-tat-tat of rifle fire, saw the bodies lying in the dirty snow. *You're old enough now for death but you're too old for guns.*

He pressed gently on the door handle, held his breath as he pushed the door, padded silently inside.

The steel-barred gate in front of him stood open. The voice came from inside the door to his left. The door was ajar.

The voice from inside went on: commanding, mocking.

Reder raised the Walther, stood in the half-open doorway.

The voice inside was saying, 'Time to move.'

The speaker had his back to Reder. Reder saw the birthmark, like a blot on the lined neck. He heard his daughter's voice, tried to hide from his mind the hands on her.

'Any tricks,' the voice was saying, 'and I'll kill you right here.'

The Walther made a soft, apologetic sound as Reder pulled the trigger.

The gurgling noise from Dover's throat died abruptly. The dark, spreading stain on the back of his coat was matched by another on his front as the bullet exited. There was a pinging noise and the radio fell silent.

No one spoke in the small office. They watched the trickle of blood from the corner of Dover's mouth, watched him crumple to the floor.

General Reder broke the silence. 'Everyone OK?' He was talking to Miller and Dieter.

They nodded, watched him put the safety on the pistol.

Klaus Kneesestrecker was wheezing, almost gasping for breath. The air in the office was heavy, fuggy with the odours of blood and burnt flesh.

Reder stepped over Dover's body, reached for the bottle of water on the desk.

'Sit,' Reder said. 'Drink.'

Kneesestrecker sank on to the chair, drank from the bottle.

Above the tilted bottle his eyes were big with fear.

'You.' Redgrave flinched before Reder's voice, before the pistol in his hand. 'I know you.' *You're one of the men in suits, manipulating lives from behind a distant desk – which is where you should have stayed, just a face in our files.* 'What are you doing here?'

'Files.' Redgrave trembled, looked at Dover's body, at Reder's pistol. 'The Americans wanted files . . .'

'And you thought you'd come along for the ride and see if you could pick up something also?'

Redgrave didn't – couldn't – answer.

'Hans.' Urgency in Dieter's voice. 'They've opened all the border crossings.'

'What?'

'The border crossings – it was on the radio.'

Heads turned to study the transistor, silent, smashed by the bullet that had exited Dover's chest.

'It's no problem, honestly.' Kneesestrecker looked as if he might crush the water bottle between his pudgy hands. 'I was going to get a new radio anyway.'

'It's a relief to know that,' Reder said, deadpan.

In spite of himself, Miller smiled, wondered how he could smile with a corpse on the floor.

'Where does that leave us?' Reder asked.

Miller heard the extra meaning in Reder's question, caught the long look that passed between him and Dieter.

'Did you know this announcement was coming?' Reder's question was addressed to Redgrave. 'Did this?' Reder poked with his toe at Dover's corpse.

'No, I swear it – he knew nothing – I knew nothing.' Redgrave swallowed. 'There's a man in the van, an extra hand to carry files out.'

'Leave it to me.' Dieter was already moving. Miller was staring at the gun in Dieter's hand. At Dover, lying on the floor like a pile of crumpled clothing.

Outside, a car door opened, quietly closed.

Dieter shepherded a dungaree-clad fellow into the office: small, wiry, a grey ski cap on his head. Alarm in his small eyes as he almost stumbled over the remains of Dover.

'Your name?' Reder asked.

It took a few moments before the croaked answer leaked out.

'Donat, Thomas Donat.'

'Is that your real name?' Reder was examining the fellow's ID.

'Yes, sir.' A whisper.

Reder looked at Redgrave.

'Yes,' Redgrave said.

'You will never again speak of this night.' Reder raised his pistol. 'Understood?'

'Yes, sir.'

Reder pointed with the pistol at the corpse on the floor, turned to Redgrave and Donat.

'Take off his coat.'

The men stared at him.

'Now!' Reder said.

While the man knelt, labouring to remove the charred, bloodied coat from Dover's corpse, Dieter whispered to Reder that Rosa had the Volvo outside.

Reder nodded, barked at the kneeling men to hurry up with the fucking overcoat. The look they gave him – furtive, fearful – reminded Miller of frightened curs.

Reder was removing Kneesestrecker's civilian overcoat from a hook on the back of the office door.

'A nice warm coat.' Reder fingered the padded material of the parka, spoke to Kneesestrecker. 'Have you any objection if we borrow it?'

'No, sir, please, sir, take it, it's yours,' Kneesestrecker spluttered, waving the water bottle about.

'Thank you.' Once more Reder turned to the two men on the floor beside the dead Dover. The American looked smaller, legs splayed like a wireless marionette.

'Stand him up,' Reder said, holding Kneesestrecker's coat at the ready.

The corpse was hauled upright, arms wide, a scarecrow in jeans and boots and a black sweater that was holed and bloodied. Miller moved to help Reder draw the sleeves on to the ungiving scarecrow arms.

Reder surveyed the corpse front and back, said it would do. He knew the body would go on leaking but he knew also – *hoped* – they'd be rid of it soon.

'You can go now.'

Donat looked relieved at Reder's words; the look on Redgrave's face was one of apprehension.

'You can go,' Reder repeated. 'Just remember,' this to Redgrave, 'that this file,' he nodded at the file marked 'Janus', lying on the desk, 'contains all the details of what you did to this man.'

He doesn't even use my name, Miller thought, because this handyman Donat guy doesn't need to hear it.

'The file contains enough detail to incriminate you and your colleagues and leave you open to criminal charges of coercion of a citizen of your own country. Understood?' Reder's voice was mild as a kindergarten teacher's.

Redgrave nodded, avoided Miller's eyes.

'You can hand our friend over now,' Reder said.

Miller and Dieter took the weight of the corpse between them.

'Now get out of my sight.' Redgrave and Donat backed

towards the door. 'If the crossings really are open,' Reder went on, 'then I suggest that you get yourselves to the other side of the Wall as quickly as possible,' he paused, 'and don't let me catch either of you on *my* side again.'

The door to Block 5 opened, closed quietly behind the men.

'Take him out to the car.' Reder was drawing the hood of the parka up on Dover's head; it was too big, fell forward, down to his eyebrows. 'Sit him in the back seat between you. Rosa will know soon enough who it is, just don't blurt it out to her.'

He paused, listening: the van was pulling away.

'I'll be out in a moment,' Reder said. 'Now get going.'

'Yes, General!' Dieter spoke with smiling emphasis.

'Yes, General,' Miller said quietly. *Now you could see the leader of men in the old boy.*

Reder watched them stagger through the doorway, dragging the corpse between them.

The door closed. Reder turned to Kneesestrecker.

'Sir!' Panic-striken, Kneesestrecker got to his feet. 'Sir, I won't tell anyone – I promise!'

Reder laid a hand on the quartermaster's shoulder, pushed him gently back down on the chair.

'But can I trust you?' Reder asked.

'I swear it, sir, honest!'

But, Reder thought, if you were, for any reason, subjected to Stasi interrogation, you'd break like a twig. *To be on the safe side, I ought to kill you.*

Reder eased the safety of the pistol to off.

'Please, sir, please!' Kneesestrecker was weeping.

There was a fresh smell in the office to go with the blood and the cordite. Christ, the fellow had soiled himself.

'Listen to me,' Reder said. 'If you breathe a single word of this to anybody, I'll come back and chop your balls off before I kill you. Understand?'

Kneesestrecker blew his nose into a dirty handkerchief, wobbled precariously on the chair.

'Yes, sir, I understand.'

'You have disinfectant here, soap, a scrubbing brush, a mop?'

'In the lavatory, sir.'

'You will get them and you will scrub these stains away,' Reder indicated the brown stain on the floor, 'until you can see your face on it, until the floor is shining.'

'Yes, sir.'

'When you are relieved in the morning, not a trace will remain. Understand?'

'Yes, sir.' A glimmer of hope in the small eyes. *He's not going to kill me.*

'What are you waiting for?'

Kneesestrecker scurried from the office. Reder heard his footsteps hurrying towards the lavatories at the front of the building. He put the safety on, put the pistol in his pocket. He blinked, tried to push from his mind the image of the bodies in the snow. Dover deserved to die for what he had done to Rosa but this poor fat slob in the shit-soiled trousers?

Reder took his penknife from his jacket. He'd already seen where the bullet had lodged in the wall. He pushed the blade of the knife in beside the bullet, levered gently. He looked at the small, misshapen slug that tumbled into his palm. So small, so deadly. *Never again.*

Kneesestrecker was back, the water slopping over the rim of the bucket, a bottle of disinfectant poking from one pocket, a hard-bristled scrubbing brush from another.

'Spotless,' Reder said, 'you hear?'

Kneesestrecker nodded, already on his knees.

As he stepped out of the office Reder was thinking of the

Wall. What did they mean, the border crossings were open? And what did that mean for the men and women throughout the GDR who were ready and willing, waiting for his command?

Thirty-five

Thursday, 9 November 1989, 9.35 p.m.
East Berlin – West Berlin

Rosa pulled the Volvo out of the Normannenstrasse complex at a sedate pace.

'What's going on?' General Reder pointed at the Stasi blocks, at the windows lighting up in the buildings.

The general was sitting in the front beside Rosa; in the rear the silent stranger was sandwiched between Miller and Dieter. She'd looked but the stranger's face was almost hidden by the hood of his parka. She'd said nothing, just watched in the rear-view mirror as Miller and Dieter sat on either side of the fellow.

She wrinkled her nose, eased the window open.

Small groups of Stasi – twos, threes – were emerging from every entrance, a soft hum of conversation rising with their cigarette smoke in the night air.

General Reder turned the radio on. Rosa closed the window; the smell was darker, thicker.

The general fiddled with the dial, edged from static past pop music into a news report. The reporter's voice was shrill with excitement:

Crowds are gathering at the Bornholmerstrasse and Zimmerstrasse crossing points. The crowds are noisy and excited. The border guards seem puzzled and nervous but, in accordance with Herr Schabowski's announcement at tonight's press conference, everybody is being allowed through at the crossing points. I would add that the crowds here are growing by the minute . . .

Static filled the car. General Reder moved the dial but, for the moment at least, reception on the car radio was lost. General Reder turned the radio off.

The silence in the car was profound.

Dieter broke it. 'Hans?'

Reder didn't answer at once, went on staring out at the night as though the dark streets might hold the answer to his question: what did it mean?

Rosa inched the car forward in a low gear; nobody had told her where they were going.

'We must go west,' Reder said at last. 'We have to find out what's going on.'

'It's dangerous,' Dieter said. 'Our passenger?'

'He won't bother us,' the general said.

Rosa looked then, adjusted the rear-view mirror, tried to focus on the hooded figure in the back seat. The hood slipped and she saw the face of her nightmare. She shivered; the car jolted to a holt.

'It's OK.' The general's voice was husky, comforting. 'It's OK,' he said again. 'Are you able to drive?'

She turned the mirror away, nodded to Reder.

'I'm OK, Papa.' *It's not the first time I've sat in a car with a body in the back. I ought to be glad he's there, lifeless, propped up between my lover and my oldest living friend, but I'm not. The killing has to stop some time.*

She rounded a corner, swung the Volvo west. Miller caught her eye in the rear-view mirror, tried to smile. He wondered at her, at himself. Rosa knew – he could read it in her eyes – that their passenger was a corpse. *And you – you've seen a man killed tonight and still you sit there as if you'd witnessed nothing more significant than a minor traffic accident.*

It's this city, Miller told himself, as they moved through the dark streets. He'd been forced to come here – allowed himself to be forced – but still he'd arrived in Berlin full of hope, full of heart. And after nine years he could sit beside a fresh corpse without fear or concern. Somewhere along the way he'd lost a piece of himself and the thought crossed his mind that that piece might be gone for good. He looked at Rosa, at the dark hair escaping from under the peaked cap, saw the tender curve of her cheek and the way her fingers curled on the steering wheel and Miller told himself, maybe you've lost something but you've also found something precious here. Hold on to what you've found and you'll find yourself again.

He reached forward and touched her dark hair and Rosa half turned and smiled at him. It was enough.

As they neared the Wall and its environs the night air began to throb with a kind of humming and the sky seemed brighter. Rosa let the window down; from ahead came the murmur of many voices. Hundreds of voices, maybe more. And the lights were spreading, up and out into the night sky. They heard laughter, shouts. Torch beams flashed across the sky. Car horns blared, honked in unrehearsed concert. And yet somehow rehearsed.

In the middle of the road, caught in the beam of the Volvo, two men linked elbows and swung each other crazily, faces broad with laughter, beer bottles raised in their free hands. On the pavement, looking baffled and confused, a Vopo stood watching with folded arms. He caught sight of the Volvo and spread his hands, palms out: *what can I do?*

'Should we turn back, Papa?' As they nosed ahead, the press of people was thickening.

'No.' General Reder looked back at Dieter. 'Our friend should also go west if the crossing is open.'

Dieter nodded. Better if the crap is found on a Western doorstep.

The crowd was greatest along the Potsdamer Platz, right up to the Brandenburg Gate in the forbidden zone. The gate was illuminated; its great horizontal arch, scarred and wounded in the war, was lit up in a noonday blaze. The spotlights were beamed from the Western side of the wall.

'Why now?'

Nobody could answer Dieter's question.

'The flag is still there,' General Reder said, pointing to the banner of the GDR on top of the gate. In the cold, calm night the flag hung limp against the white pole.

'But for how long?'

Nobody answered Miller's question either.

Rosa swung the car away from the crowds.

'It might be easier at Charlie,' she said.

No place was easy that night. Crowds were surging towards the checkpoints from all sides.

'We need to get out of this car,' Dieter said.

The crowd was loud, animated. Whoops of joy punctuated the steady hum of noise. But you never knew; even amid such excitement the sight of the Volvo might tip high spirits into violence.

Rosa spotted an open gate, pulled into a dark yard. The smell of garbage clogged the night. She coasted the car to a halt beside the rubbish bins, looked questioningly at General Reder.

'Our friend,' he pointed at Dover's remains, 'is going to walk through Checkpoint Charlie.' He looked at Dieter, at Miller.

'I'm not able to do this.' They could hear the apology in Reder's voice. 'Can you handle it?'

They manhandled Dover out of the car on Dieter's side. Rosa stood apart. Miller and Dieter held Dover upright while Reder drew the hood of the parka lower over the waxen face. Reder fastened all the toggles on the coat, bent to pull the ends of the parka below the knees. The heavy parka concealed the faint ooze of blood from Dover's torso. Reder was wheezing from the effort.

'Papa.' Rosa turned to him. 'Let me.'

She tried not to look at the face as she arranged the coat below Dover's knees. Reder whispered his thanks, knew what it had cost her.

The weight astonished Miller. He grunted, locking his right arm more tightly around Dover's shoulder.

'Gently,' Dieter said. 'It's easier if we lift rather than pull and drag.'

Their bizarre procession seemed an organic element of the sea of people borne towards Checkpoint Charlie. Rosa and General Reder linked arms, walked ahead of Miller and Dieter with their lumpen cargo. Their neighbours in the crowd, good-humoured, joshed them about the drunken companion being carried between them.

'Pissed!' someone said.

'Pissed on freedom!' his neighbour said.

Someone was pushed too close, wrinkled his nose.

'He's not just pissed, he shat himself as well!'

Miller and Dieter joined in the laughter. They stopped a number of times, pressed close to the wall, Rosa and Reder shielding them from the crowd as they changed shoulders.

'Careful now.' Dieter's whisper barely audible in the throng.

Ahead lay Checkpoint Charlie. The roundabout queuing

system had been abandoned; now the press of people pushed forward towards the West across a wide, single front. The border guards, under the lights, looked pale, puzzled.

'They're not checking everyone's ID.' Miller, taller than the others, could see over the heads. If the Grepos tried to hold back the crowd to check every ID, he thought, there'd be a riot.

They reached the head of the line, felt themselves scrutinized by the four Grepos on duty. No eye contact. Miller looked beyond the guards, at the lighted West, hoisted Dover higher on his shoulder, heard himself tell a corpse – loudly – to sober up, saw Rosa and the general ease back a step as if to obscure Miller and Dieter and their lifeless burden.

It wasn't working. One of the Grepos was advancing purposefully, small eyes fixed on Dover.

'Herr Miller!' The advancing Grepo was almost shouldered aside by a beaming Sergeant Heinz-Peter Reibert. 'You are enjoying a night out with your friends?' Heinz-Peter looked as if he'd been doing a little celebrating himself. Cap pushed back on his head, cheeks flushed. He stood close to Miller, smiling. 'And your friend here has enjoyed himself a little too much, maybe?'

Miller held his breath as Heinz-Peter turned to Dover. Heinz-Peter flinched as the smell hit him. He turned his gaze on Miller, on the general and Rosa; he looked at Dieter, once more at Miller. In Heinz-Peter's eyes Miller could read puzzlement, even alarm. He saw the shoulders shrug in the greatcoat, saw the smile gleam in the frank eyes: *on this night, Herr Miller, it's not my business*.

'Have a good time on the Ku'damm, my friends!' Heinz-Peter winked at Miller, waved them through.

'I don't know what went on there,' Dieter said out of the side of his mouth to Miller, 'but thank you.'

Miller smiled. *Thank God for toiletries and sweets for the children.*

On the Western side they were engulfed by welcoming crowds. More car horns blaring. Someone trying to blow a bugle. Laughter, shouts, a medley of sound rising to the Berlin sky. Someone yelled the slogan of the candle-lit demonstrations, and the mass of people took up the chant: '*Wir sind ein Volk!*' The lines of people still on the other side of Checkpoint Charlie joined in, voices swelling in unison: '*Wir sind ein Volk!*'

We are all one people!

Miller looked back: the Grepos weren't chanting, they were motionless, statues marooned at a checkpoint that was no longer a crossing point but a meeting place.

'We have to get rid of this!' Dieter's voice urgent.

They pushed on through the crowd, past outstretched hands, past smiling faces, beer bottles proffered, hellos in the night. Even a bubbling bottle of Sekt.

And then, suddenly, unexpectedly, the sea of hands and faces eddied them into a long, narrow street, a fjord clawed between the backs of houses and lock-up garages. The silence silenced them. They went forward hesitantly into the dark cul-de-sac, as though fearful of what they might find.

What they found was a garden bench with scrolled, rusted, iron legs and the green paint peeling from its wooden laths. Incongruous, marooned in a slime of mud and wet rubbish, the bench was pushed against the high stone wall that blocked the end of the alley.

'It was waiting for him,' Dieter said.

They laid Dover there, silent on the bench, wrapped in Klaus Kneesestrecke's parka, facing the dark wall where the sun would never reach. It might be days – weeks – before the remains of

Herbert Dover were discovered.

In silence they trooped back to the bright street. It was almost midnight yet the city seemed to sing – to swing – to a communal rhythm.

'Papa.' Rosa drew General Reder into a shop doorway. 'You look exhausted, we should get you home.'

The general's smile was wan, tired. He shook his head. 'Who could sleep on a night like this?'

Miller, watching, listening, saw the history of a country in the general's tired, lined face; heard, in the general's cancered, puzzled voice the uncertainty – the fear – of what might dawn on the morning after such a night as this.

'Besides,' General Reder went on, 'Dieter and I have things to do, phone calls to make.'

Dieter nodded. 'The sooner the better.' He stopped, looked at Rosa and Miller. Miller knew. *Soon* would not come soon; *soon* was a date postponed until the smoke had cleared and the lie of a new, uncertain land could be measured, studied.

'A taxi on a night like this . . .' General Reder was musing aloud.

'The S-Bahn is running.' Dieter was smiling. 'No matter if the Wall is open, the trains don't let you down here.'

'But Papa—'

Reder hushed Rosa. 'There are things we have to do, Rosa, you know that.'

On the street someone let off a firecracker and all four of them jumped, frightened, then looked skyward to gaze at the comet of colourful stars soaring into the night above the unsleeping city.

'It's beautiful,' Rosa said.

The technicoloured stars fizzled out, vanished in the darkness.

'It doesn't last long,' Dieter said, almost to himself.

'I wonder,' Miller said, 'if the open crossings will be as short-lived.'

'I don't think so.' General Reder was still looking skyward. 'After this there's no going back.'

'All the more reason, Hans,' Dieter said, 'that you and I should get moving.'

'But where must you go, Papa? And when will you be home?'

'I'll be home tomorrow, child, unless,' he paused, shrugged, 'unless I'm not. Patrick will stay with you, yes?' Miller nodded. 'Dieter and I need to get to a secure phone, we have a few calls to make.'

Reder and Dieter kissed Rosa, shook hands with Miller.

Rosa leaned into Miller's body as they watched the two older men make their way to the station on the next corner. Miller felt the smallness of her and wanted to shelter her; felt the warmth of her and knew there was no place else he wanted to be.

A train rumbled by, unseen, overhead, behind the street of shops and houses. Another firecracker went off; another cascade of coloured stars spilled into the night.

'A secure phone,' Rosa said. She was staring at the corner where General Reder and Dieter had climbed out of sight, on to the S-Bahn platform.

'They'll get one,' Miller said into her hair. *Maybe in Charlottenburg, in the back-street lock-up that is regularly swept for bugs*. He could imagine soldiers, airmen, engrossed in TV and radio reports, picking up phones in Rostock and Erfurt and Karl-Marx Stadt, listening to the new orders that stood them down, put on hold whatever action had been planned.

He felt Rosa shiver in his arms, wondered if it was the cold or the unforgettable knowledge that someone had been killed that night.

'Patrick,' her voice was muffled in his chest, 'who did it? Was it Dieter or . . . ?'

'It was all of us.' Miller drew her closer into his arms. 'Yes, it was all of us.'

She let it go, lifted her face to be kissed.

A teenage couple with a bundle of firecrackers caught her eye, smiled at her.

'Are you from over there?' the boy called. He was pointing to the East. How does he know? Rosa wondered.

She said yes, gave him a small wave.

The boy's face broke into a broad smile; he waved to her with a firework that he was readying for the Berlin sky.

'*Willkommen!*' he called. '*Willkommen!*'

EPILOGUE

ONE YEAR LATER

OCTOBER 1990

Thirty-six

Wednesday, 3 October 1990
Berlin

The reunification of Germany didn't seem to have had much impact on ZERO. The same black walls, the same naked bulbs and cigarette-burned tables. A dinosaur refusing to die or a haven of principle too steadfast for changing?

The same old question, Miller thought; you've been asking it for the last year. *Give it a rest.*

The fellow behind the counter, pouring boiling water on instant coffee, was unfamiliar.

'Heinrich sleeping it off?' The entire population of the city seemed to have been at the knees-up along the Wall – or what remained of it – the night before, the night that East Germany ceased to exist.

The two coffee mugs sat on the counter in their own spillage. Maybe being able to splash the stuff about was a prerequisite for the job.

'The fellow before me?' The waiter looked at Miller's West German Deutschmarks, nodded. 'I think he's gone to Hamburg, or maybe it's Hanover – I'm not sure.' He shrugged; his predecessor behind the counter of ZERO had, like many others, gone West.

Rosa took the coffee from Miller, gestured at the emptiness

of the cafe. 'Maybe we shouldn't have come here, Patrick,' she said.

'I like it,' Miller said. ZERO had become their regular haunt, once or twice a week, in the months – almost a year – since the Wall had been breached. 'This is the first place we came to together.'

Rosa laughed. 'My sentimental lover.'

'I've let go of so much,' Miller said. '*Had* to let go.' He looked around once more, wondered why he should feel any affection for this down-at-heel cafe in a sunless alley. 'But we have to hold on to some things.'

Rosa smiled. 'Even if it's only a dump like ZERO.'

Miller wagged an admonitory finger at her. 'You're winding me up – I know that you feel the same as I do about hanging on to some of our past.'

'I'm a scheming, devious female, Patrick Miller.' She took his hand, stroked it. 'I just like to hear you saying these things.'

'One good thing about the changes,' Miller said, 'we don't have to worry about what we say any more.'

Rosa lifted his hand, pressed it to her lips.

'And yet,' Miller added, 'we're beginning to feel like strangers in our own city – on our own side of the city.'

Pluses and minuses: Miller had spent much of his time the night before at the city's giant outdoor party doing the arithmetic: the good, the bad – and the unknown. Even the past that he himself had lived through was largely unknown to him. Yes, the facts, the dates, the events of the years he'd lived in Berlin were known to him; what was unclear to him was whether what had been done and undone – what had been allowed or forbidden in the name of this country that no longer existed – was to be written as plus or minus in the equation.

Now, sitting in this deserted cafe, he said as much to Rosa.

'You and I,' Rosa said, 'are too close to this country to do that kind of arithmetic.'

Miller smiled. 'Neither of us comes from here.'

'That's why we're too close, Patrick.'

'Is that cryptic remark intended to stimulate class discussion, Frau Professor?'

It was Rosa's turn to smile. 'You know what I mean.'

Miller did. Separate currents of the twentieth century had washed them up in a divided city that they had come to love – and most lovers saw only the graces of the beloved.

The previous day East Germany had assisted in its own euthanasia. The vote by parliament to become part of a reunited Federal Republic of Germany had been the almost inevitable culmination of radical changes in the country since the November night when the border crossings had been thrown open. First, old Party leaders had resigned, to be replaced by younger members. Even this was not enough for the people; in the country's first free elections, the ruling Socialist Unity Party was almost wiped out, power went to a centre-right coalition aligned with Chancellor Kohl's CDU in West Germany. Kohl had his heart set on reunification; East Germany was headed in one direction only.

You couldn't ignore it. You couldn't ignore the city-wide, all-night party of the night before. And you couldn't ignore the emptiness of ZERO.

'Heinrich,' Miller said. 'Hamburg, Hanover – why?'

'Because he can,' Rosa said.

'I miss the bugger, God knows why.'

'I know what you mean.' The keeper of the coffee tin in ZERO had been liked by everyone yet nobody quite trusted him; you couldn't ever ignore the possibility that anybody – *anybody* – might be a Stasi informer.

'Maybe he's taken all the customers with him,' Miller said, 'all the way to Hamburg – or Hanover.'

'They've been going ever since the Wall was opened.'

They were both silent, contemplating the changes, the exodus. Some said a generation would leave, tomorrow's leaders lost to the lure of bright lights in the West. Some had no choice: the days of full employment under a socialist system were ended. Agencies and government ministries were shutting down, thousands of workers were workless in the reunified land.

The Secretariat for Socialist Correctness in Publishing no longer existed. A single cardboard box had been enough to hold Miller's books and pens and stapler as he exited the building in Wilhelmstrasse along with the rest of the redundant workforce. He'd passed Frau Siedel on the stairs and she'd turned her head away. Miller understood her shame: unemployment was not part of the contract in the GDR. Maybe it was for the same reason, the same sense of angry shame, that Director Hartheim himself had asked for his personal belongings to be brought to his home by one of the front desk porters.

The new waiter was standing at their table with two fresh mugs of coffee.

Rosa smiled at him, a question in her eyes.

'On the house,' the waiter said. 'You must be regulars if you know Heinrich.'

Rosa nodded, thanked him.

'Anyway,' the waiter went on, 'we have to use up that huge tin of instant coffee.'

Rosa and Miller exchanged a glance, looked at the barman.

'You don't know this place is being knocked down?' The waiter was eager, pleased to pass on his information. 'Some company from Munich has bought it – bought the whole alley,' he spread his arms, 'everything. They're going to build a nightclub here – or a car park or something.' He shrugged. 'Better than this dump anyway. Maybe they'll give me a permanent job.' He brightened at the thought. He was still smiling to himself when he took his place behind the counter, turning the pages of *Bild*.

Rosa and Miller were silent, digesting the news.

'Some go,' Miller said at last, 'and others come.'

'Like your Mr Whitacre,' Rosa said.

T. J. Whitacre of Welwyn Garden City, would-be buyer of a sizeable chunk of the GDR's publishing output, was a surprise to Miller. In April, weeks after the newly elected, non-socialist government took office, T. J. Whitacre had presented himself, by appointment, at the offices of the Secretariat for Socialist Correctness in Publishing. Miller had known that Whitacre was coming – had, in fact, handled the exchange of letters to arrange the visit – but was not invited to take part in Whitacre's discussion with the Director.

That discussion seemed to go on through the afternoon in Hartheim's office. A couple of conmen, Miller thought, bent on cheating the state – *the people* – through doctored contracts. And seemingly nothing to be done about it.

Which meant that Miller could not conceal his astonishment when, a hundred metres or so from the office, still indignant about the scam, he was hailed cheerfully by a smiling Whitacre.

'Mr Miller,' Whitacre spoke in English, 'I've been waiting and watching for you to leave the office.'

Miller's surprise was evident; so was his scorn.

'I saw you arrive, Mr Whitacre,' also in English, 'and I'm pretty certain that you and I have little to say to each other. If we have, then you can see me tomorrow at the office.' In for a penny, Miller thought. 'Although I'm sure our Director can handle the niceties – and the contracts.'

Miller made to pass by but Whitacre stepped in front of him, sleek and plump as a porpoise and smelling faintly of aftershave and deodorant. And, in his tailored, three-piece suit and shooting shirt cuffs, T. J. Whitacre looked as out of place on the Wilhelmstrasse pavement as a porpoise might in a suburban garden pond.

'Please, Mr Miller, I really would like to talk to you.' A smile – an engaging smile – lit the soft, round face. 'And it might not be to your disadvantage, Mr Miller.'

Miller's indignation turned to anger. *Does it never end?* 'You're from Redgrave, aren't you?'

The porpoise stepped back. 'Redgrave? Can't say I know any Redgrave, old chap.'

'Really? This isn't another of your people's secret arrangements, all nicely legal and perfectly stitched up?'

'Steady on, Mr Miller.' It was Whitacre's turn to look indignant. 'I've told you I don't know any Redgrave but,' he lowered his voice, the aftershave leaned closer to Miller's ear, 'I *did* want to have a word with you about certain contracts shown to me today which, not to put too fine a point on it, leave something to be desired in the matter of legality.' Whitacre paused for breath, the big, childish eyes waiting anxiously for Miller's response.

'You mean . . .' Was it possible this Whitacre really had nothing to do with Redgrave? 'You really want to discuss certain contracts with me?'

'I certainly don't want to discuss them with Herr Hartheim. The so-called amendments to contracts that I was shown today wouldn't stand up in court for five minutes.' T. J. Whitacre had regained his composure, his round face smiling again like a benevolent man-in-the-moon. 'Neither do I want to go on talking here in the middle of the street. Can't we go somewhere for a chat?'

And so to ZERO. Miller's joke, taken in good part by Whitacre. The cafe had its usual complement of students in jeans, T-shirts and military surplus. The two new arrivals were subjected to the usual inspection when they entered. Somebody wolf-whistled. T. J. Whitacre smiled, bowed slightly in his three-piece, pinstripe suit. After which the students went back to their own concerns.

'Pot.' Whitacre sniffed. 'Is this a den of political resistance?' Across the coffee mugs he looked seriously at Miller. 'I wanted to see you, Miller, because we'd spoken on the phone – and, well, because you're English. I remember reading about you when you left our shores.'

Miller sipped the instant coffee, waited.

'I was shown some publishing contracts today for the books we're interested in. Are you familiar with these contracts – and their amendments?'

Miller nodded. 'You must realize that I'm not senior enough to amend anything.'

The sleek head nodded.

'There's an English-language market for this stuff, Miller, but everything's got to be kosher.'

'But,' Miller said, 'you want to buy them for a song.' He hesitated. 'Not that it's my business.'

'So why think the worst? You think that all businessmen are thieves?'

Miller shrugged. *Who says they're not?*

'My company will pay the going rate, Miller, but we won't be doing business with your Herr Hartheim, or with the publishing director next door.'

Miller wondered only why he was being told this. 'Business decisions like that have nothing to do with me.'

Whitacre was confident, almost brusque. 'In the next few months, Miller, this country will become part of the Federal Republic. Agencies like yours will disappear. Business will be done with the people in Bonn – or maybe they'll move those people to Berlin.' He sat back in the steel-legged chair, relaxed, confident. 'I'll be doing business with the people in Bonn, Miller, with the new broom. All legit, all properly paid for. Believe me, it will happen.'

'So?' Miller made a face. 'I believe you, Mr Whitacre, but why are you telling me all this?'

'Because you're going to be out of a job, Miller, and I'd like you to work for us.'

Miller was interested but his years in East Berlin, coupled with his involvement with Redgrave, had taught him to show a blank face to most situations. He waited.

Whitacre went on to point out, gently, that Miller's years with the secretariat in Wilhelmstrasse were too few to merit any pension, even if a federal government were inclined to honour any commitments to employees of a propaganda department.

Whitacre paused. Still Miller waited in silence.

Whitacre smiled. 'I admire your ability to listen, Miller. It's a trait that's gone out of fashion.' He sipped at his coffee before continuing. 'And I have a feeling, Miller, that your old newspaper will be reluctant to take you back on a regular basis right away, yes?'

'You're well-informed, Mr Whitacre.'

'I'm not informed by anybody, Miller, just using the old nut to draw some rather obvious conclusions.'

'And they're not wrong,' Miller said. 'But you mustn't think we're destitute in the old German Democratic Republic. Rumour has it that if Kohl gets his way and swallows us whole, we'll be getting one for one on our miserable Ostmarks.' He allowed himself a shrug, a smile: the Ostmark had never achieved parity with the West German Mark, except for tourists entering from the West, who were obliged to buy twenty-five Ostmarks (non-exchangeable) for twenty-five of the West German variety.

'So you're not broke, Miller, how remarkable.' There was an edge to Whitacre's voice now. 'I'm offering you respectable, responsible employment which is rather well-paid.' He looked about the gloomy interior of ZERO and smiled. 'I don't mind being invited into a student den for a joke, but don't take me for an idiot and don't waste my time if you're not interested.'

Miller felt chastened. Besides, he was pretty sure that in a short time he *would* be looking for work.

'I'm listening,' Miller said.

What Whitacre wanted, he explained, was someone to oversee the English versions of the German books that would soon be his property. Miller was familiar with many of the books, he could locate translators in Berlin; Whitacre was of the opinion that Miller might want to continue living in the city which was OK with Whitacre. Was Miller interested?

Miller allowed that he was interested.

After that it didn't take long. A salary was agreed. An official starting date would have to be postponed until the political situation was settled but Whitacre was happy to begin paying Miller if Miller was prepared to begin work on the business in his own time.

Miller was *not* prepared to do that while he was still employed at the Secretariat for Socialist Correctness in Publishing – it didn't seem quite ethical.

Whitacre smiled ruefully at that but said that even Communist honesty was still honesty.

Miller laughed at that. T. J. Whitacre, he felt, was somebody he could work with. And if Whitacre said he would acquire rights in certain publications, Miller was prepared to believe him.

They shook hands on it.

To celebrate the deal T. J. Whitacre felt he ought to buy a round for the house. Heinrich banged on the counter with the tin of coffee and announced that their distinguished visitor was standing the house a drink. The students knocked on the tables and cheered with ironic gusto. Whitacre, still seated, bowed from the waist in acknowledgement.

Whitacre went back to his hotel.

Miller went to meet Rosa with the good news that, whatever happened in this new and unsettled Germany, at least one of them would have a job.

Whitacre's job offer also solved Miller's problem of what to do with the money in the bank in Southend-on-Sea. The 'investment adviser' of the Barclays branch had written, via the *Guardian*, to advise Mr Miller that the regular monthly amounts which had been paid into his account since 1980 had ceased some months previously; the investment adviser was also pleased to inform Mr Miller that he should consider transferring the substantial balance in this non-interest-earning current account into the bank's Alternative Goldplus Fund. The money, to Miller's mind, was soiled, maybe bloodied, but he'd wondered if he might need it to support himself and Rosa and, possibly, her father; now he could advise the investment manager in Southend – *how did Redgrave choose these banks?* – to donate the money to charities that Miller could enjoy selecting. The money was not his, any more than the boxes of belongings sent to some storage depot near Heathrow airport. That was another life.

'Whitacre was right,' Rosa said. 'And you still believe he is what he claims to be, an English businessman with no connections to,' she searched for the words, 'you know, that other world?'

'That underworld?' Miller shook his head. 'No, T. J. Whitacre has nothing to do with Redgrave and Dover and all that motley crew.' For a second he shivered. 'And I'm glad I'm free of that world too.'

'I don't have a job,' Rosa said.

Miller took her hand. 'So what, Rosa? The last time you were involved in a change of government, you were lucky to escape with your life.' He shushed her protest. 'I'm not making a joke and I'm not trying to make little of what you suffered but this is like a Sunday stroll compared to what you went through back then.'

'I know,' Rosa said, 'it's just that it's not easy when everything around us is changing.'

'We're not short of money,' Miller said. 'I have a job and I know you'll find work – and no matter what happens, we have a place to live.'

'Forgive the glooms.' Rosa kissed him; over Miller's shoulder she saw the new waiter look up from his newspaper, look at her somewhat wistfully. 'You're right, Patrick.'

'And maybe they'll leave the general in his house,' Miller said. Whoever *they* were. Miller didn't even know who he'd be paying his own rent to from now on.

'Anything is possible in this new world,' Rosa said, 'but army generals from the wrong side of the Berlin Wall are not going to be flavour of the month. And neither,' she added, 'are their daughters.'

'General Reder is old and sick,' Miller said. 'And he did no harm to anybody. Maybe they'll leave him alone.'

'And his daughter who resigned before getting the inevitable boot?' Rosa's smile belied the harshness of her words. 'You don't mind being attached to the unemployed daughter of a general without any army?'

'Which unemployed daughter would that be?'

The mocking words came from the doorway of ZERO. Neither of them had heard the door open; when they turned to look they saw Dieter smiling in the open doorway, General Reder beside him.

'I was afraid I'd never see you again!' Rosa had her arms round Dieter. 'You just disappeared.'

'You know how it is.' Dieter disengaged himself, helped Reder to be seated.

Miller signalled to the waiter, already busy with the coffee tin and a couple of fresh mugs. The last time he'd seen Dieter was the night the Wall had been breached, the night they'd walked Dover's corpse to the bench in the sunless alley in West Berlin – although he was almost sure he'd caught a glimpse of Dieter in the TV pictures of the street demonstrations in Prague that had signalled the death of Soviet rule in Czechoslovakia: a lean, blouson-clad figure just behind the front row of the excited, banner-waving, chanting, marching students. One by one the captive states of Eastern Europe had pulled themselves free of the Soviet embrace. And Miller was also guessing that Dieter had been in attendance at the funeral rites in Poland, in Bulgaria, even at the bloody end of the dictators in Romania on Christmas Day. Gorbachev had kept his word: he'd kept his nose out of satellite business and Soviet troops in their barracks. Maybe Dieter hoped to stay alive among those chanting, banner-waving crowds some seeds of the ideology that had driven him all his life; if so, Miller reflected, then like many of us he's going to have to live with the taste of disappointment.

'How did you know where to find us? Seeing you both here in this place . . .' Rosa laughed at the presence of General Reder and Dieter in the gloom of ZERO.

'You think we didn't know about this place?' General Reder was smiling.

'And our intelligence can still locate reactionaries,' Dieter said, deadpan, 'at any given moment.'

They all laughed. You could say such things now and laugh. Even though, Miller knew, such things were still true.

The waiter arrived with the fresh coffees. He placed them in front of Reder and Dieter, the mugs on saucers, not a drop spilled. The waiter stood beside Reder's chair, staring at the general, hands clasping and unclasping.

'Yes?' Reder looked up at the waiter, the black T-shirt, the creased jeans and ankle-high basketball boots.

'*Entschuldigung*.' The waiter was nervous.

All eyes focused on him, curious, observing his nervousness, the licking of dry lips.

'Excuse me,' the waiter said again. 'May I ask, sir, are you – I mean, I think you are General Hans Reder.'

Reder nodded, said nothing. You always said nothing.

'Sir,' the waiter rushed on, 'my grandfather pointed you out to me a few years ago, you were in uniform, it was a parade, my grandfather served with you in the Panzer Korps in the war – you saved his life, sir, my grandfather told me you were a great soldier.' The waiter paused for breath, seemed overcome by his own impertinence in approaching Reder. He stood, licking his dry, nervous lips.

'Your grandfather,' Reder said quietly. 'How is he?'

'He's well, sir, he lives in Magdeburg, sir, he saw you when he came to visit us.' Another pause for breath. 'He lost an arm in the Ukraine, sir, but he said that if it hadn't been for you, he'd have lost his life.'

Reder waved a hand: your grandfather was a comrade. 'And your grandfather's name?'

'Gustrow, sir, he was Trooper Jens Gustrow.'

'Ah, Jens.' Reder nodded. 'He was a good soldier, a good comrade.' He held out his hand to the waiter. 'You must tell him that I wish him well, that I send him the good wishes of a comrade.'

The waiter seemed not so much a young man as a boy; his eyes were wet as he took Reder's hand. 'I'll tell him, sir, thank you, General Reder.' The waiter backed away, bowed by the presence of a legend.

For a moment the table was silent, Reder the focus of that silence.

'Papa.' Rosa took Reder's hand. 'You made that boy happy – happy and proud.'

Miller, too, was impressed, awed. 'You have some memory, General – out of all those men, all those years ago . . .' Miller shook his head in wonder.

'The truth is,' Reder said, very quietly, 'I have no recollection whatever of Trooper Jens Gustrow.'

Miller was puzzled.

'You do what you have to do when you're a soldier, Patrick.' Reder seemed to be looking through Miller, into his own past, maybe into his future. 'I don't remember the fellow but in a way I remember them all, every last one of them, those who lived and those who died. The boy's grandfather lost an arm, he said – it's not too much to make him feel just a little bit better because a general in Berlin remembers him, is it?' He looked at them.

A soldier, Miller thought. He does what he must: takes a life when he must, tells a small lie to make an old comrade feel good when he can.

'You were right, Papa,' Rosa said. 'Sometimes a little lie means more than the truth.'

The men looked at her, struck by her odd choice of words. And as soon as she caught their expressions, Rosa herself realized the weight of those words. To varying degrees they had all lived with lies – with versions of a truth – for a long time.

Nobody spoke. What sat at the table among them was the unknowable face of the Germany of tomorrow. From his lair in Bonn, Kohl had lectured and hectored – and pleaded, too – to be allowed to make a united Germany. Now the swallowing was done, the GDR had consented to be reunited or, as some had it, to be swallowed whole, to be reduced. And nobody could tell if they had succumbed to lies or truth – or a combination of both.

Rosa said, 'I must be a witch – three men struck dumb by my words.'

'Not by your words,' Dieter said, 'but by your beauty.'

'Oh, yes, flattery gets you everywhere!' Rosa was laughing, the others joined in.

'Anyway, it's the truth, nothing less.' Miller's words made the men silent, made Rosa blush.

Dieter caught the way Rosa and Miller looked at each other, stirred in his chair, coughed.

'We should leave these young folk alone,' he said to Reder. 'But first—'

'But first,' Reder said, 'you must give them our news.'

'It's for both of you,' Dieter said, 'but mainly for you, Patrick. News from England.'

Miller groaned. 'Redgrave. What's he up to now?'

Dieter shook his head. 'Redgrave is a threat to nobody now, except maybe to himself. He went straight back to England the day after,' Dieter shrugged, 'the day after.' For a moment the darkness of blood hung over the scarred table. 'Redgrave suffered a breakdown. He's on medical leave. He'll never return to his service.' Dieter looked at Miller. 'Never.'

'And you know this because?' Miller let it hang there.

'I know this because I know it, Patrick.'

Like you knew where and how to find Rosa and me in ZERO, Miller thought. The world has changed but some things remain unchanged.

'And you've had personal news from England, Patrick,' Dieter asked, 'since we last met?'

Are you asking me or telling me, Dieter?

'Fortunately, more good news,' Miller said. The news had been anything but good when he'd phoned England in the frantic days after the Wall came down. Even getting a line out of the city had been a challenge, with the world's media scrambling for connections out of Berlin. General Reder's reach had engineered a line to Wolverhampton; the result had been his mother's usual drink-fuelled complaints and tears. *Your poor father never gets time to rest, to be home.*

Miller wasn't about to go through that with Dieter. *He probably knows anyway.*

And then, remarkably, as unexpectedly as the Berlin Wall had opened, life had changed at leafy Compton Avenue.

'A few months ago,' Miller said, 'my father had a stroke and was in hospital for weeks. He's made a partial recovery, able to speak a few words, but of course he's no longer able to work as a doctor. He needs constant care, can't walk very far, has to be pushed in a wheelchair most of the time. There's home help but the principal carer is my mother.'

He sipped his coffee, enjoying the recollection of that phone call. He was smiling now, so was Rosa.

'Something snapped – or maybe unsnapped – in my mother when my father was hit by the stroke. She was with him when it happened and she simply took charge. Called the ambulance, went to the emergency room with him, bossed doctors and nurses about and generally behaved like a dragon.' His thin smile broadened. 'My mother hasn't touched a drop since. She goes to AA and behaves with all the zeal of a converted sinner. My mother rules the roost – and my father – like a sort of benevolent, teetotal headmistress.'

Every time he phoned, Miller feared the worst. The sound of tears, his mother lost again in her personal cloud of alcohol. It hadn't happened. The Wall wasn't the only miracle: Lady Miller was still on the wagon, lording it over her straying gynaecologist husband. And Miller felt the bastard had it coming to him.

'And in case you're wondering, Dieter,' Miller said, 'I know all this because I know.' Because I'm Janus, Miller thought. *Almost a decade I've been here and I'm still not sure who's been working my strings, pressing my buttons.*

Miller felt Rosa's hand on his. At least Rosa stood for truth in his life.

Dieter and Reder were on their feet. Miller stood with them.

'Must you go, Papa?'

'I'll see you later, Rosa,' Reder said. 'I may not see Dieter again – I'll go with him to the barracks in Treptower.'

'There's a convoy pulling out shortly,' Dieter said. 'I'll travel part of the way with them; it seems the right thing to do.'

In his mind Miller saw the long line of Soviet military vehicles making their slow way across central Europe to their home in Russia. He saw Dieter in the cabin of one of the trucks, wondered how it would feel for him and the thousands of

Soviet soldiers to be cut off from the land they had occupied for forty years.

'But we'll see you again – you'll visit?' Rosa's voice held all the loneliness of parting.

'Who knows?' The same loneliness in Dieter's voice, a chink in the ascetic's armour he wore against his own dangerous world. 'My country is changing too and I may soon have to answer to new masters.' They all knew what he meant: Gorbachev's decision to play hands-off with his Soviet satellites had undermined – perhaps fatally – his own leadership.

Rosa hugged him. Miller saw her wet eyes, glimpsed the ghosts of a long-gone day, blood on a car seat, a peasant digging a grave in stony soil.

'I owe you my life, Dieter,' Rosa said.

'You owe me nothing, Rosa.' He looked at Miller. 'Be happy, you two,' he said. 'Look after each other.'

'Time to go, Dieter, unless you want to walk to Moscow.' The brusqueness of his words could not conceal the emotion Reder was feeling. He turned to Miller. 'You'll go to Pankow with Rosa, Patrick?'

'Of course, General.'

'No more "General", Patrick.' Reder grimaced. 'Back to "Major" now.'

Miller looked puzzled. 'I don't understand.'

Reder shook his hand, couldn't speak for a moment. The look he gave Dieter was hurt, wounded.

'Please, Dieter, you explain it,' Reder said.

'Your new masters in Bonn,' Dieter said, 'have outlawed the use of all titles and ranks from the National Army of the GDR.'

'Our army is being disbanded,' Reder said. 'We are not fit to serve.' He couldn't keep the bitterness out of his voice.

'Why "Major"?' Miller asked.

Reder snorted. 'It was my rank in Hitler's army.'

'You mean—'

'Yes, Patrick, titles from Hitler's army are allowed but ours are "repugnant" – or something – to the Chancellor of the Federal Republic.'

'I'm sorry, General.' Even to Miller's own ears his words sounded limp.

Rosa kissed her father on the cheek. 'You'll always be my general, Papa.'

'And mine.' Dieter smiled. 'And Colonel Kulakov would say the same.'

Kulakov: a name from the wartime snow, from Rosa's story of Reder's survival and conversion. Miller shivered as though he were caught up in that horror.

And Reder saw him tremble, allowed himself a smile. 'Yes,' he said, 'it was a time of madness, Patrick, a time when you wondered if you'd survive for just the next few minutes. I said yes to Colonel Kulakov simply to stay alive, that's true, but in time I came to understand our own madness, the Führer's madness, and I came to believe in what we were trying to do in the GDR. We got it wrong,' Reder went on, 'but I'm not convinced that our new masters have made our world any better.' He stopped, a spasm of pain shuddering across his lined face.

He eased Rosa's hand gently away from his arm, turned towards the exit. Dieter went with him. The two men were at the door when the shout came from the cafe counter.

'Sir!' The waiter was waving.

'Young man?' Reder's voice husky with cancer and tiredness.

'Thank you, General Reder.' The waiter's voice cheerful, awed. 'Goodbye, General!'

The general smiled, waved, and the door closed on him and Dieter.

Once more they were alone in the windowless cafe.

'They'll keep leaving until the entire population has gone West.' Miller was smiling. 'What used to be the GDR will be left to you and me and a few pensioners.'

'But you're smiling.' Rosa was smiling too.

'As long as you're in my world, I'm happy.'

'You're a rogue with a honeyed tongue, Patrick Miller.'

'You put the sweetness into my life, Rosa.' He'd never told her about the despair in his heart after Sophie dumped him, saw no reason to tell her now. 'Honestly, Rosa, just being with you makes me feel more alive than I've ever felt before.'

She kissed him on the lips. 'Thank you.' She laughed. 'It must be these romantic surroundings, the lush music.'

He said nothing; she knew he couldn't find the right words.

'I'll stop teasing,' Rosa said. 'I know you mean what you say and I'm happy about it. I love you – in case you haven't heard that enough already. But I think I know what has you feeling a bit raw, exposed.'

Miller looked at her, waited. He knew that she knew: Rosa *always* knew.

'We're all facing a different world here,' Rosa said, 'just as you have a new situation back home in England – in your old home, I mean. It's another adjustment, another kind of beginning.'

'It's been a long time,' Miller said. 'I really must go back.'

'So, Patrick, you're not thinking of heading off to Wolverhampton on your own?'

'You'll come?'

'You think I'd let you loose among those scheming English women on your own?'

'Oh, yeah.' Miller's expression was rueful. 'I'm such a catch!'

'You're just fishing for compliments.' Rosa's smile grew

wider. 'And fool that I am, you'll get them. You're worth having, Patrick Miller. Never forget that we're lucky: *we* are worth having. Besides,' more briskly now, 'you have a job and I intend to see you keep it – somebody has to support me!'

They kissed. They could feel the waiter's eyes on them and they didn't care.

'One other thing,' Miller said. 'If they take the house from General Reder, we can easily find a flat big enough for all three of us.'

'You think I'm going to go on living with you, Patrick Miller?'

'Well, I suppose I could search for a replacement in Wolverhampton.'

She was giggling, kissing him.

'Seriously,' Rosa tried to look serious, 'what are your parents going to think of me? Of us?'

'You know,' Miller said, 'I think my mother will love you but I don't know what I'm going to make of her. I never knew her. She was always this half-pissed woman, always made up, always polishing and shining.' He shrugged. 'Maybe I can get to know her, maybe it's not too late.'

'And your father?'

'I'm not sure I want to know him.' Miller shook himself, as though caught in a chilly draught. 'Maybe I can learn to forgive him.'

'We all have to learn to forgive,' Rosa said, 'not least ourselves.'

As though by unspoken agreement they got to their feet together. Miller helped her into her coat, kissed her neck, her hair. The waiter waved, called goodbye and they waved back before stepping outside.

The sky was bright over Berlin; for once, the narrow alley was lit by the slanting rays of the October sun. From beyond the alley came the growl of traffic, the hum of a people at work, at play. Miller clasped Rosa's hand in his and, hip to hip, they walked together into the living, undivided city.

Author's Note

First, the obvious: this book is a work of fiction. Although the framework of my story of the last days of the German Democratic Republic is built on historical fact, I have taken certain liberties here. For example, Erich Honecker's retirement as boss of the GDR was announced on 18 October 1989 while Erich Mielke's span as head of the Stasi came to an end later, in early November.

The notion of an internal coup to create a kinder, socialist East Germany is fictional. Nevertheless, after the fall of the Berlin Wall, certain East German intellectuals and activists wished for the opportunity to create a separate, new kind of society. That brief vision was soon overtaken by events and within a year the GDR had become part of a reunified Federal Republic.

A number of books have been at my elbow while writing this novel, more for dipping into than for studied consumption. *The People's State* by Mary Fulbrook is a comprehensive account of life and work in the GDR. *The Berlin Wall* by Frederick Taylor gives a detailed account of the birth, life and death of the city and the infamous barrier. William F. Buckley Jr's *The Fall of the Berlin Wall* describes that event in detailed, journalistic fashion.

Probably the book which seemed my best companion in writing this novel was a second-hand volume I picked up for a pound in one of the last pavement 'barrows' on London's

Charing Cross Road. *Guide to East Germany* by Stephen Baister and Chris Patrick was conceived and written in the lifetime of the GDR; events moved with such speed that, by the time of scheduled publication, East Germany was in its death throes but, happily, the publishers went ahead anyway.

Uniforms of the German Soldier by Alejandro M. de Quesada is the kind of book that a writer consults at his peril. More than once, dipping into this handsome, illustrated volume, I'd discover that an hour or more had passed as I was admiring the photographs and comprehensive captions while my own blank page still remained blank . . .

General Reder, in my story, would have worn more than one of these uniforms, from the Wehrmacht of the Third Reich and Nationalen Volksarmee of the GDR. And, as General Reder discovers, the use of his GDR rank in the reunified Federal Republic is forbidden, while he can happily continue to use his Wehrmacht rank.

Finally, the usual: any errors here are mine alone.